# LOVE & LOSS
## AT
# WHITMORE MANOR

*a novel*

# Anita Stansfield

Covenant Communications, Inc.

Published by Covenant Communications, Inc.
American Fork, Utah

Printed in the United States of America
First Printing: November 2017

22 21 20 19 18 17    10 9 8 7 6 5 4 3 2 1

ISBN-13: 978-1-52440-370-6

# Chapter One
# WOUNDED

*The American Colonies, 1781*

TRISTAN WHITMORE WAS REMARKABLY UNSURPRISED when the bullet hit him. He'd been more surprised by how many times he had walked away from a battlefield unharmed. In fact, he'd lost track of the months that had grown into years through which he'd been serving king and country here in these dreadful colonies, and he'd also stopped counting his close calls in facing death. Many months ago, he'd actually come to believe that he simply would not get out of this country alive, and had therefore stopped thinking about his home and family at all. If such thoughts entered his mind, he quickly forced them away, doing his best to remain only in the present. He'd even started wishing that the fatal blow would just happen so he could be finished with this horrific experience, once and for all.

When the bullet hit his leg, Tristan's lack of surprise was compensated by a great deal of disappointment. He would have far preferred a mortal wound that would have taken him quickly, if not immediately. As it was, he found himself facedown on the ground, keenly aware of the bodies around him—some dead, others uttering vocal expressions of agony. Tristan couldn't find the strength—or the will—to make a sound. He could feel the blood draining out of him, and the throbbing pain of the wound began to ease as he became increasingly weak and lethargic. Only then did he think of home, of his father, his wife, and the comfort and beauty of the English countryside and the nearby sea. He wished then that he might return there, and he wondered how his loved ones might respond to news of his death. Then he focused only on pleasant thoughts of all he held dear until he drifted into oblivion, his final thought being the fear that he might be left for dead on the battlefield and wake up again here. If he was going to die, he wanted it to be over with here and now.

* * * * *

Tristan eased into consciousness slowly. While his eyes refused to open and his body felt heavy and immobile, it took several minutes to determine that he was indeed alive. More minutes assured him that he could move his fingers and toes. Attempting to move his wounded leg let him know that he was indeed very much alive. Surely no such pain would accompany him beyond the grave. At least he still *had* his leg.

Still unable to get his eyelids to cooperate, Tristan focused on what he was hearing—and the smells. Such terrible smells! Blood, and sweat, and something rotten. There were sounds of busyness and hushed voices, but there was also the noise of agony, of men suffering. If not for the sensation of some kind of makeshift bed beneath him, to which his body seemed to have become a part, he might have believed he was still on the battlefield. But his senses told him otherwise. He'd previously been inside the large tents that constituted what the army dared to call some kind of hospital. And he'd felt then as he did now—that he would far rather perish than be sentenced to spend any length of time in such a place. But here he was: weak, in pain, and still alive.

After what felt like perhaps an hour of slowly merging into full consciousness—and a brutal awareness of the pain in his leg—Tristan managed to force his eyes open, a little at a time, as if he needed to train his eyelids to fight against the heaviness and allow him to see his surroundings. Turning his head just slightly one way and then the other, Tristan knew he was on a cot in a long line of other cots, all occupied by wounded men. It took only a few quick glances to see bandaged faces and eyes, arms and legs. And most shocking of all was the brief but brutal look he got at men who were missing a limb. He squeezed his eyes closed as the images—combined with the sounds and smells—assaulted him with a heart-pounding horror that was not unlike what he'd felt on the battlefield as men had fallen all around him, and then when he'd fallen among them. What would be his fate now? Would his leg perhaps become infected and yet have to be removed? Would he contract some horrible disease that he knew could run rampant in such places, leaving him to die slowly and painfully? He wished with all his soul that the bullet had struck him in the heart. He'd always wanted to believe what he'd learned from Sunday sermons throughout his life, that a better place existed beyond this world, and he certainly would have preferred to be there now—perhaps reunited with his mother and his grandparents, and his little brother who had died as a baby. Tristan envied his brother, who had left the world without having to know the reality of its potential heartache and suffering. And he longed to be reunited with this sibling whom he barely remembered.

Tristan lost track of time while he just listened and waited, and his thoughts swarmed like bees all competing for space within a busy hive. He wanted to go back to sleep, to be oblivious to his surroundings, but the pain was too distracting. It occurred to him then that perhaps he'd previously been given something to help him sleep in spite of the pain, and it had now worn off. Unable to recall anything beyond losing consciousness on the battlefield, he felt severely disoriented and wondered how long he'd been here. He wanted very much to speak to a doctor—or someone who knew what was going on. But it didn't take much effort to perceive that every person who wasn't bound to a cot had more work to do than seemed humanly possible. So many needs, so much suffering, so few hands to assist. Tristan's own pain seemed minute compared to the obvious and extreme suffering of others around him. So he just waited and tried to force tranquil memories into his mind so that he wouldn't become agitated by how thoroughly unhappy he was to be here in this condition.

Tristan became so caught up in his faraway musings of home that he was actually startled to feel a hand on his arm at the same time a man said kindly, "You're awake at last."

Tristan surveyed this man as he sat down on a chair he'd brought with him. There certainly weren't enough chairs to put one at every bedside, so it seemed this man took his chair with him to use whenever he might need it. He appeared to be shorter than Tristan, and a little bit older, of slightly stocky build, with hair the color of sunshine, and a scraggly beard that was only slightly darker. His appearance betrayed a lack of sleep along with a lack of attending to his personal grooming. Such things were likely luxuries in this place, but it spoke of this man's commitment to doing all he could to ease the suffering around him. His eyes echoed that commitment as he leaned toward Tristan and asked with genuine concern, "How are you feeling? Are you in much pain?"

"I'm all right," Tristan said, realizing as he tried to use his voice that it hadn't been used in a long while.

The man at his bedside showed a wan smile. "Now, that's a brave soldier talking. And while I admire such bravery, I've spent far too much time with wounded men to not be able to see through it."

Tristan couldn't deny that this man *could* see through him. He spoke with honesty. "My leg is certainly causing me pain, but I am obviously not nearly as bad off as many others here."

"That's true. You were very fortunate compared to many, but that doesn't mean your injury is not valid, and you absolutely need time and proper treatment in order to heal. I'm certain you have many questions, so I'll try to answer some of them right off, and if you have more, let me know." Tristan nodded and the man went on. "First of all, I'm Dr. Barburry, but you can call me Jack; everybody around here does. I'm the one who removed the bullet from your leg when you came in. We have been fortunate enough to have plenty of laudanum on hand—which is not always the case—which is why you hopefully cannot remember much of that painful incident. You may have spurts of memory come back to you. Try not to be alarmed by them; focus instead on getting better so you can go home."

"Home?" Tristan echoed, his voice sounding even more raspy.

"Your leg will eventually heal well, I believe, and you will hopefully have nothing but a slight limp by which to remember us. But you certainly are not going back to the battlefield. You lost a great deal of blood, which causes the immense weakness you feel, and it takes many weeks for your body to recover from such an ordeal. As far as I have been able to tell, you are past the risk of serious infection, although we will keep cleaning the wound regularly to help ensure that. In essence, I just want you to rest as much as possible. You can have some doses of laudanum to help with that, although I will be gradually reducing your dosage so you don't become dependent upon it. Once you get your strength back and you can get around on your own, you'll be headed back to England, but I have a firm policy about not putting men on ships who are weak and at risk for infection. I would prefer that you survive the voyage, which means you'll need to become accustomed to our accommodations for a while—meager as they may be. I will check in on you as often as I can, as will others who work here." He smiled and added, "There are a few female nurses, but they're too old and cranky to be much of a distraction." He winked. "Some are crankier than others, but try not to be frightened; they do good work."

"I consider myself warned," Tristan said.

"They'll help make certain you get fed and have what you need."

"Thank you," Tristan said. He glanced around and felt compelled to add, "What you do here cannot be easy."

The doctor looked mildly surprised, as if he were not accustomed to having *his* difficulties acknowledged. "No," he said as he glanced around. "But it has its rewards at times." Looking at Tristan again he said, "I'd make a poor soldier, my friend, but I'm glad to do my part—even if none of us really has any idea what we're doing here."

Tristan felt both confused and curious over that last remark, but the doctor stood up as he said, "Right now I want you to eat a little something before you're given any more medication, since it will make you sleepy. You haven't eaten for a few days so take it slow. Someone will be here shortly with what you need. We're busy but don't be afraid to speak up if you're in pain or you need help." He took hold of Tristan's hand and squeezed it in some kind of combination of a handshake and a token of comfort. "I saved your life, my friend, and I always feel responsible for those I manage to save; I don't want your recovery to be any more miserable than absolutely necessary." He smiled again and added, "I will come round to check on you when I can."

"Thank you," Tristan said.

"Do you have any questions for me?"

Tristan shook his head and watched the doctor walk away with his chair, carrying it to another bedside where he sat down to converse with another wounded and suffering soldier.

Tristan was grateful for the doctor's kindness and his thorough explanation of what had happened and what to expect. While he waited for the promised nourishment, the bees of thought began to buzz again in his head. Now he knew that he was most likely going to be all right, and he would eventually return home with all his limbs intact. But the weeks of recovery ahead felt eternal, especially given the surroundings. He had only to glance in one direction or the other, however, to be reminded quickly that it could be so much worse. Given that he *hadn't* died, he had to acknowledge his gratitude that he was likely one of the few in this place who would not go home permanently maimed.

Doctor Barburry's kindness was put more fully into perspective when one of the cranky nurses came to Tristan's bedside to help him eat some broth and a little bit of bread. He didn't want her to have to feed him, but it quickly became evident that his arms were too weak to manage this task himself. The middle-aged, plain woman didn't speak beyond giving him instructions and asking a few questions about his pain and his present needs. She was efficient and helpful, but certainly not pleasant company. Tristan observed a somewhat glazed, faraway look in her eyes, and he wondered if her lack of warmth was a result of toiling over the bedsides of so many suffering soldiers that she had reached a point of not allowing herself to care or become emotionally involved. He couldn't blame her. He just thanked her for her help and felt no resentment when she showed no reaction to his attempts at simple kindness and gratitude.

Now that he knew the reality of his situation, Tristan forced himself not to think about the utter helplessness that spurred more fear in him than going into battle. He chose instead to put his mind firmly toward patience and temperance—virtues he knew were not necessarily his strengths, but perhaps they would increase through his efforts. He could only hope and pray that such would be the case; he would surely need more strength than he'd ever possessed to survive what lay ahead. He wanted only to go home, but there was a great deal of healing and a very large ocean between him and the people he loved. And he had no choice but to endure each day with as much graciousness and dignity as any gentleman ought to possess.

* * * * *

Olivia Halstead stood solemnly in the seemingly endless downpour of English rain that ran like a waterfall over the edges of the umbrella she held. The umbrella was large and sturdy, but it still managed to barely keep dry the heads of herself and her elderly uncle who stood at her side. She could feel Walter's weakness—both in body and spirit—as he leaned heavily against her side while they stared at the casket of his daughter-in-law as it was lowered into the hole in the ground. The flowers on the casket that had looked beautiful in the church were now severely damaged by the rain, but their pathetic appearance felt appropriate to Olivia. Muriel's untimely death had occurred for all the wrong reasons, and she'd left in her absence a great deal of confusion and heartache—but perhaps not in the way that a woman's death should have done under any kind of normal circumstances.

Olivia felt Walter growing weaker, and her own ability to help keep him upright was beginning to fail. She gave a discreet nod toward Lawrence—Walter's loyal manservant—who was nearby with his own sturdy umbrella. Lawrence had looked after Walter for a few decades now, having started when he was just a young man. Olivia knew that Lawrence was keenly aware of the elderly man's failing health, and in fact he had expressed strong protests over Walter going out in this weather at all—even for the sake of his daughter-in-law's funeral. But Walter had insisted, and he'd rallied more strength than Olivia had seen in him for many weeks now—perhaps months.

Olivia was glad for the way Lawrence insisted on helping Walter back into the carriage and for the valid reason it gave her to leave the graveside herself. Once in the carriage with the two men, she took in a deep breath of relief to be out of the punishing rain—and another deep breath of relief in having the funeral over. With any luck they could now put the household back together and press forward with some kind of normalcy.

During the drive back to the grand manor house that Walter considered his legacy, Olivia questioned silently for what seemed the thousandth time her reasons for staying in this good man's home now that her cousin was gone. Walter was no blood relation to her; he'd only been related to her cousin by marriage. And it was at Muriel's invitation that Olivia—and her longtime companion Winnie—had come to live in the manor house, mostly because they had absolutely nowhere else to go, and the family her cousin had married into had been gracious enough to share their large home and offer Olivia and Winnie some security. But Muriel was gone now, and Olivia felt entirely displaced. Walter had assured her more times than she could count that he considered himself as good as an uncle to Olivia, that he sincerely wanted her and Winnie to stay, that it was no inconvenience or burden, and that he insisted upon it. He'd even said more than once that it was a selfish request on his part because she'd become a light in his life and he didn't know what he'd do without her. Olivia wanted to believe that was true; she'd grown to love Walter and *he* was certainly a light in *her* life. But she wasn't unaware of the opinion of some of the servants in the household who had concluded that she was nothing more than a destitute woman who had come from a tainted family and that she was simply manipulating Walter in order to remain in his good graces so that she and Winnie would have a home. Walter had told her to ignore the gossip and he'd assured her that he knew the truth about her character and her motives. She *wanted* to stay, but with Muriel gone she needed to do some serious searching of her soul and determine if it was really the right thing to do. With as generous as Walter had been to her and Winnie, the last thing she wanted was to ever bring any difficulty upon him or his household—even though she couldn't comprehend being without Walter's friendship, and she believed he felt the same about her companionship.

Once back at the house, Olivia left Walter in Lawrence's capable care and went to her own room to change into dry clothes that were far more comfortable than the starched black dress she'd worn out of necessity in order to show respect for her cousin—even if she personally found it difficult to feel any respect for her whatsoever. Muriel had made despicable choices in her life, and her death felt like a disgrace in the most horrible way. The worst part was that Olivia had loved Muriel deeply; they were family—and practically the only blood family that either of them had in this world. But Olivia had realized long ago that the way Muriel had chosen to live was something they could never agree on, which had only added to her bitterness in facing the grief she felt over her cousin's death. Muriel's absence—as well as her choices—had left a deep wound in Olivia. But there were deeper wounds deep within Olivia's heart, and she preferred not to think too much about any of them.

Winnie was on hand to help Olivia change into a well-worn green cotton dress that was drab but comfortable. Winnie also helped Olivia take down and brush out her reddish-blonde hair that had no hope of drying before bedtime if it weren't set free. Winnie had been a lady's maid to Olivia long before circumstances had changed their lives so quickly and drastically that they'd both become alone and destitute—literally overnight. Following her father's ruination due to enormous gambling debts—and his subsequent suicide—Olivia had turned to Muriel, the only living relative who would have anything to do with her, and she had promised Winnie that they would always remain together and take care of each other. Muriel's new family had been generous and gracious about allowing her and Winnie to reside with them, although Muriel's husband had barely been polite about it, even though his father—Walter—had always been exceptionally gracious and kind. But Walter's son had gone to war years ago, which had made living here easier for Olivia. And he was dead for all they knew. No word had come for many months, which was a great concern for Walter. It seemed the entire household had accepted that the young master would never return, but the uncertainty was difficult— especially for Walter. Olivia felt sure that if he *did* return, he would not want her and Winnie to stay—now that Muriel no longer bound them there out of familial obligation. In that respect, Olivia would prefer that he didn't return. But for Walter's sake, she hoped—and even prayed—that his son was alive and well and would come home.

"Are you all right?" Winnie asked, moving the brush slowly through Olivia's very long and very rippled hair. "It must have been difficult; I should have gone with you."

"It *was* difficult," Olivia admitted. "But you should *not* have gone with me. You're barely past that terrible cold, and I won't have you getting pneumonia or worse." She added in a teasing tone that was common between them, "Fat lot of good you'd be to me if that happened."

"Indeed." Winnie smiled, showing the deep dimples in her slightly plump cheeks. Olivia returned her smile in the reflection of the mirror they were both facing and silently thanked God for allowing this good woman to be in her life and by her side at this time, just as she'd been with her through many years and many difficulties. Olivia didn't know what she would have ever done without her, but she'd said it to Winnie so many times that she feared saying it again now would only dilute the sincerity of her gratitude.

Winnie looked nothing at all like Olivia. She was short and full-figured with dark, curly hair that she had difficulty taming into the tight bun she wore at the back of her head. Olivia was a head taller than her faithful companion and thin with lanky limbs. Her fair skin and light hair were a stark contrast to Winnie, but their personalities were well matched and Olivia could have never asked for a more true or devoted friend. She just hoped that Walter would continue to allow them to stay, and she refused to think about what might happen when Walter's deteriorating health finally did him in. Given how deeply she'd grown to care for him, the thought of his demise felt unbearable. But without his loving generosity, Olivia feared that she and Winnie would once again find themselves homeless and impoverished.

Winnie left Olivia to rest, although Olivia was far too consumed with anxiety to be able to relax. She was surprised to come awake and realize that she had indeed drifted off to sleep and the room had grown more dim. She didn't know if that was due to the sun going down or the clouds having grown heavier. She stood up in order to see the clock on the mantelpiece clearly, relieved to find that—according to the clock—it was still afternoon. Her thoughts immediately went to Walter, since she never wanted too many hours to pass without checking on him to make certain all was well, and to let him know he wasn't alone in this huge, dimly lit house. On rainy days like this, it was almost impossible to distinguish daytime from late evening unless you were very near a large window, and there were far too few of those.

Olivia hurried to Walter's room and knocked lightly before she opened the door carefully. She knew the knock was enough to alert Lawrence if he were in the middle of helping Walter with a personal matter, and Lawrence would call for her to wait. If Walter was sleeping, the knock was not loud enough to disturb him, and even if he were awake, he likely wouldn't hear it due to some decline in his hearing ability, a side-effect that had come with his advancing age. All his faculties had diminished dramatically over the last year or so, which she knew Walter found depressing. Olivia couldn't turn back time or alter the impact of old age, but she could make the old man smile, and nothing in life had ever given her more fulfillment than his genuine gratitude for her efforts and the way they had grown to care for each other. He was more of a father to her than her own father had ever attempted to be; in fact, he was the only man she'd ever known who had treated her with sincere respect—with the exception of Lawrence and some of the other men employed by Walter who had followed his example in accepting Olivia and Winnie into their household and treating them kindly.

Olivia found Walter relaxed, with his head on a stack of three pillows— just the way he liked them—but she knew he wasn't asleep due to the distinct lack of snoring. She sat on the edge of the bed, which alerted him to her presence, and he opened his eyes. He immediately smiled and reached for her hand. She took it and kissed his brow, all of which had become their familiar routine of greeting one another.

"How are you, old man?" she asked and he smiled at what had become a lighthearted term of endearment between them.

"I'm tired," Walter admitted, "as I'm certain you are."

"Yes," she said, "although I'm not as old as you." Her teasing tone brightened his eyes, and she added, "So I'm likely not as tired." More seriously she continued, "I still don't think you should have gone out. If you get ill I will be very angry with you."

"I had to go," Walter said and his eyes became distant in a way that Olivia knew well. It wasn't just the faraway look in his eyes that let her know what he was thinking but the overt sorrow and uncertainty she saw there as well. "For all that she did to cause so much hurt, she was all I had left that linked me to Tristan."

Olivia was stunned. They had talked about Muriel's betrayal, but he'd never admitted to such thoughts before. She wondered if having Muriel finally dead and buried made him feel more comfortable in being completely honest about the situation.

"That's not true!" she quickly pointed out. "He's your son; your hearts are irrevocably connected. Muriel betrayed Tristan in the worst possible way, and she betrayed the rest of us, as well. I know they were married, but if her being gone now makes it all right for us to be completely honest, I will no longer pretend that their marriage was anything more than a technicality to her. She never deserved Tristan, and she didn't deserve the love and acceptance you gave her in spite of all she did to hurt *you!*"

Olivia became aware of the rising anger in her own voice when Walter squeezed her hand in a way she knew well as his effort to keep her calm. He'd become accustomed to her tendency to let her emotions overtake her, but he always remained composed and collected, and she was trying to learn from his example to do the same. He'd told her a number of times that acknowledging how she felt was always important, and she had a right to her own emotions, but it was important to not allow those emotions to rule her choices or control her behavior. She knew he was right; his wisdom and insight had made her want to be a better person, in spite of everything she believed she had stacked against her in that regard.

Olivia took a deep breath and met Walter's compassionate eyes just as he said, "Your cousin hurt and betrayed you every bit as much as anyone else—even if the reasons vary. But you must forgive her. She's gone now, and we must go forward and not let her actions dampen our future."

Hot tears gathered in Olivia's eyes as she heard herself admitting her worst fear. "And what future do I have when you leave me too? What will—"

"I've told you that I've made provisions for you, my dear, and you have no need to worry."

"You *have* told me."

"But you don't believe me."

"I believe you are the best of men and your intentions on my behalf are the noblest. I also know that when you are gone, your wishes might not be carried out exactly as you wish them to be. When Tristan comes back, I'm certain he will *not* agree with your regard for me, and—"

"You mustn't worry about something that's not even possible, my dear," Walter said, his voice taking on a raspiness that implied his difficulty in even uttering such words. "It's been so long since we've heard from him; I have to believe the worst has happened."

Olivia measured her words carefully, knowing the sensitivity of the topic. "Listen to me, Walter. Why do you not believe *me* when I tell you that if he had died we would have received some official notification?"

Walter's internal torment became more evident by the deepening sorrow in his eyes and the increased gravelly quality of his voice. "Then why no letters, Livy? Why no word from him at all for so long?"

Olivia looked down to avoid having him see the guilt she knew would be evident in her eyes. She reminded herself that Muriel was gone now, and it was time to put all she had done behind them and to stop keeping secrets that Olivia had often felt were necessary in order to keep peace in the house.

"Walter," she said, drawing courage, "I can't be certain . . . I have no proof . . . but . . ."

"But what?" he demanded. "Out with it, child. What are you not telling me?"

His insistence compelled her to look at him again. "Beatrice told me that on two different occasions a large number of letters arrived and she delivered them into Muriel's hands, as she knew she was supposed to; they were addressed to her, but I'm certain he would have wished for her to share them with you. He surely would have assumed she would do so."

"What are you saying?" Walter looked almost panicked.

"I think Muriel received letters and burned them." Walter gasped and Olivia hurried to finish her explanation; she'd been holding this information inside far too long. "I found her burning papers once and she said it was nothing . . . but she said it in that haughty, defensive way we both knew so well, and it usually meant she was lying or trying to hide something. I came right out and asked her more than once if she'd received letters, but she denied it—and again I believe she was lying. I asked Beatrice, knowing she handles all the mail when it arrives. She told me letters had come, but she was concerned about going against Muriel's word. You and I both know there isn't a servant in this house who wouldn't go to great lengths to avoid her wrath."

Walter squeezed his eyes closed and Olivia felt his grip on her hand tighten. She gave him some moments of quiet to take in what she'd just told him before she offered him a serving of his own advice. "She's gone now; we must move forward. But now that she *is* gone, it's time to be realistic about the situation. I didn't tell you that to add to the burdens you feel over Muriel's behavior; I told you so that you would know—as I do—that there is a distinct possibility that Tristan is alive and well. Until we know for sure, you must not give up hope."

Walter sighed and opened his eyes. Olivia saw a glimmer of hope there that offered some balance to all the heartache that had been weighing on him. "Oh, that girl!" he said, more with confusion than anger. "Why did he ever marry her? I'll never understand."

Olivia looked away, not wanting Walter to see how the question struck a deep nerve for her. "Nor will I," she said, forcing a steady voice. "When he *does* come home, I fear how he will be impacted to learn how deeply she has wounded him."

"I fear the same," Walter said. "She has wounded us all, but no one more than Tristan."

"But wounds heal," Olivia said, forcing a smile that softened Walter's expression. "How many times have you told me that when I've come to you in tears over my tattered life?"

"Yes," Walter said with a wan smile, "wounds heal. I know it's true. But healing can be painful; and deep wounds take time and patience."

"So, take your own advice, old man," she said more lightly. "Be patient . . . with yourself, and with me. And we'll heal together."

"Yes, we will," he said with such jubilance that she might have thought he was declaring they'd be going on holiday or something equally grand. "And we will not let go of the hope that Tristan is alive and well."

"I'm certain he is," Olivia said, again forcing a smile. She had deeply mixed feelings over the thought of Tristan returning and how that might impact her life. But in spite of that, she hoped and prayed with deep desperation that he was alive and well. She believed that if he *were* dead, she would have felt the emptiness in her heart. Surely when Tristan Whitmore's spirit left this earthly realm, she would feel it, and she would know.

# CHAPTER TWO
# ASSAULTED

Tristan quickly grew restless and impatient with his healing. He pushed himself to master his own care as soon as he could reasonably manage it. There were so many men far worse off than he; surely the attention of the medical staff was much better used in their behalf. Within a few days he was able to feed himself, and a couple of days after that—with the help of some crutches that were made available to him—he was able to get in and out of bed without assistance and see to his own needs. Less than a week after waking up in this wretched place, he'd become fairly self-sufficient and able to function without any pain medication. His leg certainly hurt, but it wasn't unbearable, and again he believed that the medicines available could be put to better use on others whose pain was much more extreme.

Once he was up and about, Tristan's restlessness turned to a need to feel useful. He was well aware of a group of officers in different stages of healing who spent their time at cards or dice, often with an air about them that he knew well. They'd obviously been raised with privilege, and with the expectation to be waited upon, even though they were capable of caring for themselves. These men—who not unlike himself had likely purchased their commissions into the army due to some level of wealth or title—mostly kept themselves separate from those of lower ranks who had no wealth, title, or subsequent rank. But Tristan abhorred their attitude and chose to steer clear from their type, just as he'd done back in England whenever possible. Never more than now had Tristan been so brutally aware that all men were equal when it came to the suffering of the human body, and the impact of surviving the battlefield. All blood was red, all pain was real. And gangrene was no respecter of persons.

While avoiding the distractions of those men with whom Tristan had no desire to associate, he was drawn to giving what little help he might be able to offer in easing the suffering of the men still bedridden with varying degrees of wounds and pain. At first the stodgy nurses protested against his attempts to assist in simple tasks, but Dr. Barburry told them firmly that these men could use all the help they could get, and he expressed his appreciation to Tristan for being willing to assist.

Tristan began to feel less restless and depressed as he spent his days sitting at the bedsides of wounded soldiers, sometimes helping them eat, sometimes reading to them, sometimes helping them write letters to loved ones, sometimes just listening to them tell their stories of the battlefield and offering compassion. After more than a month of living in this place that could barely be called a medical facility, Tristan was limping about without the use of crutches, and the doctor had declared him to be healing well but still weak from the loss of blood. Tristan had come to know the names of all the doctors and nurses, and most of them had come to be more kind toward him and appreciative of his efforts to help. He'd seen men heal and leave, either to go back to England or back to active duty—depending on the severity of their injuries. Barburry had not yet approved Tristan for travel due to the obvious weakness and fatigue he still felt. He emphasized again that the journey back to England was rigorous, and he wanted his patients to not waste all of his efforts in saving them, only to not survive and end up buried at sea. Tristan couldn't argue with his logic, and while a part of him longed to go home, another part of him dreaded it. Addressing the reasons for his complicated emotions felt more difficult than surviving the battlefield, so for now he focused on his physical healing and figured he would have weeks at sea to contend with how he felt about going home before he arrived there.

Tristan soon became accustomed to the flow of soldiers going out and coming in. Some men died, some healed and left, but there were always more wounded who were brought in to fill the space. The more he observed the pain and suffering, the more he began to contemplate the senselessness of war. He considered his own position in Britain's efforts to keep these rebel colonists in line, and he realized that he had honestly forgotten why he had so firmly believed in this cause when he'd initially enlisted. He considered himself a true Englishman to the core, willing to fight on behalf of king and country as any decent, able-bodied British man ought to do. But all this suffering and death had changed his view of the need for war. Personally he didn't care anymore who lost or won, or what might be at stake; he just wanted it to end.

When an especially large influx of wounded soldiers arrived, Tristan found himself standing back and observing as the medical personnel were overwhelmed and struggling to deal with far too many needs at once. He finally forced himself past any fear of getting too close to the ugliest part of the workings of this hospital and stood next to Barburry, who was frantically trying to get a wound on a soldier's neck to stop bleeding.

"What can I do?" Tristan asked him.

Barburry glanced up, surprised but quick to say, "I need you to press your fingers here—firmly." He guided Tristan's hand with his own, which was covered with blood; within a moment Tristan's hand was covered with blood as well. "Now, just hold it there; don't be afraid to press too hard. He's going to be in pain no matter what we do right now, but we've got to stop the bleeding. You hold it while I try to get some stitches in him to close the hole in his artery."

Tristan nodded, even though he barely understood what that meant. He felt a little dazed looking at all that blood, but he tried to focus on his hope of being able to help save this man. When observing Barburry's efforts to put stitches in this man's neck became a little too much for Tristan to handle, he shifted his focus to the wounded soldier's face. With his clean hand he put a hand on the soldier's brow and looked at him closely, speaking to him in a voice that he fought to keep calm and steady.

"It's going to be all right," Tristan said, but the man was in too much pain to notice. More loudly and firmly Tristan said, "Look at me; try not to think about the pain. Look at me." The young soldier did so and Tristan moved his face closer so they could easily maintain eye contact. "Good. Now think about something else. Think about home. Think of going back there. Don't think about the pain."

The soldier nodded slightly, and Tristan saw tears leak from the corners of his eyes. Within a few painful minutes Barburry had closed the hole from which this young man's life had been draining out. Once the emergency was over, Barburry turned the soldier over to a nurse to make certain there weren't any other life-threatening wounds. Barburry quickly moved on to another patient's urgent needs, and he nodded slightly toward Tristan in a way that seemed an invitation for his help. Tristan went with him and followed his instructions once again. A few hours later he had lost count of the men he had tried to help while standing at Barburry's side. He'd seen a few men die, and he'd marveled at how Barburry could so quickly accept that death had occurred and be able to move on. But what else could he do? He had to focus on those who could be saved.

When all that could be done had been done, Barburry sat down with a long, deep sigh, as if he were finally allowing himself to fully breathe. He nodded again with a silent indication that Tristan sit next to him. Both men leaned their forearms on their thighs, which brought to Tristan's attention how much blood they both had on their hands. It seemed that the doctor needed to rest before he could even find the energy to get cleaned up; at least that's how Tristan felt and he assumed Barburry might feel the same way.

"Are you all right?" Barburry asked him.

"I think so," Tristan admitted. He forced a humorless chuckle. "I don't feel as squeamish over the blood as I did earlier today. I suppose that's progress."

"I suppose," Barburry said with a heavy voice. "I've often thought that a man shouldn't become insensitive about the blood and the death, but I don't know how it would be possible to cope otherwise." Tristan couldn't comment on that; he could only consider the abhorrent truth of the statement. Barburry continued with a glance toward Tristan. "You did amazingly well, Tristan. I believe we would have lost many more than we did today if you'd not been at my side."

Tristan felt a little taken aback. Recalling many critical moments throughout the day, he couldn't reasonably argue, but it was difficult to imagine himself having that much impact on men's lives.

While he was still trying to take that in, Barburry turned to look at him and asked, "Have you ever considered going into medicine? I believe you could take to it well. You have steady hands and a clear head, and your ability to relate to the patients and help them feel calm is quite remarkable."

"Is it?" Tristan countered, the tone of his own voice alerting him to how startled he felt over such a comment. He'd never considered himself to be *remarkable* in any way.

Still trying to mentally process what Barburry was saying, he was further surprised to hear the doctor add, "I'm going to guess that you were raised a gentleman, and pursuing a profession of any kind would be considered unseemly."

"You would guess correctly," Tristan said. "And as you verbalize it, the ideology sounds even more prejudicial than I've always believed it to be."

"Well," Barburry drew the word out, "I think you should consider it; you could do a great deal of good. There are always people suffering somewhere, and there are never enough good doctors." He stood up and stretched with a moan that indicated stiff muscles and exhaustion. "Thank you for your help, Tristan. You'd best get cleaned up and get some rest."

Tristan remained as he was for several minutes, digesting the conversation he'd just had, and the enormity of the many hours preceding it that he'd spent at the doctor's side. He didn't feel like the same man he'd been yesterday at this time. In fact, he knew he would never be the same again. Whether or not the doctor's advice was right for him remained to be seen; he couldn't even think of such a possibility when he was so far from home and had no idea how things there might have changed in his absence. In that moment he felt a sudden longing for England, for the beautiful estate where he'd been raised, and to be with the people he loved. But looking around himself, he felt an equivalent longing to remain here where he could do some good.

Exhaustion quickly overtook his tumultuous thoughts and he forced himself to seek out some soap and water and some clean clothes. But washing away the physical evidence of the horrors he'd observed this day could never erase them from his mind. He just didn't know how to cope with how all of it made him feel.

\* \* \* \* \*

Olivia spent the morning reading to Walter, and Winnie brought lunch to his room for the three of them to share. Walter enjoyed Winnie's company as well, and he refused to allow society's dictates of the separation of social classes to prevent him from spending time with the people who helped lift his spirits; those he called friends, which was a term he didn't use lightly. Walter included Lawrence in that category, and his loyal manservant often shared meals with Walter. The two men also played chess and checkers and other games at which Walter became ludicrously competitive in a way that provoked much teasing from Lawrence. Their games were very entertaining to Olivia and Winnie, and sometimes they would while away hours absorbed in such simple pleasures that helped pass the time for Walter and keep him distracted from his deteriorating health and how it kept him mostly bedridden.

After lunch, Walter settled in for his usual nap while Lawrence hovered in the next room with a good book in case he was needed. Winnie went into town with a couple of the kitchen maids to have a little outing while procuring supplies. Olivia took advantage of the clear skies to take a stroll through the gardens. It had been raining for days and the grass was still damp, but the sunlight beamed down at a perfect temperature to compensate for the lawn's coldness. Olivia found a concealed spot that was her favorite and lay back on the grass and closed her eyes. She concentrated on the sound of birds chirping, the aroma of nearby roses, and the contrast of the cold ground and the warm sun. She allowed herself to think only about Muriel for a minute. Olivia had once envied her sleek dark hair and her voluptuous figure, but she'd long ago ceased envying anything about her cousin. Despite her outer beauty, Muriel had proven to be very ugly on the inside. She'd been gone for over a month, and Olivia could almost feel guilty for acknowledging how much more pleasant life had been since her death. She pushed the guilt out of her mind, along with any thoughts of her deceased and disgraced cousin, and her mind went to Tristan. She wondered about him often. Instinctively, she believed he was still alive, and she prayed that he was well. Her own internal conflicts over this war and the motives providing impetus to both sides also perpetuated some guilt when she thought of Tristan's place in the midst of it all. But she pushed that away as well, along with every other challenge over which she had no control. If she thought about it, she could feel angry all over again for the way Muriel had treated him and betrayed him. And she felt even more angry to think that Muriel had likely burned his letters without ever letting Walter know they'd been received. Olivia wondered, as she had too many times to count, what he might have written, and she wished the letters still existed. She'd imagined finding them in a drawer in Muriel's room and taking the liberty of reading them now that Muriel was gone. But Olivia had already searched through Muriel's belongings, and there wasn't a trace of any evidence that she'd even had a husband.

Aware of her own rising turmoil over the matter, Olivia pushed all thoughts from her mind and focused again on the pleasantness of the moment, concentrating all her senses on just taking this blissful respite into her spirit while she offered up a prayer in her heart that Tristan would come home safe and well; that Walter would remain living for a good, long time to come; and that they would all be able to make peace with the damage Muriel had left in her wake.

\* \* \* \* \*

Once Tristan had recovered from the initial shock of how traumatic medical care could be in an army hospital, he felt compelled to follow Dr. Barburry around as much as he could manage while he still felt weak from his own need to recover. The work of saving lives and healing wounds went on and on, ebbing and flowing in direct proportion to what was taking place on the battlefront. Over time, Tristan became stronger and less aware of his own pain, compelled by an unseen force within himself to follow Dr. Barburry around day and night, whenever and however he was needed. He quickly became immune to the sight of blood, and the smell of gangrene simply became evidence of a patient's condition rather than an odor that turned his stomach. He lost count of how many men he'd held down with his own weight while their limbs had been removed with the hope of saving their lives, just as he could never recall the number of men he'd seen die—or found dead when he'd gone to check on them—but he would likely never forget their faces.

While Tristan became completely immersed in a world he'd never even imagined, he began to consider aspects of life he'd never even thought about. First and foremost, he realized that in truth he had absolutely no idea why this war was even happening, and why men were dying and suffering because of it. And he was surprised to discover that he was far from alone in his feelings. The men who came through this place were— for the most part—fiercely loyal to the crown and would honor their country above all else, which was no doubt an honorable trait. But when conversations turned to the politics of this war—and the cause for which they fought—few if any of them had any understanding of the reasons for it. Still, a loyal Englishman would never dare speak treason, and Tristan was careful in the way he asked questions and gave answers. In spite of it all, he *still* considered himself an honorable Englishman; he just didn't know if he agreed with the motives of the king—even if he had no idea what those motives were, exactly. If he had his way, Tristan would call a truce and send everyone home—wherever home might be—to live in peace.

Tristan became good friends with Jack Barburry, and they often spent the few available hours of leisure time together playing friendly games of cards or just chatting. Tristan also came to be on good terms with the nurses, even if most of them were too stuffy to ever admit it. He gravitated less toward the men of his own class, mostly because they had a way of keeping themselves separate and above everyone else. But when it came to medical needs, there was no distinction between classes—at least not with Jack Barburry in charge.

Tristan became so caught up in his self-appointed position as a doctor's assistant that it came as a complete shock when he received orders to return home. And if he had any hope of getting to the coast before the ship on which he would travel was sailing, he had to leave early the following morning.

"I can wait until the next ship," Tristan told Jack. "You need my help here."

"I have greatly benefitted from your help, my friend," Jack said. "But you need to go."

"What will you do?" Tristan asked, horrified to think of the lives he'd helped save and how many might die without an extra pair of hands at the ready.

"I will do what I've always done," Jack said. "I will do the very best I can and continue to pray that this blasted war will end." He offered a wan smile and put a hand on Tristan's shoulder. "And I will forever thank God for your help while I had it, and for having found such a fine friend amongst all this madness."

"I will do the same, of course," Tristan said. "But . . . surely . . . my leaving can be postponed, and—"

"It would only postpone the inevitable," Jack said. "Search your heart and tell me that you do not need to return home." He tightened his gaze on Tristan. "As I have said many times, my good man, your help has been priceless and much appreciated, and I stand by my original suggestion that you should consider going into medicine. But I've come to know you well enough to see the truth."

"*What* truth?" Tristan demanded, sounding more defensive than he'd intended.

"This is your friend talking, Tristan," Jack said, lowering his voice to the kind of gentle tone he used when telling a wounded soldier that his condition was not good. "You avoid speaking of home by changing the subject; you're very skilled at diverting the topic. I know little except that you and your father had some kind of falling out, and I suspect your marriage is not all you had hoped it would be. I can only guess that it's much more complicated than that. But you cannot remain here and ignore the fact that you do have a wife and a father, and you have no idea what is going on with them." Jack took hold of *both* Tristan's shoulders.

"Go home, my friend; put your house in order and be as good a soldier to them as you have been to your wounded comrades—and to me. Go home and make peace with it. Until you do, you will never be able to be at peace in the journey of your life."

Tristan wanted to make a joke about Jack taking on the role of his vicar now, as well as his friend and his doctor. But even as the thought came to his head it seemed one of those diversion tactics Jack had mentioned. Letting the words settle into himself, he couldn't deny their truthfulness, but he could only nod at Jack to indicate that he had heard them, and he hoped Jack knew he would take them to heart.

As a going-away gift, Jack gave Tristan a collection of medical instruments that each had their place in the pockets of a length of canvas that rolled up neatly and was tied so it could be easily carried. Jack told him they were an extra set that had never been used, since there were fewer doctors than the instruments that had been allotted. Jack also gave him a small leather case which contained some other medical supplies. He suggested a little more seriously, "With your long journey home you might find yourself in need of them."

Tristan thanked him and graciously accepted the gift, even while he silently prayed that he would never encounter a situation where he might need them. However, if he ever decided to pursue training in medicine, he would be very glad to have them, especially since they were a gift from Jack.

Saying good-bye to this pathetic excuse of a hospital was far more difficult for Tristan than he ever would have thought, and saying good-bye to Jack felt even more difficult than it had been to say good-bye and bid farewell to his wife and father before he'd left home to go to war. Considering the comparison, Tristan had to ask himself if he'd felt some relief in being able to leave home—and if perhaps that was the very same reason he had avoided returning. He and Jack promised to write letters, with the hope that anything Tristan posted would ever find its way to him. But they both now knew where to find each other in England, and they committed to meeting up again someday when the war was over.

"Godspeed, my friend," Jack said when their farewell could not be delayed another moment. Other soldiers heading out were now waiting for Tristan.

"And the same to you," Tristan said, and they shared a brotherly embrace before he forced himself to turn around and walk away, barely aware of the slight limp he was taking with him as a souvenir of his time here.

* * * * *

Tristan restlessly endured one day short of six weeks on the ship that took him and many others from the American colonies back to England. It hadn't taken him long to appreciate what Jack Barburry had said about not putting soldiers who were weak or ill onboard a ship too soon. But he was very glad to never have cause to use the medical supplies Jack had given him, even though the conditions were nigh to miserable and a breeding ground in which illness could flourish. He was glad to feel strong and healthy as opposed to being in the pathetic condition that some men were in who had obviously been sent home by doctors who possessed less wisdom and foresight than Jack Barburry. Tristan tried to make himself useful by looking out for those who were struggling. He changed bandages and cleaned wounds to try and keep infection to a minimum, and he did his best to try and encourage those who were going home permanently maimed. He felt like he was doing some good, which strengthened his desire to follow Jack's advice and pursue some training in the field. But at night when he was alone and trying to sleep, thoughts of home haunted him—especially in light of all that Jack had said about the evidence that Tristan had been trying to avoid the issue. He couldn't deny that his relationship with his father had been somewhat strained for years, but it all seemed so trite now. Their personalities were dramatically different, and therefore they had different priorities. There was, however, only one major issue that had ever truly come between them, but Tristan didn't even want to think about how right his father had been in telling Tristan he should not marry Muriel. Tristan had been prideful and defensive toward his father's advice, but now it all felt so foolish. Having stared war and carnage in the face, whatever had been amiss between him and Walter no longer seemed to matter. Once he came to that conclusion, Tristan found himself eagerly anticipating a reunion with his father, and he prayed that all was well with him and the home he'd left behind.

The situation between Tristan and his wife was not so easy to resolve. He felt deeply confused over his feelings for Muriel, and sometimes he even wondered why he'd married her. His father had clearly been right, but that only made Tristan feel more like a fool. His reasons for marrying her had felt sound at the time, and he'd truly believed that he loved her and that they would make a good partnership in shouldering the burdens of life. But the relationship he'd shared with her *after* their marriage had borne little resemblance to what they had shared *before*. He'd been so confused over the reasons—and frustrated over trying to solve the problems—that he'd instead embraced the opportunity to align himself with king and country and go to war. That decision now felt as confusing to him as his reasons for marrying Muriel. In both cases it almost felt as if he'd been under some kind of spell, as if he'd not been completely himself. And now he wondered if he *could* be himself as he returned home to face the consequences of both choices.

Once the ship docked in England very early in the morning, Tristan felt no desire to waste any time. He was glad the distance to his home wasn't terribly far—at least not compared to that of most of the men he'd sailed with. He acquired a horse and headed toward home, almost as if he could smell it or feel it in the wind. He stopped a few times barely long enough to eat and give the horse some rest and feed and water. When he came to the crest of a hill that he knew overlooked his home, he wished the night wasn't so dark. But there was no moon to illuminate the lofty house and elegant grounds. He could see nothing but a dark outline of the gables and chimneys against the sky. He hurried on until he arrived at the stables, which were dark and devoid of human life due to the late hour. Tristan unsaddled his horse and put it into a spare stall, making certain to meet its needs before he closed up the stables again and walked around to the front door of the house, wondering as he did so what his reasons might be for seeking a formal entrance to his own home. He concluded that after having been gone so long, he felt more like a guest, and he didn't want to just walk into the house in the dark and give anyone a fright. Noting light in a few windows, he knew that not everyone had gone to bed yet, but he had no idea what to expect after showing up at this late hour.

Tristan found the door unlocked, which meant that the head butler had not yet done his final rounds for the night; it also meant that Tristan didn't have to actually make use of the knocker and wait for someone to come and answer the door. For a long moment, he stood in the open doorway, all his senses just soaking in the feel of home. He was glad for the lamp that had been left burning in the foyer. He closed the door loudly, hoping to alert someone to his presence.

"Who's there?" he heard a woman call a moment later, and a moment after that the familiar form of Mrs. Higley came scurrying into the foyer, bringing a smile to Tristan's face even though she couldn't see him yet. Mrs. Higley had been in charge of the household for more years than he'd been living. Her presence in his life and her loving guidance were every bit as much a part of his growing up as those of his parents. Considering the untimely death of his mother when he'd been just a boy, it seemed only natural that Mrs. Higley had assumed a more prominent place in his life and had taken on a somewhat maternal role. There was between them, of course, the expected division of their social classes, but it was kept in careful balance with her not being afraid to keep him in line if she saw fit, and she certainly wasn't afraid to tell him what she thought. For those and many other reasons, he loved her dearly, and he laughed now to see her coming toward him.

"And now I know that I am indeed home," he said as she came into full view.

He saw her stop and heard her gasp. "Is it true?" she asked, stepping more into the light with her hands on the sides of her face. "Is it really you?"

"It is, indeed," he said. "I might ask you the same."

"Oh, my dear boy!" she exclaimed and rushed forward to wrap her arms around him in a way that no ordinary housekeeper would dare. He lifted her off the ground with his embrace and turned a circle before he set her down, making her laugh. "We'd about given you up for dead," she murmured, now setting her hands to the sides of *his* face.

"I sent letters," he said, confused. "Many letters."

"They were not received, my darling," she said, and he saw tears in her eyes. "Oh, you're really here!"

"I really am," he said, moving past his frustration of the poor efficiency of the post in order to enjoy this reunion.

"Oh, you look exhausted, my boy!" she declared. "And you must be starved! I'll get you something to eat and—"

"That's not necessary," he insisted. "I stopped for supper; I'll be fine until morning. You mustn't fuss. I know it's late, Mrs. Higley—and I don't want to disturb anyone. I'm certain you should be off to bed yourself. But I would like to see my father before I go to sleep, and I'm anxious to see Muriel, of course." Tristan squelched the voice in the back of his head that told him he was lying; he *did* want to see his father, but during his journey he had come to face the truth that the majority of his reasons for avoiding home were due to Muriel. He'd told himself he needed to return with a positive attitude and do everything he could to revive their marriage and make the most of it—and he was determined to do so. He focused on that need to be positive now. He'd drilled his determination into his mind so thoroughly that he was convinced his wife would be happy to see him and their reunion would put a new spark back into what they'd once shared, and perhaps their relationship might once again be like it had been when they were courting.

Tristan became momentarily caught up in his own efforts to shift his thoughts and it took him a few seconds to pick up on the shadow that overcame Mrs. Higley's countenance. He was about to inquire over the reason for such a dramatic change in her mood when he saw her eyes shift to look past him. He turned around and didn't know whether to be thrilled or angry, or if one emotion was attempting to suppress the other.

"Olivia," he said, keeping his tone of voice even so as not to let on to having any reaction at all to seeing her here. A long braid hung over the front of her shoulder, and she wore a dressing gown and nothing on her feet.

"You're alive," she said, and he couldn't tell if her breathlessness was due to quickly coming to see who had arrived or to the fact that it was him.

"I am," he stated.

* * * * *

Olivia knew she should say something else, but she could only stare at Tristan while her mind attempted to adjust to the reality that he was here, he was alive, and she had no idea how his return would affect her own future. His dark, unruly hair looked as if it had seen many hours of riding in the wind. It was barely long enough to be tied back into a stylish ponytail, but it was typical of him to *not* tie it back, as if not doing so might declare his resistance to society's expectations. His face looked much the same, but his eyes looked as if they'd seen decades of hardship and horror. He was wearing his uniform and holding his hat; both looked as if they too had seen a long journey and much hardship. It took only a moment for her eyes to take in his appearance and accept that he was really here. And it took only another moment for her heart to quicken and her stomach to quiver, and she cursed herself for not being able to forget what it had been like between them before Muriel had set her sights on him and everything had changed. Now she was nothing more than his cousin by marriage, a burden to his household, and likely a thorn in his side.

"What's wrong?" Tristan demanded, startling Olivia. He glanced at Mrs. Higley, then back at Olivia. "Something's wrong. Tell me."

Olivia saw Mrs. Higley silently pleading to be relieved of giving Tristan the bad news. She took a deep breath to draw courage into her lungs and reminded herself that she'd been acting as the lady of the house since long before Muriel's death. Now, more than ever, she needed to act like it—even if Tristan would completely disagree with her having any right to do so.

"You should get your sleep, Mrs. Higley," Olivia said to her. "I will give Mr. Whitmore a proper update on all that's happened in his absence."

"Very good, miss," Mrs. Higley said, the relief all too evident in her voice. She added with enthusiasm, "It's truly grand to have you back home, my boy."

"Thank you," Tristan said, nodding toward the housekeeper. "It's good to be home," he added, yet sounding as if he didn't really mean it. "I will see you in the morning."

Mrs. Higley nodded and hurried away. Tristan turned to glare at Olivia, silently demanding that she tell him the truth. He had rightfully sensed that things were not as they should be, but it was difficult to know where to begin to tell him all he needed to know. As much as she hated having to be the bearer of bad tidings, she would far prefer to do it herself as opposed to leaving Walter to have to tell him. For Walter's sake, she could do this.

"Perhaps we should sit down," Olivia said and turned to lead the way toward a nearby parlor, carrying the lamp with her that she'd brought down the stairs when she'd heard a ruckus in the foyer and had come to investigate. Any unusual happenings in the house had spurred both the hope and the fear that it could be Tristan returning, but she'd felt that way for so long that she'd honestly stopped wondering how it would really be when he came home—and how she would tell him all that he needed to know.

In the parlor, Olivia closed the door on the chance that any of the servants might have some inclination to eavesdrop. She set the lamp down and sat on a sofa, pulling her cold feet up beneath her, wishing she'd taken the time to put on some slippers, and wishing even more that there was a fire. In spite of it being summer, the nights were cool, and the stone walls and floors of the old house were cold. Without looking directly at Tristan, she was aware of him studying her, as if he could somehow surmise what she needed to say. He tossed his hat onto one chair and sat on another, crossing his legs and setting his hands firmly onto the chair's arms.

"Tell me," he insisted, and she forced herself to look him in the eye. Before she could speak he asked, "Did something happen to my father? Is he—"

"Your father is very much alive," Olivia said and heard him let out a strained breath. "However, his health has declined a great deal over the last year or so. We don't know if you received any of our letters."

"Not for a long time," he admitted. "How bad is he?"

His question sounded more relaxed, less intimidating, and Olivia steadied her breathing. "He's very weak and suffers from many aches and pains. He rarely leaves his rooms, and spends most of his time in bed simply because he does not feel well enough to get up. But his mind is sharp and his spirits are good. Your return will do him much good; he has worried a great deal and feared the worst."

Tristan stood up, saying, "I need to see him. I need to—"

"We need to let him sleep," Olivia said, and he sat back down, which surprised her since she'd expected him to argue with her. He'd become very good at that prior to his leaving. "He has difficulty sleeping, and when he doesn't get enough rest, his pain is worse. He takes a dose of medicine at bedtime that the doctor has given him, which helps him rest better. If we interrupt his sleep now, he will not feel well enough to enjoy your company tomorrow. He is always awake early; you can surprise him before the servants have a chance to gossip."

"Thank you," he said. "I will. What else is wrong? I know there's something. Where is Muriel? Why isn't *she* telling me this? I should go up and talk to *her* and—"

"Muriel is dead," Olivia said, knowing she just had to say it as opposed to trying to lead up to it gently somehow, which she knew would only frustrate him.

Olivia watched the shock strike his face and then settle into his countenance. She heard him struggling to breathe and noted the way he pressed a hand over his chest. He stood abruptly and turned his back, as if he didn't want her to see his full reaction. "How?" he asked in a raspy voice. "Was it illness? An accident?" He turned to look at her, wearing a fierce determination on his face that she knew so well, but it didn't mask something raw and perhaps frightened in his eyes. She wished she wasn't about to open his wounds further. But it had to be done.

"Sit down, Tristan," she said, wondering how many times she had practiced this conversation in her mind, trying to be prepared for its possibility. But she'd never been able to know exactly how he would respond. She had no idea of his level of affection for Muriel. In spite of how badly she knew Muriel had treated him at times, she believed he'd married her because he loved her. Since he'd never cared to talk to Olivia about his feelings—or his reasons for doing what he'd done—she had no idea how deeply this would affect him.

Olivia noted his hesitancy to do as she'd asked and once again take a seat. She saw in his eyes that he had no idea what to expect, and she knew he didn't deal well with not being in control of a situation. Slowly and reluctantly, he sat back down. "What?" he insisted. "Tell me and get it over with. How did she die?" He sounded more angry than overcome with grief—but she knew well enough that anger could often mask grief, or perhaps it was just a part of it.

Olivia drew back her shoulders and lifted her chin slightly, as if that might give her the extra momentum she needed in order to say, "She died in childbirth, and the baby with her."

"What?" he asked, his brow furrowed with confusion, his eyes pained.

Olivia pressed forward with her rehearsed speech, much of it rooted in her prior speculations as to how he might feel or respond when assaulted with such horrifying news. "I can't imagine how this must be for you, Tristan. I've dreaded this moment even while I've prayed for your safe return. I know you are likely in shock right now, but I also know you well enough to know that you have many questions and you need to have them answered. So I'm going to tell you what I know, as difficult as it will surely be for you to hear." She took a deep breath and forged on. "I believe I must state the obvious: Muriel was your wife and you have been gone for nearly three years. You were not gone a year before she began engaging in casual dalliances, and I fear you must know that she was not necessarily discreet. When she finally admitted to me that she was pregnant, she told me she honestly did not know who the father might be."

Olivia paused in order to push away all her own ugly memories related to what she was saying. There were many details she wanted to blurt out if only to have some relief from the burdens Muriel had left upon her shoulders. But Tristan was being assaulted with a burden that he surely had not been prepared to face, and she needed to consider his feelings above all else right now. She noted that he looked visibly ill, and he was clutching the arms of the chair so fiercely that she knew he was fighting to hold back some kind of outburst.

Olivia knew she had given him all the pertinent information for now, but she felt the need to say, "I'm ashamed to be her cousin, Tristan. And I'm sorry that I ever brought her into your life. I wish there was something else—anything else—I could say to soften this for you, but there is no disguising the horror of it. Please know that I'll do my best to answer any questions you have that may arise as you come to terms with this." He said nothing and she added, "Do you have any questions for me now?"

"When?" he asked, as if he'd barely come up with enough breath to get the word out.

"In the spring; March. We had a proper burial; your father insisted upon it. As always, the goodness in him overrides all else. He never ceased trying to think the best of her, in spite of all the evidence to the contrary. I believe he wanted to honor her name and her place in the family. I have my own opinions about that, but they're likely best left unsaid."

Unable to bear the growing tension in the room as Tristan became visibly lost within his own thoughts, Olivia stood up, which seemed to startle him. "I'm sorry you had to come home to this," she said, "but I am very glad that you've come back safely. Your old room has been kept up with the hope of your return; you should find everything you need there. I would advise avoiding Muriel's room; it's not been touched since she . . . died there." He said nothing and she knew she had to get away from him before she either screamed or burst into tears. "I'll see you in the morning," she said and hurried out, leaving the lamp behind for him to use.

Olivia found her way through the darkness up the stairs and to her own room, unable to keep from crying as her anger toward Muriel flared up inside of her all over again. But far worse than her own ill feelings toward her cousin was knowing how all of this would impact Tristan. She didn't know if he'd loved Muriel enough for his heart to be broken over such news, but her betrayal was more than enough to break a man's heart—with or without love involved. And her own heart broke as she was assaulted once again with the horror of what Muriel had done to this family, and especially to Tristan.

## CHAPTER THREE
# RETREAT

TRISTAN HAD NO IDEA HOW long he sat in the parlor after Olivia left the room. He leaned his forearms on this thighs, hung his head, and clasped his hands painfully together, wringing them over and over as if doing so might help make sense of everything he'd just learned. It seemed as if a part of himself was watching another part from a distance, as if he knew he should be shouting or screaming or crying, but he could do neither. He couldn't even force himself to stand up and leave the room. Thoughts and questions and memories darted around in his head, all bumping into each other and creating nothing but chaos. He was in too much shock to think clearly and too numb to even answer his body's desperate need for sleep.

Tristan was startled by the chiming of a clock, and he knew from the sound that it was two in the morning. The lamp in the room had burned itself out and it took him a moment to become oriented to his surroundings. Aching from the hours he'd been sitting there—combined with a long day of riding hard and fast in order to get home—he forced himself to stand and stretch, determined to find the strength to get up the stairs and into his own bed. He'd dreamed of sleeping under this roof in a comfortable bed; now, ironically, it seemed just out of reach, and he had trouble mustering the energy to just get to his room.

In the hall, Tristan knew where to find a lamp on a table near the parlor doorway, and he felt around in the darkness until he found the matches in a little drawer. He lit the lamp, blew out the match, and took a deep breath before heading toward the stairs—as if he were about to climb a very steep mountain and he knew it would take every ounce of energy he possessed. Once in his room, Tristan closed the door, set down the lamp, and fell back onto his bed without even removing his boots. The next thing he knew it was daylight and he could hear the noise of many birds in the trees near his bedroom windows.

Tristan glanced at the clock and groaned, wanting to see his father before—as Olivia had suggested—any of the servants might spoil the surprise. He sat up and groaned again, aching everywhere. He longed for a very long, very hot bath, but for now he just cleaned up with the water he found in his room that had obviously been brought up the night before, after he'd arrived. It was not warm at all, but it was sufficient for him to feel more refreshed and presentable. He was glad to not have to wear his uniform, and instead chose comfortable clothing from his wardrobe that had been unused for nearly three years. He pushed his hands through his hair in an attempt to smooth it before he left the room and hurried to the wing where his father's rooms were. A clashing of thoughts assaulted him again as he walked, but his emotions still felt far away and beyond his reach. He could feel nothing but shock, but he far preferred it to any other possibility. He was so horrified by Muriel's betrayal that he could hardly even look at the oncoming tide of grief over her death that he knew hovered on the horizon of his ability to function. For the moment, he chose to focus more on his concerns over the news of his father's declining health. Their differences of the past had become increasingly insignificant during his time away, and now—especially with the evidence of Muriel's lack of character—he found them completely meaningless. He only wanted to see his father again and find in him the same unwavering strength that had always been there. The house was familiar and he was glad to be here, but only being with his father could make him feel like he'd come home.

Tristan paused outside his father's bedroom door to catch his breath, then he opened the door carefully so as not to disturb him if he was still sleeping. He was more than a little surprised to see Olivia at his father's bedside, adjusting pillows against the headboard. Neither of them had heard him enter, and he had a long moment to take in the way his father had aged more than a decade in three years. Walter Whitmore looked frail and weak, which was evidenced by the way he relied on the strength of a woman to assist him in simply sitting up in bed. Olivia still had her hair in one long braid just as it had been the night before. She wore a dark blue bodice over a cream-colored chemise, and a floral skirt that was full of enough gathers to make it possible for her to have one knee on the bed as she helped Walter lean back against the pillows and get comfortable. She glanced up and saw Tristan standing there while his father was still getting himself situated. He didn't know why he felt angry to see her here like this, but he did. Still, he reminded himself to behave appropriately and to focus on seeing his father again.

Olivia said to Tristan, "Good, you're here. He's been awake only a short while. Lawrence has gone to get his morning tea."

Tristan nodded and saw Walter look up at Olivia as if to ask for clarification of what she'd just said, as if he'd not heard her clearly. She looked directly at him and said with a big smile, "What would you think of starting your day with a delightful surprise?"

"Oh, a surprise sounds nice," Walter said, still looking at Olivia. "Do give me a hint."

"It's the most delightful surprise you could possibly hope for," Olivia said, and Tristan saw an enlightenment in Walter's eyes before he turned abruptly to see what Olivia was looking at. Tristan wondered if his safe return was truly the most delightful surprise his father could possibly hope for. He saw Walter's eyes fill with tears, and his weak arms reaching outward, and he knew it was true. A little teary himself, Tristan rushed to his father's side as Olivia gracefully eased out of the way. He sat on the edge of the bed and shared a long, firm embrace with his father, which made him keenly aware of just how frail Walter had become.

"Let me look at you," Walter said and Tristan eased back, taking both of his father's hands into his. "Oh!" Walter cried. "You've come home to me at last." He glanced down and back up again as if to surmise Tristan's physical state. "And you've come back in one piece?"

"By the grace of God, I have," Tristan said. "I have a bit of a limp by which I can remember my adventures, but I'm all right."

"Oh!" Walter cried again and his eyes turned to Olivia. "This *is* the best surprise I *ever* could have hoped for!" He looked again at Tristan. "You must tell me everything! It's been so long since we've had a word from you."

Tristan once again suppressed his frustration over the inefficiency of the post and smiled at his father. "I don't know if I have much to tell that's worth hearing, but you can ask me anything you want."

"Will you stay and have breakfast with me?" Walter asked with the excitement of a child.

"I would love to," Tristan said. "I've nowhere I'd rather be than right here."

This broadened Walter's smile, but once again he looked at Olivia, as if to share his delight with her. Tristan glanced over his shoulder to see her there and wished she would leave. He preferred to be able to visit with his father without her listening in on every word. As if she'd picked up on his agitation, she said graciously, "I will leave the two of you to visit, and I'll take word to the kitchen to send Tristan's breakfast here along with yours. Lawrence will be here soon with the tea."

She hurried out of the room and Tristan turned back to look at his father. "Olivia tells me you've been very ill. This is not news I wanted to come home to."

"I'm getting old, my boy," Walter said. "It's nothing for you to be fussing over."

Tristan wanted to say that Walter was not nearly as old as he looked, and he knew there had to be more explanation to it than that. Instead he said, "I'll fuss if I want to. I dare you to try and stop me."

This made Walter laugh, which made Tristan do the same, until Walter suddenly became very serious, as if he'd remembered something awful. As soon as Tristan wondered what it might be, his own memory took hold of what he'd learned about Muriel, and he felt a little sick to his stomach—perhaps because he was hungry, or perhaps because it was sickening; maybe both.

"Dear Tristan," Walter said. "Did Olivia tell you? About Muriel?"

Tristan looked down, finding it difficult for some reason to look his father in the eye. "She did," he said. "I still . . . can't believe it."

"I've known for many months and I still have trouble believing it," Walter said in a forthright way that made it easier to look at him. "I've worried so very much about what the news would do to you."

"You mustn't worry about *that*," Tristan said. "I admit to being in shock, but . . . I'll be all right. I've walked away from many battlefields; surely I will survive this."

"Ah," Walter said with an expression that took Tristan back in time; he knew that something sound and wise was about to come forth. He'd spent many years trying to ignore Walter's wisdom, and many times he had openly rebelled against it. But war had changed him, and he had nothing but respect for his father now. He doubted he had ever known a better man. "You must know," Walter went on, "that the workings of war and matters of the heart have little in common."

"Perhaps in this case they do," Tristan said, hearing bitterness in his own voice, evidence that perhaps the shock was beginning to wear off.

"You must talk about it," Walter said. "You must not hold such betrayal in your heart; it will only wound you more and more."

"I'm certain you're right," Tristan said, "but . . . I'm not ready yet. Right now . . . I just want to be here with you, and I don't want to even think about Muriel."

Walter smiled again, which made it easier for Tristan to do the same. Lawrence entered with the tea tray, declaring that he'd just heard the good news. Tristan stood to exchange a familiar embrace with this good man who was like family.

"You look fine as ever," Lawrence said with a laugh.

"As do you," Tristan replied. "And I hear the old man is keeping you busy." He said it with a tone of humor and a sly glance toward his father.

"Very busy winning at chess," Lawrence said, and Walter laughed.

Tristan relished the sound of his father's laughter, which helped ease his shock over how feeble Walter had become. To hear Walter laughing made it evident that he was still the same man, even if his body was giving out on him. Tristan moved a chair close to his father's bedside and settled in to spend the entire day if it worked out that way. They talked through tea and breakfast and tea again. Tristan listened to local gossip of who had been married, of babies born, and who had died. But there was an obvious avoidance of any mention of Muriel. Walter encouraged Tristan to tell him of his experiences in the colonies. He was hesitant at first, not wanting to even think about how thoroughly unpleasant most of it had been. With Walter's encouragement, however, Tristan began relating tales from his time at war with the colonies. Walter expressed honest compassion for the hardships Tristan had endured, which made it easier for Tristan to gain momentum and keep talking. He told his father all about getting wounded and of his experiences in healing and how he came to help Jack Barburry—and how they had become friends.

"So, are you going to do it?" Walter asked.

"Do what?" Tristan countered, sincerely having no idea what he meant.

"Study medicine? Become a doctor?"

"I . . . don't know," Tristan admitted. "I'd like to do *something* of value with my life, even if pursuing a profession is not considered respectable."

"I would respect it very much," Walter said, "for what it's worth."

"Your opinion is of more value to me than any number of people combined." As Tristan spoke he looked directly into his father's eyes to make certain he knew Tristan meant it. Every past disagreement between them, whether large or small, became washed away with the undeniable acceptance and forgiveness that Tristan saw in his father's countenance. They shared a warm smile before Tristan went on. "I believe I'll look into what would be required. For now, however," Tristan put a hand over his father's, "I need some time to just catch up with being at home and becoming reacquainted with everyone and everything. And I need to know how the estate is faring. I know that when I left, you had competent overseers who were good men, and I assume that such is still the case."

"It is," Walter said. "Everything runs very smoothly with very little input from me, but given my condition, I won't try and pretend it's not important for you to remain abreast of what your responsibilities will be when I'm gone. There are many people depending upon us for their security."

"Of course," Tristan said "We'll work on that, but . . . what exactly *is* your condition, Father? I know nothing more than what I've observed. You're far too young to be . . ."

"So old?" Walter suggested and laughed. "Yes, well," he became more serious, "there are some things we have no control over in this world, and a deteriorating body is one of them." He sighed loudly. "It's my heart, the doctor tells me. I certainly don't understand the full nature of the problem, but it's just not working as it should, and there's really nothing to be done. I just have to make the most out of each day and hope that it holds out longer than expected."

"And how long is that?" Tristan asked, suddenly afraid at the prospect of actually losing his father. He felt closer to him now with the hours they'd been visiting than he had in the whole of his life; he wasn't prepared to lose him when they were finally finding the opportunity to share the kind of relationship which should be shared by a father and son.

While it became evident that Walter had no answer to his question, lunch was brought for both of them and they talked lightly of the household staff—those who were still there that had been a part of Tristan's life for many years, and those who had left, and some who were new. Tristan enjoyed hearing his father tell stories of his interactions with the people who worked for him, and how much he treasured having them be a part of his life. But not long after they'd finished eating, it became obvious that Walter was exhausted. Lawrence appeared as if he knew this would be the case and told Tristan that after a nap Walter would be up for more company. Tristan squeezed his father's hand and kissed his brow before he thanked him for the visit and returned to his own room, feeling rather tired himself.

Once alone, thoughts of Muriel's death—and her betrayal—assaulted him freshly and he put a hand over the tightness in his chest. He knew he needed to talk to his father about it; he needed to know the whole story from Walter's perspective and how it had affected him. He wondered if his father might be able to help him even begin to feel anything at all. Walter had had months to come to terms with Muriel's death, and he would have known of her promiscuity long before then. Tristan had only known for a matter of hours, but he still felt nothing. Perhaps he was so in the habit of having an ocean between him and Muriel that it still felt as if she was just far away. And as of yet, the only evidence he had of Muriel's betrayal and death had been what Olivia told him. He'd long ago stopped trusting Olivia, and he wondered if something in his mind was luring him to believe that Olivia was lying to him, that it couldn't possibly be true, and therefore he had no need to react at all.

A rising anger over Olivia even being here distracted Tristan from his confused shock in regard to Muriel. Olivia and her companion had come to live here because she and Muriel were cousins and they'd always been close. Muriel had gone directly to Walter to ask if Olivia and Winnie could come to their home, and of course he'd agreed. Tristan admired his father's compassion and his willingness to help someone in need. But he would have far preferred to find a different way to help them—as opposed to having them under his roof. Now that Muriel was no longer here, he couldn't fathom why Olivia would believe she had a right to stay. In his mind, if she had any decency, she would have gracefully left with Winnie long before now, and he felt certain his father would have found a way to provide for them. Even now he found himself formulating a plan to give her some money—an amount that would more than compensate for any obligation he might feel over caring for his deceased wife's cousin. And with money in hand, Olivia and Winnie could be on their way to begin a new life elsewhere, and he would never have to see them again.

Tristan felt tired and pulled off his boots, attempting to take a nap. But an hour later he'd grown weary of battling his restlessness and got up. Feeling a little hungry, he went down to the kitchen and enjoyed reunions with members of the staff he'd known before his departure, as well as meeting a few new people who had been hired since. He teased with those he knew best and skirted around any talk of his time at war. And he noticed that no one mentioned Muriel or even hinted at her place in his life. But he preferred it that way—at least for now.

After having a hearty snack and enjoying some good conversation, Tristan went back upstairs to see if his father was still resting. It occurred to him that before he'd gone to war, he and Walter had often gone riding together, and they would have surely done so today if not for the dramatic decline in his health. The entire situation would certainly take some getting used to.

Approaching his father's room, Tristan turned the corner and came face-to-face with Olivia, who had apparently just left there.

\* \* \* \* \*

"He's awake," she said without looking at him. "And of course he's anxious to see you again."

Olivia tried to subdue the pounding of her heart, which she knew was more a result of his presence than the fact that he'd startled her. She moved around him and kept walking until he said, "Could you tell me why it is exactly that you are still here? With Muriel gone I see no cause for you to continue living in this house."

Olivia swallowed her temptation to get angry and fought back her worst fears before she turned to face him. "I *knew* that would practically be your first thought once you returned home," she countered. "Don't go thinking that I'm not well aware I am penniless and have nowhere to go, but that doesn't mean I would be here if I knew I was not welcome. Your father *wants* me here, and he needs me. If you—"

"Oh, I'm certain you've done a marvelous job of convincing him that he needs you. How convenient for you."

"There is nothing *convenient* about any of this, Tristan. I am brutally aware every day that Winnie and I are at your father's mercy, and when he leaves this world we will be at *your* mercy. Nevertheless, I—"

"Then you surely must be hoping that he will live a very long time," he interrupted snidely.

"I certainly *do* hope for that," she snapped, "but not for the reasons you're implying. It is a marvel that you could have been gone for so long and come back as big a fool as you ever were." She saw his eyes flare at the comment, but she hurried on before he could respond. "Do you really think your father is so spineless or blind that he would allow himself to be taken advantage of by some poverty-stricken waif who was simply trying to manipulate him? He's not only the best man I have ever known but he's sharp and wise, and you could do well to pay more attention to his wisdom and learn some manners."

"You are an insolent little—"

"I revert to insolence when it's the only method that will get *your* attention. Your behavior in light of the obvious truth is astonishing! Given the cold, hard facts about the way Muriel lived her life, you still choose to believe that everything she told you about me is true. You're a *fool*, Tristan Whitmore! You were a fool when you married her, and you're an even bigger fool now. She *deceived* you, and there's no shame in that. But if you can't look back now and be able to see the truth, you *should* be ashamed. Now, excuse me. I need to get your father's tea."

Olivia turned and hurried away, grateful he'd not launched into a tirade to convince her that he was *not* a fool—which in her opinion would have only made him look more foolish. But she knew their argument had not ended; it had only been postponed, and she wondered if she would be able to live here in peace now that Tristan had returned and was so seemingly determined to hate her. She shouldn't have been surprised, but still it broke her heart and she knew she couldn't think too hard about it without making herself upset. And she didn't have the time or energy to be upset.

* * * * *

Tristan watched Olivia walk away and felt furious. Her having the nerve to call him a fool made him want to hurry after her and put her in her place. She *was* a penniless waif completely dependent upon his father's mercy, which made her attitude toward Tristan entirely appalling. But his father was waiting for him, so he forced his anger away and tried to breathe a sense of calm into his lungs before he walked on to his father's room and knocked lightly at the door before he entered to see Walter sitting up in bed as he had been earlier. A wide smile brightened the old man's face as soon as he saw Tristan, who was pleased at being able to give his father some pleasure simply by being here—especially when there was nowhere else he wanted to be.

"Did you get some rest?" Tristan asked, taking his seat in the chair beside the bed.

"I did, thank you," Walter said. "I just can't get through the days without a good nap. It's frustrating when I've always been so active, but I'm learning to adjust."

"And how have you learned that?" Tristan asked, unable to imagine just how frustrating it must be.

"Gratitude, my boy; gratitude. Whenever I start feeling sorry for myself, I just think of all the many ways I am blessed. Before I run out of things to be thankful for, I'm usually distracted by someone or something else. I get lots of company; I have many friends in this house."

"Yes, you do," he said. "I was just in the kitchen . . . catching up with many of our old friends. We *are* very blessed."

"Indeed," Walter said and fixed his eyes firmly on Tristan. "And today I'm feeling especially blessed to have you come home safely to me. Now I can die happy."

"There will be no talk of dying, Father. We have a great deal to catch up on."

"Well, I've no intention of going anytime soon," Walter said with a little chuckle. "But I'd be unwise not to be prepared. And I'm glad to know my son will be here in my absence to carry on with all that I've devoted my life to."

"I will certainly do my best," Tristan said. "But for now . . . I'm just going to enjoy your company."

"Excellent," Walter said with another smile before his expression darkened. "However," he added, motioning for Tristan to come closer. He moved his chair a little so that he could sit close enough to the bed to take hold of his father's outstretched hand. "We must talk about Muriel."

Tristan looked down, wondering why he felt ashamed. "Yes, I suppose we must."

"Talk to me," Walter said. "You must be in shock."

"I admit that I am," Tristan said. "I hardly know how to feel."

"A man cannot control what he feels, only how he responds to those feelings. I fear your feelings will catch up with you when you least expect it. The shock will be gone and it's bound to be a difficult thing for you to face. That's why I think we need to talk about it—and talk about it a great deal—rather than trying to ignore what's happened. It can be tempting to try and pretend that the most trying times of life didn't occur, but it does no good. It only festers and becomes more painful. So, talk to me, son."

"I . . . don't know what to say," Tristan admitted and finally looked up again. "I . . . I'm so sorry."

"Sorry?" Walter echoed, surprised. "Sorry for what?"

"I don't know," he said in full honesty. "That's just . . . how I feel. I feel like I need to apologize to you."

"And what on earth should you be sorry for? For falling in love with her? For marrying her?"

"Perhaps," Tristan said. "You didn't want me to marry her. You clearly could see something that I was oblivious to."

"I expressed my opinions and I left you to make your decisions, Tristan. I hold no hard feelings over your marrying her, especially when she was so clever in her deception."

Tristan tried to find comfort in his father's words, but in his present frame of mind he just couldn't. He added instead, "I should surely apologize for going off to war and leaving her here to cause you grief."

"Well, I do not accept your apology!" Walter insisted. "Because you have nothing to apologize for!"

"Don't I?" Tristan countered, unable to let go of the one point that truly weighed on him. "You told me before I married her that you didn't necessarily like her."

"I said it once and I let it go. I respected your choice."

"I know you did, but I let it come between us. And I shouldn't have."

"It's in the past, Tristan," Walter said firmly. "We must accept what's happened and move forward." He sighed and added, "I want you to know that I never showed her any lack of acceptance or kindness—even when her behavior was unconscionable."

"I wouldn't expect anything less of you," Tristan said, then he forced himself to ask the question that was haunting him the most. "So . . . how long did you know? That she was . . . unfaithful?" The word came through his lips with a bitter taste.

"You'd not been gone six months when I noticed her flirting with other men at social events." Walter's matter-of-fact attitude made it easier for Tristan to believe he could get through this conversation—even though what he was hearing sickened him. "I talked to her about it—kindly and discreetly. She listened and didn't argue, but it didn't deter her flirtations. Not many months after that she began taking excursions to London—to stay with friends, she told me. I wasn't aware that she'd had any friends in London; at least she hadn't had any when she married you."

"None that I ever knew of," Tristan said, feeling a rising nausea.

"But what was I to do?" Walter asked. "Lock her away?"

Tristan sighed and turned to look at the wall, finding it difficult to face his father. "Forcing someone into being faithful really doesn't make them faithful, does it?"

"No, it certainly doesn't."

"I want to say I'm surprised, but I'm not sure that I am. Still . . . even though it had crossed my mind that she might be the kind of woman to engage in inappropriate behavior, I think I convinced myself that such thoughts were only some kind of . . . paranoia . . . and that she would never really lower herself to such a thing." Tristan sighed and pressed his free hand into his hair and tugged at it as if that might clear the fogginess out of his mind. "And apparently she was not discreet; I assume the entire county knew."

"Most likely," Walter said. "It's a good thing I never cared a whit about what other people think. I know some people who would have been undone by such a scandal." He tightened his hold on Tristan's hand. "I want you to know that I am *not* undone by it, Tristan. Her choices are no reflection on you *or* me." Tristan looked again at Walter, struck deeply by his conviction—and his compassion—especially when he added, "Of course I was upset when she told me she was pregnant—but not entirely surprised. But I want you to know that I made it clear to her this child would be born with the Whitmore name and I would do everything in my power to make certain that it never knew shame or a lack of love and acceptance."

"You are surely a better man than I am, Father."

"Am I?" Walter asked. "I was deeply concerned over the thought of you returning home to discover that your wife had a child. I knew it would be shocking and difficult, but I know you well enough to be certain you never would have punished that child for its mother's poor choices."

Tristan swallowed hard. "I suppose you're right. I never could have done that."

"It was my intention to write and tell you everything after the baby was born, with the hope that you would be able to have some warning before you returned. And then they both died. I wrote with news of her death but left out the reasons for it, given the circumstances. But you never got that letter."

"No," Tristan said, wondering how it would have felt to open a letter from home and read the news of Muriel's death. "The mail came in spurts, and often it would be just about the time we might be expecting mail when we would have to move on."

"I knew as much. I could only write and hope for the best. I'm only sorry you had to come home to such dreadful news."

Through minutes of silence Tristan tried to take in everything his father had said, but he still felt little except a numb blanket of shock that nearly smothered him. Walter allowed him the quiet he needed for his thoughts to catch up. Tristan finally said, "I find myself thinking that I'm relieved over her death. I wonder how I would have faced up to her betrayal otherwise."

"Oh, you would have found a way," Walter said. "And dead or not, you will still have to face up to it."

"But it's much less complicated this way, is it not?" Tristan said, hearing a hint of anger in his voice that led him to believe the shock was beginning to wear off. "Should I feel guilty for being glad that I don't have to even have the conversations with her that would have inevitably followed my returning home to discover she had lived like a harlot in my absence?"

"If you feel the need for guilt, then we shall be guilty together, my boy. I struggled for weeks over how very relieved I was to never have to speak to her again. I would have had no trouble loving the boy, but it would have been very difficult to make peace with her—especially when she had no apparent remorse."

"It was a boy?" Tristan asked, realizing this was the first thing he'd heard that had actually made the child seem real.

"Yes," Walter said, genuinely somber. "He came too soon, and things went wrong. The doctor told us the baby didn't even take a breath, and Muriel . . . bled to death."

Tristan squeezed his eyes closed against the image and let out a burdened sigh. For a moment he thought of how he'd once loved her, how he'd put all his hopes into sharing his life with her. But he couldn't think about that right now—not if he wanted to be able to keep putting one foot in front of the other. He could feel the numbness slipping away and he knew he needed to keep his emotions under control until he could be alone.

"Tristan, my boy," Walter said gently, again squeezing Tristan's hand, bringing him out of a brief stupor. Tristan looked into his father's eyes and saw such perfect compassion there that it lured his suppressed grief closer to the surface. "Listen to me, and listen well," Walter went on in a voice even more soft and merciful. "You must allow yourself to grieve over these losses, my boy. It's for no one else to say how all of this is defined for *you*. No one but you knows the full picture of your relationship with Muriel, nor how the impact of her choices—and her death—have affected you. It's impossible for others to understand, so don't expect them to. You have trouble understanding all of it yourself. But I tell you this: God understands, my boy. He knows your heart, and He is merciful toward any way you may have fallen short in any of this. Do whatever you have to in order to make peace with this so that you can move beyond it and find a good life. I'm here if you need to talk it through, or perhaps you just need time alone. Or both. But hear an old man who has faced grief many a time: it will not be squelched or ignored; it must be faced. You have faced many battlefields with courage; face this one, acknowledge the wounds, let them break open, and then allow them to heal. You've come to know much about how that works with physical wounds; let the same apply with your wounded heart and broken spirit. You may feel a great deal of anger—and rightly so. She betrayed you in the worst way. But don't let that anger become misdirected." Walter sighed and his eyes took on a distant sadness. "When I lost your mother, I went through a time of great anger. There was no one to blame for her illness or the way it took her so quickly. But I was very bitter for many weeks . . . perhaps months. The servants all wanted to avoid me, and I know that I was not a good father to you or your sisters during that time. Eventually I was given some sound advice from our vicar at the time; he's passed on now and I doubt you'd even remember him. But he was a good man, and he warned me of the dangers of allowing anger to disguise my sorrow and tempt me to ignore it." Walter looked again at Tristan. "Don't make the same mistake I did, Tristan. Acknowledge your sorrow and allow yourself to feel it. Anger will only bring regret. Do you understand?"

"I think so," Tristan said, recalling his angry outburst toward Olivia earlier. Even if he disagreed with her being here under the circumstances, getting angry had surely not been the right way for him to handle the matter. He intended to discuss it with his father at another time—when their conversation wasn't already heavy with all that he had to come to terms with.

Silence allowed Walter's words of wisdom to settle into Tristan, and with them that blanketing numbness dissipated a little more. His chest tightened and his stomach smoldered with a distinct nauseous sensation that came with thoughts of Muriel's blatant disregard of what he had held most sacred in his marriage to her. He thought of the many opportunities he'd had to be unfaithful during his years away, and how strongly he'd held to his convictions and avoided all temptation, even while many of his comrades had given in. He deeply resented Muriel's behavior and how it had impacted his father—and tarnished their good name. Anger quickly rose inside of him as a result of such thoughts, and he wondered how he might learn to rein it in so that he could face the real emotions beneath it with more clarity. He appreciated his father's advice more than he could say, and he knew it came from sound experience. Still, he suspected that actually getting through what he knew he had to face would be far from easy. It was, as Walter had suggested, a battlefield of the heart and spirit, and it would take great courage to forge ahead and not let the enemy of anger consume him.

Making an effort to suppress the anger, still aware of his father's hand in his, Tristan was taken off guard to feel tears burn his eyes. *Muriel was dead.* His sorrow over facing *that* already left him overwhelmed with confusion. He squeezed his father's hand and said in a trembling voice, "I'm very grateful for your advice, Father; I truly am. I . . . think that . . . I do need to be alone." He stood up and pressed a kiss to his father's brow. "Perhaps you could have Lawrence send some supper to my room." Even as he said it he wondered if he'd be able to eat, given the ever-increasing sickness overtaking him. "I think the staff will understand my need for some seclusion—given that they all know the truth."

"Of course," Walter said. "You take as long as you need. Lawrence will take good care of the both of us."

Tristan nodded, finding it more difficult to speak without unleashing his emotions. They were hovering in his throat now, threatening to explode, and he felt an urgency to get to his own room and lock the doors. But he knew—as his father did—that Lawrence had been so personally involved in their lives for so many years that Tristan had no qualms about allowing this good man to mediate between him and the household while he sequestered himself away. Lawrence had seen him at his worst many times; whatever state Tristan might be in while this battle ensued, he could feel comfortable with Lawrence making certain he had what he needed in order to be able to avoid the other servants.

Tristan nodded again and hurried away, certain his father understood his hasty retreat. By the time he got to his room he was gasping for breath, as if the grief and horror might swallow him whole and leave him completely incapable of breathing at all. In his room with the doors locked, Tristan sank to his knees by the bed, both from physical weakness and a sudden, desperate need to beg God to help him through this, to face the monsters threatening to devour him. In that moment he couldn't fathom ever being able to leave this room again. He could see no end in sight, and he was overcome with unspeakable terror. In that way he felt very much as he'd felt each and every time he had faced battles in the past. But somehow this was worse. The idea of facing physical death had not ever been any more frightening than what he was feeling and thinking now, all of it clashing together inside of him with a deafening cacophony of pain, grief, and the fear that he would never get past this unscathed and, therefore, he would be permanently scarred.

# CHAPTER FOUR
# HEALING

OLIVIA HEARD TRISTAN LEAVE WALTER'S room, since she'd been relaxing in the sitting room next door with a good book. It had become her habit to spend most of her time here, so that she could give Walter privacy when he needed it and allow him to rest when he was tired but also to be on hand if she was needed. Lawrence's rooms were on the other side of Walter's, and he too had cultivated a similar habit of reading while Walter rested or had company. Walter had become completely comfortable with Lawrence through his many years of loyalty and service, and Lawrence was always at the ready to assist Walter with personal matters. But Olivia knew that Walter was frustrated by his confinement to bed, and she enjoyed visiting with him whenever he needed company and no one else was available. Lawrence was eager to do whatever Walter needed, but Olivia actually enjoyed traversing the stairs and hallways back and forth from Walter's room to the kitchen—appreciating the exercise if nothing else—whereas Lawrence was glad to *not* have to go back and forth any more than necessary. Maids from the kitchen were efficient in bringing Walter's meals to his room and bringing enough food for visitors as well. But there were often other needs that required someone to go to the kitchen on his behalf when he had a craving for tea or a snack at an odd hour. Olivia was so deeply grateful for all Walter had done for her that she would gladly wait on him hand and foot; she would do anything just to help him feel more comfortable and at ease. He had not only given her and Winnie a place to live and met their every need graciously and kindly, but he had also taken them both into his heart and treated them with respect. He had given them a home, the first *real* home either of them had ever known, given their less-than-positive experiences with their own families.

Walter had taught Olivia much about life and love and the goodness of God—things no one had ever bothered to teach her before. For as long as Walter remained on this earth, she would devote herself to caring for him in every way possible—while Winnie was equally devoted to making certain Olivia had all that *she* needed and helping out elsewhere in the house in any way that she could. Winnie was comfortable among the staff and had many friendships there. They were both living a good life— thanks to Walter. And God willing, he would continue to live a good, long time—and find joy in his life, even with its limitations. Beyond that, Olivia believed that if it were up to Tristan, he would surely send them on their way. But in spite of his making it clear to her where he stood, she was determined to continue on as she had been doing for years now. She knew that Walter would certainly defend her position, but she had no desire for him to even be aware that there was a problem. She didn't want any ill feelings between Walter and Tristan—for any reason—and especially not because of her.

Now that Olivia knew Tristan was no longer visiting with his father, she set aside her book and knocked lightly at the door between the sitting room and Walter's bedroom, waiting the standard few seconds in which Lawrence would call out for her to wait if he was helping Walter with a personal matter. Walter's hearing was generally sufficient when it came to conversation, but he didn't hear well enough to hear a light knock on the door, so it was a well-established signal between her and Lawrence. When she heard nothing, she opened the door slowly and peered in to see Walter sitting up in bed, his eyes distant and thoughtful.

"Hello there," she said, approaching the bed.

"Oh, hello!" His face brightened and he reached out his hand. "What have you been doing while I've been enjoying my son's company?"

Olivia sat in the chair where Tristan had likely been sitting. "I have been enjoying a *very* good book. In fact, it's good enough that I might need to read it again—and if you're lucky I'll read it to *you*."

"I'll be hoping for some luck then," he chuckled.

"It must be wonderful for you to have Tristan back," she said.

"Oh, it is!" Walter said with an exuberance that contradicted his frailty. "And . . . he's changed . . . in many good ways. For now, at least, it seems our differences from the past have gone away, and I'm glad for it. Perhaps we've both come to appreciate the value of life . . . and the importance of family."

"I'm so glad to hear it," Olivia said. "If he's ever unkind to you, just say the word and I'll challenge him to a duel."

Walter laughed. "I daresay you would. But I wouldn't want to lose either one of you, so it's probably best that you don't."

"Probably." She tipped her head and winked. "In that case, I'll just slap his face."

Walter laughed again. "If I ever think he needs to be put in his place, I'll let you know." He laughed once more as if he found the idea terribly amusing. But his amusement became replaced very quickly by an especially somber expression and a weighted sigh. "For now, however, I believe he needs only patience and compassion." He looked directly at Olivia. "I've dreaded this very thing for a long time, my dear, as you well know."

"Yes, I know."

"And now he's back—and I'm so very glad for it—but I cannot imagine how it must be for him to contend with all that's happened. It will surely take time for him to accept Muriel's death. And I presume it will be even more difficult to accept her betrayal."

"Yes, I would think so," Olivia said, her heart hurting on Tristan's behalf. She too had dreaded his coming home to face all of this. She recalled her argument with Tristan in the hall not so long ago and knew she'd been too hard on him. He had far too much to face right now for her to be calling him a fool—even if she believed he *was* a fool, he certainly didn't need to hear about it right now, or perhaps ever. Perhaps it was just better to keep such feelings to herself.

Olivia stayed with Walter and talked a long while, both of them repeating thoughts and feelings in regard to Muriel's impact on their lives. They often said the same things over and over, but Walter had declared months earlier that doing so seemed necessary to come to terms with difficult events, and he had given both her and himself permission to talk about it until they no longer needed to. They both expressed concern for Tristan, and they both knew him well enough to know that it was best to just allow him to remain secluded if he chose while he faced his grief.

Lawrence and Winnie both joined them in Walter's room for supper. It was a fairly common occurrence for the four of them to gather there. They were a comfortable little group, and it was easy to talk and laugh and keep Walter engaged in life and distracted from his physical discomforts. Olivia wondered if Tristan might show up, and she was prepared to make a gracious exit if he did, not wanting to interfere in his relationship with his father—or his oversensitive emotions. But he didn't come and she felt concerned to think that he had likely shut himself away to contend with all that had occurred during his absence.

When it was time for Walter to get ready for bed, Olivia and Winnie went to the sitting room that joined their two bedrooms and talked mostly about the novels they'd been reading. They both loved to read, and the enormous library in this house had been a huge blessing for them. Prior to coming here, their access to books had been extremely rare. They talked until they both grew tired, having said very little about Tristan. Winnie knew every detail of Olivia's entire history with Tristan, and Olivia told her about the argument that had taken place earlier. Beyond that, they had both expressed their concern for him, and the conversation had gone elsewhere. Olivia had no desire to analyze any aspect of Tristan's return and how it might affect their lives. She preferred to just take on one day at a time and make the most of all that was good while it lasted.

\* \* \* \* \*

Tristan completely lost track of hours that merged into days. If not for Lawrence bringing meals—which Tristan could barely manage to eat—he would have had no sense of time passing at all. Keeping the heavy drapes closed, he was barely able to distinguish between daylight and darkness. At times he paced like a caged animal as a swirling force of anger and raw sorrow felt as if it would consume him if he didn't allow an outlet to release the growing pressure. At other times he cried like he never had. Even when he'd lost his mother, he couldn't recall crying like this. Of course, he'd been very young, and the tears of a child couldn't be compared to those of a man. Or could they? He *felt* like a child—a lost, lonely, frightened child. He frequently swayed his thinking in the direction of blaming himself for being taken in by Muriel's deception and the impact it was having on him now—and on his father and the entire household. And at other times, he was swayed toward a grievous, unbridled anger toward Muriel and her blatant disregard for any kind of integrity; for her moral and ethical disregard for the sanctity of marriage and the basic, decent need to be trustworthy.

Tristan slept only intermittently when exhaustion overtook him, but he was plagued with the dreams of grief that assaulted him—even in sleep—with confusion and pain and a horrified disbelief. He kept telling himself that he knew he needed to endure all that he was feeling; he needed to encourage these emotions to the surface and face them, as opposed to ignoring them and hoping they would go away. The memory of his father's words of wisdom kept him pressing forward, luring his heartache into the light rather than burying it in the darkness of his aching soul.

While the pain and confusion seemed endless, Tristan prayed often and urgently for help in navigating his way through this battlefield where cannonballs of fury would unexpectedly explode right in front of him while he was attempting to dodge an almost continual barrage of bullets, all aimed for his heart with growing evidence that he'd chosen badly when he'd made the decision to marry Muriel and that he'd allowed himself to be deceived by her—both before and after their marriage. He'd been a fool—just as Olivia had said. And her words haunted him right along with everything else he didn't want to face.

A moment finally came when Tristan suddenly felt desperate to get out of this room. His need for complete isolation screeched to a halt, and he ached for conversation with his father that he hoped would help put everything he'd learned about himself into perspective. When Lawrence brought breakfast, looking as deeply concerned as ever, Tristan asked him to send up enough hot water for a bath. Lawrence's countenance brightened, and he said he'd get right on it.

Tristan felt an increased appetite as he consumed his breakfast, and after days of personal neglect, the bath felt cleansing to his spirit as well as his body. Once he felt he was presentable, he went to his father's room and was gratified to see Walter's face light up just to see Tristan there.

"Oh, my boy," Walter said, reaching out a hand from where he sat propped up in bed in the usual way. "I've been praying for you and missing you terribly. Now that I know you're home, it's been difficult not to see you, but I knew you needed time to yourself. I hope it's been productive."

Tristan sat down on the chair near the bed and took Walter's outstretched hand. "I believe my time *has* been productive." He sighed. "I feel as if I've descended into the depths of hell, but I suppose that's necessary when it comes to facing such . . . betrayal . . . and deception."

"I'm certain you're right," Walter said. "I had my own experience of having to face all she did that was so hurtful, but I'm certain I can't imagine how much more difficult it must be for *you*."

Tristan sighed again. "Now that I've come this far . . . I wonder if I might talk through some of what I'm feeling. I respect your wisdom, Father . . . and I need to know if I'm thinking clearly."

"Of course," Walter said, visibly warmed by Tristan's expression of respect. Tristan wished he'd been man enough to offer it years ago, or to even appreciate how blessed he'd been to have such a good father.

"I think I've gotten past feeling guilty for how relieved I am that she's gone and that I don't have to live with the results of her behavior. If she were still alive, I have no idea how I would contend with trying to make peace with her betrayal, but that is absolutely irrelevant and I believe it's a waste of time to try and analyze something that isn't even relevant."

"I agree," Walter said. "And I absolutely believe you have nothing to feel guilty about."

"I don't know about that," Tristan said. "I don't feel guilty about my relief in not having to face her, but I'm having trouble with the fact that I married her in the first place. I was clearly blind to her character flaws, and I feel like I opened the door to allow a poisonous serpent into our family."

"Listen to me, Tristan," Walter said with an intensity that drew Tristan's full attention. "Muriel *deceived* you. She purposely used her beauty and charm to manipulate you into believing that she shared your beliefs and values . . . because she wanted a rich husband."

Tristan felt like he'd been slapped in the face. Even though he'd recognized that Muriel had deceived him, he'd never looked at it quite like that, and hearing it put into words so bluntly evoked more pain inside of him. He cleared his throat in an attempt to be free of the knot that had suddenly gathered there, but his voice still trembled when he asked, "Do you really think that was her thinking all along? Do you think that's all she saw in me?"

"I think she was very fond of you, Tristan," Walter said gently. "But I do not believe that her motives were ever honorable. Again, however, you cannot be hard on yourself for having been deceived. She was a very good actress." Walter leaned forward a little and his brow furrowed. "Now listen, son, and listen well. You must forgive yourself. It's important for you to forgive *her* so that you do not carry this burden with you throughout your life. But it's equally important for you to forgive yourself. Muriel set out with conscious intentions to deceive you and to live her life in a way that became her undoing. *You* only had the best intentions, and even if you chose to look past any signs that something wasn't right, I believe you were only trying to see the best in her. You have *nothing* to feel guilty about."

Tristan looked down and tried to take all that in. "I don't know about that," he said, "but I do appreciate your insight . . . and the perspective it gives me. Still . . . I'm certain it will take time for me to come to terms with my own decisions . . . and I believe I need to understand how exactly I allowed myself to be deceived. I need to understand it because I don't want it to happen again. If something in me has been so gullible and naive, then I certainly need to learn to be more wise and discerning."

"I agree," Walter said. "But I would caution you to be kind to yourself . . . and to others. Muriel's lack of trustworthiness does not mean other people do not deserve your trust."

Tristan looked up again, struck deeply by a question that he realized in that moment had been haunting him. "And how do I tell the difference, Father? How do I know if someone is being deceptive? Or if I am merely being suspicious because of these experiences?"

"You must trust your instincts as you pray for guidance. And you must never allow anger to cloud your judgment. It's easy to feel angry when something like this has happened, but you must never allow it to rule you."

Tristan nodded to indicate he'd heard. He understood the principle in theory, but he still felt too much brewing anger to fully believe that he was capable of getting past it enough to not allow it to cloud his judgment.

Following a silence that grew long enough to become mildly awkward, Walter said, "I'm certain you have more than enough to think about, and you must allow yourself time to heal. But I'm always here for you if you need to talk."

"Thank you, Father," Tristan said.

"Perhaps we should talk about something else," Walter added after more silence. "Perhaps getting your mind off all of this for a while would be wise."

"I can't argue with that," Tristan said and tried to think of something to say that had nothing to do with Muriel. "Talk to me about the estate. How is it faring? You've told me only a little since I returned."

Tristan was glad for the way that Walter dove in to discuss details of his responsibilities regarding the vast estate he had inherited—responsibilities that would fall to Tristan upon Walter's death. Tristan listened carefully and tried to learn, wishing he'd paid more attention to such things in previous years. He prayed it would be a good, long time before this responsibility fell on his shoulders, mostly because he couldn't imagine how he would cope with losing his father, especially when he'd somehow become his best friend in the days since he'd returned home. Tristan knew that the overseers would continue their work with their same efficiency, and there was also a trusted solicitor who had helped oversee business matters for many years. But he knew that he needed to get to know these men and learn to work with them. It occurred to Tristan as he talked with his father that he shouldn't wait for Walter's death to begin taking over. Walter was in poor health and could only manage the estate from his bed. Tristan was here now and he needed to step up and learn the full breadth of his responsibilities—now while his father was still here to guide him. He'd made some horrible mistakes by letting Muriel bring shame to this household, and she had certainly tarnished the Whitmore name. Tristan hoped that by honoring his father's legacy with the estate he might somehow be able to make up for wherever else he had fallen short.

Walter also brought up the importance of always being aware of those who worked in the household and how vital it was to remain abreast of their personal lives and any unusual needs that might arise. He cited a couple of examples of how one of the kitchen maids had become seriously ill the previous year, and it had taken her many weeks to recover. Walter had made certain she'd been properly cared for, had good medical care, and that her wages had not been diminished for her time off. The young woman had subsequently proved to be even more loyal and hardworking than she had before. Walter also talked about a young man who had worked in the stables, who had gotten word that his mother had passed away, leaving his younger brothers without parents. Walter had given him the time off that he'd needed to travel to his home for the funeral and to take care of whatever needed his attention. Walter had also given him some extra money to help meet his added expenses, and he had offered work to the younger brothers so that they could return here with their brother and remain together, making it possible for this young man to properly look after his family. Again, Walter made it clear that all three of these brothers were hardworking and dedicated.

"If you take care of your own," Walter said, "they will be much more likely to remain loyal and make a positive contribution to the household. When servants are treated unfairly and given no concessions for the challenges of life that inevitably arise, they are more likely to neglect their work, spread gossip, and even leave to seek employment elsewhere—which makes it necessary to find new help and start over in the difficult process of bringing someone new into the household and working out their level of commitment as well as their integrity."

Tristan listened, and his admiration for his father grew, along with his gratitude that Walter was alive and well enough to offer these wise lessons, which would make it less likely for Tristan to fumble over such matters when they were left to him.

When Walter seemed to be done making his point, Tristan brought up something that had been gnawing at him. "I must ask," he said, "why Olivia and Winnie are still here in the house. With Muriel gone, surely it makes better sense for them to move on. We can provide some financial assistance for them, of course. I understand that we have some obligation to see that they are not destitute, but—"

"Let me stop you there," Walter said with the firm authority of a father who was exerting self-discipline to hold back his temper. The tone reminded Tristan of his youth and completely caught him off guard. They had been speaking as equals with great mutual respect, and Tristan suddenly felt like a child being put in his place—which sparked a defensiveness that also took him back to his youth. He cautioned himself to listen and behave with maturity and not make a fool of himself, but he already knew he wasn't going to like whatever his father intended to say.

"First of all," Walter said, keeping a firm gaze on Tristan, "given the obvious point that you have been gone for nearly three years, I would advise you that it's likely more appropriate for you to approach such a subject by *asking* about the situation with Olivia and Winnie, as opposed to *assuming* they are merely here because of some kind of charitable obligation on my part." Tristan couldn't argue with that, and he had to order his defensiveness to stand down as Walter continued. "You have told me in this very conversation that you're having difficulty discerning whether or not someone is trustworthy, which is completely understandable given what you've learned about Muriel. You deserve to have time to come to terms with all of this, and I gladly allow you that time, son. Your humility and respect are much admired and appreciated, I assure you. However, it's my opinion that your difficult feelings toward Olivia are far more complicated than her simply being in the house when her cousin is no longer here. Given your history with her, it's impossible to separate Olivia's place in your life from Muriel's—but that does not equate with Olivia deserving any degree of the mistrust or anger that you feel toward Muriel. While you are currently in a place where it is difficult to discern a person's motives, trust your father when he tells you that Olivia is the finest young woman I have ever had the privilege of knowing; and Winnie is like unto her. Apart from your sisters—all of whom I do not see more than once a year, if that, and whose letters are sporadic at best—there is no other young woman on the earth who deserves my love and devotion—because she has earned it!"

Tristan felt increasingly uncomfortable with what his father was saying, but he couldn't tell if it was because he disagreed, or because he was being put in his place—however kindly and appropriately. He leaned back in his chair and folded his arms, maintaining his silence while Walter said what he needed to say.

"I would assume you've noticed," Walter went on, "that my mind has not been altered in the slightest by my physical maladies."

His silence implied that he was expecting an answer. "You are indeed as sharp as you ever were," Tristan said with all honesty.

"Do you think for one moment, my boy—given what you've known about me throughout your entire lifetime—that I would be fool enough to be taken in by someone who only wanted to be in my good graces for the sake of financial gain? Olivia's care and concern are genuine; she has become one of my dearest friends and most loyal companions. I would no sooner turn her out than I would Lawrence or Mrs. Higley or any of the others who have served me faithfully. Forgive the comparison, son, but I must make it. Ignoring the truth will not help you come to terms with all that's happened. *Muriel* only wanted to be in my good graces for the sake of preserving her luxurious lifestyle—which is exactly why she married *you.*"

Tristan took a sharp breath. He knew it was true, but hearing it put into words so bluntly was like a knife in the heart. Still, he just listened, feeling increasingly humbled by his father's speech.

"She spent our family money on frivolous belongings and her vulgar lifestyle, and not once did she ever express a word of gratitude to me, nor did she ever make any effort to nurture any kind of camaraderie or close-ness between us. When you married, I hoped for a daughter who would live in my home and fill the void left by your sisters having to leave here upon their marriages. Muriel brought little else except havoc and misery to this household. And Olivia is everything that Muriel was not. She is selfless and kind, and she has proven her dedication to me." Walter sighed loudly, as if to catch his breath after speaking what he surely must have been wanting to say for days but had known it would be difficult. "Now, let me be clear, Tristan. You are your own man. You are not required to like Olivia—or Winnie. You do not have to be in their presence any more than absolutely necessary. But this is still my house and I do expect you to be tolerant and respectful toward them—for my sake if not for the sake of common decency. They have asked for nothing but a roof over their heads and food to eat, and yet they have given as much to this household as any of our most devoted servants. They both work hard, and they brighten my life. You should know that I have made a provision for them in my will. It cannot be altered by you or anyone else. But I would hope that you carry out my wishes graciously and respectfully, and not begrudgingly. Perhaps you should consider your need to heal your wounds with Olivia, as much as you need to heal your wounds with Muriel—when you are ready." Walter took a deep breath. "That is all I have to say on the matter, and I hope this will not cause any discord between us. I've come to cherish our time together and the honesty we have been able to share. I don't want to lose that, Tristan, but I must speak the truth as I see it."

Tristan took a deep breath, swallowed his bruised pride, and said with resolve, "I would not want you to speak anything but the truth, Father, and I *do* trust and respect your wisdom. I apologize for making assumptions as opposed to asking you about the situation. I can't make any promises in regard to my own standing with Olivia, but I promise you that I will be kind and respectful to her—and to Winnie."

"Thank you," Walter said on the wake of a long sigh of relief, as if he'd truly feared that Tristan might be angry and this issue might have come between them. Tristan was grateful that he'd matured enough to not allow this—or any other petty matter—to cause friction with his father.

Tristan changed the subject back to matters of the estate, which he could discuss without facing any kind of internal battle. He knew he needed to fully digest everything his father had said, and he surely *did* have issues with Olivia that had nothing to do with her actually being here—except perhaps for the reminder of those issues that came up every time he saw her.

The servants were all eager to make everything as smooth and comfortable as possible for the master of the house, and they brought lunch to Walter's room, with enough for Tristan as well. As always, a newspaper was on the tray with the midday meal, and once they'd eaten, Walter asked if Tristan might read to him from the paper. He read a couple of stories that were of interest to Walter, including one on the ongoing challenge of smugglers who were apparently taking goods from this very area and putting them on ships to be delivered to the American colonists.

"I can't believe," Tristan commented, "that treason would be taking place right under our noses."

"It's astonishing," Walter said.

"The community is not so great in number," Tristan added as he thought it through. "Does this mean that we are actually acquainted with people who are assisting these smugglers?"

"I suppose it's possible," Walter commented, "but it's not for us to worry about."

"Well, I hope they come to swift justice," Tristan said, setting the paper aside. "I don't relish the thought of my own countrymen being wounded or killed with weapons smuggled to the colonists by people with whom I associate."

"It's certainly a quandary," Walter commented sincerely, "but I'm learning more and more that I can only control my little portion of the world, and there's no good in getting worked up over things that are simply far beyond our reach."

"I'm sure you're right," Tristan said, trying to block out the memories of bleeding on the battlefield and all the suffering he'd observed from his comrades. He wondered how Jack was doing and actually missed him. He hoped and prayed that all was well with him in his continued efforts to spare lives and ease suffering.

Tristan was glad to have his father change the subject, and he enjoyed the lighter conversation they shared before he left to give Walter time for his usual afternoon nap. He went back to his own room and immediately found it stifling after the days he'd been holed up in here with his grief and confusion. He turned around immediately and went outside to the beautiful array of gardens that stretched out from the west side of the house, which he believed had been done on purpose many generations ago, so that the setting sun would illuminate this area in a way that could make its artistry even more pleasing. Tristan had memories of observing many sunsets from this place throughout his life. Right now, the afternoon sun shone down with a pleasant warmth, and the aroma of a variety of flowers met his senses as he strolled slowly through the many pathways banked by neatly trimmed shrubberies. He found a bench that had shared many hours of his life with him, and he sat there to face the western horizon, trying to recall everything his father had said. He felt eager to learn the business matters of the estate so that he could grow in confidence in that regard, and also to help ease his father's burdens. But there was no anxiety or concern over that; it was all that Walter had said about Olivia that weighed on him. In his present state of feeling so weighed down by trying to make sense of all that Muriel had done and its impact on him—and his father, not to mention everyone who lived here—he could hardly begin to mentally process how Olivia fit into all that and what he should do about it. The only thing he could recognize now was the fact that he owed her an apology. He'd been sharp and unkind when they'd last spoken, and he'd said things that completely contradicted all that Walter had told him. And he couldn't deny that Walter was right. Even if Tristan didn't like Olivia or want her around—whatever his reasons might be— he absolutely needed to respect his father's wishes and be respectful and kind. He had no personal issue with Winnie; even though they'd known each other a long time, he'd rarely engaged in direct conversation with her. She'd always been a part of Olivia's life, but she had remained in the background as servants often did. The issue here was his relationship with Olivia—and the complicated history they shared. He believed he still had much to do in unraveling the tangled mass of troubles Muriel had created. But in the meantime, he could behave like a gentleman and offer Olivia the apology she deserved—and the respect his father had requested. If nothing else, he would exhibit his own devotion to his father by doing as he wished. Walter Whitmore was a good man—the best Tristan had ever known—and Tristan knew that however foolish he might have been in the past in regards to taking advice from his father, he needed to be wise enough to see that his father had a deep understanding of life and people, and Tristan would do well to pay attention to what he said.

\* \* \* \* \*

Olivia spent Walter's nap time in the kitchen, scrubbing the stove and then assisting with the preparations for the evening's supper. She enjoyed being busy and helpful as much as she enjoyed the company of those who spent their days in the kitchen, combining their skills and hard work to prepare fine meals for everyone in the house. But today Olivia didn't feel as engaged as she usually did in the conversations going on around her. She knew that Tristan had spent most of the morning with Walter and that they'd shared lunch. She was glad to know that Tristan had come out of hiding in his room; she'd been deeply concerned for him, and hoped and prayed that he would be able to find his way through the impact of what Muriel had done to his life. But she couldn't deny that having him keep to himself had been easier in the respect that she hadn't needed to avoid spending time with Walter so that he could be with his son, nor had she feared coming upon Tristan and having to face his wrath toward her. Even though she'd not said a word to Walter about what Tristan had said—and she never would—she knew that Walter would defend her, simply because she was clear on where their relationship stood, and she had a clear conscience in her own motives. Walter was like a father to her—the kind of father she'd always wished her own father could have been. And it warmed her heart more than anything ever had to know that Walter regarded her much like he would a daughter, and their time together was as much a treasure to him as it was to her.

She knew that Walter was awake when Lawrence sent one of the house-boys to get tea for him, so Olivia finished the task she'd been assigned by the cook, removed her apron, and went upstairs, hoping that Tristan wouldn't have returned to Walter's room. She found Walter and Lawrence drinking tea and chatting, and they were both pleased to see her and invited her to join them. An extra cup and saucer was *always* on Walter's tea tray, since he always wanted to be prepared for more company.

Lawrence left Walter in Olivia's care once he'd finished his tea, having a few things he needed to take care of on Walter's behalf. Olivia enjoyed her time alone with Walter, although he said nothing about his visit with Tristan except that it had been nice to see him again after his needing some days alone. Olivia wondered how he was doing but didn't want to ask, even though a polite inquiry might have been deemed appropriate. She preferred to not bring up the subject of Tristan at all with Walter, if only so she could assure Tristan that she had not talked about him with his father since he'd returned home. It was better that way. For now, she was determined to simply avoid Tristan and hopefully waylay any further opportunity for him to be unkind or express opinions that were diametrically opposed to those of Walter. Olivia knew Tristan was grieving and that he was surely horrified by the news he'd come home to, and she chose to give him the benefit of the doubt and believe that his anger toward her might settle with time. But whether or not it did, all that really mattered to her was doing everything she could to brighten Walter's life. Even though he wouldn't admit it and rarely even hinted at it, she knew that his confinement to bed was depressing for him. He'd been active all his life, and it was often difficult for Walter to remain cheerful and positive when he felt useless and heavily reliant upon others. Olivia was committed to doing everything she could to help ease his frustrations in that regard and to give him back a portion of the joy he had given her by allowing her into his home and his heart.

When suppertime came and Tristan had not returned, Olivia was glad to remain in Walter's room and share a meal with him. Winnie and Lawrence joined them, and they had a lovely visit that included much laughter—mostly because Winnie could tell stories in a way that was usually funny, even though she didn't try to make them that way. She could talk about an exchange she'd overheard in a shop in town, or a mishap in the kitchen, or a stable hand being outsmarted by a horse, and stories of general observations of life turned into hilarious anecdotes— even though she didn't stretch the truth.

When Walter's fatigue alerted them all to the fact that it was time for him to be getting ready for bed, Winnie took the dinner tray to the kitchen, after which she intended to do some personal laundry before retiring to her bed. Lawrence remained with Walter to assist him as he always did, and Olivia embarked on a leisurely stroll through the quiet hallways of the enormous house. The long days of summer had left the house still light enough for her to find her way without a lamp. She gravitated habitually to one of her favorite places, especially when the weather was favorable. Still, she'd many times stepped out onto this particular balcony even when it was freezing—if only for a few minutes—to look out over the gardens toward the west horizon. She'd enjoyed many beautiful sunsets from this spot, and it had come to be a place of sanctuary where she could find inner peace even when the drama of life had been overwhelming.

Olivia opened one of the glass doors that led to the balcony and stepped out, closing the door behind her. She moved to the railing and set her hands on the smooth, cool marble, looking toward the horizon where only a tiny bit of the sun was still visible. Breathing in the beauty of the sky, painted with intermittent clouds that brought the sun's light to colorful life, Olivia felt calmer than she had since Tristan's return. His very presence in the house had been weighing heavily on her, perhaps because she knew that he was opposed to *her* presence in the house. But in that moment she felt as if many prayers were being answered. She watched until the sun disappeared, leaving behind a light that still radiated across the sky with a warm glow. In her heart, she believed everything would be all right, even if she couldn't imagine how that might come to pass.

# CHAPTER FIVE

# AWAKENED

OLIVIA GASPED AND NEARLY JUMPED out of her shoes when she heard Tristan say, "It's a lovely view."

"Good heavens!" she said and pressed a hand over her pounding heart. "You might have made yourself known!"

"I didn't want to disturb you," he said from where he sat in one of the chairs that was always on the balcony, but he'd scooted it close enough to the rail for him to stack his booted ankles there. Due to the curve of the railing he was sitting far enough behind her that she'd not been able to see him. "Sunsets are fleeting; I wouldn't want you to miss the moment."

Olivia had no response; she was more preoccupied with getting her heart to slow down and was a bit miffed with the way he'd completely evaporated her calm mood. She moved to a chair at the opposite end of the balcony and sat down, fearing her legs might give out otherwise.

"You don't have to stay," Tristan said with no hint of the anger he'd exhibited the last time they'd talked. "Or if you'd like me to leave . . . I will. You clearly came here to be alone."

"But you were here first," she said.

"If you must know, I'm glad you came. Perhaps it was an answer to my prayers. I need to talk with you, and I'm hoping I might sleep better if I have the opportunity to do so now."

Olivia steeled herself for another conversation about her reasons for being here, and his belief that she and Winnie needed to leave. Even if he was now less angry over the matter, she couldn't expect him to have changed his mind.

"Very well," she said and stood, moving again to the balcony. She felt more confident standing and more stable by holding to the marble railing. She also didn't have to look at him if she was looking out at the gardens in the fading light of day. "Say what you need to say," she said when he didn't speak, "and then I'll leave you in peace."

"There's no need for you to get upset before I've even started," he said, and she was dismayed to realize how defensive she'd sounded. "Before you get all riled, hear me out. I owe you an apology." Olivia turned to look at him, as if that might convince her that she'd heard him correctly. "Your reasons for being here are between you and my father; it's none of my business. I want you to know that I will honor his wishes—even after he is gone."

A wave of relief washed over Olivia with such force that she had to grip the railing more tightly, glad that it was becoming too dark for him to see her expression. She'd invested so much energy into worrying about what might happen to her and Winnie once Tristan was in charge; with that worry now dispelled, she wanted to cry like a baby. She managed to keep her dignity intact, but she found it impossible to speak.

Olivia heard Tristan sigh loudly, indicating there was more he wanted to say, but he wasn't finding it easy. "My years away have changed me, Olivia. War is a humbling experience. I'm trying very hard to be a better man and not to fall back into old habits. First and foremost, I can see now that I rarely gave my father the respect he deserved. I'm glad to say that while I may be lacking in wisdom and discernment in many respects, I have become wise enough to pay attention to what my father says."

"He is a very wise man," Olivia said, filled with gratitude to hear him make such a powerful and tender declaration.

"We agree on that," Tristan continued and sighed again. In the dusky shadows she saw him remove his feet from the railing and place them on the floor. He leaned forward and clasped his hands. "I confess that I am . . . reeling over Muriel's death and . . . all that led up to it, and I'm certain I haven't even begun to understand it or come to terms with it. I ask for your patience in that regard."

"Of course," Olivia said, glad to be able to express how she really felt without the fear of his anger. "I can't imagine how difficult it must be for you. I think I'm *still* reeling over it . . . sometimes. But I'm doing better than I was a few months ago. With time I'm certain you will come to terms with it . . . even if it's impossible to truly understand."

"I hope so," he said, "because I certainly don't want to spend my life feeling this way . . . which brings me to my next point. I have to say that . . . you were right. I was so angry with what you said to me, but . . . I can see now that you were right. And maybe that's the most difficult thing to accept."

"I'm afraid I don't know what you mean exactly," she admitted when he didn't explain.

"You said that I'm a fool—that I was a fool when I married her and am an even bigger fool now. You are absolutely right about that, Olivia."

"Thank you for being willing to admit it," she said, "although I'm certain it can't be easy; in fact I daresay it must be very painful."

"And what makes you think that?" he asked with mild sarcasm.

"Because I had to admit it in regard to myself," she said and saw his head turn more toward her. "I always tried to give her the benefit of the doubt; I always tried to see the best in her, to be a good friend to her, hoping that I might have some positive influence. But I was a fool, as well. I ignored so many signs. I looked away when my instincts were telling me that she was lying to me. She willfully deceived me. I told you there was no shame in being deceived, and I believe that; I really do. But I've had trouble convincing myself that I shouldn't be ashamed, that maybe if I'd handled the situation differently she might still be alive. And yet there's a part of me that is deeply relieved to not have to contend with her bad behavior and poor choices, and with my relief comes guilt. What kind of person am I to be relieved that my cousin would die?" Hearing her own voice crack, Olivia cleared her throat, a little embarrassed with how candid she'd become, especially when she didn't know for certain how Tristan might interpret everything she was saying—in spite of his own humble admissions. She turned back to look out over the gardens. "Perhaps one day I'll be able to sort all of this out and find the strength to forgive myself."

"Well, when you do, let me know how you did it," Tristan said. "Right now that feels utterly impossible."

"With God all things are possible," she said. "Isn't that what we believe?"

"I *want* to believe that," he admitted.

"I *have* to believe that," she said. "Otherwise I don't know if I could cope with all that's happened and my place in the midst of it."

"I'll try to take that into consideration," he said in a tone that implied he didn't want to talk about it anymore—or perhaps he *couldn't* right now. She completely understood.

A stretch of silence came to the brink of becoming awkward before Olivia asked, "Would you like to be alone? I can—"

"Your being here is not bothering me," he said. "It's a big balcony."

Olivia sat down again, not wanting to leave. It was a perfect evening and she enjoyed this spot that offered fresh air without having to traverse the hallways and stairwells required to actually go outside. She also felt a great and enormous relief over the conversation she'd just shared with Tristan. She knew there was likely a great deal they still disagreed on, and their path of healing might well bring such things to the surface. But for the moment, she didn't feel uncomfortable in his presence and was glad to share this brief reprieve with him.

The silence stirred up Olivia's thoughts and she hated where they were taking her. While she was desperately trying to think of something to say that might begin a conversation that would distract her, she could only think of how much she wanted to say, *You broke my heart, and I don't know if I'll ever get over it.* Olivia thought back to the night he'd come home, and his very presence had extinguished all her efforts to convince herself that she could face him and not be reminded of all they had once shared. When he'd been married to Muriel, she had prayed very hard to stop seeing him in any kind of romantic light, but there had always been an awkwardness between them from the time she and Winnie had come to live here at Muriel's insistence, and until Tristan had gone to war. She'd even wondered if part of his reason for leaving was to get away from the tension between them, and she suffered some guilt over the possibility that he might have purposely put himself in harm's way just to get away from her. Olivia thought of how difficult it had been upon his return to not throw herself in his arms, just to hold him close again. Since Muriel's death, she'd tried very hard to keep her thinking in the mode that he was not available to her, and that she needed to think of him as a cousin—or a mere acquaintance. But all her efforts had vanished the moment she'd seen him, and all the feelings she'd struggled to subdue for years came rushing back. It had taken every bit of strength she had to maintain an appropriate demeanor while she'd taken on the role of telling him all of the bad news he'd needed to know. She'd longed to offer comfort, to talk to him the way they'd once talked. But that was no longer her place, and she'd certainly come to know her place; Tristan had made that very clear when she'd come to live in his home, at the mercy of his father. He'd been anything but pleased at the time, and in spite of his kind apologies here tonight on the balcony, she felt certain they had been initiated by a desire to honor and respect his father more than anything else. He obviously hadn't held onto any of the feelings he'd once had for her, which made her feel like a fool.

She'd accused him so unkindly of being a fool, but was she not the same? Tristan had never deceived her, but he'd treated her cruelly once he'd fallen under Muriel's spell. She'd spent years trying to forgive Muriel, putting the blame all on her. She knew that Muriel had deceived Tristan, but she never would have believed he would have been gullible enough to fall for it. And whatever Tristan may or may not have done, Olivia considered herself a fool—for falling in love with him in the first place and believing that he could ever love someone like her. And she'd especially been a fool to hold onto her feelings all these years. Her conscience was clear in regard to her thoughts and feelings toward him during the time that he'd been married to her cousin, but in the months since Muriel's death, she'd not been able to think about him without remembering a time when everything had been much different between them—which was surely the biggest reason why they were so easily agitated with each other. And now, here they sat, surrounded by a silence that was anything but comfortable. She could hear crickets chirping in the garden, but they weren't as loud in her ears as the sound of Tristan's silence and the echoes of her own thoughts while she wondered what *he* was thinking.

"I should go in," she finally said and stood up, unable to bear the tension another moment.

"Don't leave on my account," he said and seemed to mean it.

"I'm just . . . very tired and . . . thank you . . . for the things you said; it means a great deal." Olivia heard her own stammering and hurried toward the door before she made a fool of herself. "Good night."

"Good night," she heard just before she closed the door behind her. She paused to draw in a deep breath, but it took a few tries before she could fill her lungs with air. Then she hurried to her room to get ready for bed, doubting that she would ever be able to sleep.

\* \* \* \* \*

Tristan didn't sleep at all that night, following his conversation with Olivia on the balcony. He'd said everything he'd felt the need to say. He could now look his father in the eye and say that he had respectfully apologized to Olivia, and he'd committed to honoring his father's wishes on her behalf. So, why didn't he feel better? He had expected to feel a weight lifted, to feel somehow lighter. But he didn't. Of course, he was still heavy with grief over Muriel's death—and perhaps more so over her betrayal. More than anything, however, he felt confused. He believed he should feel more grief than he did—considering that his wife had died. He should be mourning and preoccupied with such an enormous loss. But he found it difficult to mourn the loss of her life when he knew that another man's baby had been buried in the casket with her—and indeed her giving birth to that baby had been the cause of her death. He'd wondered many times how he might have felt if she'd been a loyal and loving wife and she'd died giving birth to *his* child. If that were the case, he wondered if he could even go on living. But conjuring up such a fairy tale only added bitterness to the reality.

Tristan tried to force his mind completely away from thoughts of Muriel. He felt as if his head would implode with the debilitating force behind such rancorous notions. But when he managed to get Muriel out of his mind, Olivia rushed in to fill the void. He recalled sitting on the balcony with her this evening, and he couldn't lie to himself and pretend he'd not been affected. But why? After getting out of bed around three in the morning and wandering restlessly about the room until nearly four, he sat down and faced the question straight on. *Why?* He'd admitted to her that he'd been a fool for marrying Muriel in the first place, and an even bigger fool now. Thinking back through their argument over that matter, and his related apology earlier this evening, Tristan recalled exactly what Olivia had said, and something painful struck his heart. He pressed his hand over his chest and struggled to take in a deep breath. Her words echoed over and over in his head as if someone or something beyond himself was forcing him to hear her clearly until he understood what she'd meant.

*Given the cold, hard facts about the way Muriel lived her life, you still choose to believe that everything she told you about me is true. You're a fool, Tristan Whitmore! You were a fool when you married her, and you're an even bigger fool now.*

"Good heavens," Tristan muttered aloud. He *was* a fool. He'd spent years being angry with Olivia—and believing he could never trust her—because of things Muriel had told him about her. He had no evidence to support Muriel's allegations. Olivia's father had been a scoundrel, always gambling and continually accumulating debts. But Tristan had known all of that long before Muriel had intruded upon his relationship with Olivia. He'd always told Olivia that it didn't matter, that her father's bad behavior was no reflection on her own character. And then Muriel had started flirting with him and had told him in supposed confidence that Olivia was involved in her father's schemes and was as dishonest and selfish as he was. Muriel told him that Olivia was conniving and manipulative and a very good actress. And he had believed her. He had *believed* her! Following his marriage to Muriel, Olivia's father had taken his own life, adding more shame and scandal to her burdens, and everything she'd owned had gone to pay off his outstanding debts. Olivia and Winnie had come to live here at Muriel's insistence. Muriel had played the compassionate cousin, appealing to Walter's charitable nature, and she'd taken Olivia and Winnie under her wing. Or had she? What had resulted was a series of tense and awkward moments as Muriel had flaunted her marriage to Tristan, along with the wealth of the family, always doing so under a guise of kindness and with just enough politeness that he'd always just passed it off. But Tristan could look back now and see that Muriel had been cruel to her cousin in every possible way. Olivia had likely been smoldering inside, and Walter had surely seen exactly what had been going on—while Tristan had been completely blinded by his infatuation with his wife and oblivious to the underlying drama that had been taking place. He *was* a fool! He was a pathetic, blind fool! And now that he was beginning to understand exactly what that meant, he felt literally sick. Nausea smoldered inside of him for a long while as he reviewed the memories over and over, assessing the accuracy of his new deductions. The sickness inside of him increased until he had to run to the chamber pot and throw up. Given his empty stomach, having eaten very little supper several hours earlier, he mostly heaved painfully as if he could somehow retch up the painful realizations assaulting him and be free of them.

When the heaving stopped, he sat on the floor, weak and drowning in a cold sweat. "Oh, help!" he murmured and hung his head, overcome with a dizziness that accompanied the hovering nausea. "God, help me. . . . God, forgive me. What have I done?"

The room was filling with the light of dawn before Tristan managed to drag himself up off the floor and back to his bed. Exhausted as he was, he still couldn't sleep. Intermittently praying for help and guidance and forgiveness, he took his mind back to when he'd first met Olivia, and how quickly and deeply he'd fallen in love with her. He'd met her at a social she'd attended with her father, a man who had barely been considered acceptable at such gatherings but invited because he was believed to have great wealth—even though he had earned his fortune as opposed to inheriting it. Tristan had no problem with that. He believed that a man should be enterprising and seek out education and occupations. But it was more Mr. Halstead's daughter that had caught Tristan's attention. Olivia was an only child whose mother had died more than ten years earlier. It had taken Tristan very little time to win the favor of both Olivia and her father, and Tristan and Olivia were soon officially courting. And it hadn't taken much time after that for Tristan to realize that Olivia's father was not nearly as well off as he professed. It was true that he had earned a fortune, but he had a terrible gambling habit and the money was dwindling away. Olivia had confided to Tristan how ashamed she felt for her father's lack of scruples and her fears that he would gamble away every last shilling until they had nothing. She had confessed to Tristan that she knew her father was not only adept at cards and dice—and losing more money than he made—he was also adept at cheating. He'd gotten into trouble for it more than once, but he'd also gotten away with it many times.

Tristan had felt a strong desire to marry Olivia and take her away from the fear and shame she suffered. He wanted to make her his wife and give her the security she deserved, and he also wanted to put distance between her and her father's bad habits. Tristan was on the verge of proposing marriage to Olivia when Muriel came to live with her cousin and uncle after the passing of her mother. At first, Tristan had considered Muriel ostentatious and annoying; he'd avoided her and mostly ignored her. He'd initially been oblivious to the fact that she'd actually been flirting with him, and then she'd tearfully confided to him the concern she felt for his well-being if he had serious intentions toward Olivia—due to the things she knew about Olivia's deceptive ways and the unseemly behavior she'd not allowed Tristan to see. Tristan could now see that Muriel had been describing herself. She'd purposely put herself between him and Olivia because *she* had wanted to marry into a wealthy family as opposed to having her cousin marry for love. With Muriel's parents now gone and with no other living relatives, she was dependent upon her uncle—Olivia's father—for her living. Their lifestyle had been comfortable, but they all knew that he was heavily in debt and there was certainly a fear for how that might impact them all. Through Muriel's repeated lies, Tristan had come to believe that Olivia had only wanted to marry him for financial security. And Muriel had professed her love for Tristan that she'd tried to keep secret so as not to hurt her cousin. But now the truth stood before him, bare and blatant—and utterly horrifying. He couldn't get over just how big a fool he had been and how Olivia and his father had been innocent victims to Muriel's fiendish character—and his own gullible stupidity. He couldn't believe it. He just couldn't believe it!

After marrying Muriel, Tristan had forced all thoughts of Olivia out of his mind, believing that she had deceived him. Then a day came when Olivia's father could no longer put off his debtors and he took his own life. Olivia and her lifelong companion, Winnie, were abruptly left with practically nothing except their clothes. They had no means to make a living, and nowhere to go. Muriel had spoken to Walter about having them come to live at Whitmore Manor. It was Walter's home and it was certainly his decision to make, but Tristan had been angered by the way that Muriel hadn't spoken to *him* about it as well. And so it had just happened. While he felt increasingly uncomfortable with his marriage, and unable to accept that he'd made a mistake, Olivia was there at every meal, and he never knew when he might encounter her anywhere in the house. He'd run away to distant battlefields, and now he'd returned home, desperately praying that there could be redemption for such foolishness on his part.

When Lawrence came to check on Tristan and ask if he'd like to have breakfast downstairs or with his father, Tristan declared that he would pass on breakfast altogether since he wasn't feeling well. Tristan assured Lawrence that he would ring if he needed anything because he was hoping to be able to rest and therefore didn't want to be disturbed. The truth was that Tristan couldn't bear to face *anyone* until he could process these new discoveries through his reeling mind and try to come to terms with this new perspective of the truth.

Tristan finally slept and woke to realize that it was the middle of the afternoon. He rolled over and sighed as the thoughts he'd fallen asleep with rushed back into his head. He groaned and put his hands over his face, as if he could hide from them. Lost and confused as he felt, he turned his mind to prayer, knowing he could never do this without God's help. He'd always believed in God, and he'd always prayed—the way his father had taught him to. He prayed now harder than he ever had. He needed God's forgiveness in a way he had never needed it before. He'd always been aware that he was far from perfect and that the need for God's forgiveness was an essential aspect of life. But he'd always tried to be a good man, to have integrity and behave with the moral values he'd been taught in his youth. He'd always tried to live the teachings of the Bible and make decisions based on those principles. But he'd been deceived by a wolf in sheep's clothing, a serpent in skirts with impeccable beauty and beguiling ways.

And his choices had caused immeasurable suffering to so many others. At the top of the list was Olivia and his father. But there was also Winnie, who surely would have suffered over his decision to choose Muriel instead of Olivia to be his wife. And what about every person in this household who had had no choice but to follow Muriel's orders and put up with her insolence? And what of the people in this community who had interacted with her? Surely every single person who had come to know Muriel as the wife of Tristan Whitmore would have been disgusted and horrified. And now that Tristan could see the truth, *he* was disgusted and horrified.

While Tristan prayed, he recalled clearly Olivia saying to him just last night, *With God all things are possible.* The memory of her words crept over him with a soothing comfort. In spite of all he'd done to hurt her, she had treated him with kindness and respect, and she had reminded him of the very thing he needed now more than he ever had: faith! He had to believe that through his faith all things were possible—even forgiveness for making such an enormous mistake. And the very fact that his father and Olivia could forgive him—and he believed they would—made it easier to believe that it was possible for God to forgive him. And perhaps one day he could actually forgive himself. Of course, he had a long road ahead and he wasn't even sure how to begin, but by suppertime his stomach was growling and he felt enough strength and motivation to get cleaned up and go to his father's room, hoping he wasn't too late to share supper with him.

Tristan entered the room to the sound of laughter, and he quickly assessed that Lawrence, Olivia, and Winnie were eating their supper at the table that had always been here in the room, a short distance from the bed. Walter was sitting up in bed, as usual, with a dinner tray over his lap. And they were all laughing—until Tristan's entrance brought it to an abrupt halt.

"Forgive me for interrupting," he said, wondering if his countenance looked as bad as he felt, which had brought on the sudden sober mood, or if perhaps they had been laughing at his expense. "I'll come back after supper, Father, and—"

"Not at all," Lawrence said, motioning toward the empty chair across from him at the table. "There's enough here for you; we were hoping you'd join us."

"Indeed we were," Walter said. "It's good to see you, my boy."

Tristan noted that Olivia and Winnie didn't comment, but he couldn't blame them—especially in light of all he'd just figured out about how they must have viewed him for the last five years. Was that really only how long it had been since he'd married Muriel? It seemed a lifetime ago!

"Thank you," Tristan said and sat down while the other three at the table each put helpings of food on his plate from the covered serving dishes.

Lawrence made himself comfortable again and said, "We were just talking about the vicar's sermon last Sunday."

"We take turns going to church so that one of us stays here with Walter," Winnie volunteered, as if she had no ill feelings toward Tristan whatsoever. Either she was incredibly forgiving or a very good actress.

"Someone's got to tell me what goes on at church," Walter said.

"Indeed," Olivia interjected with a smile toward Walter. "Although I daresay you prefer our interpretation of the vicar's sermons as opposed to actually having to sit through them."

"There are advantages to being bedridden," Walter said as if it were very funny.

"But no one repeats the sermons better than Winnie," Lawrence said with a chuckle, and Tristan recalled how witty and clever Winnie could be.

"You must fill me in," Tristan said, relieved at least to know they'd been laughing about something that had nothing to do with him.

"The thing is," Winnie said, looking at him since the others had obviously already heard the story, "the poor man stumbles over his words; he means well and we all know he's a good man, but preaching at the pulpit certainly does put his nerves to the test." Winnie chuckled warmly and the others smiled. "So, he was talking about the parable of the lost sheep, and he actually said . . ." She broke into laughter that made it impossible to speak, and the others laughed with her. Tristan laughed too, unable to keep from doing so when it was so infectious. It felt good to laugh, as if all the tension bottled up inside of him was being given an outlet for release.

"He does get the wrong word sometimes," Lawrence managed to say.

"And the congregation tried so hard not to snigger," Olivia interjected. "Or so I heard; I wasn't actually there."

"We heard it secondhand," Walter said, still laughing along with the others.

"Spit it out," Tristan said to Winnie. "I can't bear the suspense."

Winnie managed to calm down enough to speak, breathless from her laughter. "The vicar said that . . . when we choose to come back to the fold . . . we would not only no longer be lost, but . . ." She laughed again. "We would be blessed with . . . immorality."

They all broke out into hysterical laughter again, while Winnie managed to say. "It's really not *that* funny, but . . ."

Tristan couldn't help once again joining in their laughter over the vicar using the wrong word. After a good minute or more of just laughing, which prevented everyone from eating or speaking, Lawrence finally wiped his eyes and said, "The poor man turned red as a beet. The congregation was trying so hard to remain polite. He quickly corrected himself, making it clear that he meant *immortality*, but the damage was done. Dear fellow. He does mean well."

"Afterward," Winnie said, "I heard many people telling him it was a lovely sermon and reassuring him that he'd done fine; people for the most part are very kind. I myself told him the same."

"As did I," Lawrence said. "God bless him!"

The conversation turned elsewhere while they all finished their supper, and Tristan felt surprisingly comfortable among the small group. He credited that mostly to the laughter they'd shared, especially considering how weighed down he had been feeling in regard to Olivia. As his thoughts returned to the regret he felt over his choices and the way he'd behaved, the room felt suddenly stifling and Tristan excused himself, telling his father he would see him tomorrow. Needing to get out of the house, he hurried to the gardens, glad for the familiar reprieve that engulfed him as he slowed his pace to amble among the pristine shrubberies and flowers. He stood in a favorite spot and watched the sun go down, thinking of how it had risen and set each day he'd been away, just as it had each day since he'd returned. The decisions and drama of his own life had not changed the absolute consistency of the world he lived in. He found comfort in the notion that God had created this world and He was surely in charge. And perhaps with time, Tristan could find forgiveness through his faith in God. But he knew that he first needed to seek it with the people in his life who had been most affected by the way he'd hurt them—even if he'd never intended to do so.

\* \* \* \* \*

Olivia remained in Walter's room until he showed signs that he was ready to go to sleep. Winnie took the tray of supper dishes to the kitchen, Lawrence stayed to give Walter the help he needed, and Olivia wandered to the balcony, hoping there might be a picturesque sunset this evening. Even more so, she hoped she might find Tristan there. Since their last conversation, she'd been thinking about him far too much. Against her will, memories of all they had once shared had come rushing back. She'd slept little as she'd fought to banish such thoughts from her mind to no avail. She knew that to admit her love for him, that she'd never stopped loving him, was to make herself vulnerable to the possibility that he would reject her again. Remembering the love and tenderness that had once existed between them also meant remembering how he had humiliated her and broken her heart. Everyone she knew had believed that Tristan Whitmore was on the verge of proposing marriage to her. She too had believed it— and for good reason. He'd not hesitated to make his feelings known to their families and to others he associated with in the community. And Olivia had never been happier; the anticipation she'd felt over becoming his wife had filled her with perfect joy. And then Muriel had stepped between them with her beguiling, deceitful, and conniving ways, and Olivia's world had come crashing down. Tristan's mistrust of her became quickly evident, and then he had accused her of being involved in her father's underhanded schemes, making it clear that he could never marry her knowing what he had come to know about her lack of integrity. Her attempts to tell him that Muriel had been lying to him had been boldly squelched, and Olivia had been left to stand by and watch as he'd courted Muriel—and then married her. Olivia had grieved deeply as she'd fought to forgive them both and find a way to be happy. She had barely begun to believe it was possible to move forward and find happiness when her father's debts suddenly rose up to swallow him and he'd taken his own life, leaving her to face the brunt of his lifetime of poor decisions. She'd sold everything they had to pay off his debts, which had left her and Winnie with very little to live on and no place to live. Muriel had been her only living relative, but coming to her—and the family she'd married into—for help had been the most humiliating experience of her life. And now here she was. She never could have foreseen Muriel's depth of betrayal, nor her death. And she never would have believed that after all that had happened, her feelings for Tristan could be so easily awakened. At moments she felt angry over feeling this way, as if her love was some kind of curse meant to punish her. At other times she felt elated at the possibility that their love could be rekindled. But she had no idea where Tristan stood. He'd come a long way in the days since his initial angry outburst toward her, but he was surely still off balance with grief and shock, and she knew she needed to be patient and allow time to heal their wounds before she could assess whether these feelings were worth encouraging, or better abandoned.

Olivia stepped out onto the balcony and closed the door behind her, disappointed to not find Tristan there. At the very least she would have enjoyed a little casual conversation with him. Focusing on her usual reason for coming here—the grand view of the setting sun—she looked toward the west horizon. The sky was cloudless, which made the sky rather colorless as the golden circle of light eased effortlessly out of sight. Just before the last glimmer of the sun disappeared beneath the edge of the earth, Olivia glanced down to the gardens, and she drew in her breath when she saw Tristan standing there. He wore his typical attire of dark breeches and black boots, and a dark waistcoat over a white shirt with blousy sleeves. His unruly hair was being teased about by a subtle breeze, and his hands were clasped behind his back while he too watched the sun go down. Her heart quickened at the sight of him, and she felt the somber thoughtfulness of his aura. She hurried back into the house and down the stairs before she had a chance to talk herself out of this opportunity to just be with him—if only for a few minutes. And she prayed that—at the very least—she might be able to share some comfortable conversation with him, anything that might help ease them toward healing the wounds of the past they shared. Even if there was nothing in their future beyond friendship, she wanted it to be free of any burdens of regret. For now, she just wanted his company in any way that he might be willing to share it. And with any luck, they could find some common ground and work toward mending the tattered years that had passed since he had been the center of her life, and she had been the center of his.

Olivia hesitated at the edge of the garden and slowed her breathing. She didn't want him to know that she'd practically run from the balcony with the hope of getting here before he had a chance to leave. She could see him in the distance, still in the same place. He couldn't go back into the house without having to pass her. She steadied her breath and walked toward him, praying that she could conceal all that had been reawakened in her and that she might avoid making a fool of herself in any way.

Olivia stopped a few steps behind him, noting that he hadn't heard her approach. Secretly hoping to startle him, she said, "Hello," and wasn't disappointed with the way he turned abruptly, his expression betraying momentary fear.

"Don't sneak up on me like that!" he said before resuming his comfortable pose.

Olivia stood beside him and laughed softly. "Sorry," she said. "I couldn't resist."

"What are you doing out here?" he asked, glancing toward her. His tone of voice held no hint of displeasure, which she considered a good sign. But she was surprised to see unmasked evidence in his expression that he was glad to see her, although his eyes exuded deep sorrow.

"Same as you, I assume," she said, not willing to admit that she'd come here with the sole purpose of initiating more conversation with him that might yield some positive results.

"I love this time of day," he said, sighing and looking around. "Right after the sun has gone down but its glow leaves everything in a hushed kind of light. I love it when the horizon is a line across the sky. You can see the outline of the hills and trees, but no details. It's as if . . . everything is clearly defined; there is an absolute distinction between the earth and the sky. It's that moment when the space between darkness and light is very clear. Sometimes I think that in this space I'll be able to make sense of that very place in my own life—that place between darkness and light."

"Between the difficulties and the joy?" she asked with the hope of trying to clarify exactly what he meant.

"Perhaps," he said, looking at her again. "It's difficult to define."

"I think you just did a lovely job of explaining it," she said, soaking in the relief of his being open and warm toward her. "You always had a way with words."

"Did I?" He made a mildly scoffing sound. "Now and then, perhaps."

Olivia heard him sigh loudly, and she sensed the burden he carried on his shoulders. She wanted to offer some words of comfort and hope, but couldn't come up with anything that didn't sound trite or patronizing. In truth, she had no idea where he was at in coming to terms with all he'd been assaulted with, and she didn't want to make any assumptions. She heard him clear his throat in a way that she knew usually meant he was trying to work up the nerve to say something, so she remained silent and waited.

"Olivia," he finally said, "I owe you an apology."

Olivia was surprised by this ongoing evidence of his humility. "That's how you began our last conversation," she said.

Tristan wished he could see her expression in the growing dusk. He felt increasingly nervous over what he knew he needed to say, and he was taken off guard somewhat by how her mere presence was affecting him. But he needed to take on one thing at a time. "Clearly I have much to apologize for," he countered. "It could take many conversations."

"Could it?" she asked as if she hoped so, or perhaps she had a clear understanding of how very much he had done that was worthy of regret—especially in regard to her.

* * * * *

Tristan drew back his shoulders as if that might help him forge ahead, and he was surprised by the memory of how it had felt to march into battle. Bringing himself fully back to the moment, he said what he knew needed to be said before he could ever hope to move forward. "When I told you that you were right . . . about what a fool I had been . . . the full depth of what that meant had not occurred to me. As I have looked back . . . trying to understand what happened . . . and everything that led up to things being the way they are now . . . I was horrified to see exactly what you meant." He heard his voice tremble as it had skidded over those last few words, and he was actually afraid he might start to cry. Taking a deep breath to try and steady his emotions, not wanting to make an even bigger fool of himself, he carried on. "You said that . . . given the evidence of how Muriel had lived her life . . . I was still foolish enough to believe that everything she'd told me . . . about you . . . was true."

Tristan's voice trembled more obviously and he felt a little lightheaded as the full impact of what he was saying threatened to swallow him. Needing a moment to gather himself and genuinely fearing his legs might give out, he muttered, "I need to sit down." He hurried to a nearby bench and sat there, gripping the cold stone with his hands as he lowered his head and fought to pull air into his lungs. Speaking the words aloud had triggered some kind of emotional assault he was not prepared to handle—especially with Olivia present. But she sat beside him and put a gentle hand on his shoulder, murmuring with compassion, "It's all right, Tristan. There's no need for you to feel embarrassed simply because this is difficult. You should know that I'm not going to judge you; I certainly won't be shocked or appalled by evidence that you're human. And you should also know that I would never hold a grudge against you for something that happened years ago."

Tristan looked up at her, amazed at her goodness and wondering why he'd been so blind to it. "I *should* know that, shouldn't I," he stated, glad to hear his voice sounding more steady. He hurried to get the rest of what he needed to say out in the open before there was any chance of him crumbling. "I just need to say again that you were right. I can see now how I fell headlong into Muriel's trap, and no one was hurt by my behavior more than you. I can only say how very sorry I am and express my deepest hope that one day you will be able to forgive me."

Tristan heard her sniffle and knew she was crying even though he could barely see her face in the growing darkness. She took a handkerchief from her pocket and wiped it over her cheeks. "Thank you," she said. "It means more than I could ever tell you . . . that you would say that to me." In a voice that was more steady she added, "But you need to know, Tristan, that I forgave you a long time ago. And I've forgiven Muriel, as well. Clearly there are lessons to be learned from all of this, but it's in the past."

Tristan could hardly believe what he was hearing, or the way it affected him. What had felt like an impenetrable wall of despair and hopelessness had now become a hill that he felt capable of climbing. "Oh, Olivia," he murmured and impulsively wrapped his arms around her. An embrace seemed the most appropriate way to express the depth of his gratitude that he could never put into words. She returned his embrace, and he tightened his arms around her before he realized what he'd done and how she might interpret it—and how it affected *him*. Holding her in his arms this way had once been so easy and comfortable, and now the memories of all they'd shared rushed over him. Her forgiveness—along with her kindness and compassion—had soothed his wounds and aided his healing in great strides, leaving his heart open enough to acknowledge what he'd lost with Olivia—and perhaps the hope that he might still be able to get it back. But he had to be careful to not make assumptions and get ahead of himself. Her eager forgiveness did not necessarily equate with any reason for him to believe that her love for him might be rekindled. He tried to focus on the conversation they'd been having so that he could proceed with admissions that he knew were mandatory in order to press forward.

# Chapter Six

# LONG OVERDUE

Tristan relinquished his embrace and sat up straight, again taking hold of the bench. Olivia once again wiped her handkerchief over her cheeks and sniffled. He knew there was more he needed to say, and he managed to avoid being distracted by her nearness enough to say it. "I've come to accept that I'd fallen out of love with Muriel even before I went to war, but I didn't know how to admit it—even to myself. I look back and see that she'd shown her true colors very quickly once our vows had been spoken, but how could I allow myself to feel the despair of having given my life, my name, and all that I have to a woman like that?" His eyes closed as if the pain of such a statement still felt unbearable. "I now know that I separated myself from her in my mind and in my heart—perhaps in some bizarre means of self-protection—and I was glad to be able to go to war, to not have to face her every day. Or worse, I didn't have to face myself with the consequences of my own foolishness."

"You must let go of your regrets, Tristan; you must forgive yourself." She put a hand on his arm in an attempt to offer some comfort.

Tristan glanced down at her hand, then at her face. "So you keep telling me. Perhaps if you tell me often enough, I might one day be convinced."

"I've struggled with this myself," she said. "I've wondered a thousand times and more what I might have done to prevent the damage she caused."

"How could it ever be your fault?" he insisted.

"I *introduced* the two of you," she said in a voice laced with the depth of her regret over that fact. "I should have warned you; I should have never let you marry her."

"As I recall, you told me very plainly that I should not marry her."

"I should have tried harder."

"I should have listened," he said. "I was blinded by my own pride, Olivia."

"And it's in the past." Her voice softened, but she kept her hand on his arm. "We need to leave it there and move forward."

Tristan looked directly at her face, taken in by the soft glow of her features in the minuscule light of day that remained. She looked up at him, and their gaze connected in a way that took him back in time. He was startled to realize how close her face was to his, but not at all disappointed. He wanted to kiss her, and he couldn't say he hadn't thought about doing so long before he'd encountered her here in the garden. He'd long ago let go of his love for Muriel, and news of her death and betrayal had only cemented what he had felt for years. Olivia had once been the center of his life, and now it seemed she had very naturally stepped back into that place. He couldn't think of a single reason *not* to kiss her—except for the possibility that she might not want him to. The last thing he wanted was to offend her. He leaned slightly toward her, which he hoped might give her some warning of his intention—and an opportunity to back away or turn her face if she had no interest in his affection. His heart quickened when she responded to his gesture by doing the same. She moved her face just a little closer to his, silently inviting him to kiss her. The very fact that she too wanted to cross this bridge—after all that had happened—left him feeling somewhat giddy, which was a soothing contrast to all the grief and regret he'd been contending with.

Tristan touched his lips to hers, tentatively, cautiously. The evidence of her response encouraged him, and he kissed her in a way that stirred memories of all they had once shared. They had courted, they had fallen in love, and he'd been on the verge of proposing marriage when Muriel had put herself between them with evil designs. He forced himself not to think about Muriel in that moment. He was here with Olivia, and he had the hope of believing that they might be able to once again find all they had lost.

"Tristan," she whispered as their lips parted and she looked up at him. She put a hand to his face and once again lifted her lips to his.

"Olivia," he murmured and kissed her again. "We remember each other's names," he said lightly. "That's a good place to start over."

"Yes," she said, her voice dreamy, but a moment later he felt her become tense, and he wondered what might be wrong.

Tristan was startled when Olivia stood abruptly and turned her back to him. He could hear her sharpened breathing and knew that she was upset, but he had no idea exactly why. He had to begin with the most obvious conclusion.

"Olivia," he said and stood behind her, "forgive me. It was never my intention to offend you . . . or to make you uncomfortable. If I've overstepped my bounds . . ." He allowed her a long moment to finish the sentence but she didn't. "I got the impression that you *wanted* me to kiss you; if I misunderstood, then you must set me straight."

"I *did* want you to kiss me," she admitted, "but that doesn't necessarily mean it's prudent for us to be . . . crossing such boundaries when . . ." She hesitated and let out a harsh sigh. "Our history together is complicated, Tristan. Muriel's death does not necessarily mean she isn't still there between us. Obviously we must be committed to complete honesty in order to go forward, but that doesn't mean it will be easy for either of us to say the things that *really* need to be said. And we cannot ever hope to find real happiness if we simply pretend that she never came between us, and she will remain there until we fully come to terms with all that's happened and why."

Olivia finally turned to face him, but he could barely make out her expression. "You've scarcely had time to begin to accept that she's dead—and the horrible reasons for it. Do you even know *why* your affection for me has suddenly rekindled? Have you come to realize that you love me still and you hope for the possibility of a future together in spite of all that's happened? Or am I a comfortable and convenient source of comfort?" She hesitated long enough to prove that her question had left him speechless. "I need you to be able to know the answer, Tristan. I need you to be honest with me, and with yourself. The damage Muriel did to our lives is not just going to magically dissolve because we want it to. I know because I've been trying to make that happen for a very long time. The thing is . . ."

Her voice broke and she hung her head; he knew she was choking on something she wanted to say—or perhaps *needed* to say—but it was obviously difficult. He wondered if it would be more difficult for her to say, or for him to hear. Either way, he knew this conversation couldn't stop here—not if they ever hoped to get beyond the chasms between them. "Just say it, Livy," he said. "For what it's worth, I agree with you. We have to face up to how we got here and why. So, say what you need to say."

Olivia took a deep breath and said, "First of all, I need you to answer the question."

"Which question?"

"Is this . . . what's happening between us . . . because it's comfortable? Because I'm here and convenient? Or are you implying that there is still something between us? Something to hope for? Because I'll not be investing hope in something that will only . . ." Again she hesitated and her breath quivered; he suspected she'd once again come upon wanting to say words that were having trouble coming out.

Tristan knew she deserved a fair answer to her question, and he was prepared to give it. He wouldn't have kissed her if he hadn't understood his own motives. He readily admitted, "The answer is both, Livy. You are *here*, and now that I've had the good sense to get past all my illusions, it seems a miracle to me that you are. I'm grateful for all that we once shared, which makes being with you now comfortable and easy to accept. But you need to know that in spite of my deplorable behavior toward you in the past, I would never take advantage of your friendship and affection for the sake of appeasing my own comfort. I *do* have hope that we can rebuild what we once lost, because I love you, Olivia. I know now that I've been trying to suppress my feelings for you beneath the anger I felt because I believed everything Muriel had told me about you. I believe now that it was easier to think that *you* had betrayed *me* somehow than to acknowledge my own foolishness. I ask for your patience and for your continued commitment to being honest with me."

His declaration was followed by a silence that allowed his own words to reverberate through his mind, keenly illustrating his vulnerability and culpability. His thoughts immediately took him to Muriel's betrayal and what a fool she'd made of him. He knew that Muriel's lack of integrity had no connection to Olivia—but he'd believed for a very long time that it did, and he had to steady himself against the realization that he felt afraid of being set up all over again to be manipulated and taken advantage of.

When her silence began to make him feel as if he were on the verge of some kind of outburst, he cleared his throat and tried to calm his mind before he said, "Now you know where I stand. Please tell me what you need to say."

\* \* \* \* \*

Olivia looked up at Tristan in the darkness and knew that she absolutely needed to say it. The words had been hovering on her tongue since the moment she'd come face-to-face with him the night he'd returned. She doubted she could say it without betraying how upset she'd been—for years—over this cold, hard fact at the core of all that had happened and all they had yet to get past in order to heal. She summoned her greatest courage even while she felt her chest tightening as the threat of tears lay just beneath the surface. Determined to just get it over with, she said on the wave of a sob, "You broke my heart, Tristan!" She sobbed again and forced herself to keep going. She would hate herself if she left anything important unsaid. "You had sworn your devotion and eternal love for me, and then you believed all of her lies and . . . and . . . you were so cruel to me!" She heard her own voice escalating into anger—or rather the pain beneath it—but she had to press forward. "I *never* gave you any reason to not trust me. Never! I *hated* my father's bad habits, and the way they had caused so much pain for *me*! And then you had the nerve to accuse me of actually being *involved*. How could you have ever believed such a thing? I didn't understand. I still don't understand." She sobbed in a way that she knew was a warning that she was about to lose complete control. "You broke my heart!" she managed to say one more time before she hung her head and sobbed helplessly. A part of her felt embarrassed by her reaction, even humiliated. But something more true and sound deep inside of her knew he needed to witness a glimpse of the pain he'd caused in her life.

Olivia wondered if he would have anything to say, or if he would just walk away. Needing to sit down, she took a step toward the bench, startled by the way Tristan took her into his arms and guided her face to his chest, silently inviting her to cry as much as she needed to while he supported her. It took her only a moment to recall how comfortable she had once felt when crying in his arms. He'd been there for her when she'd been hurt and terrified by her father's bad behavior. He had once been her rock, her strength, the center of her life. She had found the strength inside herself to stand strong in spite of her hurt and then to recover from her father's death and the debts and humiliation he'd left in his wake. She'd found financial security through Walter's kindness and generosity. But she'd forced herself to forget how perfectly safe and loved she'd once felt in Tristan's arms. Now she held to him and cried years' worth of tears, praying inwardly that this was not the beginning of more disappointment and heartbreak. Refusing to think about the uncertainty of the future, she just basked in the moment and the relief pouring out of her. She *wanted* a future with Tristan—not because he was heir to a great fortune, and not because it was convenient. She loved him; she'd loved him for as long as she'd known him. And she wanted desperately to believe that he loved her enough to move beyond all they'd been through. But she needed to be wise and cautious and not get ahead of herself.

When Olivia was finally able to calm down, she attempted to ease away from him, but he tightened his embrace. "It's all right, Livy." He pressed a kiss into her hair. "I can't predict the future, but I can tell you that I want more than anything to go back to the way we used to be. No," he corrected, "I want us to share what we once shared, but to be able to add to that the wisdom and strength and courage to never allow anything to ever come between us again." He took her by the shoulders and looked firmly at her. "I am so, so sorry, Livy—for the way I hurt you. There are no words to express the depth of my regret." His voice cracked. "I will prove myself a better man, Livy. I swear to you that I will. You're right when you say that you have never given me any reason not to trust you. Forgive me . . . for being such a fool. No one was hurt more than you by my foolishness. I pray that you can forgive me."

"I forgave you a long time ago, Tristan," she admitted easily. Trying to explain how that could be true, given her recent outburst, she added, "But I suppose forgiveness doesn't always mean that the pain is magically erased. And I've learned that forgiveness does not necessarily equate with trust. I forgave Muriel too, but that doesn't mean I would have ever trusted her. I suppose we need to learn to trust each other again . . . and we both need to make peace with the pain of what we've experienced."

"Perhaps we can work on that together," he said with a humble sincerity that filled her soul with a hope and peace she'd not felt since she'd first realized he had been falling prey to Muriel's deception.

"That would be lovely," she said with equal sincerity.

* * * * *

Tristan was glad for the progress they were making, but he didn't want this conversation to end without understanding exactly where they stood with each other. More accurately, he knew he needed to make his intentions unmistakably clear, and he hoped to know with the same clarity how she felt. He guided her back to the bench where they sat close together, and he turned to face her.

"Olivia." Tristan took both her hands into his. "I know that we both have healing to do, and I know we must be prudent, but . . . I would like to propose that . . . well, I would like it very much if—at the very least—I might once again be allowed to officially court you." He heard her gasp softly and hurried to explain himself fully. "We both know that the purpose of courting is to determine whether marriage is feasible, and I want you to know that I sincerely hope that's the case. If I had been deeply in love with my wife and had learned of her death only days ago, then my request to court you would be ludicrous. But we both know such is not the case, and there isn't a person in this household—or in the county for that matter—who doesn't know the truth. And I'm not going to pretend to be in mourning over her death when doing so would be a mockery."

Tristan waited in silence for some kind of response, resisting the urge he had to just drop down on one knee and propose marriage to her here and now. He should have done it years ago; he'd known then that they were well matched and their love for each other was sound and true. Muriel had come between them and deceived him, but he'd been fool enough to believe her lies, and he'd made some horrible mistakes as a result. He wanted to go back in time and erase all the bad pieces of these past years. Knowing that was impossible, he only wanted to start over and make it right. Logically, he knew that Olivia had been right when she'd said they needed to learn to trust each other again, and they needed to make peace with all that had happened. Still, he hoped with all his heart that she would agree to let him court her, and he prayed that the outcome would be marriage—as it should have been long ago.

"Your lack of response is making me nervous," he finally said. "Are you opposed to—"

"No," she said, "I'm not at all opposed." He breathed in some relief that was only slightly marred when she added, "I only ask that we take time . . . that we exercise caution. We are not the same people we were before. We know nothing of each other's experiences during these years you've been away. I want to be with you, Tristan," she said, putting a hand to his face. "I just need to be certain that nothing stands between us that has the potential to tear us apart. I doubt that I could bear going through that again."

Tristan couldn't imagine *anything* coming between them after all they'd endured. If they had survived what Muriel had done to them, surely they could survive anything.

"Of course," Tristan said. "We will take all the time we need."

Now that it seemed they had said all they'd needed to, he was relieved when she placed her head on his shoulder and relaxed. He put his arm around her and was glad to hear her say, "It's so good to have you back,

Tristan—and back in my life. I missed you dreadfully, even if I didn't want to admit it."

"I missed you too," he said, glad to now be able to speak with her in complete honesty. "Being a married man, I focused all my loyalties—including my thoughts and feelings—on my wife. But there were many times when I wished there wasn't this chasm between us. I missed your friendship; I've never had a truer friend than you."

Olivia sighed and wrapped her arm around him. "Nor I," she said. "Winnie is the truest of friends, certainly. But with you it was different. It's my hope that whatever happens, Tristan, we can always be friends."

"I hope for the same," he said, although he couldn't imagine ever being content with friendship alone. Now that his love for Olivia had been sparked to life once again, he had to believe that he could have her in his life in every way for as long as he lived. Any other outcome felt unbearable.

Olivia admitted to being very tired, and they walked back to the house together and up the stairs. He kissed her good night at the cross section of hallway where she needed to go one way and he the other in order to get to the opposite wings of the manor where their rooms were located.

Tristan didn't want to be apart from her at all, and he had trouble sleeping as the warmth and comfort of this reawakening completely suppressed all the grief he'd been swimming in since his return home. Now he could only think of Olivia, and he wanted to spend the rest of his life making up for these years they had lost due to his foolish choices. He wanted to mend her broken heart and devote himself to her happiness, knowing she was a good woman with every quality he could ever hope for in a wife—and he loved her.

Tristan finally slept, blanketed with thoughts of Olivia. He awoke to daylight with his first thought being of her, and he realized he'd slept better than he had since he'd come home to the news of Muriel's death—and her betrayal. Now he felt as if he could fully put Muriel behind him and move forward. He simply needed to honor Olivia's wish to take their time, which meant that he needed to discipline his impatience.

Once he was dressed for the day, Tristan went to his father's room, relieved to see Olivia there. They shared a long gaze and a warm smile, which soothed his spirit, even though he soon realized that his father had noticed their intimate exchange, and his mild smirk implied his pleasure over what he was seeing. But Walter didn't comment, and as soon as he and Tristan had exchanged their customary greetings, Lawrence brought breakfast and they all ate together and chatted comfortably.

After Lawrence had left to take the tray back to the kitchen, Tristan said to Walter while looking at Olivia, "Father, do you think it's too soon for me to be courting? Do you think that people might say I've not had adequate time to mourn my wife's death before moving on?"

"I'd say," Walter began with a stoutness in his voice that declared his serious intent, "that you should know me well enough to know that I don't care a tittle what anyone thinks or says. And as for what *I* think: if you're talking about our Livy, then I'd say it's long overdue. There is no finer woman to help you find your way home."

"I *am* home, Father," Tristan said, wondering if Walter's mind might be showing signs of confusion.

"You're getting there." Walter smiled at him, and Tristan knew he meant something more metaphorical than literal. He looked at Olivia and felt sure his father was right.

The three of them spent much of the morning engaged in pleasant conversation, even though Walter talked some about Muriel and how difficult it had been to deal with her being a part of the family, especially when she'd become less and less discreet about her infidelity. Tristan recognized—and respected—his father's need to talk about how all of this had affected *him*. But it was also evident that Walter was trying to get Tristan to open up about how *he* felt about all that had happened, and now that Walter knew Tristan and Olivia had made peace with each other and were moving forward, the three of them were able to talk openly about these things. Tristan preferred any other topic, but he knew this was necessary and so he endured it and did his best to be honest with his father and the woman he loved.

"I do wish," Tristan said at one point, "that more of my letters would have made it home." He thought of all he'd poured into those letters, and how it had been his only connection to all he'd left behind. He noticed a strained glance between Olivia and his father and realized they knew something he didn't. "What?" he demanded.

Olivia said to Walter, "I assumed that you had told him."

Walter replied, "I assumed that *you* had told him."

"And once again there is trouble from *assuming*," Tristan declared, agitated over what exactly they had both assumed.

Tristan waited while Olivia and Walter seemed to be silently battling it out to decide who had to tell him whatever he didn't know. Walter finally said, "Just tell him what you told me."

Olivia looked directly at Tristan and said, "I believe that Muriel burned your letters . . . without ever sharing them with your father."

"What?" Tristan muttered, assaulted with a new sense of betrayal. "Why would she do that?"

"I don't know," Olivia said. "I've tried and tried to make sense of it. What did she have to gain by depriving your father of hearing from you?"

"What exactly led you to this conclusion?" Tristan asked.

"Beatrice told me that letters had come . . . several at a time . . . more than once . . . and she'd known from talk in the house that Walter was concerned over not having heard from you, so she told me. I once saw Muriel burning what appeared to be a pile of letters. I confronted her with my suspicions. Of course she denied it. But what other explanation could there be? I know that some mail can get lost—especially in situations of war—but not *that* many."

"I'm stunned," Tristan admitted, wishing the word could begin to describe how he felt. He took a deep breath and reminded himself that it was in the past. Looking directly at his father, he said, "I shared so much that was far more for you than for her, but she had asked that I send the letters to her; she said that with her being my wife it was more proper. And she promised to share them with you. When I look back, I don't know how I was convinced by her reasoning, but I suppose that summarizes the entire problem." He sighed and shook his head. "I can only say once again how sorry I am."

"You've nothing to apologize for, my boy," Walter insisted. "You're home now and I have the joy of hearing you tell me of your experiences face-to-face."

"But if I'd not made it home . . ." Tristan said. "The very idea of you never knowing just . . . well, it makes me sick."

"Which is entirely understandable," Walter said. "And I can assure you that both Livy and I know how you feel. We've had to contend with our anger and frustration over these things, but time does make things better; you must be patient with yourself."

"Yes, I suppose I must," Tristan said and impulsively stood up. "You know . . . I've been thinking that I've not once gone riding since I got home. I've been so caught up in . . . other things, that . . . I've not even been out to the stables . . . or the carriage house . . . to say hello to the people there I've missed. And . . . I think a good ride would help clear my head."

"An excellent idea," Walter said as Tristan bent over and kissed his father's brow in a way that had become common and comfortable for them both.

"I'll see you both later," Tristan said, bending over to kiss Olivia's brow as well.

She took his hand to squeeze it, silently expressing her concern for his mood. "Be careful."

"Of course," he said and forced a smile. "I'll see you later."

Olivia nodded and he left the room, hurrying outside and toward the stables. By the time he got there he was able to push away his initial anger over the news that Muriel had actually had the nerve to burn his letters and keep his written words from ever getting to his father. He greeted the stable hands he knew well with laughter and brotherly embraces. Wagner and Seymour were both a couple of gruff fellows who shared a common sense of humor and much laughter. One was as tall and dark as the other was short and blond, and both had been here since Tristan's childhood. They asked Tristan questions about his time away and blurted out some typical jokes that made them all laugh. They also introduced Tristan to a couple of new lads who had begun working there more recently. Tristan apologized for not coming sooner to see them, but they all understood that he'd come home to face some difficult news. He talked comfortably with the small group of men for nearly half an hour, and he appreciated how straightforward they were about Muriel's indiscretions and how disappointed and disgusted they had been, but how not one of them regarded it as any negative reflection on Tristan or their respect for him. It meant more to Tristan than he could say, and he hoped their feelings were shared among the community. Even though the opinions of others mattered little to him, he didn't like the idea of people judging him based on the behavior of his deceased wife.

Tristan turned the conversation to catching up on all that had happened while he'd been gone. Among the group a marriage had taken place, two of them had become fathers, and one of them had lost his mother to death. Tristan offered his congratulations and condolences respectively before he saddled his own horse and headed out into the warm summer air, galloping on a once-familiar stallion across the vast meadows that stretched out around the perimeter of the house and gardens. He rode for nearly an hour, reacquainting himself with his home, with all its vastness and beauty that was so comfortingly familiar. Before returning, he halted at the crest of a hill where he could look down and see the house. It looked much smaller from here, and it was difficult to imagine how massive it was, and how easy one could become lost among its endless hallways and staircases and the separate wings that felt like different houses all linked together. He thought of the large number of people who lived and worked there, and how dear they all were to him. He pondered the responsibility resting on his shoulders of seeing that each and every person within his stewardship was well cared for. They all worked hard to earn their wages, and they deserved a good life in return. He was grateful beyond words to have his father still living, but he couldn't look at Walter's condition and not be reminded that stepping into his father's shoes would likely come sooner than later, and Tristan needed to be prepared. It was easy to imagine Olivia at his side in that role; in fact, he couldn't imagine being able to do it without her. But he'd only been home less than a week—even if it felt like much longer than that—and he needed to be patient, as both Olivia and his father had cautioned him.

Recalling his reasons for needing to ride and clear his head from the ever-growing disillusionment of his deceased wife, Tristan was glad to realize that it had worked. He felt much calmer in regard to all that he was trying to put behind him, and much more hopeful in regard to the future. He returned home with a sudden desire to see Olivia, and found no workers in the stables. He took his time removing the saddle from his horse and giving the animal a proper brushing while it enjoyed feed and water as a reward for being Tristan's loyal companion on their outing.

Tristan then went to the carriage house, hoping to see the men who worked there keeping all the family's vehicles in good condition. He found Lloyd and Hewitt both there and was glad to see them. They were not many years older than Tristan, and he remembered well when they'd been hired, coming on together as established friends following the death of the previous caretaker of the carriages. Tristan shared similar conversations with them to those he'd had with the men who worked in the stables. Lloyd and Hewitt left together to pick up some supplies in town, but Tristan remained in the carriage house, soaking in childhood memories that added to the comfort of being home. Then he realized that something felt strange. He stood in the center of the huge carriage house, looking at the variety of wheeled vehicles all resting in the same places they always had. Tristan had played here as a boy a great deal, and he'd come here often throughout his adult life. He knew this place well, and something wasn't the same, but for the life of him he couldn't figure what. Examining every detail of what he saw and trying to compare it to his memories, he stood there for a ridiculous amount of time until he finally noticed what looked unfamiliar—but in such a subtle way that he might never have noticed if he'd not been keenly observant.

Tristan could clearly see how there was less floor space between the carriages backed up against one wall and the smaller vehicles backed up against the opposite wall. Considering the possible reasons, he noticed that one of the walls looked different. But why would a wall have been replaced? Had there been some kind of damage that had necessitated rebuilding a wall in the carriage house? Something troubling settled into him as he walked between two carriages and put his hands on the wall, as if doing so might answer his questions. Of course, he could just ask someone. Surely there was a reasonable explanation. He knocked on the wall for no specific reason and was startled to hear a hollow sound. The outer walls of the carriage house were solid; they always had been. But a close examination of the wall showed him no other apparent abnormalities, and he convinced himself that he was becoming obsessed over something ridiculous and insignificant, most likely to distract himself from other things he didn't want to think about. He made a mental note to mention it to his father and left the carriage house, wondering where he might find Olivia this time of day.

Knowing that his father was likely still napping, Tristan went to the sitting room next to Walter's bedroom where he knew Olivia often sat to read in order to be nearby if Walter needed her. He found Lawrence there, who suggested that he might find Olivia in the kitchen or the laundry. Assuming she had made friends there and might be known to go there to visit with them, Tristan went first to the kitchen, but she wasn't there. He spent a few minutes visiting with the cook and her helpers before he went to the laundry—a room filled with large tubs for washing, stoves for heating water, and clotheslines where clothes and linens were hung to dry. He'd come here often as a child but couldn't recall ever coming here once he'd reached maturity. The women working there all looked surprised when he entered, and he was ashamed to realize that he didn't know any of their names. He spoke a kind greeting to them and was surprised himself when Olivia turned at the sound of his voice—from where she was bent over a laundry tub, busy scrubbing something against a washboard.

"Oh, hello," she said but returned her attention to her task after she pushed back a stray lock of hair from her face with her dry forearm. Tristan wondered if she considered it necessary to do her own laundry, not wanting to be a burden to anyone else. But she lifted up a table linen to examine as if to be certain it was adequately cleaned. "I'll be finished shortly," she added.

"No hurry," Tristan said, wishing he didn't feel so awkward here—or so taken aback by Olivia feeling the need to work in the laundry to earn her keep. He wanted to talk to her about it—but not here, and not now. Given that it hadn't been so many days since *he* had accused her of taking advantage of his father's hospitality, he felt once again humbled by his own foolish arrogance.

"I told her she don't need to come down here and help like this," Tristan heard a woman say and turned to see a smiling, plump face—shiny and pink from the warm steam that rose from the laundry tub over which she was working. "But she insists, just as she insists on washing pots and pans in the kitchen."

"Does she, now?" Tristan asked in a tone that he hoped would keep the mood light.

"I enjoy the company," Olivia said while wringing out the linen in her hands with a vigorousness that contradicted her declaration that company was her sole reason for being here. As if she sensed his discomfort, she smiled at him and said nonchalantly, "I don't know if you ladies have ever met the honorable Tristan Whitmore—recently returned from war." His awkwardness increased at becoming even more the center of attention, but he was touched by the way that Olivia had referred to these hard-working women as *ladies*. "But here he is in the flesh."

"Not a myth or a legend as we might have thought," one of the women said and they all laughed.

"'Tis a pleasure," another said and the others added similar remarks.

"Likewise," Tristan said, nodding toward each of them.

Olivia told Tristan all of their names, but he knew he would have to hear them multiple times before he had any hope of remembering them. He'd prided himself on once believing that he knew the names of every person working in his father's household, but in his arrogance he had completely overlooked the laundry. And here was the woman he loved hard at work among them, when no one would have thought it was necessary for her to do anything but read and lounge about, given her relationship to the deceased mistress of the house, and her role as a companion to Walter in his confinement.

While Olivia was hanging up the linens she'd just washed, Tristan impulsively decided to take some steps to eliminate the strain in the room, and to remedy what he'd just come to realize was a problem—at least *he* considered it a problem. Before Olivia could declare that she was finished here and urge him to leave, he hurried to roll up his sleeves before he grabbed another piece of linen from the obvious pile of what needed to be washed. He took up a washboard and set to work, which created a sudden stillness in the room as everyone stopped for a moment to stare at him, aghast—including Olivia.

"What?" he asked her. "I did a great deal of this sort of thing at that dreadful army hospital. Someone had to wash the sheets and bandages."

Olivia smiled and picked up another item in need of cleaning and got back to work. And thankfully the other women did as well. "I never imagined you doing such a thing," she said quietly to him.

"I confess I never imagined it myself," he said, offering her a gentle smirk. "Let's just say you inspire me."

Olivia paused and leaned over the laundry tub to kiss his cheek, and Tristan chuckled. Who would have guessed even a few days ago that he could actually feel happy while working in the laundry of his own home? But he *did* feel happy, and he also felt hopeful. Given all that had happened, he considered such feelings a miracle, and he was glad to think that tomorrow was Sunday and he would be able to attend church for the first time since returning home. He owed a great deal to God, and it seemed fitting that he could now return to a habit of attending church on the Sabbath. The thought of being there with Olivia almost made him giddy—even if he suspected it might cause whispers and speculations among the community. But he didn't care about that. He could see nothing now but a bright future on the horizon—even if that horizon was somewhat distant. Still, he could see it and he could keep moving toward it with the hope that all would be well.

# CHAPTER SEVEN
## SECRETIVE DEALINGS

OLIVIA GAZED AT HER REFLECTION in the mirror while Winnie rolled her long plaited hair into a bun at the back of her head and pinned it into place. It was only for special occasions or attending church that Olivia cared to put her hair up; it always felt heavier when pinned in place as opposed to just allowing the braid to hang down her back, which kept it out of the way and tidy. Lawrence would be remaining with Walter today while she went to church with Winnie as she had done countless times. But today would be different. Tristan had told her he would be going with them. She'd expected him to go to church; he always had before. And this was the first Sunday since he'd returned. Considering all that had happened in less than a week heaped an added sense of disorientation to the reeling sensation already rumbling through her. For all that she felt good about moving forward in her relationship with Tristan—even deeply relieved considering her ongoing love for him—she wasn't certain that a public declaration of their courtship was a good idea. No words would be necessary for such a declaration. Their arriving at church together would start the rumors flowing, and all he had to do was touch her back or her arm to imply that he wanted people to know the two of them had some kind of understanding. Perhaps if Olivia knew that marriage would inevitably be the outcome, she might not feel so hesitant. But she had trouble believing it could be possible. Perhaps it just felt too good to be true after having accustomed herself to the fact that he'd married her cousin. And given how he'd come to see her in such a bad light—all thanks to Muriel's lies—Olivia had never thought it would be possible for them to achieve such a level of forgiveness. Even with her hope that he might one day see the truth and be able to apologize for his misgivings, she hadn't dared hope that he could come to love her again the way he once had. But he'd declared his remorse, his understanding of all that had gone wrong, and most importantly, he'd declared his love. Olivia had no reason to question his sincerity, and she had examined her own instincts enough to know that this was the right course for herself. Perhaps it was simply the speed at which all of this was happening that left her unsteady and bewildered. A week ago she hadn't even known if Tristan was alive, or if he would ever come home. Now they were officially courting once again and about to go to church together!

"You look as if you're going to the gallows," Winnie said wryly, startling Olivia from the deep pool of her thoughts.

Olivia inhaled loudly as she came up for air. "Do I?" she asked.

"I'm not sure what you're stewing about, but I think I could guess," Winnie went on. She moved to Olivia's side and knelt on the floor, taking hold of her hand in a way that was common with the perfect friendship they shared. "I know a lot has changed very quickly with Tristan coming back. But he's the love of your life, Livy! He's come back a better man, and he's been given a fresh chance at a new life; a chance to erase the mistakes he made with Muriel. And he's choosing to start that new life with you. This is not impulsive or irrational, my dear. You've loved him since you were a girl."

"I have, haven't I," Olivia said and couldn't help but smile at the memory of the first time she'd seen Tristan Whitmore. She'd barely been old enough to be out socially, and she'd been invited to attend a ball more grand than she'd ever imagined possible. Her gown had paled in contrast to the lavish creations worn by the other women there, but she hadn't cared. She'd just relished every bit of the experience, enjoying the fact that more than a few young men had asked her to dance. And then she'd seen Tristan across the room, and she couldn't keep herself from staring. When he'd casually glanced in her direction, he'd caught her at it, but even then she hadn't been able to look away. And he'd stared back. She'd known just from looking at him that he was older than she was, wealthy and well-bred, and very much admired by nearly every woman in the room. Her heart had nearly exploded as he'd walked toward her. He'd asked her to dance, and then to dance again, and then he'd guided her outside to get some fresh air and they'd started talking. After that, he quickly became her friend, calling on her and her father often, and including her in social gatherings whenever the opportunity presented itself, but always keeping her at a certain distance, as if to declare that they were friends and nothing more. It had been nearly two years before he'd asked her father's permission to court her, and months later Olivia had known he was on the verge of proposing marriage; he'd been hinting at it for weeks. Then her cousin Muriel's mother passed away and she had come to live with Olivia and her father. Muriel had barely met Tristan before she began spinning her evil web around him. And Olivia's efforts to warn Tristan of Muriel's questionable character had all fallen on deaf ears. And now here they were, years later, much heartache to contend with and many lessons learned.

"There you go again," Winnie said, startling Olivia. "Your mind wandering off into who knows what dark places." She put her hands on Olivia's shoulders and laughed softly. "This is a happy day, Livy; a happy time in your life. Enjoy it!"

"There are things he doesn't know," Olivia said, not wanting to even think about how Tristan might react if he ever found out about certain facets of her life that had evolved during his years away.

"It doesn't matter!" Winnie said, but Olivia couldn't ignore how *her* expression became dark. "We both know it's far better that he *doesn't* know; he must *never* know—for his own protection."

"Of course," Olivia said. "But I hate the feeling that I'm deceiving him—when I've been so angry with Muriel for *her* deception."

"It's not the same," Winnie insisted and stood up, pressing her hands down the front of her dress as if to add emphasis to her words. "It's *nothing* the same. We are engaged in a noble cause, and we must finish what we've begun. Muriel had no motive except her own gain and her own pleasure. What we are doing requires sacrifice and commitment—neither of which Muriel could have even understood."

"I know you're right," Olivia said. "But thank you for reminding me. We will just pray that it can all be taken care of before Tristan has a chance to even suspect that anything is amiss."

"Yes, we will," Winnie said. "And everything will be fine. He's back now, and he's already exceeded our hopes that he might be able to see the truth and come to his senses." She handed Olivia her gloves and hat. "It's time to go. Remember that you're the best thing that ever happened to him, and he's blessed to have you in his life."

"It is *I* who am blessed to have *him*," Olivia said.

"Yes," Winnie drawled as if it were debatable, then added with a smile, "but he's still getting the better deal." She picked up her own hat and gloves. "Come along. I'm sure the carriage is waiting."

Olivia hurried down the stairs with Winnie at her side. She had to slow her pace when she saw Tristan pacing slowly in the foyer. The sight of him simply took her breath away—just as it had when he'd returned home less than a week ago. He'd been wearing his uniform then, and he'd been weary from travel and understandably unkempt for his journey. Since then she'd seen him dressed in his most comfortable attire, which certainly suited him favorably. But now he was dressed in his finest, with his hair more in place than it had been since his return. The fine brocade waistcoat he wore beneath a sharply tailored coat complemented the high collar of his white shirt and his dark breeches and highly polished boots. He was everything fine and masculine, and she was overtaken by a fluttering in her stomach to think of how it felt when he kissed her and to know that he loved her. The sensation increased when he looked up to see her and his eyes betrayed that he was equally affected by *her* appearance. She too had been wearing her most comfortable attire since he'd returned, but now she wore a skirt and bodice and jacket that were her finest, all in varying shades of cream and green. She pulled the cream-colored gloves onto her hands as she descended the last few steps and smiled to greet him.

"Don't you ladies look lovely," Tristan said, nodding kindly toward Winnie and then taking Olivia's gloved hand to kiss it.

"You look rather dashing yourself," Olivia said, allowing her gaze to mingle with his for a long moment, cherishing the way it renewed her hope that all would be well between them.

"While the two of you are gawking at each other," Winnie said lightly, "we'll be late for church and interrupt the sermon when we go in."

"We wouldn't want that," Tristan said and offered his arm to Olivia. She put her hand there and they followed Winnie out to the waiting carriage.

When they were on their way, Olivia said to Tristan, "I wonder if people have even heard that you've returned. You could be assailed by well-wishers after the meeting."

"Or," Tristan said, "they could ignore me rudely due to my poor choice in a wife and the scandal she created in my absence."

"*Or,*" Olivia countered, "they could be astonished that you would so quickly following your wife's death show yourself in public with *me*. Everyone knows we once courted. Does this not have the potential to come across as some kind of comedic melodrama?"

"Hardly comedic," Tristan said. "And need I remind you still again of how little I care for what people say *or* think?"

"Perhaps," Winnie interjected, looking at Olivia, "you should stop trying to predict what will happen, or speculate over what people are thinking. Simply enjoy yourself."

"Amen to that," Tristan said, winking at Winnie.

Olivia noticed the smile they exchanged and recalled how comfortable they had once been with each other. Winnie had always been a close companion to Olivia, and Tristan had been the center of her life for years. She was glad now to see bridges mended between Tristan and Winnie as well. The evidence of that further soothed her anxiety and she admitted, "You're both right. I just need to enjoy this." She looked at Tristan and took his hand. "It's so good to have you back—back home, and back in my life."

"It's good to *be* back," he said and kissed her brow, "in both respects."

"Amen to that," Winnie said, mimicking the exact tone in which Tristan had said it a moment ago, which made him chuckle.

They arrived at the church before the meeting began, but with only enough time for them to be seated. Whispers and glances made it evident that people had noticed Tristan Whitmore's arrival, but it was impossible to know if they were pleased to see him safely returned from war, or if his presence reminded them of Muriel's scandal. Or perhaps they'd noticed how Tristan had entered the church holding Olivia's hand possessively over his arm. As soon as they were seated, Olivia scolded herself for once again trying to predict and speculate. For the moment she just focused on being here with Tristan on one side of her and Winnie on the other. As they sang hymns and listened to the sermon, she was overcome with a warm combination of hope and peace. She held the sensation close to her heart and prayed that it would last.

\* \* \* \* \*

Tristan loved being back here in the church where he'd come every Sunday throughout the majority of his life. The opportunity for any kind of worship service was rare in the midst of war, and he'd sorely missed the blessings of having this one day a week set aside to be different from the other six, and especially to be able to listen to a carefully thought-out sermon and to sing hymns with a congregation—even if he was well aware that many of them were whispering and speculating over him. His decisions had certainly given the locals much to gossip about. Everyone knew he'd once courted Olivia; she had attended church here with him many times, and it had been expected that they would marry. And then he'd attached himself to Muriel, blind to her unsavory motives, and gossip had run wild over that. He'd married Muriel; and then her cousin—the woman he'd previously been expected to marry—had moved into their home. And now he'd returned from war to find himself a widower—and everyone knew the full extent of Muriel's betrayal. And better still—at least in regard to fodder for gossip—he had shown up at church with Olivia and her well-known companion, less than a week after his return. But Tristan sincerely didn't care. He quietly considered how members of the community might view his actions, but he brushed all of that aside, focusing on his gratitude to have come so far in so short a time. The sermon was focused on the need for each individual to turn to the Lord in order to attain the peace that He had promised. The vicar talked of how heartache and sorrow were an inevitable part of the experience of this life, but Jesus had taught us how to find peace in spite of that, and He had sacrificed Himself on behalf of all of humankind. Tristan felt as if the vicar had written this sermon especially for him—even if he'd only been following his own instincts without realizing that his words were an answer to Tristan's prayers.

In the middle of the sermon, Tristan put his arm on the back of the pew behind Olivia. He wasn't actually touching her, but he knew that everyone seated behind them would interpret the gesture as some kind of declaration that he and Olivia were officially a couple. And that was exactly what he wanted. He turned to look at her for a long moment while her attention was focused elsewhere. Her soft, pale skin and rippled hair—neatly drawn back from her face and pinned into place—made him want to touch her. His gaze was drawn to her lips and he wanted even more to kiss her. He marveled at how quickly and easily his love for her had come rushing back into him once he'd chosen to break down the barriers that had held it at bay. He looked back over the years since he'd allowed himself to believe Muriel's lies about Olivia, and he almost felt as if he'd been possessed by some kind of evil that had distorted his thinking and smothered his truest instincts. Now that he'd been set free from such distortions, every cell in his being drew him to Olivia. He wanted to marry her; he wanted her to be a part of his life—officially and permanently.

Olivia turned and caught him looking at her. She smiled, but she also gently nudged him in the ribs to remind him to pay attention to the sermon. He focused on what the vicar was saying, but he truly believed both in his heart and in his mind that marrying Olivia was the best and most right decision he could make for his future—and hers. And with that thought came a surge of added peace. He took hold of her hand to squeeze it, wanting to propose this very day. But he knew she would think it was too soon; she would insist on being cautious and taking some time. He couldn't argue with her reasoning, and he certainly needed to respect her wishes. If only he didn't feel so impatient! In his heart he believed that Olivia could soothe away whatever residue of grief and sorrow remained inside of him. She seemed to be the answer to his every question, and the relief to his every heartache.

After the meeting ended, Tristan wasn't surprised to be surrounded by people who wished to express their pleasure over his safe return. The majority of greetings were genuine and kind—even enthusiastic—and he reprimanded himself for having jumped to the conclusion that people would be judgmental over his past choices and all that had happened. There were, however, a few who spoke to him with a false politeness that barely hid their disdain. These were the same people who ignored the fact that Tristan was holding Olivia's hand; some pretended to not even see her, which angered Tristan. But there were others who greeted her kindly and seemed pleased to see them together. They finally managed to escape the small throng and found Winnie waiting by the carriage, and Tristan was able to hold onto the kindness that had been offered to them and simply disregard anything else, knowing it didn't matter.

Once they were inside the carriage, the three of them casually discussed their views on the sermon, and some light comments were made about the gossip they'd likely fueled. Tristan was more preoccupied with holding Olivia's hand and with his delight over the implication in her smile that she was equally pleased. He pressed her gloved hand to his lips and took note of the sparkle in her eyes. How blessed he was to have her in his life!

Back at the house, Winnie quickly excused herself and went inside ahead of Tristan and Olivia, as if she intended to not intrude upon their time together. As they entered the foyer, still holding hands, Olivia said, "I want to change my clothes before lunch. Will you be eating with your father or in the dining room?"

"I'll be eating wherever you will be," he said.

"I far prefer your father's room—and his company—as opposed to that enormous, stuffy dining room."

"Then, my father's room it is," Tristan declared.

"You should know . . . I made some changes to the meals on Sundays."

"Did you?" he asked, feeling amused. "So . . . you've just taken over running the household."

"With your father's permission and guidance, of course."

"Of course," he said in a light tone that he hoped would take away the hint of defensiveness he'd sensed in her comment. "Someone had to do it." More soberly he added, "I'm guessing Muriel didn't take her position as mistress of the house very seriously." He didn't like mentioning her, but they were committed to not avoiding the truth of their circumstances, and like it or not, Muriel's impact was a part of their lives.

"Or perhaps a little *too* seriously," Olivia said. "She had the staff on edge much of the time, all waiting on tenterhooks to do her bidding in order to avoid her wrath."

"Truly?" Tristan asked with astonished gravity; there was no way to lighten such a statement.

"Truly," Olivia said.

"They must have all hated me for marrying her and leaving her here in charge."

"No one here *ever* hated you, Tristan," she said with sincerity. "Don't think they couldn't see through her enough to understand how convincingly sweet she could be in order to get what she wanted."

"Everyone could see through her but me, apparently," Tristan said, wondering how they'd gotten into such a serious conversation. But he couldn't deny that it was necessary; he needed to understand all that had happened and why.

"You were in love with her," Olivia said as if that made everything make perfect sense.

"Was I?" Tristan asked. "I look back and it feels more like I was under some kind of spell. Are you certain your cousin wasn't a witch of sorts?" He said the last with a flippancy that he hoped would lighten the mood, but Olivia only scowled.

"If I believed in such things," she said, "I would love to be able to say that she was."

"So, we can both admit with no distorted sense of guilt that we are glad she's gone, that her death was a blessing."

"I have no trouble admitting that," Olivia said. "And she certainly dug her own grave; forgive me if the cliché is perhaps too literal."

"No need to forgive anything," he said. "I've had the same thought." When they thankfully seemed to have nothing more to say about Muriel at the moment, Tristan added, "You were saying . . . that you'd made some changes to Sunday meals."

"Yes," she said. "Our Sunday meals are now very simple and mostly prepared the day before so that the staff can also attend church if they choose, and no one will have more than just a little bit of work to do on the Sabbath. So, be warned that we'll be dining on cold lamb sandwiches for lunch."

"It sounds delightful," he said and hastened to add sincerely, "And your Sunday changes are brilliant. I wish I'd have thought of it myself— years ago."

"Funny," she said with a self-satisfied smile. "That's exactly what your father said." She eased her hand out of his and headed toward the stairs. "I'll see you shortly in—"

"Wait," he said and grabbed her arm. "Come with me for just a moment."

Tristan urged her into the parlor just off the foyer and closed the door before he drew her completely into his arms and kissed her. Her startled surprise quickly melted into an eager response and he reminded himself to behave like a gentleman and not get carried away.

"I've wanted to do that ever since I saw you coming down the stairs earlier," he admitted, hearing the dreamy quality in his own voice.

"That's when I wanted it to," she said and smiled, pressing her hands over the front of his waistcoat. "You look so . . ."

"What?" he asked when she hesitated.

Olivia looked into his eyes and he was surprised to see the glisten of tears there. "You wore this very waistcoat the first time you kissed me."

"Did I?"

"I'll never forget it," she said, turning her attention to the fabric as she examined it with her fingers.

"I'm so sorry," he said and she looked up at him again.

"There's no need for you to keep apologizing, Tristan. It's in the past; all is forgiven."

"I'm grateful for that, but . . . we should have been married a long time ago." He nearly added that they should just get married as soon as it could be arranged, that there was no reason to wait, given the history they shared. But her eyes turned downward in a way that made him uneasy. "What is it?" he asked.

"A great deal has happened during these years, Tristan," she said, still not looking at him. "There are things that have happened in *my* life while you've been away, things that have nothing to do with Muriel. I need time to sort things out, and . . ." She looked at him in a way that seemed to take great courage, and the severity in her eyes caught him off guard. "I can't tell you about it, not now, perhaps not ever. I can only ask you to trust me and to believe me when I tell you that I would never do anything to hurt you."

"I don't understand," he said, trying to sort out what she was saying. "Just . . . trust me."

"About what?" he asked. "I don't even know what we're talking about."

"And it's better that you don't . . . for your own protection."

"My *protection*?" he echoed, astonished. "If you're not going to tell me what's going on, why are you telling me at all?"

"Because I don't want to keep secrets from you; I don't want you to sense that something is going on and believe that I'm hiding something from you . . . that you can't trust me, because you can."

"And yet," he said, taking a step back, "you *are* hiding something from me. Everything you just said is full of contradictions, Livy."

"I know it sounds that way, but—"

"Is there someone else? Does this have to do with another man in your life?"

"No!" she said firmly and with a little laugh. "It's nothing like that. I promise you, Tristan, you are the only man I have ever loved. There's never been anyone else. But I have an obligation, something I've committed myself to; and I need to follow through on my commitment, but for the sake of protecting everyone involved, I can't talk about it. Please . . . just . . . trust me."

Tristan felt frustrated—and even tempted to get angry and insist that she tell him. But she had been perfectly forgiving of his own foolish choices, and he knew he had hurt her deeply. He couldn't begin to imagine what she might be talking about, but he recalled her telling him that she'd never given him any reason not to trust her. And she was right. He nodded hesitantly and said, "I will do my best. I hope that eventually you might trust *me* enough to tell me whatever it is you're involved with. I don't like the very idea of our keeping secrets from each other."

"I don't like it, either," she said, "but this has nothing to do with you. It's *my* commitment to something that began while you were away, and you must know that I never imagined Muriel would die and you and I would come back together this way. I had no reason to believe that what I'm doing would ever impact *your* life at all. Please . . . just trust me."

Tristan nodded again, unable to say anything more. Her explanation had only made him more confused and frustrated, but he loved her and he was willing to commit his entire future to her. He owed her the respect of heeding her request, even if the reasons for it left him entirely baffled.

Olivia kissed his cheek, squeezed his hand, and hurried out of the room, saying over her shoulder, "I'll see you in your father's room as soon as I've changed."

"I'll be there," he said, but he remained where he was standing for more than a minute, trying to make peace with all that Olivia had just said. Realizing he couldn't, he told himself that he just needed to do as she'd asked and trust her. Beyond that, he could only pray that whatever she had gotten herself into wouldn't bring trouble into her life. After all they'd been through, he couldn't bear to lose her now.

\* \* \* \* \*

Olivia rushed to her room with such zeal that she was completely out of breath when she got there. She sat on the edge of her bed and gripped the bedspread tightly while she lowered her head and attempted to slow her breathing. Somewhere in the middle of the vicar's sermon, it had dawned on her that she could not go forward with any kind of serious relationship with Tristan and not have him know there was something going on in her life that could cause complications—even if she was sworn to secrecy to not tell *anyone*. He was sharp and perceptive and he knew her well. He would have inevitably become suspicious and would have pushed for answers, which would be more likely to create a stir—which was the last thing anyone needed. During the carriage ride home, she had come up with a way to say all that she could possibly say without compromising his safety or her own—or that of anyone else involved. But she'd hardly given him a moment to react; in truth she thought it best that he have some time to let it sink in. Her relief in having said what she'd needed to say was overshadowed by her fear of how he might respond after he'd been able to ponder it. But she couldn't think about that now; she had to just go on with her day as normally as possible and pray that he would trust her—as she had pleaded with him to do—and respect her need to keep the details to herself.

Winnie came in from the sitting room and immediately asked, "What's wrong?"

She sat on the bed right next to Olivia, who was glad that her breathing was now almost normal. "I told him."

"Told him what?" Winnie looked panicked.

"I just . . . told him there was something going on in my life, but I couldn't tell him anything else. I asked him to trust me."

"And?" Winnie asked, now alarmed.

"I believe he *will* trust me," Olivia said with firm resolve. "He's frustrated, and I can't blame him for that. If it were the other way around, I would certainly be frustrated. But it's better this way. I could never keep a secret from him. By at least acknowledging that there *is* a secret, we are more likely to keep the matter hidden, as it should be."

"I hope you're right," Winnie said and stood up to open Olivia's wardrobe in search of a comfortable dress that she could change into for the remainder of the day.

"Thank you," Olivia said as Winnie handed her one that was dark green with a pink floral pattern embroidered on the front of the bodice.

After changing and freshening up, Olivia and Winnie both went to Walter's room where Lawrence and Tristan were already there with him, talking and laughing. Tristan stood to greet Olivia with a kiss on the cheek and they exchanged a smile that *almost* seemed normal. She saw concern and frustration in his eyes, but he also showed an obvious determination to not let on to anyone else that anything was out of the ordinary. Even if he had to contend with some feelings of vexation toward her, his knowing this much was more likely to make him behave in a way that would divert any suspicion should anything unusual arise—which it inevitably would.

They all enjoyed eating lunch with Walter while filling in the highlights of the vicar's sermon for Walter and Lawrence—along with a comical rendition of the way people had reacted to Tristan and Olivia showing up at church with non-verbal declarations that they were once again a couple. Walter concluded the matter by saying, "Let them think what they want. The two of you being together is a good thing for all of us here. Nothing else matters."

Olivia saw Tristan smile at his father in response to the comment, then he turned to look at her and his smile widened. She saw no hint of frustration or suspicion in his eyes; only his love for her. She had to believe that everything would be all right.

* * * * *

The new week began with a more settled mood in the atmosphere. The household had adjusted to Tristan being home, especially since he had settled into a more normal routine—as opposed to having locked himself in his room. Olivia mostly went about her days as she had before, spending time with Walter when it was most convenient for him, along with helping out in the kitchen here and there, or the laundry, or sometimes the gardens. Occasionally Tristan came along and pitched in to help as well; at other times he went riding or conducted estate business on behalf of his father. She liked seeing him take these steps toward the inevitability of being heir to all his father's holdings, but even more so she appreciated his humility and obvious sense of responsibility in doing so. Prior to leaving for war, he had been somewhat begrudging about such matters, which Olivia knew had been concerning to Walter, if not disheartening. They had both known that Tristan was a good man and that he had the potential to fill his father's shoes very well. But it was as if Muriel had brought out the worst of him in every way. He'd had more of a tendency to avoid any responsibilities that didn't suit his mood, and he'd become terse and testy with practically everyone in the house. It was easy to look back now and see how Muriel had been monopolizing his time and even manipulating his choices and attitudes. But there had been no getting through to him, and Olivia had worried that he would only become more and more unhappy and unfulfilled. Now he was a different man; he was very much the Tristan she had fallen in love with years ago, although he also had a depth of humility and strength of character that being a soldier had instilled in him. And Olivia felt grateful on many levels.

Weeks passed with a sweet tranquility as Walter's health actually seemed to improve now that his son had come home and all past wounds were healed between them. Occasionally Lawrence and Tristan helped Walter to sit out on the patio near the garden, and he began eating some of his meals in the dining room, often declaring how good it was to get out of that bedroom—even if he did need a great deal of help to get anywhere else. But Tristan and Lawrence were both strong men and glad to be of assistance, and there were other men who worked in the household who were always eager to help Walter in any way.

About a month after Tristan's return, Olivia realized she'd never been happier. Tristan had naturally struggled with coming to terms with Muriel's impact on his life, and they often had long talks where they were both able to express their astonishment at her appalling behavior, their grief over all that had been lost, and sometimes even anger toward her. But each conversation brought them closer to being able to talk about all that had happened and simply accepting it as something that was more and more easily left in the past.

With the passing of time, Olivia saw new evidence every day that Tristan was indeed a new man, and that the misgivings and lack of trust he'd once displayed toward her were completely gone. Now that he understood the full truth, he had accepted it readily, and his love for her was impossible to discount. Olivia's own difficult feelings toward Tristan over the way he'd been so gullible in regard to Muriel, and how cruelly he'd treated Olivia as a result, had also settled into complete forgiveness and peace. She'd forgiven him a long time ago, but she'd also lived in fear of what might happen when he returned, still holding to his false beliefs. She'd seen a glimpse of the man she'd feared right after he'd come back, but she'd not seen so much as a hint of such attitudes since. On the contrary, he was attentive toward her, deeply respectful, and clearly in love. The overall result was that her love for him—which she had kept locked away all these years—came forward fully and blossomed. They began to speak of marriage more seriously, and she believed it was inevitable—although she still thought it best to allow more time to pass. She told Tristan it was simply a more prudent approach to marriage—to give courting and engagement a proper time to serve their purpose. What she didn't tell him was that her involvement in things she could not share with him would be much less complicated once the summer was over. By then she would be in a better position to put her secretive dealings into someone else's hands and be able to marry Tristan without having any of that hanging over them.

About once a week Tristan brought up the secret she wouldn't share with him, expressing his concern and frustration—and his curiosity, since he admitted that he couldn't possibly imagine what she could be involved with that might be so serious. She just kept telling him the same things: it was better that he didn't know, for his own protection as well as for others, and he needed to trust her. Eventually they always changed the subject, since they had agreed to just focus on all that was good in their lives and look forward to a bright future together. For Olivia, that future was bright and close to perfect as she imagined living out her life here in this home with Tristan and all the other people she'd grown to love. And she prayed that Walter would live a very long time. He'd started making jokes about Tristan and Olivia giving him grandchildren. Tristan's sisters all had children, but they lived very far away in different directions, and he was lucky to see any of them more than once every couple of years. Walter's comments would always make Tristan chuckle and say, "All in good time, Father," while he usually winked at Olivia, which inevitably made her blush with mild embarrassment. But the idea of being able to have Walter live long enough to be a part of her children's lives gave her great joy, and she prayed every day that it might be possible.

# CHAPTER EIGHT

# TRAITORS UNDERFOOT

TRISTAN RETURNED FROM A LONG morning ride in the summer sun and felt unusually tired. He hadn't slept well for some reason, so once the horse was cared for, he sat down in the clean straw in the stall with the idea that he'd rest there for only a few minutes, just enough to give him the momentum to go up to his bedroom and take a proper nap before lunch. The soft straw was more comfortable than he'd anticipated, and the horse didn't seem to mind his being there. He quickly fell asleep and woke up to the sound of men's voices; two of them, no—three. He recognized the voices and knew that one of these men—Hewitt—worked in the carriage house, and the other two—Wagner and Seymour—in the stables. And Tristan knew all of them very well. He wouldn't have thought twice about them taking a break to have a little chat, except that their voices were hushed and laced with a tone of urgency, as if they didn't want to be overheard, and whatever they were discussing had great importance.

Tristan couldn't hear everything they were saying, but he definitely knew that these men would all be going out late in the evening to take care of something vital they'd been planning for weeks, and he distinctly heard the words at *high tide*, which led Tristan to believe that they would be going to the beach to do whatever it was they were doing, and the obvious place was an inlet less than ten minutes' ride on horseback from the estate.

The men dispersed and returned to their work, but Tristan was left with his heart pounding, wondering what on earth these men were up to—men he trusted and looked up to; men who lived and worked within the bounds of his father's household, of *his* household. Hearing sounds to indicate that at least one of the men was still in the stable, busy at some kind of task, Tristan had to remain hidden or they would discover that he'd overheard their conversation. He stayed huddled in the corner of the horse's stall long enough for his heart to slow to a normal rhythm, and for his mind to assess the possibilities of what could be happening. He tried to think of anything—*anything*—else that might be the slightest bit suspicious that had occurred since his return. He thought of what Olivia had told him—that she was committed to something she couldn't tell him about, but for the life of him he couldn't possibly connect her secret to whatever these men were doing. He dismissed any possible relationship between the two, but couldn't stop thinking about the strange differences he'd noticed in the carriage house. There was a new wall, and the interior of the structure itself was smaller. He knew it! Instinctively he knew there was a connection; he just had to figure out what it was. A part of him wondered if it was better to just pretend he'd not overheard this secretive conversation and simply allow these men to go about their business— however untoward it might be. Perhaps he should just remain uninvolved and ignorant. On the other hand, how could he not consider himself responsible for these men? They weren't simply employees of his father's household; they were like family. What if they were getting themselves into some kind of trouble? Or what if they already had? Perhaps Tristan needed to intervene and would regret not doing so if whatever they were up to brought difficult repercussions into their lives. And who was to say such repercussions might not affect the entire household?

Tristan tried to keep his mind from getting carried away, but without knowing the truth, his imagination went wild with all kinds of possibilities. He was startled to hear the stable door closing, and the ensuing silence led him to believe he was finally alone. He moved with careful slowness and silence to peer over the edge of the stall and make certain no one else was there. Only the animals were there with him, and none of them seemed to care that he'd been hiding and eavesdropping—however unintentionally.

Tristan went discreetly out the *back* door of the stables, which was rarely used, being careful to peer out first and look both ways to be sure that no one saw him. Until he decided what to do—or if he should do *anything*—he didn't want anyone becoming suspicious of his being aware that something was amiss. He went to the nearby carriage house, hoping no one would be there, but prepared to behave as if his appearance there was completely normal on the chance that he came across anyone. He entered to find the place devoid of people, but he was immediately taken aback to see that the carriages and wagons were facing in opposite directions to where they'd been the last time he'd been here. Something about having two wagons backed up to the new wall led Tristan to believe there was a connection, and a purpose. He stood there for a moment putting pieces together in his mind, and logic told him this wasn't just a *new* wall; it was a *false* wall. The diminished space was due to the wall allowing space behind it for *something*, and whatever it was would be loaded into the wagons that had been placed strategically near the wall for easy access.

In spite of being afraid he might get caught, Tristan went to the edge of the new wall and felt his way all the way up and down where it met with the wall that had always been there. He felt nothing out of the ordinary. He pressed his fingers to the bottom of the wall, feeling for anything unusual while he went the entire distance of the wall, moving like he might have on the battlefield, crouching down and easing forward stealthily. Still, nothing unusual. But he was deeply convinced that this wall was not what it appeared to be, and he wondered what his father would think if he knew there were strange goings on here among those who worked for him. He felt angry to think of men they'd always trusted taking advantage of Walter's poor health to become involved in something their employer would surely disapprove of—and conducting some kind of secretive business right here under their own roof, relatively speaking. For all Tristan knew, what they were doing was criminal; if not, then why all the secrecy?

Tristan came to the end of the wall and carefully pressed his fingers up the other side, desperately feeling for some evidence that might prove his theory correct, while at the same time beginning to believe he was letting his imagination put things together that had nothing to do with each other. He gasped when he felt something strange. He couldn't see it, but he examined it carefully with his fingers. *A latch.* "Unbelievable," he whispered under his breath, and the latch sprung open when he pressed on it just so. He peered in every direction, suddenly *very* afraid of being caught. He no longer trusted men he had believed he could trust, and he feared what he might have stumbled upon. Might he have put himself in danger? Would he himself face criminal charges if whatever was taking place were to be discovered by legal authorities?

Heart pounding once again, Tristan sucked in a harsh breath as he realized that a significant portion of the wall could be opened like a large door, and a quick glance showed that this long, narrow *room* which had been built here was stacked with crates. With only the daylight from the windows on the opposite side of the carriage house, Tristan couldn't see anything more than that, then he noticed that just inside this strange door he'd opened, there was a lantern and matches. Again he looked all around himself to make certain he was alone before he lit the lantern, then held it high and walked into the room. There was barely enough space for a man to move past the long line of stacked crates, varying in shapes and sizes. He wondered what might be inside them, and what on earth could be happening here. *Smuggling?* he wondered. Could these men who worked for his father actually be *smuggling?* He recalled their mention of high tide and plans that had been in the making for weeks. But what would they be smuggling, and to *whom?* Were they just trying to make money by avoiding taxation on exported goods? Or was there some other purpose to this endeavor?

Tristan noticed that the crates were nailed shut, but he also saw a claw hammer sitting idly on top of one of them. He set the lantern down and picked up the hammer, using the claw to loosen a couple of nails and then lift the lid.

"Merciful heaven!" Tristan muttered under his breath, blinking several times to be certain his eyes weren't deceiving him. This particular crate held a number of rifles. Weapons implied war, and there was only one war going on right now that he knew of. If these weapons were to be loaded on a ship—secretly—there was only one logical place they could be going. *The colonies.* And that meant only one thing. *Treason.* "Merciful heaven!" Tristan murmured again, more breathlessly. These men were traitors, and treason was taking place right here under their noses. As memories of being on the battlefield facing colonist soldiers catapulted through his mind, he felt literally sick to his stomach. He glanced at the other crates and surmised by their shapes and sizes—and some of them were actually labeled—that they contained various supplies; likely ammunition and nonperishable food. And who knew what else? Blankets? Tents? Clothing? Whatever was here, he knew its most likely purpose was to aid a cause that went against king and country, and against everything Tristan had spent years risking his life to fight for. The sickness inside of him increased.

A stark fear overcame him suddenly. Whatever was taking place, he could never find a way to stop it if he was discovered here. He had to pretend he knew nothing; he had to figure out a way to prevent these supplies from being delivered to the enemy. Something inside told him his assumptions might not be correct, that there could be some other explanation. But his deepest instincts shouted in his mind that he knew *exactly* what was going on here, and he had to find a way to stop it.

Tristan hammered the crate closed again and returned the hammer to where he'd found it. He doused the lantern and put it back exactly where it had been. He once again looked out carefully in every direction before he left the secret chamber and pushed the large door closed, hearing the latch click firmly into place. Again he chose to go out the back door, looking both ways before he exited, and hurrying toward the garden where he could have some time to think of an excuse for where he might have been all this time. With rows of high shrubberies, a person could easily remain unseen among them if they chose to, and if anyone questioned his whereabouts, a nap on the grass in the gardens gave him a sound alibi. He sat down on a bench and tried to catch his breath, but thinking through what he'd just discovered only made it more difficult to breathe. He pressed a hand over the center of his chest as it tightened in response to the inner conflict growing there. He planted his elbows on his thighs and pressed his head into his hands, wondering what on earth he was supposed to do now. Should he talk to his father about this? As soon as the question entered his mind, he knew he couldn't; he just couldn't. Walter's health was so fragile. To learn something like this would be devastating to him! How clearly Tristan recalled his father's declarations—all throughout Tristan's life—of his loyalty to the crown, of the importance of honoring the British Empire, of never forgetting how blessed they were to live in glorious England. Tristan recalled clearly how proud Walter had been of Tristan's decision to enlist and fight in this war against the colonists. He'd expressed the tender concerns of a father sending his son off to battle, and his fears in that regard. But his pride had still been readily evident. Walter's pride and devotion to country had often kept Tristan going. In spite of all the differences between Tristan and his father at the time, they had been in complete agreement concerning their loyalties and the ofttimes necessity of defending them.

No, Tristan couldn't go to Walter about this. In this respect he needed to step up and be the master of this estate and figure out how to handle the problem himself. He wondered who he could turn to for help and realized he couldn't trust *anyone*. If these men he'd believed he could trust without question were actually traitors—as he suspected they were—then who else might be involved? He didn't even entertain the idea of seeking out assistance from the law. If he implicated these men at this point, he had no idea who else he might be implicating. And regardless of anything else, these men lived and worked on *his* family's estate; the illegal goods were being stored in his carriage house and delivered by his employees. The family name had already suffered more than enough scandal as a result of Muriel's deplorable behavior; they didn't need something like this added into the mix.

The only possible solution that Tristan could see was to somehow get more information and try to stop whatever was going on before someone got into serious trouble. He knew the punishment for treason, and no matter what anyone might be doing or not doing, he had no desire to see them hang for it. He might not be able to stop what was taking place tonight, but if he could figure out exactly what was going on and who else was involved, he could surely stop it from ever happening again. He was as good as master of this estate; he needed to make certain the people who worked for him knew he would never tolerate such goings-on. He would give them fair warning and pray that would be the end of it.

Thinking the matter through, he knew approximately what time the goods would be loaded up and removed from the premises in order to get to the beach at high tide. Deciding it would be better for everyone to believe he had no suspicions whatsoever, and that he was gone for the evening, he set himself upon a plan and finally found the fortitude to enter the house and behave as if everything was perfectly normal. Hearing his stomach growl, he realized he had missed lunch.

Wondering where Olivia might be—since he knew his father would be napping by now—Tristan went first to the kitchen, hoping to talk the cook into giving him some buttered bread or something equivalent that he could eat while he searched the usual places. He considered himself fortunate to find Olivia there, drying a freshly washed pot with a clean towel.

"Hello there," he said, proud of himself for how perfectly normal he sounded while his insides were churning.

"Oh, there you are," she said. "You missed lunch."

"Were you worried?" he asked with a smile and approached her, nodding a silent greeting toward the other two women working nearby.

"Not terribly," she said.

"I confess that after my ride I went for a walk in the gardens and got suddenly sleepy. I laid down on the grass with the intention of staying there for a few minutes and woke up with my stomach growling."

"Good thing you found your way back," she said with a smile. "You could have been lost there for days."

"Yes, I could have been," he said and gave her a quick kiss. "I don't suppose you could help me find a little something to eat without upsetting anyone's routine."

"I think I could manage that," she said and put the clean pot away before she told him she'd meet him in the breakfast room in a few minutes.

He was glad for a chance to freshen up, which also allowed him to once again consciously will his smoldering thoughts to remain at bay, and to try and subdue the sick feeling hovering inside of him.

He found Olivia in the breakfast room—a small, pleasant room with big windows, an ideal place for eating a light meal. The small, round table there had four chairs around it, and there was little else in the room that served any practical purpose. There was a tray on the table from which she was removing food and dishes and setting them on the table. He hoped that eating something would help calm his nausea and was pleased to note that the cold pork and thick slices of dark bread looked appetizing. There was also cheese and some sliced tomatoes; he knew the tomatoes were growing in abundance in the garden right now.

Tristan sat across the table from Olivia as she said, "I haven't eaten yet; I was hoping to eat with you. I left Lawrence to share lunch with your father."

"Everything all right since I left?" he asked, thinking how much had gone wrong for him since he'd walked out of the house right after breakfast.

"Yes," she said, sounding surprised. "Why wouldn't it be?"

"Just wondering. I confess that I always worry that my father will get worse. I don't want that to happen."

"Nor do I," she said. "But you say that as if you've never said it before. Of course, it's a concern. But we'll keep making the most of every day and pray that he will continue on as he is for a good, long time."

"Of course," Tristan said, while he imagined his father finding out that treason was taking place within his household, which news would send him into heart failure and immediate death.

"Are you all right?" Olivia asked.

"Yes," he said and looked at her directly. "I'm fine," he added convincingly. "I think I'm just a bit dazed from such a deep nap so early in the day. For some reason I didn't sleep well last night."

"The usual?" she asked, and he knew she meant his previous confessions to sometimes having bad dreams associated with memories from the war, which could often mix into his ongoing efforts to make peace with Muriel's death and the reasons for it. And sometimes he simply couldn't sleep due to the same reasons.

"Yes," he said. "Nothing to worry about. As you often tell me, I'm certain it will get better with time."

Tristan wished in that moment that his greatest concern was what it had been earlier today: difficult memories of war and his wife's betrayal. Now, he had a very real problem right in front of him.

Considering the plan he'd come up with, Tristan said casually to Olivia, "I've been thinking that with all the weeks I've been home, I've not once gone to the pub. I used to go there once or twice a week, mostly to visit with the locals. I found it enjoyable and relaxing, and I think it's good for me to associate with people and not appear to set myself above them by never showing my face in public."

"Then I'd say it's high time you went." She smiled wryly and added, "I trust you won't be getting into any trouble."

"Me?" he countered facetiously.

"It's good timing, actually," she said. "Winnie asked me to help her with a sewing project she's working on. I'll devote some time to that while you're away."

"Excellent," he said, glad to know that Olivia and Winnie would be occupied and not have any reason to think that his being away from the house this evening had any suspicious purpose.

Tristan had supper with his father; Olivia, Winnie, and Lawrence were there as well. He told them all of what he'd told Olivia at lunch, and Walter told him to have a good time and to give his regards to any old friends there that Tristan might encounter.

"I'll do that," Tristan said, hoping it never got back to anyone that he wouldn't actually be at the pub this evening. For a moment he thought of how difficult it must be for his father to not be able to go out and do things that had once been so common and easy for him. In the weeks since Tristan had returned, Walter had received visits from a few of his old friends, but Walter had told him there were many people whom Walter had considered to be his friends but who hadn't once come to visit or even written to inquire over his well-being since his health had taken a sharp decline. The thought saddened Tristan; it was certainly evidence of how quickly life could sift out the true friends from those whose association was merely shallow and meaningless.

Tristan went to the stables where he managed to behave completely normal in his interactions with the men working there—men he'd overheard discussing treasonous plans earlier today. He saddled his own horse—as he always had—and graciously accepted their well wishes that he have an enjoyable evening at the pub.

"Don't get drunk now," Wagner said teasingly as Tristan headed toward the stable doorway.

"We don't want to have to come looking for you." Seymour laughed.

Tristan laughed too. There had been one incident in his life when he'd not made it home because he'd been drinking too much, and Walter had sent these men to find Tristan and bring him home. But Tristan would never live it down. He really didn't care; he'd grown far beyond that kind of behavior and they all knew it. He was more focused on keeping up the pretense that he actually *was* going to the pub and that he wasn't aware of something dreadful taking place this evening.

Tristan rode a good distance toward town before he eased the horse into a thick patch of trees that was out of sight from any homes in the area. He rode back in the direction from which he'd come, staying mostly in wooded areas and off the main road until he came to the perfect place where he could tie off the horse in the trees and allow it to graze comfortably while he hid himself behind a cluster of large rocks, with a perfect view of the beach below. He had the advantage of having grown up in this area. This was the very spot where he had often spied on his sisters when they'd gone to the beach to have picnics and play in the waves as they rolled up onto the sand. There had been no purpose in his spying except to appease the mischievous nature of a little brother. But now he was glad for the experience he'd gained from his childhood mischief. As he settled in, trying to get comfortable but still keeping a good view of the cove below, he wondered how long he might have to wait before he saw anything. Or what if he didn't see anything at all? What if he'd misunderstood what he'd overheard? Or perhaps he'd put the pieces together wrong and this was *not* the place where whatever was happening would take place.

Tristan had only been there a minute or two when he saw by the light of a partial moon two heavily loaded wagons moving slowly onto the beach. If these were indeed the wagons that had come from his own carriage house, then they would have already been loaded when Tristan had left home just a while ago. He could see a rider on horseback leading the way, one man driving each wagon, and another rider on horseback coming behind; four men altogether. He still couldn't believe it! But he prayed that his stumbling upon all of this might be the means to help protect his household and prevent anyone from getting into any serious trouble. The wagons and riders stopped at a point that was just barely beyond the rush of the waves as they rolled in and out. Tristan knew the tide hadn't yet reached its highest point, but it soon would. He had perhaps expected there to be a ship on the horizon and longboats on the beach that might have come in to collect what was in those wagons. But there was no sign of any sailing vessel within his sight. Tristan thought of the firearms and ammunition that were among the supplies and felt a little sick. How could he not think of how he'd been wounded by a colonist soldier? The irony that guns were being smuggled from his own home to aid the colonists was literally nauseating. He thought of all the suffering he'd observed during his time spent recovering from his wound and assisting Jack Barburry, and the nausea increased. Trying not to think about that, Tristan watched as the four men quickly and efficiently unloaded the crates from the wagons and carried them to a place that was blocked from Tristan's view by a huge outcropping of rock that formed a cliff that rose high above the sea. Then he realized that he knew *exactly* where the crates were being taken. There was a cave beneath that cliff; he'd played there as a boy and knew it very well. At high tide it was impossible to get in or out of the cave without getting wet, but the interior of the cave itself always stayed dry. It was the perfect place to store something that could later be loaded onto a ship via longboats that could row to the shore.

Tristan watched as the unloading took place very quickly, and he wondered what—if anything—he was supposed to do about it. He wondered when the next stage of this process might take place and how he might find out about it without purposely eavesdropping on the men that he knew were involved. Again he considered confronting them, but he no longer trusted them at all—nor anyone in the household for that matter. He had no idea what he was dealing with, or who knew about it. And if he didn't trust them, he didn't like the odds of four to one if he let on that he knew what was happening.

With the unloading completed, the men quickly moved the wagons off the beach, and Tristan noted that their timing had been perfect, and obviously planned this way. The waves that had just begun lapping at the wagon wheels now completely erased their tracks and any evidence that anyone had been there, or that anything had taken place. Another few minutes and they might not have been able to drive the wagons off the wet sand. It had been well-timed, indeed.

Tristan watched as the wagons were driven out of his sight, again with one rider ahead of them, and one behind, obviously to keep a lookout for anything amiss. He quietly left his hiding place and mounted his horse, even though he was too far away to be seen or heard. Riding slowly and with care, Tristan waited in a patch of trees until he saw the little caravan emerge from the well-hidden road that led down to the beach.

He followed at a safe distance, remaining hidden by trees and moving too quietly to be noticed. He was struck with another wave of disbelief just to see the evidence of how the wagons were returned to his own carriage house. He waited with his horse in the woods at the edge of the groomed lawn where he had a perfect view of the carriage house and stables. He tied the horse off so that he could focus fully on what he was observing while he again wondered if he should intervene. He prayed in a whisper to know what to do, not even knowing for certain what he wanted the outcome to be—other than protecting his household. Given that he had criminals working for him, he couldn't be sure whether they should rightly be turned over to the law for their crimes. But his first instinct was that it would be better to give them fair warning and simply stop this madness from going any further. And no one need ever know what was going on. He found himself wondering if he would lie to protect his home and the people who belonged there, which would technically make him a traitor too. He was surprised—though perhaps he shouldn't have been—to realize that his deepest self demanded that he choose the protection of his home and family over his duty to his country. The decision made his objective clearer; he needed to find a way to put a stop to this, and then he would do everything in his power to protect these men and forgive them for their misguided actions—if they vowed to never again engage in treasonous activities.

Tristan watched as all four men went into the stables with the horses that had been pulling the wagons and those that had been ridden. After the amount of time passed that would be required to see the horses cared for, two of the men left the stables and headed toward the entrance of the house that was used mostly by the servants, since it was the door closest to the stairs that led to the servants' quarters where the majority of the unmarried staff each had their own rooms. A minute later, a third man left the stables and went in the same direction, but Tristan waited, knowing there was a fourth man. He wondered if his prayers were being heard when he realized that he felt a lot more confident about confronting *one* man, as opposed to four, and three of them had already gone into the house. He waited several more minutes, wondering if he'd just missed the fourth man somehow—except that he'd been watching so closely. He wondered if this fourth man was remaining in the stables for some reason. To keep watch? To wait for someone? Tristan had no idea, and his heart began to pound as he wondered what else might be planned in regard to this entire operation.

The fourth man finally came out of the stables, closing the door securely behind him before he too headed toward the house. Tristan acted on an impulse that felt more like a hefty nudge. He left the horse tied to a tree and ran quietly toward the lone man, slowing his pace and sneaking noiselessly as he got closer. In the dark, he had no idea which one of his servants this was, but once he was only a few steps behind him, Tristan could see he had the advantage of height over this man and could easily subdue him enough to at least get him to pay attention and have a serious conversation—one that involved threats that were already ricocheting in Tristan's head. Fearing he would be detected if he didn't act quickly, Tristan was glad for his military training as he closed the gap between himself and the man he was following. With strength and stealth, Tristan put one arm around the man to disable the use of his arms, and at the same moment put his other hand over the man's mouth to keep him from making a sound. It was a tactic he'd used more than once in taking prisoners of war; he'd hated doing it then, but he'd been acting under strict orders. He hated doing it now, knowing that what was about to follow wouldn't be pretty—even if he had no idea how it would go exactly. Would he be met with defiance? Anger? Or remorse? But remorse for treasonous actions, or simply remorse for getting caught? Tristan would never know until he just faced it head-on.

The man now in Tristan's grasp was understandably startled, and squirmed and groaned. Tristan hurried to say close to his ear with harsh firmness, "Don't make a sound. I'm not going to hurt you, just . . . be still!" The squirming ceased, but he could feel the man breathing sharply, as any man would who had been startled in such a way. "I assume you know who I am," Tristan added, still keeping one arm firmly around his captive and the other hand over his mouth. "I want to know what's going on and why, and you're going to tell me. I'll move my hand if you give me your assurance that you will remain quiet." There was hesitation, then a firm nod, and Tristan moved his hand. He then let go of his tight grasp around the man's middle but quickly took hold of his arm firmly to keep him from leaving. He wished it wasn't so dark and that the man's face wasn't shaded by the tricorn he wore on his head. He hurried to get to the point while he had the chance.

"I followed you . . . and the others. I saw what you did . . . where you hid the goods that have been stored in *my* carriage house, and transported with *my* wagons. Tell me this isn't what it appears to be. Convince me!"

Tristan waited impatiently for the man to speak, certain that once he did, Tristan would recognize his voice and know to whom he was speaking. But the man said nothing.

"Tell me!" Tristan said through clenched teeth, tightening his hold on the man's arm. Still he was met only with silence. "I will *not*," Tristan went on, allowing his anger to come forward more fully, "allow people among *my* household to engage in treasonous activities. I will *not*! Now, tell me what's going on. It's the only chance you've got to possibly avoid having all of this turned over to the authorities. If you want my help to undo this as quickly and quietly as possible, you will talk to me, and you will do it *now*!"

"And what if it can't be undone," he heard Olivia say, and he suddenly lost the ability to breathe. He yanked the hat from her head and tossed it to the ground before he tilted her face toward the stingy portion of moonlight available, completely disbelieving of the evidence before his very eyes.

"What on *earth* are you doing?" he demanded, practically hissing, maintaining his firm hold on her arm.

"It's a *very* long story, Tristan." Her voice was strong with courage, but the quaver of fear in it couldn't be disguised. "And I wanted very much to keep you out of it . . . for your own sake. Now you know, so there's no point in trying to keep it a secret any longer. I'll tell you everything, but . . . not like this. You're hurting me." She attempted to yank her arm from his grasp, reminding him that he was holding it very tightly. He let go, no longer worried about his captive running away and too stunned to even think clearly.

"I can't believe it," he said. "I can't even imagine what would lead you to do something so . . . *deplorable*."

"How do you know it's deplorable when you just admitted that you don't know what's going on or why?"

"I can guess, given what I *do* know. Tell me you're not involved in some form of smuggling guns and supplies out of the country. Tell me they aren't intended to be used by the American colonists. Tell me! Give me some other explanation! Because I was shot by a colonist, Olivia! I laid on a battlefield bleeding from a bullet that came from one of their guns! I spent many weeks in a pitiful excuse of a hospital while men lost their limbs and their lives. Tell me that what you're involved with doesn't put you on the opposite side of everything I risked my life for!"

She sighed and hung her head. He waited for a response, realizing that with each second of silence that passed, she was admitting to everything he'd just accused her of. If there was some other explanation, some way she could defend her actions, she would have jumped to do so.

"I can't believe it," he said again, this time barely getting the words out on the wake of a strained breath. "So, you *are* a traitor." Still, she didn't deny the accusation; she only continued to look at the ground. The hurt and anger he felt quickly spread to his every nerve. He used all his willpower to remain calm, but he couldn't keep himself from saying, "And I had just convinced myself that I really could trust you."

"Tristan!" she finally spoke, finally looked up at him. He took a step back and was struck with the reality that she was dressed in a man's clothes, and they were just baggy enough to conceal the fact that she was not shaped like a man at all. He could not get his mind to accept everything he was seeing and hearing. "Listen to me," she added and he tried to focus. "*This* has nothing to do with you and me."

"Doesn't it?" he countered. "You keeping secrets from me isn't supposed to—"

"I told you there was something in my life I needed to see through to its finish. I never lied to you."

"This is not just a little secret, Livy," he snarled. "This is *treason*! You could *hang* for this! And did you not think about how absolutely contrary all of this is to who I am and what I believe in?"

"I've thought about it far more than you could ever imagine. And don't go assuming that I am not torn, or that I would think this easily explained. That's why you need to give me the chance to explain; I'll tell you everything. But not here; not while you're so angry."

"And you think I will have stopped feeling angry by breakfast? Ever?"

"Perhaps you might at least calm down a little," she said as if *he* had done something wrong.

"Don't count on it," he said, realizing his anger was rising and he knew she was right about not pursuing the conversation any further right now. He picked up her hat and handed it to her, saying with disdain, "If my father knew about this, it would *kill* him. Do you hear me? It would *kill* him!" He walked away before he completely lost his temper, going back to the woods to get the horse he'd left there. He felt every bit as sick inside as he had when he'd come home to find out that Muriel was dead—and buried with another man's baby. He only wished that he could begin to know what to do about it.

# CHAPTER NINE

# PARTNERS IN TREASON

OLIVIA LAY IN HER BED in the darkness while a steady stream of tears ran from the corners of her eyes into her hair. She'd been worried about Tristan finding out; she'd been praying that he never would. But he knew, and the means by which he'd discovered her involvement in all of this couldn't possibly have gone any worse. She feared now that whatever the outcome might be in regard to this smuggling scheme, she had likely lost Tristan forever. He'd broken her heart once before, but now that it had been broken again she feared it would never recover. She couldn't blame him, really. Last time he'd believed Muriel's lies and his cruelty toward her had been without just cause. But this time he had good reason to be angry with her. She knew well his loyalty to his country, and how her going against that so boldly could be nothing but a huge offense to him. She understood, and she couldn't lay any blame at his feet for simply being who he was and believing in what he believed. The simple fact was that when it came to such loyalties, they were on opposite sides. She'd known it long before he'd returned from war, and she'd struggled with the great dilemma of knowing that she—and others in the household—were involved in something that might actually bring harm to Tristan, if only indirectly. She'd lost track of the hours and days she'd spent harrowed up by the ironies, the guilt, the quandary of it all. But she had truly believed it was best for everyone concerned to keep Tristan from knowing anything. And yet he'd found out. She couldn't imagine how that had happened when they had all been so careful; not as careful as they'd believed, obviously. And if Tristan had discovered the truth, was it possible that others might as well? Were they in more danger than they'd allowed themselves to believe?

Olivia rolled onto her side and hit her pillow hard in a futile attempt to release some tiny degree of the turmoil consuming her. She tried to settle into a comfortable position and relax, but her entire body felt tense and constricted. "Please help me, God," she muttered aloud. "Show me the way. Keep us all protected and safe as we press forward in our cause, and . . . please . . ." Tears overtook her voice but she pressed on. "Please . . . I would ask for a miracle . . . that Tristan might find it in his heart to forgive me . . . that he might know how very much I love him. Please, God! Please!"

Olivia squeezed her eyes closed against the memories of Tristan's angry words, his disappointment, his very legitimate hurt over the trust that had been broken between them, and she couldn't begin to imagine how they could ever get beyond this.

\* \* \* \* \*

Once alone in his room, Tristan pulled off his boots and threw them across the room, as if that might somehow express the roiling anger that grew steadily more explosive inside of him. He removed his stockings and his waistcoat as well, tossing them with equal vigor before he began to pace the room in bare feet, rethinking every tiny bit of information he knew about what he'd discovered today and trying to combine it with everything he'd known about Olivia prior to what he'd just learned about her. The love he felt for her clashed violently inside of him against the absolute absurdity—and horror—of the way she had just broken his trust in ways he never could have imagined. He paced and stewed and fretted until his feet hurt and his back and neck ached from the tenseness of his every muscle. He finally succumbed to the only thing he knew how to do when faced with the challenges of life that were far too big for him to handle; he dropped to his knees by the edge of the bed, clasped his hands together, and pressed his face into the bedspread, praying aloud in sputtering bursts of expressing his anger, his fear, his disappointment, and—he had to admit it—his broken heart. He pleaded for guidance to know how to handle all of this correctly. On a practical level, he needed to protect his household, and he needed to protect Olivia. He didn't agree with her choices *at all*, but now that he knew what he knew, he would never leave her to suffer the brutal consequences that would face her if her actions were discovered. On a more personal level, Tristan asked God to help him sort out his confused feelings toward Olivia. He loved her; he'd believed he could trust her. Learning what he'd learned didn't make him love her any less; it only made him wonder whether or not loving her was wise, or if he would be better off to just close his heart and stop pursuing any hope for a future with her. Of course, people knew they were courting. If he were to break off their relationship, it would spur questions from the people around them, and perhaps even suspicion. But could he pretend that everything between them was the same as it had been before he'd discovered that the woman he loved was a traitor?

While he prayed and prayed and continued to stew and mull everything around in his mind over and over, a thought occurred to Tristan that seemed significant—even if it felt overwhelming and difficult to process in the midst of such disturbance. But he realized completely and fully in that moment that he'd never really loved Muriel. He'd believed that he had, but it became remarkably clear to him in that moment how carefully she had manipulated him with her beguiling and provocative ways into misinterpreting his own feelings. He'd been attracted to her, drawn to her; he'd even felt like he'd needed her. But all of those feelings had quickly faded after the wedding when her true nature had come to the surface, and he had long ago let go of his distorted beliefs. What struck Tristan as odd was the fact that this clear and undeniable epiphany would come to him now, in the midst of fervent prayer, while he was trying to come to terms with things that had nothing to do with Muriel. He asked God that question and kept asking it over and over for what felt like a very long time, while his knees began to stiffen and the ache in his back and shoulders returned. But he felt inclined to remain there in solemn prayer until he received some kind of guidance, something to help him go forward, to know what to do—if only just enough to get him through one day, and then he could evaluate the matter again and get through another.

Tristan gasped aloud and lifted his head as another epiphany—even more clear and strong—appeared in his mind, seemingly out of nowhere. Throughout his entire life, he'd sought to follow God's guidance, and he'd many times felt answers to prayers come to him, but he'd learned even in his youth that such answers generally came very quietly as feelings of peace and calm, or hushed ideas that just felt right; perhaps it was a combination of the two. Rarely had Tristan received answers with such force as that which overcame him in that moment. But he was up against some enormous dilemmas, and he believed that God understood the need for divine guidance that he could rely on without doubt or hesitation. Still, the answer surprised him somewhat, even though he could clearly see the best path to addressing what was most important and most urgent. The enlightenment in his mind was immediately accompanied by an extraordinary sense of peace, and he felt remarkably calm—especially in contrast to the explosive fury that had been with him when he had gone to his knees an hour or so ago. He knew now that he'd needed to recognize his lack of love toward Muriel so that he could appreciate the real and true love he had for Olivia. And he knew that no matter how much he might disagree with her, he had to honor his love for her, and he also had to take into account his entire history with her, and all that he knew about her character as a whole. He couldn't allow what he'd just learned to erase all that he knew to be good and noble about her. He *knew* that every negative thing he'd believed about her had come from Muriel's lying lips. He knew it! So, why would a woman so full of goodness become involved in something so treacherous? He concluded that he had no idea, and he would never know if he didn't ask her. She had earned the right to speak her piece; she'd proven over and over to him that she was a woman of integrity. She *had* told him she was involved in something, and he could see now that her motives in not telling him had been to protect him. Could he not appreciate that as a sign of her love for him? He'd been gone for a very long time. He had no idea how all of this had come about. And while he still wholeheartedly disagreed with it, and he also felt legitimately afraid that terrible legal repercussions could result, he could not expect his own beliefs to be shared by someone else—even the woman he loved.

Tristan bowed his head again and thanked God with all the energy of his soul for such clear enlightenment and for the presence of mind and clarity of spirit to help him face what needed to be done. He then rose abruptly to his feet, taking a moment to stretch his aching muscles when his stiff knees and tense back rebelled. Without any hesitation, he took up a lamp and left his room, going quickly and quietly to the opposite wing of the house where Olivia's room was located. He had no idea what time it was, and he didn't care if he woke her. They needed to talk, and it had to be now. Now, while his mind was clear; now, while the household was quiet; now, before any further action occurred in the smuggling business that was underfoot.

* * * * *

Olivia became distracted from her ongoing disagreement with her bed—and her futility in trying to get comfortable in it—when she heard a very quiet knock on her door. She gasped and sat up, knowing it could be no one but Tristan. "Oh, help," she murmured, not wanting to call out to him and perhaps awaken Winnie, whose room was just on the other side of the sitting room, and she couldn't remember whether the doors between the rooms had been left closed.

A moment later, the door came open and Tristan entered carrying a lamp, wearing only a shirt and breeches and nothing on his feet.

"What on *earth* are you doing?" she asked in a harsh whisper. "You can't just burst into my room like this in the middle of the night and—"

"I assumed you would be sleeping and I would have to wake you," he said with no hint of apology in his voice.

"And do you really think that sleep would be possible after all that—"

"No," he said, "that's why I'm here. We need to talk, and we need to talk now." He glanced around until he saw her dressing gown draped over the footboard of her bed. He tossed it at her and turned his back. "Put that on and get out of bed. We need to talk."

"Winnie might overhear us," she whispered in the same petulant tone he was using. She didn't doubt that they needed to talk, but she certainly wasn't looking forward to facing more of his wrath.

"That's why we're going somewhere else . . . somewhere in the house where we won't be overheard. Hurry up."

"I'm hurrying," she insisted, tying her dressing gown around her waist.

She barely had slippers on her feet before he took her arm and murmured, "Let's go."

"You don't have to drag me," she said in the hallway once they'd passed Winnie's room. "I'm not going to run away."

Tristan eased his grip and slowed his pace, but he didn't let go. They moved in silence down the stairs and into the library, where he finally let go of her arm before he quietly closed the door and set down the lamp. Olivia drew all of her courage together and tried not to think about how she'd forfeited any possibility of sharing a life with him. She knew he would never trust her again, and she couldn't blame him. Still, her heart was broken. But she couldn't think about that now or she would melt onto the floor in heaving sobs. She had to keep herself under control and maintain her dignity. Whatever he had to say she would take it as graciously as she could possibly manage, and with any luck he would be willing to hear her side of this story and not cause any problems in regard to their current mission being seen through to its conclusion.

Olivia had no desire to sit down, feeling more strength and confidence by remaining on her feet. Tristan stood to face her, his hands on his hips, his expression stony and unreadable. She steeled herself for an inevitable verbal assault, completely unprepared to hear him say, "I love you."

"What?" she countered with a breathy gasp.

"Did you not hear me?" he asked, sounding less angry than she'd expected. In fact, now that she really looked at his expression and considered his tone of voice, she detected no anger at all.

"Of course I heard you, but . . ."

"Listen to me, Olivia," he said and took her shoulders into his hands. "I love you. Nothing matters more than that." She put a hand over her mouth, which only partially muffled a sudden, uncontrollable sob. "I don't agree with what you're doing, and I certainly can't begin to know why you're doing it. But my being angry over it will solve nothing. I need you to understand that beneath my anger is . . . fear more than anything. I'm confused; I'm upset. But mostly I'm afraid. I'm afraid of what might happen to you . . . to us . . . to whoever is involved. I need to understand what's going on so that I can do everything in my power to keep you safe, to protect my household. Do you hear what I'm saying?" She didn't respond, due to the fact that she was still holding a hand over her mouth, and he persisted, "Olivia, do you hear me?"

Olivia nodded and he went on. "You've told me you're committed to something and you must see it through. So, whatever the destination might be for what was put into that cave . . . I will help you meet your commitment if that's what it takes to keep you safe. And then . . . we're done with it; we're finished. There will be no more treason—not here, not under my roof, not with the people I love. We will do whatever it takes to see this through and put it behind us, and God willing, no one with the power to harm us will ever know. Do you understand?"

Olivia nodded again, so overcome with what he was saying that she could hardly breathe, let alone speak. When he said nothing more, she pressed her face to his chest and just allowed her tears to rush forward, relishing the way he wrapped her in his arms and pressed a kiss into her hair. It was a miracle! His pledge to help her meant more than she could ever tell him, but his declaration of love for her in spite of their differences felt like the parting of the Red Sea. With him in her life and by her side she felt capable of conquering anything—even treason for the sake of a cause she deeply believed in. And even if Tristan didn't believe in the same cause, he believed in her, and for now that was enough.

\* \* \* \* \*

Tristan held Olivia desperately close and silently thanked God for granting him the compassion and understanding that had allowed him to get past his anger over the situation. He was so grateful to be holding her in his arms and offering her the strength she needed, as opposed to arguing with her and lashing out as a result of his own fears. He *was* afraid; he couldn't even count the reasons he had to be afraid over all he'd discovered just today—and to know that Olivia was right in the middle of it. But he needed to be rational—for both their sakes—if he hoped to keep her safe and see all of this undone as quickly as possible.

When her crying calmed down, Tristan urged her to one of the couches and they sat close together, holding hands. "Now, tell me, Livy; tell me everything. If I'm going to help you, I need to know everything."

She looked hesitant and thoughtful, then turned away and wouldn't look at him at all. "I'm more grateful than I can say that you're willing to help me . . . and that you trust me; and most of all to know that you still love me. I pray that never changes. But . . ."

"But?" he pressed.

She looked at him then, and he saw fierce determination in her eyes. "I appreciate that you want to protect me, Tristan; therefore, you must understand that I want to protect you too. There are things I know that could cause a great deal of trouble for myself; I understand that. But I *do* know them, and I can't erase that knowledge; I'm responsible for that knowledge. I will tell you what you *need* to know about what's going on right now, but there are some things I need to keep to myself—for your own safety. The less you know, the more you will be able to claim innocence if we are ever discovered."

"And if we *are* discovered, I claim innocence while I let you go to the gallows? That's not going to happen!"

"I pray that it does not," she said, tightening her hold on his hand. "But I *am* breaking the law; I know that. I knew it when I got involved. But I believe in this cause, Tristan. I completely understand why you are on the other side, and I do not expect you to adopt my beliefs. I'm grateful for your help, but you need to remain loyal to your own convictions—and you and I need to keep our convictions on this matter out of our relationship—if you think that's possible."

"It has to be," he insisted, not willing to lose her for any reason. "And there has to be a way to keep you safe and make all of this go away so that you can *stay* safe. I want to marry you, Olivia. I want us to have a family and grow old together. I don't want to lose you to this or anything else. I will help you, and I accept your terms—that you only need to tell me what is absolutely necessary. But I'm asking you to stop; once you finish your current obligation—whatever it may be—I'm asking you to remove yourself from this. Whatever your beliefs and convictions, war is temporary; the war will end—soon I hope. But we have our whole lives ahead of us. I'm begging you, Livy, to disentangle yourself from this."

He could see that she was thinking about it and he allowed her the time to do so. She finally nodded and said, "If that's what you ask of me, then I will stop. But I *do* need to finish what I've started. I must make certain that it's taken care of—because people are putting their lives on the line, and I cannot be responsible for putting someone else in danger because I didn't do what I committed to do. Please tell me you understand that."

"I *do* understand it," he said. "Again, I must make it inescapably clear that I don't agree with what you're doing, but I will help you complete your obligations with the agreement that once this is done, you are retiring—for good."

"Very well," she said. "That's more than fair."

"And promise me, Livy . . ." Tristan leaned closer to her. "You must promise me that you will not keep secrets from me—for any reason. I respect your reasons for not telling me everything, but even with that exception, I need to know what's going on in your life. If any repercussions from this *ever* arise at any time in the future, promise me that you will tell me, that you will let me help you. No more secrets!"

"I promise," she said.

"Thank you." Tristan took a deep breath of relief. "Now," he said with firm resolve, wanting to know what was going on and how they were going to do what needed to be done, "talk to me. You can be vague if you must, but tell me how you got involved in this."

Olivia looked down as if she were ashamed—or hiding something; maybe both. But she'd already said she wouldn't tell him everything, so he just waited patiently for her to decide what she could and couldn't tell him. "It's a long story, Tristan. And one day I will tell you everything— when it's behind us, when the war is over and the outcome is settled. For now, I'll keep it simple."

"I'm listening," he said, managing to push away his inner conflict over this whole thing. He felt confident and calm about helping her and standing by her, but he still couldn't believe it. *Treason? Smuggling goods to the enemy?*

"In essence . . . I will summarize by saying that I felt conflicted over this war even before it began. Everything I read in the newspapers . . . everything I heard being discussed by the people I associated with . . . just made me feel like there was a blindness to what was *really* going on. If the king wants to colonize the world and rule other lands beyond the British Isles, then he should be willing to protect and defend the people of those lands—not persecute and oppress them. I don't agree with it; plain and simple. If the American colonists want to be free of the king's tyranny, then they should have that right. And you should know I do not use the word tyranny lightly. But I am well informed, Tristan. I'm not blindly following the ideas of fanatics. I believe this with my whole heart. If my circumstances were different, I would likely be living in America and fighting for the cause there—as an American. As it is, I'm here and I dearly love my homeland—but I do not agree with the politics of our king. So, yes . . . that makes me a traitor. And yes . . . I understand the price for treason if my actions were to be discovered. But I could not stand idly by and do nothing while I felt haunted by what the colonists are trying to achieve. My *only* regret in this, Tristan . . . my *only* misgiving has been you. I knew you were over there fighting on the opposite side. I've felt literally sick at times thinking of you there, wondering how I could ever face you with what I'm admitting to right now. I have prayed and prayed for your safe return—even though I believed you would return to Muriel and I would have to continue living with my broken heart. Better that than living with the guilt of wondering if your demise might have been the result of my efforts to aid the cause of the colonists."

Olivia took a long, deep breath, and then another. He saw her shoulders droop as if she'd just unloaded a great burden from them. He wondered how long she had been wanting to say what she'd just said. He was a little startled to realize how what she'd said didn't spark his anger— at all. In fact, the effect was quite the opposite. Her words had sparked his curiosity. He wanted to know more of what she knew of the colonists' cause. But he wasn't ready to admit to her just yet about his own inner conflicts over what he'd experienced in America and how he'd felt about it. Right now, he had to focus on the matter at hand—keeping them all safe, because no matter what either of them felt or believed, what they were doing was still illegal. And the same went for the other people who worked here who were also involved. He had many questions about who became involved first, and who talked whom into being a part of a smuggling operation. But they were both exhausted; it was the middle of the night. They needed to focus on what needed to be done *now*.

"Thank you for telling me that," he said and she looked up in surprise. "I respect your convictions, whether or not I agree with them." He saw tears pool in her eyes, as if her fear of telling him was now showing itself after she'd forced the confession into the open. "We can table the rest for now. Tell me what happens next. What is the plan for the large amount of goods you've hidden on the beach? What can I do to help? Is there any potential problem I should be aware of?"

\* \* \* \* \*

Olivia took another deep breath of relief, overcome by the miracle of Tristan's acceptance and support. And the evidence of his love for her that he was proving this very moment to be stronger than any disagreement between them. She could never express her gratitude; at least not in this moment when there were so many thoughts racing around in her head, and she was so exhausted in every way. Needing a minute or two to sort out what she needed to tell him—and what she should avoid—she leaned her head on his shoulder and wrapped her arms around him, murmuring softly, "I love you so much, Tristan. Thank you . . . for not . . ." She attempted a chuckle, hoping to keep the mood light, but it came out sounding more like a sob. "For not completely disowning me." He tightened his arms around her. "I couldn't bear to lose you again; I think *I* would die of a broken heart." Hearing the depth of her own admission, she felt in awe of how far they'd come—in spite of being on opposite sides of a great war.

"I love you, Olivia," he said and pressed a kiss into her hair. She loved it when he did that and eased slightly closer in response. "I've always loved you. I'm trying to stop regretting how badly I behaved toward you, and how I hurt you. I don't want to break your heart, and I know you don't want to break mine. If anything were to happen to you as a result of what's going on, I think that I would die of a broken heart. That's why I'm going to do whatever it takes to keep you safe." He eased back enough to look at her. "So, tell me what I need to know."

Olivia sat up straight and cleared her throat, determined to get it over with. "A ship is coming into the cove this evening at high tide, and longboats will come to shore to get the goods. We have very little contact with these people, so tonight will be the only opportunity I'd have to speak to the captain of the ship—the man who is overseeing all of this—and tell him that I will no longer be assisting him."

"This . . . captain; is he British?"

"Yes," Olivia said.

"And a privateer, obviously."

"Yes."

"And how did you come to know him?"

"I think that's information I prefer to avoid . . . for now. He's a good man; he's smart and he's careful. His men will mostly take care of what's happening tonight. We will go there on horseback, through the woods as much as possible, to simply help make certain all goes well. I can speak to the captain and that will be the end of it."

\* \* \* \* \*

Tristan internalized the information, thinking that it sounded simple enough. He asked exactly who was involved or aware of what was taking place. She told him of the three men he'd overheard talking, and also that Lloyd was aware and supportive. Winnie also knew because there was nothing in Olivia's life that Winnie didn't know about. He was most surprised to realize that Mrs. Higley was also well aware and supportive, and she had done her fair share of discreetly delivering messages and covering for the absence of Olivia and the others when they were going about their treasonous activities. She told him that goods were often collected discreetly when household supplies were being picked up in town. Food and supplies for the house and feed for the animals had frequently concealed weapons and ammunition and other supplies they'd been acquiring from different people in town who were also involved. Olivia refused to tell him the identity of anyone else involved, but she did admit that there were some people he knew well who were firmly aiding the colonists and willing to die for the cause as much as any colonist soldier fighting on the battlefront in America.

Tristan took all of this in, focusing on exerting his willpower toward remaining emotionally detached and simply taking in information. He could deal with his emotions later.

"Is there any reason for concern?" he asked, making certain their eyes were connected firmly so that she knew how serious this question was. "Anything at all that has been suspicious or might give you cause for alarm? *Anything?* If there is, I need to know."

Olivia nodded stoutly and he was dismayed to see in her eyes that there *was* cause for concern. He was hoping she'd tell him that all of their deception had gone unnoticed.

"There has been some talk that a British officer has been assigned to root out any possible smuggling in this area. He and two other officers in his command have been about town, asking questions, making their presence very boldly known—as if doing so might stir up the nerves of anyone with something to hide."

"And has it? Do you think they have suspicions about anyone specifically?"

"I don't know; none of us have any idea of what they may or may not know. There is a woman who works at the inn where they've been staying. She often serves them drinks and meals and flirts with them just enough to make them feel at ease with her. From what little she's overheard when they've had too much to drink, she believes they're certain that smuggling *is* taking place, but they don't have any specific leads and they are actually quite frustrated. Or rather . . . the man in charge is frustrated. The other two seem to be enjoying what they see as an easy and relatively pointless assignment."

Tristan considered the information Olivia had just shared and found himself trying to imagine how these soldiers might be thinking. Given the fact that he had been a British soldier, he knew much about their training and their methods—although fighting on the battlefield in another country was dramatically different than trying to track down treasonous activities right here in England. His thoughts only led him to a muddle of confusion, and he realized he was exhausted. The silence that had fallen between him and Olivia made it clear that there was nothing more to say that couldn't wait until they'd both gotten some rest.

"Come along," he said, taking her hand. "Perhaps now we will be able to sleep; we both certainly need it. We'll talk in the morning and decide exactly what to do."

"Wait," she said and tugged on his hand to stop him before he reached the library door.

"What?" he asked and turned to face her.

"Thank you," she said and lifted her lips to his. He could see tears in her eyes as she added, "I thought I had lost you . . . forever. Thank you . . . for giving me another chance."

"You certainly gave *me* another chance," he said. "We'll get through this . . . together."

She nodded and they left the library together and went quietly up the stairs. He escorted her to the door of her room and kissed her once more before he left her there and went to the other end of the enormous manor house with the hope of now being able to sleep. He felt enormously better and far calmer now that he'd made things right with Olivia. And God willing, everything would go smoothly tonight and all of this would be over in less than twenty-four hours.

\* \* \* \* \*

Olivia awoke to sunlight, surprised at how well she'd slept. It took her only a moment to recall everything that had taken place the previous evening that had all gone so horribly—and then the miraculous conversation she'd shared with Tristan that had turned everything around. She felt literally lighter since she'd finally been able to tell Tristan what she'd become involved with and why. He didn't know *everything*, and it was certainly better that way. But he knew enough that she no longer felt like she had to be continually on guard with him about what she said. And his convictions about helping her complete her obligations and keep her safe—despite his firm disagreement with her convictions—was so thoroughly touching that it took her breath away even now.

A glance at the clock let her know she'd missed breakfast, but her desire to see Tristan overpowered her hunger. She hurried to get dressed and make herself presentable before she went to Walter's room, eager to check in on him but also hoping she might find Tristan there. She entered Walter's room to see him sitting up in bed as usual and Tristan in a nearby chair, one ankle crossed over his knee and his arms folded over his chest, laughing at something his father had just said. Just seeing him increased Olivia's heartbeat. For a long moment they just looked at each other. She could see in his eyes the barely discernible evidence that they now shared very dangerous secrets, but the smile on his face genuinely expressed his love for her.

"Good morning, my dear," Walter said as she closed the door behind her and Tristan came to his feet.

"Hello," she said, moving toward Tristan who greeted her with a quick kiss. After he'd discovered her treasonous activities the previous evening, she never would have believed that even such simple affection would ever pass between them again. The fact that all was well in their relationship seemed nothing short of a miracle. "And what are you two chortling about?" she asked, kissing Walter's brow while Tristan set another chair next to where he'd been sitting.

They both sat back down and Tristan repeated the humorous anecdote that a friend of Walter's had told him the previous day when he'd come to visit.

"And what friend was this?" Olivia asked. She'd become very familiar with Walter's friends, and she was grateful for the few men who came to visit him since his health had declined so dramatically.

"Cornaby, of course," Walter said. There were a couple of gentlemen who each came about once a month, and Walter always enjoyed their company. But Kenneth Cornaby had proven himself the truest of friends and had come to visit Walter at least once a week, sometimes more. Tristan had known Mr. Cornaby his entire life, and he too was glad for the evidence of this man's ongoing friendship with Walter.

They continued chatting with Walter through lunch, and Olivia was proud of herself for behaving as if nothing at all was out of the ordinary. But Tristan also proved to be an excellent actor in the way he appeared completely relaxed—as if he'd not been assaulted with horrible drama the previous night and was about to help her embark on a secret smuggling mission this evening.

After they left Walter in Lawrence's care for his usual afternoon nap, Tristan went with Olivia out to the carriage house where they found Hewitt and Lloyd working together on some repairs.

"Oh, hello," Hewitt said brightly at the same time Lloyd nodded toward them in greeting.

"We need to talk," Olivia said gravely, and Hewitt's bright manner disappeared immediately. Both men stopped what they were doing and Lloyd's brow became deeply furrowed. "He knows everything," Olivia added, glancing briefly toward Tristan.

"I see," Hewitt said with a loud sigh, setting his hands on his hips. "I can't say I'm surprised."

"I told you he'd find out," Lloyd said to Hewitt.

"We've discussed our concern that you would figure us out," Hewitt said directly to Tristan. "I don't suppose it matters *how* you found out." When Tristan said nothing, Hewitt added, "So, will you be letting us go . . . or turning us in to the law, or—"

"Neither," Tristan said, and the two men showed visible relief. "I'm going to help make certain that everything goes as smoothly as possible this evening, and then there will be no more treasonous activities among my household. Is that understood?"

"Yes, sir," both men said.

They talked for a few minutes about their specific plans for their late-evening rendezvous with the ship and Olivia's intention to speak with the captain. Then Olivia and Tristan went to the stable to speak with Wagner and Seymour, but they were told by one of the young lads who now worked there that the two older men had taken a couple of horses out to exercise them. Tristan held Olivia's hand as they walked the short distance to where they found Wagner and Seymour, and they shared a conversation with them that was almost exactly that which they'd shared with the men in the carriage house. Details of their plans were again clarified, and these men also agreed that after tonight there would be no more smuggling or any other treasonous activities taking place among them.

When there was nothing more to say to these men who had been working with Olivia in her endeavors, Tristan again took her hand and they walked together in silence to the gardens where they found a bench. Sitting side by side, Tristan asked her, "Are you all right?"

Olivia considered her answer carefully. "I'm very grateful that I'm not facing this day with a broken heart. I don't know if I would have been able to get out of bed." She tossed him a wan smile, then looked away. "I confess that I'm nervous about this evening. I've always had some nerves about it; I'd be a fool to think there isn't danger involved. I don't know if I feel more nervous because you're now at risk too, or if my instincts are telling me something will go wrong."

"Has anything ever gone wrong before?"

"No, never," she said. "But I *have* been concerned about these soldiers probing about, and I really have no idea what they may or may not know. I can't deny that I've felt some concern in considering how many people are involved. It would be impossible to acquire such a variety of goods and supplies without having people aware of what's going on. We've been careful to assess trust and personal convictions before involving any individual, and as far as we know, they are all loyal and would never betray our activities." Olivia sighed loudly as she got to the truth of her biggest concern. "But I don't know these people personally. These men who work here . . . who are our friends . . . have been careful in their individual communications and connections. But who is to say that someone might not be vulnerable to bribery? Or simply weak when being questioned by an officer who is forceful and intimidating?" She sighed again. "We can only hope and pray that no one has betrayed us—whether intentionally or otherwise."

"Yes," Tristan said with concern. "We can only hope and pray."

Olivia looked directly at Tristan. "I couldn't bear having anything happen to you—not now; not when we've come so far."

"And I feel the same about you," he said, brushing a stray wisp of hair back from her face. "We will do our best to be careful and pray that it will all be over very quickly—and without incident. That's all we can do."

\* \* \* \* \*

"Yes," she said and sighed, putting her head on his shoulder. He put his arm around her and she wished there were words to express her gratitude for his love and support. She began praying in that very moment that all would go well tonight. She wanted more than anything for this to be over.

## CHAPTER TEN
# THE SCOPE OF DANGER

AFTER SUPPER TRISTAN TOLD HIS father he was going to take a long walk in the gardens with Olivia. He winked at Walter and told him that with any luck they'd get very lost and be gone a very long time. This made Walter chuckle before Tristan bid him good evening and left the room. Olivia had left a few minutes earlier, as soon as they'd finished eating. They'd thoroughly discussed their plan to discreetly leave the house at different times after it was dark. Tristan didn't like the part of the plan where Olivia intended to speak to the captain alone, but she'd been stubbornly insistent about the need to do so in order to protect everyone involved. As Tristan rode away from the estate under the ruse that he was once again going to the pub, he felt an increasing panic over the very idea of leaving Olivia alone for even a minute to conduct these transactions.

Tristan headed toward town for a short distance, then discreetly moved into the woods and eased his horse slowly and carefully toward the sea. He met up with Olivia—once again dressed like a man—and Hewitt, and they proceeded together. Riding close to Olivia's side, Tristan once again expressed his concerns. "I just don't feel comfortable with your having to speak with the captain alone and—"

"I won't be alone," she said, barely loud enough for him to hear while they rode slowly and steadily, hoping to not be seen or heard by anyone who might be watching out for smugglers in this area tonight. "Hewitt will be with me when I speak to the captain," she continued in a tone that implied a mild impatience over how many times they had already talked about this. "But it must be *me* that speaks to him."

"What if you were ill . . . or unable to come for some other reason? Isn't there some kind of . . . code or something that could let him know a message came from you even if it was delivered by someone else?"

"That's a good idea, Tristan," she said with mild sarcasm. "I would put such a secondary plan in place if I were going to continue doing this sort of thing, but I'm not. Tonight is the end of it—or at least it will be once I can speak to the captain. Let's just . . . stop talking and get this over with."

"Fine," Tristan said, "but please . . . be careful."

"You know I will," she said more gently.

"I'll be watching out for her," Hewitt said from where he was riding just ahead of them.

"I know," Tristan said, wishing they hadn't been overheard. "Thank you."

According to their plan, Tristan left Olivia to ride down to the beach with Hewitt while he returned to the same spot from which he'd been spying on them the previous evening. He had two loaded pistols in his belt, which he hoped he wouldn't need. It was his job to watch for anything that might be suspicious and to whistle loudly if he observed anything amiss. He couldn't shake a certain paranoid sensation that made him fear that British soldiers patrolling the area might know more than they believed, and that this evening's activities were far more dangerous than any of them had been willing to accept. He was haunted by Olivia's own concerns that they might have been betrayed by someone who knew what was going on. While Tristan knew very few details, it seemed evident that the people secretly committed to aiding the colonists were not trained soldiers or spies; they were simple shopkeepers and townspeople. It wasn't difficult to imagine how easily one of them might be intimidated by an officer intent on digging deep for information and badgering people for the truth. Given what he knew of human nature, he felt increasingly concerned that tonight's rendezvous might not be nearly as secretive as they all hoped and believed.

Once settled into his familiar place behind the cluster of large rocks, Tristan got comfortable and took in the view below. He'd brought a spyglass, which might help him see details more closely, but he knew he also had to remain aware of the entire scope of all that was visible on the beach below. The sky was heavy with clouds, which blocked any possible light from the night sky and prevented him from being able to see details, but perhaps that would work to their advantage. He immediately saw the outline of the ship some distance away, and there were already three longboats resting on the sand, with the waves of high tide licking against them each time the breakers rolled in.

Tristan's pulse quickened and his senses heightened in a way that reminded him of many similar experiences when he'd been in the colonies as a soldier. He never would have believed that he'd come home and find himself engaged in dangerous activities in support of the other side. But the feeling was the same—that incomparable sensation that while he was attempting to keep himself and his comrades safe, the enemy could very well be breathing down their necks without their even knowing. He couldn't count the times he'd embarked upon following the orders of his superiors with the knowledge that he might not survive to see another day. He had that feeling now. A part of him wanted to believe that he was just being paranoid, that everything would go smoothly, and this would all be over without incident. But something else inside of him felt prickly and keenly aware, making him wonder if they had any comprehension of the scope of danger to which they were exposed.

It began to rain, which made the experience of lying in wait more miserable, but it was far from the first time he'd endured bad weather while fulfilling a dangerous assignment. This was different, however; this time people he cared about were in danger. The woman he loved was in danger. He couldn't think about it too much or he would have difficulty breathing. He knew from his training that he needed to remain emotionally detached in order to keep his mind clear so that he would be able to act quickly and efficiently if necessary.

Tristan watched as Olivia arrived on the beach with Hewitt, Wagner, and Seymour. They spoke for a moment with some men who rose up out of the longboats like strange apparitions. Tristan was now able to distinguish Olivia from the others as they all walked back and forth from the cave to the longboats, carrying and loading the crates of supplies. She might be dressed like a man, but she certainly didn't walk like one. When the longboats were loaded and began heading back toward the ship, Tristan breathed a sigh of relief until he saw Olivia jump into one of them, and Hewitt along with her.

"What?" Tristan muttered under his breath. Had the captain not come ashore? Did she actually need to go to the ship to be able to speak with him? His concern heightened along with his sense that danger was afoot. This was going to take too long! He tried to keep an eye on Olivia while at the same time regularly scanning his entire view for evidence of anything out of the ordinary. The rain was making it difficult to see as it ran off the brim of his hat, but he fought to remain keenly focused.

He saw Wagner and Seymour leave the beach, but he knew they were headed to predesignated places where they could hide and also watch out for Olivia and Hewitt until they returned safely.

After what seemed like an eternity, Tristan could see the single longboat returning to shore. He had trouble not holding his breath as he watched it finally come to rest on the beach only long enough for Olivia and Hewitt to step out. At the very moment Olivia's feet hit the sand, a shot broke the air, coming from the trees somewhere to Tristan's right. He couldn't tell whether it was Olivia or Hewitt who went down, but the other dropped immediately to the ground while the longboat moved hastily back toward the ship. Tristan scrambled over the rocks and ran down the steep slope toward the beach while he pulled out both pistols and tried to tune his hearing to detect the source of danger through the sound of the falling rain. As he ran, he could see who he now could recognized as Hewitt trying to remain close to the ground while he tried to help Olivia—who was clearly injured—toward safety. The way she held to Hewitt let him know she wasn't dead, but he had no idea how bad off she might be otherwise. Another shot rang out and Tristan heard a bullet whiz past his ear. It was far from the first time he'd heard that sound and realized how close he'd come to dying when a slightly different aim of an enemy's gun would have put a bullet in his head. He dropped and turned toward the source of the shot and returned fire, which he hoped would give Hewitt enough time to get Olivia off the beach where they were sorely exposed.

With his pistols now empty, Tristan turned and ran toward the trees, glad to not be able to see Hewitt and Olivia at all. They'd made it into the woods, and if he couldn't see them, no one else could either. But he felt sick to consider that Olivia had been wounded. His pounding heart threatened to render him incapable of functioning, and he forced himself to a practical state of mind. It took him only a minute to realize that he was never going to be able to actually find Hewitt and Olivia; he had to trust that Hewitt would get her safely home. With the training of a skilled soldier, he moved carefully and quietly back to where he'd left his horse, praying continually that the animal had not been discovered, that he could ride home without being followed, and especially that the others would get home safely and that Olivia would be all right. He now blessed the rain for the way it would obliterate any tracks that might lead soldiers to his estate. He only hoped that everyone involved would be able to avoid detection as they each returned home discreetly along different routes while staying off the main road.

Tristan found his horse but waited silently for more than a minute before he approached it and mounted. He started carefully toward home, pausing every minute or two to listen intently and be certain he wasn't being followed. It seemed an eternity before he finally returned home and went quietly into the darkened stable to quickly unsaddle his horse and hope there would be no evidence that anyone had been coming or going from here this evening. While he was easing the horse into its stall, he heard Wagner whisper to him, "You're the last to come in. I don't think we were followed, but we'd best hurry inside and do away with any signs that we've been out and about."

"Olivia?" Tristan asked while Wagner tried to catch his breath, making his nerves evident.

"Bullet in the thigh," Wagner said, still whispering.

Tristan winced. He knew it could have been much worse; at least she was alive. But he found it ironic that he'd endured the same wound and he knew exactly how difficult the recovery would be.

"Mrs. Higley and Winnie are already caring for her, but I confess I'm not sure what we're gonna do if—"

"See that everything is closed up here," Tristan ordered and hurried out the back door of the stables and toward the house. He knew what Wagner was trying to say; they couldn't trust the doctor, and Olivia had a bullet in her leg. But there was still hope that everything would be all right. Thanks to Jack Barburry. Tristan felt both confident and terrified as he left his wet coat and boots in a place where they weren't likely to be discovered before he returned tomorrow to fetch them. Before going to Olivia's room he hurried to his own. He reached into the back of a drawer and grabbed hold of the canvas packet in which a variety of surgical instruments were rolled up tightly, each in their individual pockets. He also found the small leather case that Jack had given him, which contained some other medical supplies, including pain medication. He then ran to Olivia's room where he knocked lightly on the door while saying in a low voice, "It's Tristan."

Winnie pulled the door open, looking understandably frantic. But his eyes were drawn more to Olivia who was on the bed, writhing in pain, while Mrs. Higley held a blood-soaked towel over the wound on her leg. Olivia was still dressed in her disguise—a man's clothes that were wet from rain.

Tristan set his things down and leaned over Olivia to look directly into her eyes. "You're going to be all right. Do you hear me?" She nodded slightly and he hurried to add, "I've told you about my experiences in the colonies, Livy. I know what to do. I have medicine to help the pain, and everything else I need. I'll take care of you. Do you understand what I'm saying?"

"Yes," she murmured and tears leaked from the corners of her eyes. "I'm so sorry, Tristan. I . . . I . . ."

"Hush," he said gently and kissed her sweaty brow. "I love you. Everything's going to be all right."

She nodded again and Tristan turned to the women in the room who were gazing at him with fear and expectancy. They were waiting for him to tell them what to do, but it took him half a minute to think through the situation and come up with a firm plan.

"First of all," he said, noting the obvious, "I'm going to leave you two women to help her out of these wet clothes and into something warm and dry. Fold some clean linens beneath the wounded part of the leg, and cover her otherwise so she'll stay warm." He didn't vocalize the remainder of his thought—that he'd never assisted in any medical procedures on a woman and he certainly wanted her to remain modest in his presence.

Tristan stepped out into the hall where he paced and went over in his mind—again and again—what he needed to do. When he was let back into the room, he was prepared to give orders.

"Mrs. Higley," he said. "I need one of the men to assist me—one of those who already knows Olivia is injured. You know them all well. I need someone who is physically strong but won't become squeamish at the sight of blood."

"That would be Seymour," she said.

"Excellent," Tristan declared. "Bring him here. Make certain he washes his hands—better than he ever has in his life."

"Consider it done," Mrs. Higley said and rushed out of the room.

"Winnie," Tristan said to her, noting that she was trying very hard not to cry, "I need alcohol—liquor—a lot of it. Brandy, whiskey, anything; it can help ease her pain if necessary. I know there's liquor in the house. Bring all you can carry, and then find me clean rags and towels. And a couple of clean bowls or basins."

"I'll hurry," she said, looking relieved to have something specific to do that might help.

Alone with Olivia, Tristan examined the wound briefly, glad to note that it wasn't bleeding terribly profusely. He then sat on the bed beside Olivia and had her drink an abundant dose of the medicine that would ease the pain and help her rest. She coughed, and he offered her some water, but she coughed again before she relaxed her head against the pillow. Tristan leaned close to Olivia's face again and repeated, "You're going to be all right."

"You have to . . . get the bullet out," she said with her courage barely masking her fear.

"Yes, I do," he said, and she nodded resolutely, showing evidence that her courage was far stronger than her fear.

"You . . . have been through this," she said.

"Yes." He smiled and attempted to lighten the mood. "We will have matching scars."

"Not funny," she said, and again he noted tears trickling from the corners of her eyes. She took hold of his hand. "I'm scared, Tristan. I'm not . . . as strong as you. I . . ."

"You are *strong*! You're far braver than I am in many ways. I have medicine to give you for the pain. It's still going to hurt, but not as much as it would otherwise."

"How bad . . . did it hurt . . . when you . . ."

"I don't remember; I'd lost a great deal of blood—which made it much more difficult to recover. Don't think about any of that now. Just try to relax. I'm going to get some things ready, but I'm not leaving the room."

She nodded and closed her eyes as if she wanted to shut out the reality of what was happening. Tristan hoped the medicine would work quickly and efficiently. He'd seen it render some men practically unconscious, while others were hardly affected and remained in a great deal of pain. He prayed it would be the former for Olivia; otherwise, he would use the liquor to give her some relief. He forced himself to breathe deeply and think calm thoughts while he took advantage of the clean water and soap in her room to scrub his hands thoroughly. He tried to gather memories of the countless times he'd assisted Jack Barburry in removing bullets, while at the same time he attempted to push away all he'd witnessed of men suffering and dying. He wished that Jack was here now and wondered for a moment how he was doing, and if he was still adhering to his duty in that wretched hospital in the colonies. Forcing his mind to the present, Tristan silently rehearsed every step he needed to take, finding confidence in the way that Jack had taught him the basic skills that would make such a procedure go as quickly as possible and with the least likelihood of infection.

Tristan was drying his hands when Winnie entered the room with four bottles of liquor that she set down before she hurried away again without a word. He sat down on the edge of the bed and was pleased to note that Olivia was asleep. He could hear her breathing, but she didn't respond when he spoke her name. Mrs. Higley came in with Seymour and declared firmly, "His hands are clean. I scrubbed them myself."

"Indeed she did," Seymour said with some mild chagrin. He then looked right at Tristan and asked, "Will she be all right?"

"Yes!" he insisted. "I've given her medicine for the pain and she's asleep, but I don't know how effective it will be once I'm actually trying to get that bullet out." Looking intently at Seymour he said, "I need you to hold her shoulders down so that she doesn't move in response to the pain. It will go much more quickly and painlessly if she can't move. Do you understand?"

Seymour looked terrified but he nodded stoutly. "I understand," he said. "I won't let you down—or her."

"Good," Tristan said, and Winnie entered the room again with everything Tristan had sent her to find.

Mrs. Higley locked the door and reported, "The rest of the household is asleep. I'm certain no one will have seen or heard anything to cause suspicion."

"Good," Tristan said and took one of the basins Winnie had brought and put the instruments he would need into it. Then he poured an entire bottle of whiskey over them to make certain they were sterilized.

"Oh," Winnie said. "I thought she was going to drink it."

"She's already asleep," Tristan said. "No need to get her drunk."

Tristan assigned Winnie to kneel on the bed opposite him and hold Olivia's leg down to keep it from moving during the intervals when he was doing what he needed to do. He prayed that Olivia would not feel much—if any—pain, but they had to be prepared. Even if she slept, she still might respond physically to the pain.

Winnie showed the same kind of courage that Olivia had shown; he knew she was afraid, but she was willing to do whatever needed to be done.

Tristan assigned Mrs. Higley to hand him what he needed when he needed it and briefly explained the plan. He hesitated just before cutting into Olivia's leg, marveling that his hand was so steady when his heart was pounding. Olivia *did* react to the pain but Seymour and Winnie did well at holding her still and Tristan blocked out everything except what he needed to do. It took only a matter of minutes to get the bullet out—which was thankfully not very deep—and to stitch up the wound. But it seemed like at least an hour or more. As soon as he was finished, Olivia sank quickly back into a strained sleep, and the rest of them exhaled almost in unison as if they'd all been unable to draw a deep breath since they'd realized what needed to be done.

"And now what?" Winnie asked, looking at Tristan as if he should have all the answers. "How do we conceal from the rest of the household that Livy has been shot? It will take time for her to heal."

"We simply tell everyone that she's taken ill," Mrs. Higley said, "and that she refuses to see the local doctor because she doesn't like him, and that with Tristan's medical training during the war, she trusts that he knows how to care for her."

"That part about the local doctor is certainly true," Winnie said.

"In fact," Mrs. Higley said with a conspiratorial smirk—and she had clearly thought this through—"I can personally vouch for Miss Olivia and the fact that she started feeling ill soon after supper and came to me for some assistance. And that both of you were here with her all through the evening as the fever set in."

"How very . . . sneaky you are, Mrs. Higley," Tristan said, implying it as a compliment.

"And since the two of you are already exposed to whatever might be ailing her," Mrs. Higley continued, "you've both volunteered to care for her and not expose anyone else in the household."

"I'll pass the news on," Seymour said, "of Miss Olivia's illness to those that work in the stables and carriage house."

"Thank you," Tristan said to him, "for everything. And with any luck, no one will have any suspicion toward us at all."

"But if they do," Seymour said, looking directly at Tristan, "you mustn't forget that we built that secret storage area in the carriage house to hide extra feed and supplies due to the thefts we'd been having."

"Did we?" Tristan asked. Seymour winked and left the room.

Tristan turned his attention back to Olivia, who was breathing evenly. He bandaged the wound carefully while he gave instructions to the women on how to go about cleaning up the room so that no hint of blood or injury remained. Olivia's clothes and the bloody rags were burned, and

Mrs. Higley left with the dirty linens, declaring that she would soak the blood out of them in her own personal bathing room and then add them to the household laundry in a way that would never make anyone suspicious.

When Tristan was left alone with Winnie and there was nothing more to do, she said, "I'll stay with her. It might be more . . . proper."

"Except that I'm acting as her physician and she's ill . . . and according to Mrs. Higley, she's contagious. I'll rest on the couch in the sitting room with the door open. But you should get some rest as well."

"I'll stay right here with her." She motioned toward the large bed on which Olivia was lying. "It wouldn't be the first time we've kept near each other when one of us was ill. I'll let you know if she needs anything."

"Thank you, Winnie," he said, and she started to cry, as if her tears had come as a delayed reaction.

"No, thank *you*," Winnie said and sniffled. "I don't know what we would have done without you. If we'd needed to call on the local doctor, he surely would have reported her injury to the law . . . and who knows what would have happened?" She sniffled again and wiped a hand over her cheeks. "I can't even think about that."

"Nor can I," Tristan admitted. "We can just be grateful that our prayers have been answered, and all will be well."

Winnie nodded and Tristan reluctantly left the room after a long glance toward Olivia. He hurried to his own room where he freshened up and changed his clothes, marveling that he'd managed not to get any blood on himself, thanks to how high he'd rolled up his sleeves. He took a pillow and blanket back to the sitting room next to Olivia's room, looking around as he wondered how many nights he might be sleeping here. He prayed that Olivia wouldn't contract any kind of infection and that her healing would go well.

Holding a lamp, he peeked into Olivia's darkened room and saw Winnie on the bed opposite Olivia. He was glad to know that Winnie would be near enough to be aware of any change in Olivia's condition, when it wouldn't have been appropriate for him to remain so close. He went back to the sitting room where it took him a while to get comfortable, but when he finally did, he slept deeply from the sheer exhaustion of all that had transpired during the last couple of days.

Winnie awakened Tristan while it was still dark to tell him that Olivia was awake and in pain. He gave Olivia more of the medicine and tried to assuage her fears by telling her that he had removed the bullet, everything had gone well, and no one would suspect that anything was amiss. Winnie told Olivia Mrs. Higley's plan and how it gave both Olivia and Tristan an alibi for the time that the skirmish had taken place on the beach. By the time Winnie was wrapping up her explanation, Olivia was drifting back to sleep. Tristan tried to go back to sleep himself, but he only managed to doze off and on briefly while the sun came up and the day began.

Mrs. Higley herself brought tea and breakfast for Winnie and Tristan, and she quietly reported that all of the servants were very worried about Olivia's *illness*, but they understood the need for her to remain secluded, with Tristan and Winnie caring for her. Only Mrs. Higley would bring food and other necessities back and forth and wash the dishes herself in order to avoid any contagion. The ruse of Olivia being contagious was causing more work for Mrs. Higley, but she declared that she'd assigned some of her usual chores to others and that nothing was more important than caring for Olivia.

"Has anyone said anything to my father?" Tristan asked her.

"Not yet," she said. "I wondered if you would want to talk to him, even if you need to pretend that you shouldn't get too close."

"Yes, I think I will," Tristan said and wondered for a moment if he should tell his father the truth. But he believed now as he had when he'd first discovered what was going on: such knowledge could likely worsen his father's condition. He would tell Walter what the rest of the household believed, that Olivia was ill and he and Winnie were caring for her.

As soon as he'd finished eating some breakfast he went to his own room to try and make himself look presentable before he went to Walter's room, but he remained some distance away and on his feet as he reported, "Olivia is ill."

"What?" Walter said with concern. "No! What is it?"

"Some kind of fever," Tristan lied. "I'm not sure. But she refuses to see the local doctor, and I believe I have enough knowledge to be able to look after her; Winnie and Mrs. Higley are also helping care for her. But only Winnie and I have been in the room with her; we don't want anyone else becoming ill, so I'll keep my distance."

"Do you think it's serious?" Lawrence asked from where he was sitting near Walter's bed.

"She's miserable," Tristan answered, "but I don't believe it's anything that won't run its course. We'll pray that she doesn't become too ill."

"Indeed we will," Walter said gravely. "Give her my love."

"I will, of course," Tristan said. "I should . . . get back. I'll check in with you every day and keep you updated."

"Take care of yourself as well, my boy," Walter said.

"And you do the same," Tristan said and hurried back to Olivia's room.

He found Olivia still sleeping, but in the light of day the pallor in her face and the dark circles around her eyes were evidence of all she'd been through. Winnie was in the sitting room reading, with the door between the rooms open. Tristan moved a chair close to the bed and sat down, holding Olivia's hand while she slept. Now that the trauma was over and he'd gotten some rest, his mind rehearsed last night's events in explicit detail, over and over. Never would he have imagined when he'd begun courting Olivia—again—that something so dramatic and dangerous would have been a part of their relationship. He felt horrified to recall the pain she'd endured after being shot, and even more so when he'd been removing the bullet. But gratitude filled him as he considered how much worse it could have been. Her injuries might have been something beyond his ability to repair. Or she could have been killed if the shooter's aim had been just a little different. He wondered exactly *who* the shooter might have been. Mostly likely one of the officers who had been investigating local smuggling. And it seemed evident that Olivia's concerns might have been well-founded; someone who knew what would be taking place had clearly given that information to these officers. Still, it could have been so much worse. He felt confident that they had done well in keeping their escapade a secret, and he prayed that no suspicion would be drawn toward his household. They could only hope that the betrayal of information had only been in regard to last night's rendezvous, and it had not included any reference to the people involved. At least it was over now; Olivia had completed her commitment, and there would be no further reason for her to be involved in anything dangerous.

As Tristan considered the possibility that he might have lost Olivia, he wasn't surprised to feel tears moisten his eyes, and he quickly put his hand over them on the chance that Winnie or Mrs. Higley might come into the room. Thankfully they didn't, and he quickly got control of his emotion, but he felt certain it would take him as long to recover from the fear and shock he'd experienced as it would for Olivia to get back on her feet.

\* \* \* \* \*

Olivia eased reluctantly into consciousness, fighting the heaviness in her head that she knew was a result of the medicine Tristan had given her to help ward off the pain. Pain. The pain in her leg made it difficult to think of anything else. The throbbing ache reminded her of the horrifying experience of being shot and then having the bullet removed. The procedure itself felt hazy in her memory, but not hazy enough for her to forget how painful it had been in spite of what she'd been given to help dull her senses.

Olivia reached beneath the covers and put a hand over her bandaged thigh, as if touching the source of the pain might ease it. She thought of Tristan enduring a similar but much more serious wound, and his many weeks of recovery. She'd been given a hearty dose of empathy for his experiences, while knowing she still couldn't comprehend what he'd been through. He'd been left on the battlefield to bleed, and he'd only had a narrow cot on which to rest in that dreadful excuse of a hospital he'd told her about. Olivia was in her own bed with every possible comfort, with people around her who loved her and would do anything to keep her safe and comfortable.

Tears of gratitude leaked from the corners of her closed eyes as Olivia considered how blessed she was and how much worse it could have been. Surely her survival was a miracle! Thinking back on all that had happened before and after she'd been shot, Olivia marveled over the fact that she was even alive. She was glad to know that it was over. The captain she'd been working with was disappointed by her need to no longer be involved, but he understood; he was a good man and he didn't want anyone to get hurt. But Olivia wondered if it was *really* over. Given the complications that had surely been caused by her getting shot, she wondered if they had managed to avoid detection, or if she—and the others involved—might still be facing some serious trouble. The very fact that someone had known they would be on the beach that night was certainly cause for concern.

Olivia's anxiety took her abruptly back to the continuing pain in her leg and she groaned as she attempted to open her eyes, very much wanting more of that medicine as much as she needed to know if everyone else was all right or if this drama was still not over.

"I'm here," she heard Tristan say at the same moment she felt him squeeze her hand. "Are you in pain?"

"Yes," she murmured, "but . . . I have to know . . . is everyone all right? Did we . . . ." She couldn't put the words together to finish her question.

"Everyone is fine," Tristan said and she felt him kiss her brow. She managed to push open her heavy eyelids enough to see his face close to hers. "It was raining so I believe we all got back here undetected. I don't think there is any cause for concern."

Olivia sighed. "Oh, I'm so glad," she said, her voice raspy.

Tristan helped her drink some water before he asked, "Do you feel hungry? Do you want anything to—"

"No," she said. "I just . . . I'm hurting, and . . ."

"I understand," he said and gave her a dose of the medicine. Now that she knew everything was all right—at least for the moment—she only wanted to sleep and be oblivious to the pain. Just before she drifted off she heard Tristan telling her that within a few days she should be feeling better. She prayed that he was right. She only wanted to get past all of this upheaval and have life go back to normal.

\* \* \* \* \*

Tristan and Winnie took turns sitting with Olivia—or sometimes they both hovered near her, sharing very little conversation. Tristan knew that it was as important for Olivia to keep up her strength as it was for her to rest, so he requested that warm broth and tea be brought up from the kitchen each time Olivia awakened with the need for more medicine. At first, Olivia refused to eat anything, but Winnie talked her into it with an authoritative insistence he'd never seen in her before. She obviously had no difficulty taking charge when she needed to, especially when it came to Olivia's welfare. While Olivia was awake, Winnie would help her see to any personal needs, and then Tristan would help her drink the broth and tea before giving her more medicine that lured her back to sleep and kept her from feeling the pain.

Within a couple of days, Olivia was already feeling a little better. She was sitting up in bed some, and there were longer intervals between her doses of medicine—and she was taking smaller doses. She admitted to having some pain, although not as bad as the first couple of days, and when Tristan explained the importance of not becoming too reliant upon the medicine, she agreed and thought it best to only take that which she absolutely needed.

Now that Olivia was more conscious and aware, Winnie had taken over the task of checking the wound and replacing the bandaging regularly. Tristan had told her what to look for as far as any signs of infection, and she reported to him that according to what he'd taught her it appeared to be doing fine. Tristan was deeply grateful that the bullet had not penetrated as deeply as the one that had wounded him, and that she'd lost very little blood in contrast to how bad it might have been. All things combined, he expected her to recover quickly, and an hour didn't pass when he didn't thank God for preserving Olivia and for giving him the skills to be able to help her. His own suffering back in the colonies now felt entirely worth it if only for the experience it had given him to work with Jack Barburry and to have the knowledge and instruments and medicine he'd needed to be able to help the woman he loved.

Three days past Olivia having a bullet removed from her leg, she reached for Tristan's hand while he was sitting in silence next to the bed. "Now that I'm staying awake more . . . and I've had some time to actually think about all that happened . . . I need to thank you." She got tears in her eyes and tightened her hold on his hand. "Without you I can't imagine what would have happened. I know I could have died; it's likely a miracle that I didn't. And . . . if we'd needed to call on that dreadful excuse of a doctor to help me . . . he surely would have informed the authorities and I would have gone to prison—or worse."

"I'm just glad it's over," he said, not wanting to talk about the details—or his lingering confusion over her reasons for even becoming involved in such an endeavor. He chose instead to simply say, "I'm glad that I can take care of you . . . and that you're safe."

"I love you, Tristan," she said, her eyes becoming moist again.

"I love you too, Olivia," he said with all the intensity he felt after almost losing her. "I can't bear to think of living my life without you."

"Then that gives us something in common," she said with a wan smile.

Olivia drifted back to sleep, but Tristan remained at her side, lost in thought, wondering if the passing of a few days without any further incident meant they had escaped any suspicion from the law. He began to doze off in the chair until Winnie nudged him awake and said with mild panic, "Mrs. Higley asked me to tell you that a Lieutenant Wixom is here and he wants to speak with you."

"Heaven help us," Tristan said, shooting to his feet.

"We've been careful," Winnie said in a firm voice of courage that contradicted her terrified expression. "We have proper alibis in place. It will be all right."

"I pray," he said and turned toward the mirror to straighten his waist-coat and push his fingers through his hair in an attempt to not look as if he'd been asleep—even though he had. "However, Olivia wouldn't have been shot if someone hadn't betrayed us. And we have no idea how much information might have been given up."

"Oh, I don't like the sound of that," Winnie said.

"Nor do I," Tristan said and took a deep breath and left the room. He went slowly down the stairs, giving himself some time to put himself in the proper frame of mind—completely innocent and baffled over such a visit—and to rehearse the story of the night in question as it had been agreed upon by all involved. He had been attending to Olivia, who had taken ill right after supper, and the men in the carriage house and stables who had been involved were all willing to vouch for each other with the ruse that they'd been playing cards together in one of their rooms.

Tristan took another deep breath before he entered the drawing room and closed the door behind him. A man in uniform turned from where he'd been looking out the window. Memories associated with having worn a very similar uniform left Tristan a little queasy so he pushed them away and donned his best acting skills.

"What might I do for you?" Tristan asked, sounding more like the lord of the manor than he'd ever attempted.

"Lieutenant Wixom," the officer said and bowed slightly, his hands behind his back. "I was expecting to speak to the man of the house. Is he—"

"That would be me," Tristan said and Wixom looked confused.

"Forgive me; I expected you to be older."

"If you're speaking of my father, he is bedridden and has been for a very long time. The estate is in my care now."

"I see," Wixom said. "Well, then . . . I'll come straight to the point. I am simply investigating some rumors of smuggling in the area, and—"

"Smuggling?" Tristan echoed, sounding horrified and astonished. Inside he felt deep relief; investigating rumors implied that this man had no actual information regarding Tristan's household. "Here? In this community?" he added.

"I'm afraid so," Wixom said with a subtle hint of arrogance that made Tristan dislike him—even if he wasn't the man who could put him and his household in peril.

"But . . . to what purpose?" Tristan asked as if he couldn't even comprehend the very concept. "Smuggling what . . . and to whom?"

"To aid the colonist cause, sir," Wixom said grimly.

"I can't believe it!" Tristan said with adequate astonishment. "Please . . . sit down." He motioned to a sofa while he sat in a chair, pretending to be very interested to hear what this man had to say. "I just *cannot* believe it!" he added more fiercely, calling upon his own feelings when he'd first discovered what had been taking place. "Are you sure?"

"Quite sure," Wixom said once he'd made himself comfortable on the sofa. "We've witnessed activity taking place from a distance but we've been unable to identify exactly who might have been involved."

Tristan's relief deepened and he hoped this man was telling the truth.

"Myself and two other officers are speaking with every household in the area to see if anyone has noticed anything suspicious."

Tristan responded as if he might lay down his life to assist this man in his efforts. "By all means . . . if there is anything I can do to help." He added with exasperation, "I nearly got myself killed fighting those blasted colonists. I can't tolerate the very idea of our own countrymen doing anything that might put our own brave soldiers at risk." He was surprised to realize as the words came out of his mouth that he felt as if he were lying. He'd come to terms with the need to be dishonest with this man in order to protect his household and the woman he loved. But he couldn't quite make sense of the confusion rumbling inside of him over a cause that he'd once firmly believed in. Or had he? Did he truly believe in what he'd been fighting for in the colonies? Or had he merely buried his own discomfort over the issues at stake in this war in order to be able to fulfill his duty?

"Then you will understand why it's so important that we find these traitors and root them out," Wixom said, distracting Tristan from his surprisingly treasonous thoughts.

"I do indeed," Tristan said, realizing in that moment just how dangerous a precipice he was standing upon. He had aided smugglers and he was lying to protect them. Whatever his own personal convictions may or may not be, he was now guilty of treason, and he was sitting here face-to-face with a man who had the authority to see him and Olivia—and many others—to the gallows. The full scope of danger made his heart beat ferociously in his chest, but he concealed his own inner turmoil and said firmly to Lieutenant Wixom, "Tell me what I can do to help you."

Wixom smiled, and Tristan knew that he was more likely to protect those he cared about if he made himself the lieutenant's ally—or at least pretended to be. He set his mind to put forth his greatest efforts in convincing this man that they were of one mind over the matter and that Tristan would do whatever it took to weed these traitors out of their community. He prayed that his efforts would keep his friends and loved ones safe.

## CHAPTER ELEVEN
# UPHEAVAL

"Your cooperation is very much appreciated," Lieutenant Wixom said to Tristan. "I hope you won't consider it an intrusion if I ask you some questions—and if I might do the same with your staff."

"Not at all," Tristan said.

"The questions are simply routine," Wixom said. "They are not meant to be accusatory or offensive; it's just what needs to be done to eliminate anyone here from suspicion. And perhaps someone has seen or heard something that might help us put the pieces together. People sometimes observe something that might help without even realizing it."

"Of course," Tristan said. "I understand."

"Allow me to start by asking you where you were the evening of this past Thursday. It wasn't so many days ago, but I know from much experience in questioning people that they sometimes get days mixed up in their minds. Do you recall where you were?"

"Actually, I do," Tristan said. "Thursday was the evening that Olivia became ill. She is the cousin of my deceased wife and has been a close companion to my father through his illness."

"Is this the Miss Halstead that you are currently courting?"

"That's right," Tristan said with the kind of smile a man would show when thinking of the woman he loved. "We were well acquainted before I married; therefore, when I returned from the colonies and my wife was deceased, we quickly became *reacquainted*."

Wixom didn't comment on Tristan's personal life; he returned to the original question. "You say Miss Halstead became ill on the evening in question?"

"That's right. It was around suppertime that she began to get feverish and feel ill, and I remained with her throughout the evening—along with her maid—to help care for her."

"And you didn't send for the doctor?" Wixom asked in a tone that certainly *was* accusing. But Tristan remained confident in his well-rehearsed tale.

"Not one of us in this household is fond of the local doctor. We only call upon him if we absolutely have no choice. I spent a great many weeks in the hospital in the colonies. While I was healing from my injury I assisted the doctor there and received a fair amount of training. I felt confident that I could care for Olivia sufficiently and there was no need to send for the doctor."

"And how is Miss Halstead feeling now?"

"She's improving," Tristan said and instinctively countered with a question he hoped would make his story more convincing. "Is there some reason you find Olivia's illness of such interest?" He was glad to know that Olivia had been dressed as a man and he felt certain these men would never suspect her or any other woman. They were looking for men, and therefore it was Tristan's activities that were being questioned.

"I find it of interest to know if you were actually with her all evening," Wixom said.

"Are you accusing me of something?" Tristan asked, proud of himself for how offended he sounded.

"Just doing my job," Wixom said curtly.

"Well, feel free to do your job by questioning anyone in my household, and they will tell you that I was here, although there are only two or three staff members that I generally interact with in the evenings. I doubt the girls in the laundry could verify my alibi." He added the last with sharp sarcasm.

"Oh, I'll be talking to them," Wixom said and went on as if Tristan's disdain over this interrogation meant nothing to him. "And have you observed anything at all—here at home or anywhere else in the community—that you might find suspicious?"

"Nothing," Tristan said. "Although I don't go out much. With my father being bedridden I spend much of my time with him."

Wixom asked him a few more seemingly pointless questions before he said, "I would like to speak with your head housekeeper and your butler before I leave; I believe they would be most aware of the goings on of the household and they can assist me in speaking with other members of the staff."

"Of course," Tristan said, trying to sound indifferent.

"But first we need to do a brief search of your outbuildings and a portion of your home—not the living quarters, but the kitchen, the pantries, the laundry."

"Whatever you need to do," Tristan said in the spirit of full cooperation while he hoped that there wasn't anything hidden somewhere that he didn't know about. He wished he'd more thoroughly questioned those involved regarding such possibilities. And he really hoped that Wixom would not notice the false wall in the carriage house.

"We?" Tristan asked, seeking clarification since he'd believed that Wixom had come alone.

"I would like you to accompany me, if you would," Wixom said. "And I have two officers waiting outside." The lieutenant's friendly demeanor faded into his determination to catch any guilty party by whatever means possible. With a smile that was more like an evil sneer he added, "We wouldn't want to give you or anyone else sufficient warning to dispose of any incriminating evidence."

"Good thinking," Tristan said and came to his feet, concealing his desire to punch this guy in the face. He reminded himself that the lieutenant was just following orders and doing his job, but even if Tristan was in complete agreement with him—and innocent of treason—he still wouldn't like this man. He reminded Tristan of the officers he'd been forced to associate with in the colonies who had put themselves above others because of their rank or their upbringing. He recalled those who had been treated for injuries in the same hospital where he'd recovered, and how they'd expected to be waited upon as if the doctors and nurses didn't have the work of saving lives to attend to.

Tristan forced his thoughts to the present and walked out of the room, expecting Wixom to follow him. "Where would you like to start?"

"The outbuildings if you please," Wixom said. "My officers should be waiting somewhere near your stables. Please lead the way."

Tristan wondered if he should initiate some kind of conversation while he walked with the lieutenant down long halls to a door that exited the house closest to the stables. It took him a minute to be certain that he could speak with a steady voice and a guise of ignorance over the truth of all he was guilty of. He finally said with perfect innocence, "Might I ask where you hail from, Lieutenant? Are you far from home?"

"I myself am from Liverpool," he said. "One of my comrades is from London, and the other comes from somewhere up north; I confess I don't recall where, specifically."

"I hope our community has treated you well during your time here," Tristan said while he secretly hoped they were not enjoying their stay in the area and would want to leave as quickly as possible.

"Well enough," Wixom said.

They arrived at the stables to find the two officers playing a game of dice with Wagner and Seymour, while the other stable hands were gathered around them watching and cheering. The men were all laughing boisterously until they realized that Tristan and the lieutenant were both standing there. The officers immediately came to attention, looking like children who expected to be punished. And Tristan almost sniggered to see the same expression on the faces of his own employees. They all knew he didn't care a whit about their playing dice or cards in between their chores—as long as they completed their work. He suspected that Wagner and Seymour had lured the officers into getting caught up in a game in order to make them more comfortable and perhaps keep them a little off balance in their purpose for being here.

"We have work to do," Wixom said to his officers as if they *were* children.

"We've already conducted a thorough search of the stables, sir," one of them said. "All of the hands waited outside while we did the search, as you had instructed, sir, and we found absolutely nothing amiss or out of the ordinary."

"Thank you," Wixom said, then offered Tristan a false smile. "Shall we move on?"

The stable hands got back to work and Tristan went with the officers while they searched the icehouse, the smokehouse, the garden shed, and every other nook and cranny of the property directly surrounding the manor, coming last to the carriage house, which was the place that made Tristan the most nervous because he knew there was actually something here he didn't want these men to find.

Behaving like the arrogant lord of the manor, he asked Wixom with impatience, "How long is this going to take? Given that this escapade is being done at *your* convenience, I have obligations in regard to my father and the estate that are being neglected."

"It shouldn't take much longer," Wixom said as if he didn't care at all about Tristan's obligations.

Tristan entered the carriage house with Wixom and the other two officers to find Hewitt and Lloyd working together to remove a damaged wheel from one of the carriages since it was obviously in need of repair. The men looked surprised and curious but not at all concerned. Tristan was grateful for their acting skills. Given that he had a number of employees who were guilty of treason, he was at least glad that they were all very good at feigning innocence; perhaps that was a required skill in order to be involved with illegal smuggling.

"These men would like to look around," Tristan said as if it meant nothing to him.

"Make yourselves at home," Hewitt said. "As you can see, we're a bit busy."

"Don't mind us," Wixom said and his officers started looking inside each of the wheeled vehicles while Wixom himself turned to survey the entire circumference of the huge room in which he stood. He'd done the same in the other buildings, as if he were searching for any tiny hint of something suspicious. But Tristan hadn't felt nervous in the other buildings; it was here that he knew they had something to hide. He leaned against one of the wagons and folded his arms over his chest, heaving a sigh of boredom, followed by another one that implied his impatience.

Tristan could hear his heart beating in his ears when he saw Wixom demonstrating curiosity over the false wall behind the wagons. He fought to appear calm and disinterested while he discreetly watched Wixom moving his fingers along the edge of the wall—just as Tristan himself had done the previous week. He wondered what Wixom would do if he found the secret compartment that was large enough to store a significant amount of supplies.

Tristan was taken aback when he heard Hewitt say to Wixom, "Oh, that's where we hide the extra goods."

"Excuse me?" Wixom said, turning toward Hewitt, who had finished removing the carriage wheel.

Tristan observed with amazement as Hewitt showed Wixom the hidden latch while he said, "A while back we had some trouble with animal feed and other supplies disappearing from the outbuildings. We never had any luck catching the thieves, but we did start locking things up better, and me and Lloyd here built this so we'd always have an extra store of needed supplies that no thief could ever find."

Tristan walked toward Hewitt and Wixom as Hewitt popped the latch and lit a lantern, behaving as if he were eager to show the lieutenant this space that had been created for hiding goods that would be smuggled. Hewitt actually looked proud of himself for his ingenuity, as if he enjoyed showing it off.

"Nobody's been in here for a while," Hewitt said the same moment that Tristan recalled something Seymour had said to him the night Olivia had been shot; something he hadn't understood until now. *You mustn't forget that we built that secret storage area in the carriage house to hide extra feed and supplies due to the thefts we'd been having.*

Tristan followed Hewitt and Wixom into the storage space, amazed to see it filled to the brim with sacks of animal feed as well as flour and sugar and oats. There were crates of household supplies, and tack for the horses, and parts for the wheeled vehicles that might need repairs. The claw hammer that had been laying on top of a crate when Tristan had first come here was still there, and Wixom used it to open crates and investigate their contents, to see exactly what was inside. The most amazing thing to Tristan was how everything—even the floor—was covered with a layer of dust, which boldly confirmed Hewitt's statement that nobody had been in here for a while. Tristan found it amusing to imagine these men who worked for him loading all of these extra supplies in here and then carefully covering everything with what appeared to be a perfectly even layer of dust as they backed carefully out of the room. He suspected they had probably done this the very night Olivia had been shot. While he'd been removing the bullet from Olivia's leg—with Seymour's assistance—Hewitt, Wagner, and Lloyd had obviously been very busy here on the chance that officers might show up the very next day. Tristan marveled at their ingenuity, and for a moment he actually felt sorry for Wixom. This man was *never* going to find what he was looking for. Tristan knew who was guilty of the crimes that Wixom had been charged to investigate. But those crimes had been so carefully covered that Tristan felt deeply confident they would never come to light. Even *if* someone had told Wixom of their involvement, he had no case if he could find no proof.

Wixom finally exited the dusty compartment with a firm declaration. "Nothing out of order here as far as I can tell." Tristan exchanged a quick glance with Hewitt before they followed Wixom, and Tristan felt certain that Hewitt was *extremely* pleased with himself.

Tristan led Wixom and his officers into the house where he found Mrs. Higley and turned them over to her. She not only came across as being glad to help them with whatever they needed, but she behaved like a concerned mother and insisted that they must come to the kitchen and have something to eat. Tristan thanked her and said to Wixom, "I trust Mrs. Higley will take good care of you. If there is anything else I can do, I'm certain you'll let me know."

"Thank you for your time," Wixom said, but he didn't seem to mean it. Tristan just nodded at him and hurried away, anxious to see how Olivia was doing and glad to finally be away from these men in uniform who felt like vultures circling over his home, seeking an opportunity to find any weakness and prey upon it.

Tristan found Olivia awake and Winnie sitting with her.

"Is everything all right?" Olivia demanded the moment he entered the room. "We were told that an officer was here to speak with you . . . and that was hours ago. Or it *feels* like hours ago."

"It *does* feel like hours ago," Tristan said, taking a seat. "There are *three* officers, and they are now in Mrs. Higley's care. I suspect they'll still be here for hours yet, questioning everyone in the house and searching every cobweb and speck of dust. Although I was told they won't be searching the living areas. I suppose they don't think anything could be hidden in wardrobes or under beds that could be worthy of smuggling."

"Do you think they suspect anything?" Winnie asked.

"I think everything is all right," Tristan said and repeated details of his interview with Lieutenant Wixom and the subsequent search of the outbuildings. The women laughed when he told them how graciously Hewitt had given Wixom a tour of the secret room, and how the men had left it well stocked with typical supplies for a manor house. It was the layer of dust that left them especially amused, and Tristan couldn't keep from chuckling to hear Olivia and Winnie speculating over how the men had done it. He was glad for their perspective, which helped push away the uneasiness still hovering around him since he'd been forced to keep company with these officers and their disdain and suspicion.

That evening, Mrs. Higley asked to speak privately with Tristan when she brought a supper tray to Olivia's room. He stepped into the hall with the housekeeper and closed the door.

"I just wanted you to know," Mrs. Higley said, "that all went well with the officers. I was with them every minute while they inspected every pantry and cupboard and cellar, but of course they found nothing. They didn't ask to interview anyone individually, so I was with them when they asked the staff in the kitchen and then in the laundry if they'd seen or heard anything suspicious—and of course none of them had because we've all been very careful."

"Excellent," Tristan said. "Thank you, Mrs. Higley. I can't thank you enough for helping keep Olivia and the others safe."

"You should know by now that I'd do anything for Miss Olivia." She glanced toward the door to Olivia's room, then looked intently at Tristan. "If you have any sense, dear boy, you'll not let her go. You'll never find a woman so fine in every way."

"I am in complete agreement," he said, and she smiled before she hurried away.

Tristan stood for a few minutes in the hall, recounting all that had happened today—and all that had led up to the need to be so careful and secretive. But most of all he had to examine how he was feeling. His relief over their avoiding any suspicion was indescribable. More than relief, however, something else consumed him with a confusion that he had trouble sorting out. Before he'd discovered treason underfoot in his own home, he'd been firm in his convictions. Or at least he thought he had. But now he wasn't so sure how he felt about either side of this cause over which a war was being fought with so many lives being lost.

Tristan tabled his thoughts for the moment and returned to Olivia's room where he shared supper with her and Winnie as he'd been doing for days now. He was pleased to note that Olivia's appetite had increased immensely, and she was showing very little evidence of weakness, which he took to mean that her blood loss—however minimal—had not affected her adversely. Winnie told him while they were eating that Olivia had not needed any medicine at all that day for pain.

"The aching isn't nearly so bad," Olivia reported. "It mostly hurts when I move my leg or if I happen to bump it."

"Or when you roll onto it in the night and it wakes you up?" Tristan said, recalling his own experience.

"Yes, there's that," Olivia said and reached for his hand.

Their tender moment of mutual understanding diffused into humor when Winnie said, "Matching bullet wounds are so terribly romantic."

"Indeed," Tristan said with a chuckle and smiled at Olivia, so glad to see her smiling back. He wanted to see her smile that way every day for the rest of his life.

* * * * *

Ten days after Olivia's *illness* had set in, she was up and about and feeling fine except for the obvious limp she had, since the injured leg reacted painfully when she stepped on that foot. But she was sick to death of being trapped in her room, she missed spending time with Walter, and she very much wanted to get outside and enjoy some fresh air.

"It's going to take time to heal," Tristan said. "We can't keep you hidden up here that long, obviously. But there's no disguising the limp."

"Oh, I've already figured this out," Winnie declared proudly, and Tristan marveled at the deceptive tactics of the people around him. "Miss Olivia attempted to get out of bed on her own while she was still too weak to stand and she twisted her ankle terribly when she fell." Winnie mimicked a horrified expression that made both Olivia and Tristan chuckle. "I've already passed the information on to Mrs. Higley and a couple of the maids, so the entire household will know by suppertime." Winnie shook her head comically. "I've heard that such a sprain can take many weeks to heal. We'll have to keep that ankle tightly wrapped for good measure on the chance that anyone might get a glimpse of it."

"You're brilliant, Winnie," Olivia said. "I've always said so."

"And I agree wholeheartedly," Tristan added. "Truly brilliant."

"Now that we've established the fact that Winnie is brilliant," Olivia said to Tristan, "could you take me to visit your father? I think I shall die if I don't get the pleasure of his company, and since it's so far and my ankle is so terribly sprained, I think you should be a gentleman and carry me."

"It would an honor," Tristan said and lifted Olivia into his arms so swiftly that it made her laugh. On his way out the door, Tristan said to Winnie, "Feel free to spread the gossip that Miss Olivia is well past her illness and practically back to normal."

"Everyone will be glad to hear it," Winnie said and waved them off.

* * * * *

Olivia laughed with delight just to be outside of her room, and she loved the weightlessness of Tristan carrying her.

"You don't have to carry me the entire way, you know," she said. "I *can* walk."

"I *like* carrying you," he insisted and laughed just before he pretended to drop her, which made her cry out and gasp. He laughed again as he made it clear she was completely safe and secure in his arms and he was plenty strong enough to carry her the full distance to Walter's room.

Tristan set Olivia on her feet just outside the door. He knocked lightly and waited a couple of seconds before he opened the door and Olivia limped into the room.

"Oh, my goodness," Walter said, his countenance beaming when he saw Olivia. "Come here, my dear. I've missed you dreadfully!"

"I've missed you too!" she replied while holding onto Tristan's arm, which helped her keep any weight off the ailing leg.

"You're limping!" Walter observed as she got closer to the bed. "What's happened?"

"I twisted my ankle trying to get out of bed when I was too weak," she said with sincere chagrin. "But it's nothing time won't heal." She kissed Walter's brow and sat on the edge of the bed, taking hold of his hand while Tristan sat in a nearby chair.

"I've been terribly worried about you," Walter said, "in spite of Tristan telling me every day that you were on the mend."

"No need to worry," Olivia said, giving him her most convincing smile. "I'm fine, and now that I'm no longer contagious, I can go back to spending my days making certain you behave yourself."

Walter laughed. "How very delightful!" he declared and they delved into catching up after many days of not seeing each other. Olivia was proud of herself for how well she kept up the ruse of having been ill with some mysterious fever—and having sprained her ankle due to clumsiness. Walter was just so thrilled to have her company again that he surely didn't suspect that anything was amiss.

Throughout the next few weeks, Olivia continued to heal. The pain was worse some days than others, and she quickly recognized that if she tried to walk on the injured leg too much, she would suffer for it. So she allowed Tristan to help get her back and forth to his father's room, and she ate most of her meals upstairs—which was not unusual.

Olivia was glad when the day came that she felt strong enough to get down the stairs with Tristan's help, and she could show her face in the kitchen and the laundry where many people were very glad to see her doing well. She was touched by their expressions of concern and worry, and she felt glad to know that she would never have to leave this house and all the friends she'd made here.

Tristan hovered near Olivia while she sat and visited, as if he was going to make certain she didn't overdo it or injure herself further. When she'd distracted the staff long enough from their duties, Tristan carried Olivia out to the garden and sat her on a bench, declaring that she mustn't push herself too much in one day. Given the ache she felt in her leg from her efforts thus far, she couldn't argue with him. But it felt so good to be outside, to breathe fresh air, and to feel the sun on her face! It felt especially good to have Tristan's hand in hers while she enjoyed the experience, feeling more grateful for the simple pleasure of such an experience since she'd been unable to get out of her room for so many days.

"It's good to see you doing so well," Tristan said with a seriousness that caught her attention.

"It's good to be out and about," she said, sensing there was something else—something more important—that he wanted to say. When he hesitated, she touched his face as if that might help.

"I was so afraid I would lose you," he admitted. "I've never been so afraid in my life. I don't think I could have even brought myself to say it aloud until now . . . now that you're getting back to normal and all is well. But you have to know how afraid I was. I think back and wonder why I wasn't shaking when I was trying to get that bullet out of you. I didn't start shaking until the surgery was done."

"Then we were both very blessed," she said.

"Indeed we were." He drew in a deep breath. "And now that this upheaval of life is behind us . . . I can't wait any longer to ask you to marry me."

Olivia gasped and her heart quickened. His proposal wasn't surprising, given that they had been talking about the possibility of marriage before her smuggling indiscretions had come to light. But perhaps she'd wondered if he would still be fully committed to her after all that had happened. She didn't question his love for her, and he had put himself at great risk—and had given much of himself to care for her. Still, she'd perhaps not allowed herself to think that all of this might mean he would want to commit himself to her for life. At the very least, she had believed that it would likely take time for the trust between them to be renewed. But there was no questioning the sincerity in his eyes, nor the expectation in his countenance.

"Of course I will marry you," she said, hearing a quiver in her own voice. "Nothing could make me happier . . . if you're certain this is what you want."

"Certain?" The word came out on the crest of a nervous laugh. "I've never been more certain about anything, Livy. You and I need to be together; we need to share our lives in every respect. I need you. More importantly, I love you. And I want to devote my life to caring for you and making you happy."

Olivia laughed with perfect happiness and wrapped her arms around his neck. He returned her embrace and kissed her hair, her throat, her cheek, and then her lips. His kiss was cut short by the sound of Winnie calling Olivia's name some distance away, but her tone sounded panicked.

"I'm here," Olivia called back as she stood, moving as quickly as she could manage around a corner of the length of shrubbery that had concealed where they'd been sitting. She found Tristan at her side, offering his support so that she could walk without putting so much weight on her healing leg. "I'm here," Olivia called again when she saw Winnie, who saw her at the same time and came running, her expression filled with some kind of terror.

"Something awful has happened," Olivia said to Tristan, holding tightly to him.

"I pray the lieutenant has not returned with new evidence to arrest us," he said in the long moment it took Winnie to get close enough to them to speak without shouting.

"It's Walter," Winnie said, completely out of breath.

"Oh, no!" Olivia muttered and leaned more heavily on Tristan, but she felt him lean back.

"What's happened?" Tristan demanded and Olivia feared they would be told he'd been found dead.

"The doctor's been sent for," Winnie said while trying to catch her breath. "Lawrence said that he can't speak clearly . . . and he can't move his arm; I think that's what he said."

"Go," Olivia said to Tristan, pushing him away from her. "I'll slow you down. Go. He needs you. I'll catch up with you; Winnie will help me."

Tristan barely nodded toward her before he broke into a run, and Olivia's heart sank deep into her chest as Winnie's grim news began to penetrate a sudden fog in her mind. "We can't lose him now," she said to Winnie who had taken Tristan's place at her side, giving her someone to lean on. "We just can't!"

"I couldn't agree more," Winnie said as they began to move slowly toward the house. "But if the good Lord sees fit to take him home, there isn't anything any of us can do."

Olivia couldn't argue, and nothing more at all was said between them as they made their way far too slowly to Walter's room. Olivia was exhausted by the time they arrived at the door, but she knew that Winnie was too, given the effort she'd put into finding Olivia, and then her assistance in helping Olivia walk. At times like this, Olivia hated how very huge the house and gardens were. It was all very conducive to good exercise, but not at all accommodating to a leg injury.

Olivia entered the room with Winnie at her side, and she froze for a long, shocking moment, attempting to take in all she was seeing as reality. Lawrence was pacing the room and wringing his hands; his expression implied that he feared Walter was on the brink of death. And Tristan's expression was the same. He had one foot on the floor and one knee on the bed so that he could lean over his father and look directly into his eyes.

"It's going to be all right," Tristan said as if he believed it. Olivia noticed the tight grip with which Tristan was holding his father's hand. He glanced over his shoulder briefly toward her and she saw the stark fear in his eyes before he put his entire focus again on Walter. "We're all here," Tristan added. "We're going to help you get through this . . . whatever it takes. Do you hear me?"

Walter nodded but his attempt to speak came out as a few indiscernible syllables all slurred together. Olivia was horrified to see the way that one side of Walter's face was drooping. That side of his mouth hung down into half of a frown, and his eyelid was closed in an unnatural way. She limped quickly to Walter's bed, on the opposite side of where Tristan was holding his hand—to the side that was afflicted with whatever awful thing had happened to this man she loved so dearly. She sat on the edge of the bed, and Walter turned his head slightly on the pillow to look at her with the eye that was open. She took hold of his hand and immediately realized that it too was beyond his ability to control. When she squeezed his fingers in a familiar way, she got no response. It took only a moment to realize that Walter had lost the ability to control the entire left side of his body. Olivia struggled to maintain a calm facade while panic surged through her. Was this condition permanent or would it heal with time? If it was permanent, would Walter be able to live like this? Did this mean that death would closely follow? And if he did live, how would he ever manage? She had no idea what was happening or why, and she desperately wanted answers. She knew the doctor had been sent for; as much as no one in the house was fond of Dr. Brown, he was still a doctor and she hoped that he would be able to help Walter. Seeing the fright in Walter's eyes left Olivia thinking she preferred being shot as opposed to having him suffer this way. She exchanged a long gaze with Tristan, which let her know he shared the depth and breadth of her concerns for this man they both loved so dearly.

While Olivia was wondering what she might say to Walter to offer some reassurance, a maid opened the door and Dr. Brown entered the room like some kind of human whirlwind who immediately commanded and demanded that he be honored as the most important person in the room.

"Back away from the patient," he ordered, glaring at Tristan and then Olivia.

They both bolted away from the bed to allow the doctor access to Walter. Olivia huddled close to Winnie, who had been observing the drama in silence. Lawrence stopped his pacing and sat down in a chair near the window as if he'd paced himself into exhaustion. Tristan leaned his back against the wall as if it might help him remain standing. Dr. Brown took only a few minutes to examine Walter by testing the response of his limbs and facial muscles, then he asked him a handful of questions to which Walter could barely nod or shake his head in response. The self-ennobled doctor turned toward the concerned onlookers to declare with pride, "A clear case of apoplexy."

"What does *that* mean?" Tristan demanded in a voice that indicated he was not intimidated by this man.

"A brain malfunction that paralyzes one side of the body," the doctor said as if he might be telling them about the inconvenience of a rainstorm intruding on a planned picnic.

"And what can be done?" Tristan asked, now sounding more upset than demanding.

"Nothing," the doctor said nonchalantly with a glance toward Walter that implied the kind of pity a tyrant might offer a dying peasant. "Miserable condition to be sure," he added and picked up the bag he'd brought with him that he'd never opened. "It could lead quickly to death, or he may have to suffer this way for years. Impossible to say." He moved toward the door, saying over his shoulder, "Best of luck to you all."

The moment the door closed, Olivia hurried back to Walter's side and took his hand. "Don't you listen to that wretched, wretched man! We've all witnessed his arrogance and insolence in the past, but I've never imagined he could be so thoroughly rude!"

Walter tried to speak but no one could understand him. "Try again, Father," Tristan said from the opposite side of the bed. Walter tried once more but they all just exchanged frustrated glances at not being able to discern what he desperately wanted to say.

Walter lifted his right hand—which was working perfectly normally—and made a writing motion.

"Paper and pencil," Winnie declared, and Walter made a noise to indicate that he was pleased by her figuring it out. She rushed out of the room and returned within a couple of minutes with several sheets of paper and a couple of pencils. She grabbed a book from Walter's bedside table and set it on the bed to create a hard surface on which she put a piece of paper, then she put a pencil into Walter's hand.

Since Walter had always written with his right hand, he had no difficulty writing the words: *Doctor is right. Uncle had same thing. Never recovered.*

Tristan read it aloud to the others and they all sighed.

"But we can help you," Olivia said brightly. "We will adjust to these new limitations, but we will manage. Your life can still be good . . . and you can still be happy."

"She's right," Lawrence said, moving closer to the bed so that Walter could see him. "We will figure this out, my good man."

"Yes, we will!" Tristan added with firm resolve.

Walter quickly wrote something more, which Tristan again read aloud. "'Don't want to be a burden. Already a burden.'"

They all emphatically tried to convince Walter of their love for him and their desire to have him live and continue to be a part of their lives. But Olivia couldn't help but notice that Walter wasn't convinced. She tried to imagine his fear and frustration at now feeling even more trapped inside of a deteriorating body. But at the same time she couldn't bear the thought of losing him. She held his hand and listened to Tristan telling his father how very much he loved him, and how he would gladly do everything he could to help Lawrence care for him. Olivia tried not to cry, knowing it would upset Walter. She considered the upheaval that had been caused by her involvement in smuggling—and subsequently getting shot—which now felt almost trivial in comparison. Her love for Walter and seeing him in this condition put everything else in perspective.

# CHAPTER TWELVE
# DIVINE INTERVENTION

IN THE DAYS FOLLOWING WALTER'S decline, Tristan became immensely educated on the impact of apoplexy on the human body. He had insisted that he be the one to help Lawrence care for Walter, as opposed to seeking the assistance of one of the male servants in the household, none of whom Walter knew well enough to feel comfortable with while receiving such personal care. At first Walter had protested with a combination of indiscernible noises, gestures with his right hand, and writing down his thoughts when he couldn't be understood any other way. But Tristan pushed back with as much stubbornness, and in the end Walter agreed. A few days into learning how to best help Walter with his new limitations, his father admitted to Tristan—with tears in his eyes—how grateful he was for Tristan's help. He wrote down that he'd never been so proud of him as a son; that the way Tristan treated his father with kindness and respect—despite the complete lack of dignity created by the apoplexy—had made Walter realize what a truly good man Tristan had become. Tristan read the note, then sat on the edge of the bed and wrapped his frail father in his arms and they both wept while Walter returned the embrace weakly with his good arm.

"It's my privilege to care for you," Tristan said to his father, easing back to look into his eyes. "We will get through this."

Walter nodded and offered one of his lopsided smiles that was becoming more familiar.

While Lawrence and Tristan took turns being on hand to help Walter with anything personal, members of the staff who knew Walter well came and went from his room, bringing his food and other necessities, and often sitting to visit for a few minutes. Gradually Walter became less self-conscious about the changes in his body and with his difficulty communicating. Everyone was kind and gracious in giving back to a man who had given them so much. But no one was more loving toward Walter than Olivia. Winnie too brightened Walter's eyes and was enjoyable company for him. But Olivia had a way with Walter with which no one else could compete. Tristan observed how gracefully she handled the changes in his father and how her kind words always set him straight about how much he was loved and adored no matter what his condition might be. Tristan wondered what had ever made him believe when he'd first returned from the war that Olivia being here was for her own selfish reasons—or that his father could have ever managed without her. He fell in love with her more every day, although his recent proposal of marriage had been swallowed up in this new drama. As much as they both wanted to be married, they had agreed that they needed to wait to even discuss it with Walter until he had adjusted to these changes in his life.

After more than a week of helping care for his father, Tristan felt exhausted in body and spirit. Being so reminded him of his time working in the hospital with Jack, although such memories always stirred him to deep gratitude for being in such a secure home with every possible comfort. And Tristan was glad at least that Olivia had gotten past the worst of her recovery before this had happened. He couldn't imagine how he would have cared for her—needing to keep their secret safe—and also care for his father in this condition.

During every waking minute when Tristan wasn't busy helping his father or seeing to the estate business that Walter could no longer do, he found himself praying for guidance and relief. He sensed that his father's condition was worsening, and he wished that the local doctor wasn't so blasted arrogant. He missed Jack and longed for such a doctor in *this* community. For the first time in months, Tristan thought about his own consideration of following a medical profession. If for no other reason than to give the appalling Dr. Brown some competition, Tristan felt a desire to become a doctor. But it was far more than that. In his heart he agreed with what Jack had told him; he believed that he *did* have a disposition for it. The way he'd been able to help both Olivia and his father gave him confidence in that regard. But he was so ignorant as to such conditions as that which currently afflicted his father. He'd helped dig out many bullets with Jack at his side, and he'd stitched many wounds. But apoplexy had not shown up among those wounded on the battlefield, and Tristan had no idea what to expect. Was his father truly dying? Was there something they could do to keep it from worsening? Given that he had no idea what the answers to these questions might be, he prayed at every possible opportunity, hoping for some kind of divine enlightenment that might help him know what to do and also what to say to his father to prevent him from becoming increasingly discouraged.

While everyone who cared about Walter and helped care for him all remained vigilant in trying to keep his spirits up, no one could brighten his countenance the way Olivia could. Tristan often sat across the room and just watched as she read to him or managed to carry on a conversation in a way that no one else had been able to since Walter had lost the ability to speak without extreme slurring and difficulty in forming words. But Olivia was learning to understand him, and between Walter's efforts at speech and his use of paper and pencil, she could keep him engaged in conversation in a way that Tristan found fascinating.

Tristan was watching her late in the afternoon, nearly two weeks into this new way of life, when he drifted to sleep in the chair and dreamt that he was back in the colonies, bleeding to death on the battlefield. He felt strong arms lift him up, and heard a soothing voice promise him that he would be all right, and he looked up to see Jack Barburry floating above him in a way that could only happen in dreams. He was startled awake by Winnie nudging his shoulder.

"What is it?" he muttered, still half asleep. "What's wrong?"

"Nothing is wrong," she said quietly with a discreet glance toward his father as if she didn't want Walter to overhear. "At least I hope that's the case. The lieutenant is here and wishes to speak with you . . . right away, he said."

"Oh, blast," Tristan snarled under his breath and hurried to his own room to make himself presentable before he went down the stairs, reminding himself of the attitude he'd taken on the last time he'd had to deal with Lieutenant Wixom's suspicions. Innocent, confident, and respectful—but just impatient and arrogant enough to hopefully hurry the lieutenant's visit along as quickly as possible. Tristan dismissed the possibility that something might have been uncovered to condemn someone in his household. He just suppressed his fears and entered the room where Wixom had been left to wait.

"Lieutenant," Tristan said as he entered to find this uniformed pest lounging in the corner of a sofa, and he didn't bother to stand upon Tristan's arrival. His entire demeanor had a slight smugness about it that made Tristan nervous, but he didn't show it. "To what do I owe the plea-sure?" he asked with sarcasm and closed the door before he folded his arms and glared at Wixom as if he had absolutely nothing to fear.

"I'm just doing what I always do," Wixom said.

"Chasing tall tales and making assumptions?" Tristan countered nonchalantly.

"My job," Wixom said. "And my job is following orders. I've been ordered to find the source of illegal smuggling in this area, and I will."

Tristan's instincts told him he was more likely to arouse suspicion if he came across as defensive. He sat down and said easily, "I would be more than happy to help you, Lieutenant, if I didn't feel like you were here looking for ghosts—or perhaps an innocent scapegoat. I don't know you well enough to know if I can trust you; to know whether you're a man of integrity. I must protect my household, especially when I have no reason to believe that anyone here is guilty of any crime. Are you the kind of man who sincerely wants to do what's right? Or would you be willing to send an innocent person to the gallows simply to satisfy your superiors?"

"Do you not think that wearing this uniform requires a man to follow orders with integrity and to defend what is right?"

The question sparked a bitter smoldering in the pit of Tristan's stomach, but it was a question he was only too happy to answer. "I spent years in the colonies doing my duty and following orders, and I always strove to do so with integrity. But I encountered many supposed comrades who had not a shred of integrity. Many were self-serving and only wished to further their careers by impressing those who gave the orders. The uniform means nothing to me, Lieutenant—at least not as a measurement of whether a man has good or evil intentions. What are *your* intentions, Wixom? Look at me and assure me that you are not here to stir up trouble where there is no trouble to be found? Make me believe that and I will do all that I can to help you."

"I doubt that I need your help," Wixom said in a tone that seemed meant to dismiss all that Tristan had just said, which made him believe that this man was one of those who lacked integrity, and he was diverting the conversation away from that point in order to disguise the truth. "You see . . . there is a certain young woman who worked here in the laundry . . . until last week. Were you aware of her leaving your employment?"

Tristan's nerves heightened but he kept his cool facade. "Should I be? My housekeeper oversees those employed here. Even if I *were* keeping track of every laundress or kitchen maid that might come and go—which is ridiculous—my father has taken a turn for the worse and I have hardly left his bedside for nearly a fortnight." Tristan sighed as if he were bored with this conversation. "Tell me exactly what this young woman thinks she knows; get on with it."

Wixom sounded smug as he said, "Apparently she was aware of some strange comings and goings in your household, sir."

"And what *exactly* did she observe?" Tristan asked.

"Does it matter?" Wixom asked, and Tristan knew he had nothing more specific than that. Or at least it seemed that way. He felt relatively certain that if Wixom had something to hold over him, he would boldly declare it.

Tristan let out a chuckle that perfectly disguised his relief. "Strange comings and goings?" he repeated. "How old exactly *is* this young woman? Do you think it's ever occurred to her that there might be at least one clandestine romantic tryst going on in the house? Might she be aware of the men who work here who are often out late drinking and stumble into the house and up to the servants' quarters at all hours? You're chasing ghosts, Lieutenant." He said the last with what he believed was justified anger. "Until you have something *real* on which to base your ridiculous accusations, please do me the honor of staying away from my home. I have far more important things to attend to."

Wixom looked mildly flustered and reluctant to leave, but he sighed and moved toward the door as Tristan opened it. As if to resurrect his dignity, Wixom said as he passed by Tristan, "If there's anything to find, I will find it."

"If there's anything to find," Tristan countered, "you will not find it here." He said it with confidence while at the same time knowing that treason *had* taken place here, and he among others were guilty. Was there something Wixom could find to incriminate him? The people who worked for him who had been involved in smuggling? *Olivia?* The very thought made him sick so he pushed it away and escorted the lieutenant outside. Once he was alone, he leaned against the closed door, squeezed his eyes shut, and prayed with all the fervency of his soul that they would all remain safe, and that everyone involved had been careful enough to not leave any clues that might lead Wixom back to them.

\* \* \* \* \*

Olivia was nearly to Walter's room carrying the tea tray when Winnie intercepted her and said, "Lieutenant Wixom is here again. Tristan is talking to him now."

"What on earth does *he* want?" Olivia demanded, as if Winnie might know the answer.

"Do you think there's *anything* he might have found to implicate us?" Winnie asked.

"We always took every possible precaution . . . or at least we tried. But how can we possibly know if something was overlooked? Or if someone might have betrayed us?"

"Here," Winnie said, taking the tray from her. "I'll deliver this. You're doing much better at getting around but you look a little shaky at the moment."

Olivia didn't comment; she just leaned against the wall and said, "I need to wait for Tristan. I have to know what's going on."

"Of course," Winnie said. "Lawrence and I will keep Walter occupied. Take as long as you need."

"Thank you," Olivia said and slid her back down the wall to sit on the floor. She *was* getting around much better, and with increasingly less pain. But she couldn't deny that her leg ached. That, combined with this new onslaught of worry, made it easier to just wait here rather than trying to walk any further at the moment. She knew Tristan would come this way when he returned to his father's room, and she knew that checking on Walter would be his first priority as soon as the lieutenant left.

Olivia's mind whirled with possible scenarios of what might have gone wrong that could condemn herself or those she cared for. When each possibility ended with facing the gallows, she had to force her thoughts to a more positive place. At the center of everything good in her life was Tristan. She loved him and he loved her. And she believed he would go to great lengths to defend her. She loved the secure little world in which she existed, where she and Tristan were surrounded by people who loved and cared for them. And there in the center was Walter. She enjoyed every minute she spent with him; she only wished she could shake off the feeling that her intense desire to be with him as much as possible stemmed very much from her fear that he wouldn't be with them much longer. Each morning she awoke fearing that he might have passed in the night, and each time she went to bed, she wondered if she would ever see him alive again. She sensed the old man's growing desire to be free of his mortal limitations, and with the way his body was not cooperating and was in fact getting worse, she couldn't blame him. She often felt conflicted over wanting to beg him to stay with them for years to come, while at the same time feeling such deep sorrow for his pathetic physical condition. She was glad to know that Walter's life was in God's hands, and she fought to trust that God would take Walter home when the time was right, and that all who loved him would be comforted and strengthened when that time came.

Olivia looked up when she heard footsteps approaching and she wasn't disappointed to see Tristan.

"What on earth are you doing?" he asked, looking down at her with his hands on his hips.

"Winnie told me the lieutenant was here again. I decided to just wait for you here. Has he discovered something that could—"

"I think he mostly came to try and rile me, or perhaps he believes that he can intimidate me into some kind of confession—which will never happen." Tristan sat down beside her and took her hand.

"But . . . what did he say? There must have been some reason he came? Did he—"

"Apparently," Tristan said, "there is a young woman who worked in the laundry here and recently left. Do you know anything about that?"

Olivia's mind started whirling again as she tried to imagine what one thing could have to do with the other. "Her name is May. She was hired not long before you returned home. She was shy; kept to herself mostly. Mrs. Higley told me she'd been caught stealing little things from the rooms of the other servants. She returned the stolen items, was given a firm warning not to do it again. But she did, so Mrs. Higley let her go with sufficient pay so that she wouldn't be without means until she could find other work. That's the way it's always done."

"So, she's left our household and she's likely disgruntled, perhaps distorting in her mind the reasons for her dismissal."

"Perhaps," Olivia said. "But what could she have possibly known that would be of interest to Lieutenant Wixom?"

"He said that she'd reported there had been strange *comings and goings*. That was all. He was vague otherwise. I don't know if that's because he didn't want to give away what he knew, or there was no other information. I suspect from his behavior that it was the latter, but I can't be sure."

"Strange comings and goings?" Olivia repeated. "What does that mean? We were so careful. Or at least I thought we were."

"I know, but . . . who's to say that someone like her—or anyone else in the house—might have been unable to sleep and was wandering around and happened to see wagons coming or going in the middle of the night?"

"Still, that's not proof of anything," Olivia said. "Is it?"

"I wouldn't think so."

"What did you tell the lieutenant?" she asked.

"You'll be proud to know that I laughed it off with my best acting skills. I suggested that strange comings and goings could mean men out drinking and stumbling in at all hours, or perhaps there was a clandestine romantic tryst going on."

"You said that?" Olivia asked with a little laugh.

"I did," he said. "Is it funny?"

"Maybe . . . a little. Do you think he believed that's all it was?"

"I don't know; I hope so. But we can't do anything about it either way, Livy. He's gone for now, and hopefully he has no other information he can hold over us and he'll never come back. Right now we have more important things to consider. My father needs us."

"I know he does," Olivia said, and they were both silent a long moment as if they each needed to try and catch up with the dramatic changes that had taken place in Walter's life—and subsequently theirs as well.

"I need to say something," Olivia said, tightening her hold on Tristan's hand. "What if he *is* near the end, Tristan? I know we don't want to accept such a possibility; we don't even want to think about it. But . . . maybe we need to consider it, even if it's not what we want."

"I know you're right," Tristan said. "I hate the thought of losing him, but I also hate seeing him so . . . frustrated and . . . struggling so desperately."

"I feel the same."

"But there's nothing we can do except just care for him the best that we can."

"Of course," Olivia said, "but . . ."

"But?" he repeated and turned to look at her more directly.

"Right after this happened, we decided to wait and tell him about our engagement, but now that some time has passed . . . I think . . . well . . . we both know he very much wants the two of us to be together. I think it would make him very happy to know that we *will* be married. Now I'm thinking that perhaps it might bring him some peace—and even some joy—to know the truth."

"I think you might be right," he said and kissed her. "Besides, I'm tired of keeping it a secret. We have too many other secrets to bear; I prefer that the entire household—and the county for that matter—knows that I'm going to spend the rest of my life with you."

"How divine!" she said and smiled. "And maybe we should just set a date and start working on preparations; perhaps your father would enjoy being in on the plans."

"And perhaps he might be saddened to know that he won't be able to attend the wedding."

"I daresay he will have some sadness," Olivia said. "We both know him well enough to know that. But perhaps his exposure to *our* happiness as we plan our wedding might compensate for that."

Tristan came to his feet and held out his hand. "Let's tell him now."

"Yes, let's," she said and stood with his help.

Walter was so thrilled with their news that a tear rolled down his cheek while the right side of his mouth went up into a delighted smile. He wrote with the pencil that was becoming very comfortable in his right hand: *Nothing could make me happier!*

"We are in agreement over that," Tristan said and hugged Olivia tightly while Walter looked on and beamed proudly.

Tristan and Olivia had supper in Walter's room—as they always did—and Winnie and Lawrence joined them. Walter required some assistance with eating, given that one side of his mouth was not functioning properly. He was able to feed himself with his right hand, but he often had trouble keeping food in his mouth while he chewed it, which made him terribly self-conscious and frustrated. Therefore, they had decided that it was easier for Walter if someone else helped give him bites of food and Walter could hold a napkin over his mouth while he chewed and swallowed, which made him feel more in control of the most awkward aspect of eating. Those who shared meals with him had become accustomed to the changes and they all took turns helping Walter; and Walter seemed to be getting more comfortable with accepting help and not worrying about any awkwardness.

During supper and afterward as they shared tea and visited, they all discussed plans for the wedding. They speculated on a date and talked about the celebration they would have afterward. Olivia noticed that Walter's initial delight over their plans to marry had disappeared. In spite of one side of his face being paralyzed, she was still able to read his expressions, and she knew that he was feeling some kind of uneasiness—or perhaps sorrow—even if he probably didn't want anyone to notice. But she *had* noticed, and she was not going to let it pass.

"Walter," she said, moving from her chair to sit on the side of the bed to take hold of his good hand, "is something troubling you? I know it's difficult for you to communicate, but you must speak up."

He didn't appear pleased over her observation, but he nodded and reached for the pencil and paper that were always on the bed beside him when he was awake. He wrote the words: *Get married soon, before I die.*

Olivia read it, then held it up for the others to see. Tristan immediately said, "Why do you think you're going to die? This condition is not necessarily fatal."

Walter scrambled to write: *We don't know that. I feel like I'm dying.* As he held the paper up for Tristan to read, his expression made it clear how firmly he believed that his life was coming to a close.

While Olivia was trying very hard to discern what Walter might really be feeling, Tristan said to Walter, "I can't imagine how difficult this must be for you, Father, but I can't believe it means you're dying."

"I think," Olivia said, hoping to help this conversation become more productive, "that perhaps Walter might like to say that no matter how much any of us don't want him to leave us, we have no control over when it might happen." She looked at Walter directly and asked, "I'm only guessing . . . or trying to understand. Tell me if I'm right." Walter nodded in agreement, while his expression showed encouragement for her to continue. "I'm guessing that what you're going through has left you feeling very vulnerable . . . and perhaps aware of how fragile life can be." Walter nodded again and she pressed on. "And even with the possibility that you might yet live a long while, you would like to know that your son is married and all is well."

Walter nodded again and wrote on the paper: *Olivia knows me well.* He held the paper up for the others to see.

"Indeed she does," Tristan said, sounding sad.

"Dare I say," Lawrence interjected, "that as much as none of us want to have you leave this life, because we would all miss you, we need to be realistic about the evidence that your physical body is not doing well."

Again, Walter nodded, evidencing that he was being understood. Olivia was glad to be having this conversation, and she wished they'd had it days ago—in spite of how troubled Tristan appeared. But Lawrence was right; they needed to be realistic. On that note, Olivia added, "This is difficult to face—for all of us—nevertheless I believe it's wise to be prepared, as opposed to ignoring the fact that death is inevitable." She tightened her hold on Walter's hand and smiled at him. "We need to make the most of every day we have together, and when you *do* leave us, we will have the peace of knowing that we took advantage of this opportunity to be prepared for you to go, and we will be comforted by the knowledge that you are in a better place and free of these afflictions."

Walter nodded. Tristan sighed and said, "I can't deny that she's right, but . . ." His voice cracked as he looked directly at his father. "I just don't feel ready to lose you."

"I daresay," Winnie said, "that a son would never feel ready to lose his father . . . especially when you share such a close bond. None of us want to lose you." Winnie smiled at Walter. "Even though you're such a stubborn old man."

Half of Walter's face smiled at her comment and he chuckled. The mood in the room lightened and Winnie added, "If I might offer a suggestion . . ."

"Of course," Tristan said to her.

"You'll have the wedding celebration here at the house, so why not have the wedding here as well so that Walter can be present? It would only take a couple of strong stable hands to help get him downstairs, and we can make him comfortable there. Given the circumstances, I believe the vicar would be willing to accommodate us." Winnie looked directly at Walter and asked, "Would you like that, Walter?" He nodded but his expression showed some concern.

"Are you uncomfortable with people seeing you this way?" Olivia guessed.

Walter nodded and wrote: *Not enough to miss the wedding. Don't care what people think. Going to die soon anyway.*

Olivia shared Walter's words with the others and concluded, "I guess it's settled. We will schedule the wedding as soon as possible, and we will have it here."

"I will post the banns on Sunday," Tristan said, "and speak with the vicar right away, which means we should be able to marry in less than a month."

They talked a little more about wedding plans, and Olivia noticed that Walter seemed more relaxed. His concerns had been heard and addressed, and he now showed pleasant anticipation. Olivia was glad to know Walter now felt better about their plans, and she was certainly pleased to think of marrying Tristan as soon as possible. But observing Walter's physical difficulties, she couldn't help wondering if he might not live even long enough for them to be married. All they could do was press forward with their plans and pray that he would live that long. She wanted to believe that he could live well beyond that. She wanted him to live to be a grandfather—and she knew that Tristan felt the same. But the length of Walter's life was in God's hands, and they could only do as she had declared and make the most of each day they had together.

* * * * *

Tristan had difficulty sleeping as the conversation that had taken place with his father kept rolling around in his head. He knew now that he had been denying the possibility that his father was nearing death. He'd wanted so badly to believe that Walter could conquer his physical limitations enough to remain alive that he'd dismissed the possibility of any other outcome. And now that he'd been forced to accept the possibility, he felt the monster of grief threatening to overtake him. He wanted to run and hide from it, but he had enough sense to know that doing so was impossible. Eventually grief would catch up, and the longer he fought to avoid it, the more difficult the battle would be.

As Tristan allowed the prospect of losing his father to fully settle in, his chest tightened and tears stung his eyes. He encouraged the tears to come, given that he was all alone and he felt sure they needed to be released. What surprised him most was that he'd never felt this depth of sorrow before. The grief he'd experienced as a result of Muriel's death had been practically imperceptible in contrast; his grief over her betrayal had been more pronounced. But looking back, he believed that his greatest grief had been over his own poor choices, which had created the situation, and how much difficulty they had caused for so many people for whom he cared. He'd needed to come to terms with his choices and forgive himself. But now, facing the very idea of Walter's death, what Tristan felt was entirely different. His father had always been a great strength to Tristan—even when he'd been too young and arrogant to admit it. In the months since Tristan had come home, his father had become his closest friend and confidant. With the exception of all things related to treason, there was nothing Tristan couldn't talk to his father about. Walter was kind, compassionate, and a man of the highest character. His integrity and honor were a great example to Tristan. And he was going to miss him so badly that it provoked physical pain to even think about it.

Tristan fell asleep immersed in his grief, as if his father had already died. He woke up to the realization that Walter was still alive and he needed to do as Olivia had suggested—and make the most of every day they had together. While he was getting dressed for the day, he couldn't shake a nagging feeling that more could be done for his father to help ease the symptoms of his condition and perhaps even to extend his life. Perhaps there was a way to make Walter more comfortable. He didn't know if this was simply evidence of his own unwillingness to let go and accept that Walter's days were numbered, or if there was some purpose to his thoughts.

Tristan tried to clear his mind of all worries and concerns as he walked the beaten path from his own room to his father's. He found Lawrence helping Walter drink some tea, and there was no missing the light in Walter's countenance when Tristan entered the room. A deep gratitude filled Tristan for the time he yet had with his father, and he was indeed determined to make the most of it.

Lawrence had some things to take care of and left Tristan in charge of helping Walter with his breakfast. Olivia herself brought the breakfast tray and he rose to take it from her, giving her a quick kiss as it passed from her hands to his. Tristan turned to set the tray down and caught his father smiling at them.

"Yes, I'm in love with her," Tristan said lightly.

Walter wrote with his pencil and held up the paper for them to see. *Best thing you've ever done.*

"I couldn't agree more," Tristan said.

They shared comfortable conversation throughout the course of breakfast and afterward. Walter apparently enjoyed talk of wedding plans, and he wrote down some memories of his marriage to Tristan's mother. Tristan asked some questions, which Walter seemed to enjoy answering. As Tristan noted the words written in his father's hand regarding tender moments from the past, he determined that he wanted to keep the pages on which Walter was writing. They would surely be a precious memento of their time together.

Their conversation was interrupted when Winnie came to tell Tristan that he had a visitor.

"Oh, not another interrogation from that dreadful lieutenant!" Tristan exclaimed.

"No, sir," Winnie said. "It's not him. He told Mrs. Higley that he met you in the colonies. He's a doctor."

"Good heavens!" Tristan rose to his feet and laughed.

"Do you think it's your friend?" Olivia asked in a tone that implied she shared his excitement.

"I don't know who else it could be," Tristan said and hurried toward the door, saying over his shoulder, "I'll let you know."

Tristan hurried down the stairs, hoping that it was indeed Jack Barburry. He couldn't think of any other possibility, but it felt too good to be true. Not only had he missed his friend and often wondered how he was doing, but Jack was a doctor—and a very good one. To have his expert opinion on Walter's condition didn't feel merely like an answer to Tristan's prayers; it felt like a miracle.

As Tristan entered the drawing room to see Jack Barburry there, in the flesh, he laughed aloud and declared, "What a joyous event this is!"

Jack laughed as well and the two men shared a brotherly embrace. "It's so good to see you!" Jack declared.

Tristan took hold of his friend's shoulders and looked him over. "You don't look too much the worse for wear. How are you?"

"I'm well," Jack declared, and Tristan motioned for him to sit down. "And you?" he asked as Tristan sat across from him.

"I'm very well," Tristan said. "What brings you here?"

"I confess that I've clung to your repeated invitations to come here when I returned to England. Of all the people I encountered during my time in the colonies, you are the only real friend I gained. I've wondered about you, and I'm so very glad to see you."

"As I am to see you!" Tristan declared.

"I must also confess," Jack said, looking a little sheepish, "that in truth I have nowhere else to go. We were always honest with each other, so I'll come straight to the point, and I know you'll not be afraid to tell me the truth."

"Out with it," Tristan said when Jack hesitated. "You saved my life, Jack; you're one of the finest men I've ever known. What do you need? Money? A place to stay? Name it!"

Jack chuckled, seeming a bit more relaxed. "How perceptive you are. I must admit that a roof over my head and some honest work to earn my keep would be a great blessing. With my medical training I'm certain I could find work somewhere and be able to meet my needs; however, I confess that after enduring years of war, I wanted very much to spend time with a friend. But I will not impose upon your generous nature, Tristan. I must—"

"Don't say another word," Tristan said. "It would be my pleasure to have you here; the house is ridiculously huge, and I'm glad to be able to help."

Jack chuckled again, this time sounding as if he were trying to conceal some emotion. "I do believe that divine intervention brought us together, my friend. I'm deeply grateful."

"I agree about divine intervention," Tristan said, "but I think that I will benefit far more from the arrangement."

"What do you mean?" Jack asked, looking confused, as if he couldn't possibly imagine himself being a blessing to Tristan.

"It just so happens," Tristan said, "that I am very much in need of a doctor."

"No!"

"Yes!"

"But you said that you're doing very well."

"I am," Tristan said, "but my father is not." He stood and Jack did the same. "If you are up to it, I'd like you to meet him now—before lunch, since he naps after he eats."

"I'd would love to meet him," Jack said with enthusiasm, "and I would also love to be of assistance."

"Come along," Tristan said, putting a hand on Jack's shoulder. "I'll explain as we walk."

They headed together toward the stairs while Tristan silently thanked God for sending the answer to his prayers in the form of Jack Barburry.

# CHAPTER THIRTEEN

# THE TRAITOR

TRISTAN FELT ALMOST GIDDY OVER the arrival of his friend, even while he quickly told him what he knew of his father's condition. At the top of the stairs, Jack stopped as if he needed to stand still while he asked some specific questions, which Tristan answered to the best of his knowledge. Jack was distinctly appalled with the attitude of the local doctor, and they walked on toward Walter's room with an urgency that implied Jack's desire to get to his new patient quickly with the hope of being able to help in some way.

Tristan knocked lightly at his father's door, waited the standard few seconds, then opened it to see Olivia and Lawrence sitting with Walter.

"There's someone I want you all to meet," Tristan announced and stood aside for Jack to enter.

"It *is* your friend, then?" Olivia asked, coming to her feet.

Lawrence stood as well and Tristan motioned toward Jack, saying with unreserved delight, "May I introduce my dear friend, Jack Barburry. Jack, this is Olivia Halstead." He nearly added that she was his fiancé but realized that as far as Jack knew he was still married to Muriel. They had much to catch up on. He stated instead, "I'll tell you all about Olivia later."

"Hello," Olivia said and held out her hand, which Jack kissed gallantly and smiled at her as he let go. "It is such a great pleasure. We've heard so much about you."

"The pleasure is surely mine," Jack said.

"And this," Tristan continued, "is Lawrence, my father's faithful companion and friend for many years."

"So good to meet you," Lawrence said and nodded.

"And the same," Jack replied, also nodding.

"And this," Tristan motioned toward the bed where Walter was propped against pillows, his expression showing curiosity and anticipation, "is my dear father, Walter Whitmore."

Tristan had perhaps expected some awkwardness at this point, given Walter's inability to even speak and be understood. But Jack moved directly to Walter's good side and took his hand, saying with the respect and deference that might be due a king, "It is such a great honor to finally meet you, sir. Your son has told me so much about you." Tristan saw his father nod slightly in response. He was ready to remind Walter that Jack was a doctor and was willing to render his services when Jack said, "Your son has told me a little of the medical challenges you are facing. You know that I'm a doctor." Walter nodded. "I wonder if you would allow me to assess your condition and offer my opinion." Walter nodded again, and even though his ability to move was limited, his eyes showed how eager he was for any other opinion than that which had been given by Dr. Brown.

"I would like to start," Jack said, "by simply testing the strength in your hands and feet." He glanced over his shoulder and said with a chuckle, "Would you like these spectators to leave, or—"

Walter reached for his pencil and Jack immediately picked up on his intention and waited for him to write. *They should stay. They've all suffered with me.*

Jack read it aloud to the others and Lawrence added, "I daresay he's beyond embarrassment with us."

"If this is meant to be private," Olivia said, "I can go and—"

"Nothing too personal," Jack said, and Olivia sat back down, as did Lawrence. Tristan chose to remain on his feet, intensely curious over what Jack might do and what his opinion might be.

Tristan was amazed—though he knew he shouldn't have been—at the kindness and respect with which Jack addressed his father. The contrast to Dr. Brown was incomprehensible! The tests he did were simple. *Squeeze my fingers as hard as you can. Push your foot against my hand. Look at my finger as I move it.* He did these and several other assessments of Walter's strength and movement and use of his faculties. He encouraged and complimented Walter on how well he was doing, as opposed to treating his frailty as something to be ashamed of. He then sat again on the edge of the bed and asked many questions which all of those in the room helped answer, looking to Walter each time to see if he was in agreement. Occasionally Walter added input by writing down a specific answer.

Jack then explained in detail the medical analysis of what had happened to Walter to cause this problem, and that he'd previously worked with more than one patient who had experienced the same thing. Prior to his going to the colonies to care for soldiers wounded in battle, he had worked in London, serving a variety of patients from many different walks of life. He finally declared with a note of hope in his voice, "I believe that with some simple changes to your treatment, sir, your symptoms can improve." Tristan appreciated the way he spoke directly to Walter. "The overall effect of the paralysis will never go away, but I've seen patients worse off than you regain some abilities with their limbs and also their speech. The problem often comes in simply assuming that the paralyzed side of the body is useless; therefore, it gets ignored. If we make some simple changes to your routine, and help you with some basic exercises every day, I believe you can experience some improvement. Of course, the heart condition that existed prior to the stroke of apoplexy is still a concern, and you must still be mindful of that. But you have many people here who care about you and are willing to help you." He tossed a smile toward the others in the room, then looked back at Walter. "And since your son has been generous enough to invite me to stay here for the time being, I would be honored to assist you every day in doing these things that can help you enjoy life more."

Walter looked undeniably pleased, but he wrote on the paper and held it up for Jack and the others to see as well. *Do you not have family that will miss you?*

Jack answered matter-of-factly. "I'm afraid I don't. I was raised in an orphanage and left there when I was very young. I was blessed enough to be taken in by a kind doctor and his good wife. He taught me a great deal and when I was old enough I completed my education. These good people have passed on; therefore, I have not had any place to call home for many years. I'm very grateful for the opportunity to spend some time here in your home with your family. And I promise not to wear out my welcome."

Walter wrote quickly and held up the paper. *You saved my son's life. You will always be welcome here.*

"Thank you," Jack said. "You're very kind." He looked at Tristan and grinned. "I was just doing my job, but it was the first time one of my patients insisted on becoming my assistant, and we naturally became friends." He looked back at Walter. "Your son is a good man, which I'm certain is much credit to you. He helped make an unconscionable situation almost tolerable."

A knock at the door preceded Winnie's entrance into the room with a lunch tray, and another maid following her, carrying a second tray. "Mrs. Higley told me you had a guest and suggested that I bring lunch enough for all of you."

"Thank you," Tristan said, taking the tray from her to set it on the table where he'd eaten most of his meals since his return home. "Will you be joining us?"

"Not today," Winnie said, but she hurried to kiss Walter on the forehead and say to him, "I'll see you later, old man. Behave yourself."

Walter chuckled and Winnie followed the maid toward the door. Jack looked a little confused over what appeared to be one of the servants having such a relationship with the master of the house. Tristan just smiled at him and said, "I'll tell you later."

"Also," Winnie said with her hand on the door, "since rumors spread quickly in this house, Mr. Barburry's horse is being cared for, and his bag has been taken to the guest room across the hall from your room." She nodded toward Tristan.

"Thank you, Winnie," Tristan said, and she left and closed the door.

Jack appeared humble and grateful to the point of almost looking sheepish. "That's very kind," he said as they turned their attention toward lunch.

Olivia volunteered to help Walter eat, but Jack said, "May I? I might have a trick or two that could make it easier for him." He took the plate meant for Walter—which always came from the kitchen with everything already cut into bite-sized pieces—and sat on the edge of the bed, saying to Walter, "Now, remember, I'm a doctor, and I've seen many a strange and difficult thing in my days. I'm not at all uncomfortable with this, and you shouldn't be either." Walter nodded and Tristan saw a relief in his eyes that reflected his own feelings. Jack had managed in less than an hour to ease the awkwardness of this situation and to alleviate many of their fears. He had given them hope, a gift that was deeply precious under the circumstances.

\* \* \* \* \*

After lunch, they left Walter with Lawrence, who would help him get settled in for his nap. Before she went to take care of some personal things, Olivia told Jack how very pleased she was that he'd come to Whitmore Manor. Tristan took Jack to the library where they could have some time alone to catch up.

\* \* \* \* \*

"This room absolutely has the most comfortable sofas," Tristan said, opening the door. "I've often come here to steal a nap."

Jack walked in and took a long gaze around the room, marveling at the enormous number of books. "How grand!" he said. "I do believe I could get lost in here for days."

"Feel free," Tristan said and closed the door.

Tristan and Jack sat across from each other on separate sofas.

"Now," Tristan said, "tell me all that's happened since we last said good-bye."

"There's not much to tell," Jack said. "Patching up the wounded went on much the same. I can admit to you that it became increasingly difficult. I do believe a person can work under such circumstances for only so long."

"I'm sure!" Tristan said with compassion. "I don't know how you managed to do it as long as you did."

"I'm not sure myself. Perhaps one day I'll figure it out. But thankfully another doctor was sent to replace me. We worked together for a week or so before I left, and I do believe my little hospital was left in good hands—which made it easier to leave. I've struggled with wondering if I did enough, but I know deep down that I could never give enough under such circumstances. I served my time and I was glad to get on a ship and return to my homeland. And here I am. That's all there is to tell. But I sense that your life has not been so boring since you returned."

Tristan erupted with a wry chuckle; he thought of all that had happened regarding treason and smuggling that he couldn't tell Jack. For a moment his mind wandered to the fact that he still didn't know if Lieutenant Wixom had some kind of evidence that could incriminate someone in his household, and he had no idea what the disgruntled young laundress might have observed that could have left them exposed. He hated the fear that rose inside of him at the thought and wondered if they would ever feel truly safe.

"Tristan?" he heard Jack say. "Are you all right?"

"Yes, of course."

"You were somewhere else, I believe."

"It's just . . . so much *has* happened. I was wondering where to begin."

"At the beginning," Jack encouraged. "How was your journey home?"

"Fine; miserable as you predicted, but fine for the most part. Once we made port I got home as quickly as I could and arrived late evening.

I had been anticipating some time with my father—even though it was late—and seeing my wife. I was met with the news that my father's health had deteriorated dramatically and he was already asleep."

"That must have been disheartening."

"Indeed," Tristan said. "He was strong and vibrant when I left for the war." Tristan sighed as he contrasted his father's present condition with the memory of how vital and vibrant his father had once been. But at least Jack was here now and they had some hope of dealing with the problems more effectively.

"And your wife?" Jack asked. "I've not met her yet. Is she—"

"She's dead," Tristan said quickly to get it over with. "I came home to the news that she had died . . . in the spring."

"I'm so sorry!" Jack said, astonished.

"Thank you, but . . . her death was much easier to come to terms with than . . . the reasons she died."

"I don't understand," Jack said when Tristan hesitated.

"Forgive me," Tristan said, realizing how the darkness surrounding this topic had overtaken him, slowing his thinking and his ability to talk about it. "I've made peace with it; I really have. But I admit the memories of that time are difficult." Tristan looked directly at his friend and just said it. "She died in childbirth, Jack, and the baby with her." Jack looked as if Tristan had just thrown a bucket of water on him. Tristan hurried to offer the minimal explanation. "I knew soon after I married Muriel that she was not the woman I'd believed her to be when we'd been courting, but I think I was too horrified to realize what a fool I'd been to be able to acknowledge how unhappy I was. I'm certain that part of my motivation for going to war was to get away from the marriage, and I confess that something inside of me almost hoped that I would get killed and not have to come home and face her again. Hence, there was some relief over her death, and perhaps relief that her choices had publicly illustrated the kind of woman she was. I felt . . . validated, perhaps. But I also felt guilty for being relieved that my wife had died. However, I have worked through my grief and I am moving forward with my life."

"I'm very glad to hear it."

"My father and Olivia have both been an enormous blessing in helping me make sense of all that happened and coming to terms with it."

"I'm glad to hear that as well," Jack said. "And who *is* Olivia, exactly? Some relation, apparently."

"She is Muriel's cousin . . . and my fiancé."

"Oh," Jack chuckled, "you *are* moving forward with your life."

Tristan smiled at his friend. "It's not as impetuous as it sounds. You see . . . I've known Olivia for many years. In fact, we were courting before I met Muriel."

"Oh, I see," Jack said, apparently fascinated with this story. "I think I can guess where this might be headed. Go on." He motioned impatiently with his hand.

"Looking back now and putting the facts together, it's apparent that Muriel wanted a rich husband and set her sights on me, pretending to be everything I wanted and saying all the right things. But she also lied to me about Olivia, making me believe that she was not trustworthy. And I was fool enough to fall for it. In truth, Jack, that has been the most difficult thing to make peace with—my utter foolishness and how much I hurt Olivia, not to mention my father and everyone in this house who had to put up with Muriel's arrogance and selfishness. Thankfully I am surrounded by very loving and forgiving people."

"That is a great blessing, indeed," Jack said. "May I ask why Olivia is living here? Just curious."

"Olivia and her maid, Winnie, came here after Olivia's father died and they had nowhere else to go; this actually happened before I left."

"That must have been awkward," Jack said lightly.

"Very much so," Tristan admitted with a chuckle.

"More motivation to go to war?" Jack asked.

"Perhaps," Tristan said. "While I was away, Olivia took on the overseeing of the house that Muriel neglected, and I believe she tried very hard to soften the blow of Muriel's indiscretions as much as she could. She also did a great deal to help my father when his health declined. I daresay the house would have fallen down without her. The most important thing is that I love her—and she loves me, if you can imagine that; after all I've put her through, she still loves me. She is a woman of courage and integrity and wisdom. I quickly realized I would be a fool to let her slip away again. We will be married in less than a month; funny how I was just thinking yesterday how I wished that you could be here for the wedding. And here you are!"

"Yes, here I am," Jack said. "And since I last saw you, you've been through enough drama to last a lifetime. I hope life will settle down for you now."

"That's my hope, as well," Tristan said, wishing once again that the threat of their treasonous activities was not hanging over them. He hated living in fear, but he could do nothing about it without appearing more suspicious. So he focused on his gladness at having Jack here, and the prospect of Walter experiencing some improvement and being with them for some time yet. And most importantly, he had his marriage to Olivia to look forward to. Life was good in too many ways to count, and he resolved to keep his attention on remembering that above all else.

* * * * *

It didn't take long for Jack to fit in comfortably and for everyone to be comfortable having him around. Tristan appreciated how quickly Jack felt at home among the little group of people that came and went from Walter's room as they worked together to care for the old man. Olivia and Winnie both took quickly to Jack; his kindness and respect toward them was far too genuine to not be infectious. Lawrence also liked Jack and seemed at ease with having him around, especially given the respectful way he treated Walter. Tristan quickly realized as he observed Jack interacting with his father that they had all been treating Walter like an invalid, and Jack somehow managed to communicate with Walter in a way that separated the man from the malady. Within just a few days of Jack working with Walter, his mood had already brightened considerably. Jack would talk casually to Walter as he did simple exercises with his limbs to help strengthen them, and Walter was surprisingly eager to become engaged in a series of speech exercises with Jack that were meant to help him relearn how to use the muscles in his face and mouth that *did* work in order to form sounds more clearly so that he would be able to use his voice to communicate again. Previously Walter had avoided even trying to speak, partly because it had been so ineffective, and perhaps partly due to some embarrassment. But Jack put Walter completely at ease and there no longer seemed to be any awkwardness over the situation.

Tristan enjoyed visiting with Jack, and he quickly recalled the many stimulating conversations they'd shared in that wretched hospital. Jack was well educated and he loved to read, and the two of them never ran out of things to talk about. Tristan especially enjoyed the times when Olivia would join them; his fiancé and his closest friend got along well, which he considered to be a good thing on many counts.

Tristan continued to spend time alone with Olivia every day, and he appreciated the way they could talk about anything and everything, and they could completely rely on each other. Despite his gratitude for having Jack now as a part of their household, Olivia would always and forever be his dearest friend—and he told her so. Each day they discussed the development of wedding plans, and with the help of Mrs. Higley and Winnie, everything was coming along smoothly. Tristan couldn't help but anticipate being married to Olivia for many reasons. He wanted to share every facet of his life with her, and he would be glad to be able to share a room, as opposed to living on opposite ends of such an enormous house—which sometimes felt as if she lived in another country.

Within a week, Jack seemed completely at home and Tristan found it difficult to imagine how they'd gotten along without him. He was continually kind and polite and appreciative, while at the same time more than earning his keep with the way he'd taken over much of Walter's care. They did a long series of exercises twice a day, which was always followed by working on Walter's speech. Jack also helped Walter eat his meals and was helping him to be able to eat with more control.

Jack had quickly become acquainted with the staff. He usually spent some time every day helping with the horses, since he had a great love for the animals. And more than once Tristan had found him in the kitchen doing menial tasks and teasing the cook and her assistants. On Sundays, Jack went to church with them, and he told Tristan how good it felt to be attending a service again after years away in the war, where every day of the week had felt the same in caring for the wounded and dying.

Jack was like the brother Tristan had never had, and he felt as if life had never been better—until thoughts would jump into his mind about the secrets being kept about smuggling and treason, and the possibility that the tenacious Lieutenant Wixom might yet find something to link the illegal goings on in the area back to Olivia or the others who had been involved. Tristan wished every day—many times a day—that there might be a way for all of this to be resolved and put to rest, but he wondered if it would simply take time for the threat to dissolve. Surely with the passing of time it would all be forgotten. Oh, how he wished that it could all just go away!

Walter's dear friend Kenneth Cornaby came to visit for the first time in a few weeks. His regular weekly visits had been interrupted by his traveling to take care of some business in London. He'd seen Walter soon after the apoplexy had occurred, and now he marveled at the remarkable improvement that had taken place since his last visit. Tristan gave credit for the improvement to Jack's efforts with Walter, and the gift of his knowledge of such things.

Tristan left his father alone with Mr. Cornaby to visit, knowing that Lawrence was nearby in case Walter needed any assistance. He found

Olivia assisting with the laundry and he helped her finish what she was doing before they headed toward the gardens with the intention of taking a long walk together so they could talk privately and enjoy each other's company—even though it looked as if it might start to rain. But Olivia said that she was willing to take a chance and enjoy some fresh air together. They were almost to the door when they heard Mrs. Higley call, "Oh, good! There you are!"

"What is it?" Tristan asked as he turned to see the housekeeper hurrying toward them, out of breath.

"I've been looking for the both of you. I'm glad you're together. We have a situation."

"What *kind* of situation?" Tristan demanded. "If that lieutenant is back here expecting to—"

"No, it's not him," she said, trying to catch her breath. "Just . . . come with me."

She turned and hurried back in the direction from which she'd come and they had no choice but to follow her. Tristan exchanged a concerned glance with Olivia that let him know she was as ignorant as he over what this might be about. He just kept hold of her hand as they followed Mrs. Higley, hoping that whatever this problem entailed, it would have nothing to do with treason or smuggling.

The housekeeper led them to a small parlor that was most often used when servants had visitors come for them. She opened the door, and they entered to find a young woman seated at the edge of a chair, her eyes red and swollen from crying, her hands clenched together on her lap. She bolted to her feet when they came into the room, and she looked as if she were about to face imminent doom. But Tristan had no idea who she was.

"May," Olivia said in surprise as Mrs. Higley left and closed the door behind her. At the mention of this young woman's name, Tristan knew this was the maid Mrs. Higley had dismissed, and somehow, she'd ended up giving information to Lieutenant Wixom that had created suspicion. He immediately felt angry and was grateful for Olivia's kindness as she stepped forward and asked, "What on earth has happened? You look as if you're about to faint. Please . . . sit down."

Olivia guided May back into her chair and sat down nearby. Tristan preferred to remain standing, but Olivia tossed him an icy glare, then nodded toward a chair. He knew that she was well aware of his anger and she wanted him to sit and calm down. He took a seat and drew in a deep breath, trying to heed her silent admonition, but he needed to hear what this girl had to say before he could even think about being at ease.

"Just tell us why you've come back," Olivia gently encouraged.

"I'm so sorry!" May said and burst into tears, pressing a handkerchief over her mouth.

Olivia scooted her chair closer to May and put a hand on her shoulder while she looked at Tristan with eyes that reflected his own alarm.

"Please talk to us," Olivia said, still kind but more firm.

May was clearly trying to gain her composure, but Tristan grew impatient. He tried to follow Olivia's example of using a kind voice, but he had difficulty not sounding sharp when he said, "Until I know exactly what it is you're sorry about, I have no idea how to help you."

May's eyes responded to that word *help*. She was clearly in some kind of trouble, and she'd obviously been desperate to come back here when she'd been dismissed from her job due to her tendency to thievery. But if she actually knew something that could incriminate Olivia or anyone else, Tristan far preferred to have May become an ally.

May appeared utterly terrified as she looked directly at Tristan and said, "I'm so sorry about what I told Bert. I only found out yesterday that he'd told the lieutenant, and . . ." She pressed her handkerchief over her mouth again to hold back a new onslaught of tears.

"*Who* is Bert?" Tristan demanded. "And *what* did you tell him?"

May continued to cry, and Tristan wanted to shout at her. He was once again grateful for Olivia's kindness as she took hold of May's hand, saying firmly, "I know this is difficult, May, but you must calm down and tell us everything." May looked up at Olivia. "Everything! Do you understand?" May nodded and Olivia added, "Now, take a deep breath and talk to us. We'll do everything we can to help you as long as you tell us the truth." May took a deep breath, then another. "That's good," Olivia said. "You can cry later if you need to, but right now you need to do your best to remain calm and talk to us."

"Forgive me," May said, glancing at Tristan before she looked again at Olivia, who was apparently easier to talk to. "I've been so overly emotional lately; I don't know why." She took another deep breath and wiped the tears off her face.

"Just . . . start at the beginning," Olivia encouraged.

"When . . . I left here . . . my intention was to use some of the wages I'd been given to stay at the pub in town for just a couple of nights so that

I could see if there was work to be found. I was eating a meal in the dining room when Bert started talking to me. I admit I was somewhat taken in by the uniform."

Tristan took in that bit of information and sought to clarify. "So, Bert is one of the officers that has been in the area trying to find evidence of smuggling . . . or treason . . . or some such nonsense." He watched closely for May's reaction to his treating the crimes as trivial; she showed no reaction at all. If she believed they were involved, he felt certain she would have given away some surprise or disdain toward what he'd said.

"Yes," she said, still looking at Olivia. "He was so kind to me, more than any man ever has been. He started paying for my meals, and . . . he helped me look for work, and . . ." May got emotional again, but she managed to keep her tears at a level through which she could speak. "He told me he loved me; he made me believe he loved me. But now I know it was all a lie. He knew I'd worked here. He was just . . . taking advantage of me . . . to try and get information, and . . ." Again the handkerchief went over her mouth.

"What exactly did you tell him?" Tristan asked firmly. He couldn't bear the suspense a moment longer.

"Nothing," May said, looking at him with the confidence of honesty in her eyes. "There was nothing to tell. I don't know what may or may not be going on here. I worked in the laundry and I slept in a little room in the servants' quarters. What would I possibly know? I *did* tell him I felt confident that everyone I knew here were good people, and that I couldn't imagine anything so serious taking place here. That's all. But . . . Bert told me yesterday that he'd told the lieutenant some kind of . . . distorted version of what I'd told him. He made it sound as if I'd . . . said or done something wrong; that someone here would be found out as a traitor and it would be my fault. I had to come back . . . I had to tell you what he said . . . and I need you to know that I didn't betray you. They're stretching the truth; they're making it up." May sniffled and looked at the floor. "I know I did wrong here, and I know you have good cause not to believe me, but it's the truth. I need you to know that."

"I believe you," Tristan said, so relieved he almost wanted to hug the girl. His concern shifted as he took in the many clues he'd observed from her behavior. "Thank you for coming, May, and for having the courage to tell us the truth." She looked up at him, so astonished that he wondered what she might have expected from him. Her courage became more evident; but something else also became evident. She was more afraid of something else than she was of coming back here and facing the consequences of being known as a thief, and the possible repercussions if he had been angry over learning of her association with the officers who seemed determined to find a scapegoat, no matter the cost.

Now that Tristan believed this young woman would tell him the truth, he tried to think of a way he might get information from her without appearing to be guilty. He pondered it only a moment before he said, "Lieutenant Wixom has been making a nuisance of himself around here, but I don't know if he's been as annoying to other people in the area as he has been to me. He seems to think that smuggling is going on around here, and for some reason someone here might be involved." Tristan heard the well-practiced innocence in his own voice. "I'm just wondering—given your association with these men—if you have any idea why they would even be suspicious of such a thing, and if anything has happened locally to warrant these suspicions."

May looked eager to help him and he hoped she might have *something* to say that could help him keep the lieutenant away for good. "All that I ever heard was that a local merchant—a cobbler I believe—had been somehow involved in passing goods from one place in town to another. He told the lieutenant about a rendezvous taking place somewhere nearby—but only because the lieutenant threatened him in some way; I'm not sure how. Bert and the others had come upon the rendezvous, but a little too late apparently, and they were never able to find the people involved. This cobbler gave them no other information, and he has moved away and is nowhere to be found." May took in a shaky breath. "I overheard Bert and the lieutenant talking about it, and they were angry over their lack of information. That's all I know."

"Thank you," Tristan said, so deeply relieved that it took great will-power not to let on. "I wouldn't want to think that anyone I know could be involved in such a thing, but I'm very glad to know that the lieutenant doesn't actually have any viable information."

May nodded and Tristan considered the state of her countenance once again. "I'm glad I could help," she said. "Perhaps that might in some way repay you for any trouble I've caused."

"May," Tristan said, again noting that she seemed afraid—but not of him, "might I ask what initiated the conversation yesterday when Bert told you he'd been taking advantage of you? You said he'd been kind and helpful; obviously his kindness toward you came to an end. Please tell us what happened."

Huge tears welled up in May's eyes and spilled down her face, but they fell in silence, and Tristan saw Olivia toss him a concerned glance.

"Please tell us," Olivia said.

May swallowed hard and took a deep breath before she was barely able to mutter, "I'm pregnant."

"Good heavens!" Tristan said, wanting to go and find this Bert and give him a bloody nose. The entire picture became clear. This naive young woman, left on her own, had fallen prey to a conniving and selfish officer who had only used her, hoping to get information she didn't have—so he made some up to perhaps justify his methods. Whether or not Lieutenant Wixom knew the information was false might never be known. But Tristan was relieved to know there was no proof out there—at least not from May—of anything untoward going on here. His relief went even deeper because of what she'd overheard fit perfectly with what had happened the night Olivia had been shot. But he now knew that the man who had betrayed the time and place of their rendezvous had not given up any other information, and he had left the area—presumably to avoid being pressured into giving up anything else that might incriminate his comrades in the cause.

Along with his relief, Tristan felt a deep compassion for this dear girl and her predicament. He knew the sensitivity of the issue could best be handled by Mrs. Higley, but it was up to him to make a decision, and he had no trouble knowing what to say.

"You must stay here so that we can keep you safe," he said, and May looked as if she might melt into a pool of tears and drown there. "I will let Olivia and Mrs. Higley see that you have what you need and that you are assigned tasks in the house that will not cause any difficulties with your pregnancy." He stood, an indication that he was concluding this conversation. "I trust we will never again have to worry about the problem that forced Mrs. Higley to let you go."

"Never!" May managed to say as she slipped into sobbing once again.

Tristan left the room, glad to leave May and her emotional state in Olivia's care. He felt the need to be alone and attempt to get all of this straight in his mind. His relief over the lack of evidence May had given to the officers was wrangling with his concerns for how all of this had impacted the young maid—and the ever-present hovering question of whether or not

Wixom might have intimidated anyone else into giving him viable information, or if he might even make something up just to appease his superiors. Either way, he had to wonder if there was still the possibility of danger.

Tristan decided to go outside alone while Olivia was helping May, but he passed a window and realized it was now raining—and none too lightly. He opted instead for the library and hurried there, but he opened the door to find Jack sitting on one of the sofas, reading a novel.

"Forgive me," Tristan said, not really wanting to talk to Jack right now—especially since the problems on his mind were all related to secrets he'd kept from Jack. "I'll leave you to your reading and—"

"Not at all," Jack said and put the book aside. "Come in. I thought you were going for a walk with Olivia."

"We were . . . interrupted," Tristan said, still standing near the door. "A problem with one of the maids. I've left Olivia and Mrs. Higley to take care of the details. I'll . . . see you later and we can—"

"What's going on?" Jack asked, his brow furrowed with concern. Tristan struggled to think of something to say to evade Jack's question and leave without raising any suspicion. But another moment of silence preceded Jack saying, "Something's wrong; I can tell. And it's not about one of the maids. You should know that you can talk to me about anything . . . that you can trust me."

"I do know that," Tristan said, wondering as he did if it would be better to just come clean with Jack and tell him everything. Perhaps Jack could help him make sense of all that had happened. And maybe he could even help Tristan find a solution. He closed the door and sat down, but he still wasn't certain if telling Jack was the right thing to do. He wasn't worried about Jack betraying him, but Tristan knew well enough that carrying the knowledge of treason could be a great burden—even if you weren't directly guilty.

"If it's something you're not comfortable talking about," Jack said, "I completely understand—and I respect that."

"Thank you," Tristan said. "I admit there are some things weighing on me, but I'm not sure if it would be in *your* best interest to tell you."

"Fair enough," Jack said. "Would you consider a distraction? There's something I've been wanting to talk to *you* about . . . because you've opened your home to me, and I believe I need to be completely honest with you. I don't want my staying here to ever become a problem. But, if this is a bad time . . . if you have too much on your mind already . . ."

Tristan's curiosity was piqued, and he couldn't deny that perhaps a distraction right now would be quite welcome. There was nothing he could do at present to solve his own concerns. "Go on," Tristan said, making himself more comfortable.

Jack sighed loudly and appeared to be nervous; Tristan wondered what could possibly be so serious.

"How do you feel about the war?" Jack asked. "About what's going on in the colonies and the position our king has taken?"

Tristan was stunned into a full minute of silence. It was not at all what he might have expected to hear Jack say, but he could guess where such questions might be leading. He finally answered honestly, "I admit to being somewhat . . . conflicted over the matter. Why?" Tristan recalled Jack saying he didn't want his staying here to become a problem. "Are you in some kind of trouble with the law?" he asked.

"Not as far as I know," Jack said, "because I don't think anyone knows what I did."

"What *did* you do?" Tristan asked, turning his head to look at him sideways as if that might better help him see his friend in a new light. "I won't tell a soul, Jack, but obviously it's something you think I should know."

"I *do* think you should know—for a number of reasons—but it's not easy to admit to, given the fact that I consider myself an honorable Englishman and I dearly love my country."

"Just tell me."

"I've committed treason, my friend," Jack said and blew out a long, slow breath as if verbalizing the statement had given him great relief. Tristan took in a sharp breath of surprise in response and just waited for him to go on. "I did something that would very much help the colonists' cause before I came home, and it could have very well cost many British lives. And yet I don't regret it. There; I've said it. I'm a traitor. I have no reason to believe that it will ever catch up with me, but if it does, I'm willing to pay the price. You're my only friend in all the world, Tristan, and you've practically made me a part of your family. I can't live here and not have you know the truth. I'm a traitor," he repeated. "Tell me if you want me to go and I will. I would understand, and I would never hold it against you."

Tristan took in what Jack was saying and could hardly believe the ironies of all that he'd been concealing from Jack. He felt stunned, but certainly not upset or angry. He just wasn't quite certain what to say.

# CHAPTER FOURTEEN

# THE CONFESSION

"WELL, SAY SOMETHING!" JACK INSISTED. "I've been trying to work up the nerve to tell you. Don't leave me hanging; not a very good pun under the circumstances."

"I would never betray you," Tristan said. "You should know that."

"I assumed, but it's nice to hear you say it."

Tristan stood up and started pacing. "What . . . did you do exactly? May I ask?"

"You may ask me anything you like, but I'd prefer that you sit down."

"Sorry," Tristan said and took his seat again.

"I'd prefer not to share details that might be used against us, so I'll keep it simple. As soon as I was relieved of my duties at the hospital, I discreetly acquired the means to come up with somewhat of a disguise, and I found my way to where I'd learned one of the leaders of a colonist regiment was located at that time, and I told him I had information I'd overheard from some of the arrogant British officers who had been in the hospital, healing. I led this officer to believe I'd been a patient, which would make it practically impossible to identify me. I gave him the information and I traveled a significant distance by night before ridding myself of the disguise, and I made it to port in time to board the ship on which I'd been assigned to sail home. And then I came here. That's all there is to know." Jack looked expectantly at Tristan for a reaction, but he still could only offer silence while this was settling in. "Say something, man. Are you disappointed in me? Disgusted? Do you want me to leave, or—"

"None of those things, I can assure you," Tristan said. "I confess that the temptation to do something similar crossed my mind more than once when I overheard the way those self-indulgent, egotistical swine bragged about the way they'd invaded villages and burned down homes. I thought many times that this was not the cause I'd signed up for; and even *if* the cause were worthy, this was not the means to go about executing duty and honor. I tried to just keep my head down and do what was expected of me, but I felt ill at ease many times during my years in the colonies. I suppose I'm trying to say that I understand why you did what you did. I hate the idea of innocent people perishing on either side . . ."

"As do I," Jack said solemnly.

"But . . . I can't say that I agree with Britain's stand in the argument behind this war, and I certainly don't agree with how the king's wishes are being carried out."

As the words came out of his mouth, it occurred to Tristan that he'd never spoken them aloud to Olivia. When he'd first discovered her involvement in treasonous activities, he'd told her he didn't agree with what she'd been doing, but he would do all he could to help keep her safe and to protect his household. And he'd done that. But never once had he and Olivia actually discussed their views on the matter—at least not enough for him to admit to the fact that he felt conflicted, and he had since before he'd returned home. Perhaps his own idea of needing to strictly adhere to duty and honor had kept him from being able to admit—even to himself—the full truth of such an internal conflict. But Jack's confession had spurred his own into the open.

"I can't tell you," Jack said, "what it means to me to know that you understand—at least to some degree. Even if you never would have engaged in any treasonous actions, the fact that you have some comprehension of why I did it is important to me."

"Jack," Tristan leaned forward and put his forearms on his thighs, "there's something that *I* need to tell *you*." He looked directly at his friend, now knowing that it was right to tell him exactly what was going on and why. He took a deep breath and let the words out on the wake of his exhale. "Members of my household have been involved in smuggling goods to the colonists; Olivia is one of them."

"Good heavens!" Jack said, sounding more amused than concerned. "And you came home to *that* as well as finding out that your wife had died giving birth to another man's child?"

"Yes," Tristan said. "Yes, I did. I've been wondering if I should tell you, because I fear that a certain overly tenacious officer seems intent on remaining suspicious of our household—even though I have no reason to believe he has any actual evidence. I've wondered if you might be able to help me find a solution—or perhaps I just wanted someone to talk to about it; someone I could trust."

"Well, this is indeed ironic," Jack said with a little smirk. "Tell me everything you know; surely we can find a way to set things straight."

Jack's confidence inspired Tristan to be able to tell him the entire story from the beginning. Jack laughed to hear about Olivia dressing in a man's clothes in order to be directly involved in a smuggling operation. But he was horrified to learn that Olivia had been shot. He was impressed with hearing of how Tristan had removed the bullet—thanks to the instruments and the training that Jack had given him—and he was even more impressed with the guise of Olivia's illness and her subsequent sprained ankle in order to keep the majority of the household from knowing the truth.

Tristan brought Jack up to the present by telling him of his every encounter with Lieutenant Wixom, and the most recent developments regarding May, the young maid he had just rehired in order to see that she was cared for and protected.

"It's my opinion," Jack said, "that if this lieutenant had any real evidence he would have brought it forward a long time ago. He sounds like a dog with a bone he doesn't want to let go of, and we've encountered many with the same mentality in the past."

"We have indeed," Tristan said.

"It's my belief that we need to make it clear to the lieutenant that he doesn't actually *have* a bone, and he's not only wasting his time but could be in a great deal of trouble for allowing one of his men to manipulate and take advantage of your maid. Her coming back here is the perfect opportunity to act on putting this man in his place."

"Do you not think that could bring suspicion back on us?" Tristan asked.

"That's the way a guilty man would think," Jack said.

"But we *are* guilty!"

"And yet . . . you should be thinking as if you are not. From what you've told me, you've done well at behaving completely innocently in your conversations with the lieutenant thus far. But tell me honestly, Tristan, if you were not concerned about being found out, how would you react to what young May told you today?"

"I'd be furious," he admitted. "I *am* furious!"

"And yet, I believe your fear is clouding your fury. This young woman has come to you for help, and she has given you good cause to be upset about the conduct of these officers who have been loitering like vultures in the area for many weeks. We have both served in His Majesty's army. We both know what might happen if their superior officer caught wind of such behavior. Even the threat of it might serve us well."

"What are you suggesting?" Tristan asked. "That the next time the lieutenant shows up, we threaten him with—"

"Oh, I don't think we should wait for him to show up," Jack said zealously. "I am suggesting we go and find him right now and see this matter settled once and for all."

"You're serious," Tristan said, a little breathless.

"Completely serious."

"And you believe it will work?"

"If I didn't, I wouldn't be suggesting it. I would never suggest doing anything that could put you or your family in danger."

Tristan thought about it for a moment and added something he'd overlooked saying before. "I need to clarify that . . . it's mandatory that my father never knows about any of this. He is devoutly British and loyal to the crown. It would break his heart to know what's been going on here in his own home. One of the blessings of his being bedridden is that it's easy to keep him from seeing or hearing anything that might upset him. I prefer him to die without ever knowing any of this."

"I completely understand," Jack said. He came to his feet and added, "You know, I've been thinking that with as many days as I've been here, you've not yet taken me into town for a drink. Are you ashamed of me, dear friend?"

Despite how nervous he felt, Tristan chuckled when he realized Jack intended to go here and now to the pub where he knew the officers spent a great deal of time, likely hoping to eavesdrop on the townspeople enough to finally hear incriminating information. He stood and said, "I took you to church with me, didn't I?"

"So you did," Jack said. "But I would still like a tour of the town."

"Let me find Olivia and make certain everything with May is taken care of."

"Certainly," Jack said. "I'll meet you at the stables."

Tristan tried to think of the most logical place to find Olivia, but he walked the halls of his home far too long while his mind reiterated his conversation with Jack and the vast gamut of emotions that had followed and seemed to be trying to catch up with him. He discovered that Olivia was not in her rooms, or with Winnie, or his father. She was not in the laundry or the kitchen, and the continuing rain made it highly unlikely that she had gone out. He finally went to Mrs. Higley's little office, which was near the kitchens, to ask if she might know where Olivia had gone—given that he knew Olivia had intended to take May to visit with the housekeeper. He found Mrs. Higley there with May—who was still crying—but Olivia was absent.

"Do you know where she's gone?" Tristan asked.

"She went to find you," Mrs. Higley reported.

"Grand," Tristan said with sarcasm, "I've been looking all over the house for *her.*" He sighed. "Could you let her know that I've gone into town with Jack and I'm not certain when we'll return?"

"Of course, sir," she said, and Tristan hurried out to the stables, knowing he'd kept Jack waiting much longer than he'd anticipated. He entered the stables, surprised to see Olivia visiting with Jack, while distant noises made it evident there was at least one stable hand working nearby.

"Hello," Tristan said and took Olivia's outstretched hand, "I've been looking all over for you."

"And I you," she said as he kissed her brow.

"And here you both are!" Jack declared as if the Red Sea had parted.

Tristan smiled at his friend and said to Olivia, "How did it go with May? I saw that she was with Mrs. Higley—and still very upset."

"Yes, she's upset—understandably so—but I think she's enormously relieved that we're willing to take her back. She was surely terrified of being out on the streets and pregnant."

Olivia glanced toward Jack, as if to question how much they should be saying in front of him. Tristan assured her, "I told him what's going on. It's all right."

"What exactly do you mean by *what's going on?*" she asked lightly in an attempt to disguise the concern he sensed.

"Who is here?" Tristan asked, looking more deeply into the stables.

"Only Wagner," Olivia reported.

"Well, then," Tristan said, "now is as good a time as any to let you know that I told Jack everything."

"Everything?" Olivia echoed, no longer trying to hide her concerns.

Jack spoke up quickly, keeping his voice quiet. "You can trust me," he said. "He only told me after I admitted to him that I'd committed treason in the colonies before returning home."

"You?" Olivia asked, overtly astonished.

"I could ask the same of *you*," Jack said with a little smirk.

"So you could," Olivia said, looking at Jack as if to acquaint herself with this new facet of his character. "It seems we all have much to talk about."

"Indeed we do," Tristan said. "But it will have to wait. Jack and I are going into town—to the pub. I'm not sure how long we'll be gone. I'll explain later."

"Explain what?" Olivia asked with suspicion. "What explanation is required for going to the pub?"

Tristan looked at Jack, who nodded in silent encouragement. He turned back to Olivia and said, "We're going to find the lieutenant and talk to him. I intend to let him know how disgusted I am about the way May has been taken advantage of, and Jack believes if we handle this right, it will put the matter to rest—once and for all."

"Or bring him down on us more fully!" Olivia said with alarm.

"It will be all right," Jack said, genuinely calm.

"You mustn't worry." Tristan took hold of Olivia's shoulders. "We've talked it through; we know what we're doing. Our innocence is as firmly in place as it ever was."

"Our *feigned* innocence, you mean," Olivia countered.

"If the lieutenant had any evidence, he would have come forward with it by now," Tristan said. "We just want to give him good reason to let it go and to leave the area."

"Everything will be fine," Jack asserted, once again the calm voice of reason.

Olivia sighed loudly and gave both men a hard stare. "Very well. But please be careful."

"We will," Tristan said. "You mustn't worry."

"Easier said than done," Olivia said and hurried out of the stables as if she didn't want to talk about it anymore.

"Everything *will* be fine," Jack repeated to Tristan.

"I pray you are right," Tristan said, trying not to take on Olivia's concern.

Tristan and Jack said little on their way into town since they were riding quickly in order to get there and get out of the rain as soon as possible. They tied off their horses and entered the pub, laughing with relief to get out of the downpour, which helped put Tristan into the proper

frame of mind to behave as if he'd simply come here with a friend to relax
and share a drink. They removed their wet coats and hats and hung them
near the door along with those of other guests, although this wasn't a very
busy time of day so the pub was fairly quiet. A quick scan of the room
made it clear that no military officers were present. Tristan hoped the
lieutenant would show up before too long; he wanted to get this over with.
He wasn't certain whether he wanted to encounter Bert; he felt so angry
on May's behalf that he feared he might actually do the man harm, which
surely wouldn't help their situation—not to mention he knew it certainly
wasn't the Christian way to respond to his anger.

Tristan led the way to a table that would give them a good view. He
sat where he could see the majority of the room, and Jack sat across from
him in a chair that gave him a perfect view of the door so that he could
see anyone who came in. They ordered the usual ale that was a specialty
of the house and sipped their drinks slowly, wanting to make them last.
The two men talked quietly, jumping from one topic to another. Since no
one was sitting nearby, it was possible to talk freely and not be overheard,
although they still kept their voices down. They discussed again their
justified reasons for confronting Lieutenant Wixom so that they were
adequately prepared to do what needed to be done. But they also talked
about Walter's progress and their mutual agreement that it was a blessing
for both of them to have Jack living in Tristan's home. But Tristan was
surprised when Jack started asking questions about Winnie.

"She's been with Olivia for . . . well, for many years," Tristan said.
"Long before I ever came to know them. She's a fine woman. Olivia has
told me many times that she could never manage without her. They're
very close friends, but she's also stood by Olivia through many hardships."

"Including treason?" Jack asked.

"Yes, including that," Tristan said. "Why?"

"I like her," Jack said without hesitation or embarrassment. "We've
shared some conversations in our comings and goings with caring for your
father, and of course I've had plenty of opportunity to observe her since
she's among the exclusive club that shares meals with Walter in his room."
Jack held up his glass and smiled. "I consider myself privileged to be a
member of that club."

"You've certainly earned it," Tristan said, awed by how much his father
had improved in the days since Jack had arrived. But he wanted to stick
to the topic. "When you say that you *like* Winnie, do you mean that the

two of you are becoming friends, or . . . are you implying something . . . romantic?"

Tristan chuckled as Jack looked down and actually blushed. "Both," he admitted, and he chuckled as well. He looked back up at Tristan and the rosy hue of his skin dissipated. "It's been a very long time since I've felt this way about a woman. I've asked myself if it's simply a matter of convenience . . . that we are both unattached and spending so much time together. But it's more than that. I believe that no matter where I might have met her, I would have come to feel this way."

"That's remarkable," Tristan said, laughing softly at the evidence of divine intervention being at work in Jack's coming to live in his home. "Does she know how you feel?"

"I haven't *said* anything; I've felt the need to give the matter more thought and not be impulsive. But I'm certain she suspects, and I believe she feels something as well."

"Then you should talk to her; you should court her."

"And if it doesn't work out?" Jack asked. "Then our living in the same home could become terribly awkward."

"And that's something you should talk about before you make a mutual decision of whether or not to officially court her. You're both mature, reasonable adults. I'm certain you can work it out."

Jack sighed and got a tender, distant look in his eyes, which abruptly changed to something dark and perhaps angry.

"What?" Tristan demanded quietly.

"Three officers just came in. I assume they are the ones we need to speak to."

Tristan glanced discreetly over his shoulder. "That's them," he affirmed.

"Then let's get this over with," Jack said and took a hefty swallow of his ale before he stood up and set his eyes upon the lieutenant as if he were aiming a rifle at him. Tristan took a deep breath in an effort to calm his pounding heart and put the proper attitude in place. He stood and followed Jack to the table where the three officers had barely sat down. He quickly rehearsed the plan that Jack had come up with and knew exactly what he needed to say and how he needed to say it. With any luck, this wouldn't take very long, then all of this could be forever behind them.

"Lieutenant Wixom," Tristan said and put his hands on the table so that he could lean over and look him in the eye. "We were hoping to find you here."

"And here I am," the lieutenant said with his familiar arrogant persona.

"I'm wondering which one of your two lapdogs here is responsible for compromising the young maid from my household." Tristan saw one of the officers flinch slightly and turned to glare at *him*. "So you're Bert, I presume." The officer said nothing, but guilt consumed his expression. "Is this an approved tactic of your military assignment, I wonder, to seduce an innocent young woman, lie to her about love and offer implications of commitment and security, only to try and get information out of her, which you then twist and distort with some perverse effort to throw suspicion upon my household?" Bert didn't move, didn't speak, and Tristan pounded a fist on the table and shouted, "Is it?"

All three officers flinched, and Tristan glared at each of them before he stared again at Bert, glad to know that every person in the room was now aware of the encounter taking place. That was exactly how he wanted it.

When seconds of silence still didn't provoke a response from any of the officers, it was evident they had no justifiable defense—and they all obviously knew what Tristan was referring to.

"And what will you do now?" Tristan asked Bert. "Slither out of town and leave this young woman to face the consequences of pregnancy on her own?"

"Pregnancy?" Wixom countered; he obviously hadn't known about *that*.

"Yes, Lieutenant." Tristan turned back toward him. "You and your warped determination to find something that doesn't exist has incited at least one of these two men to behave in very unseemly ways. And yet for all of his efforts at seduction and deception, he still discovered nothing—because there is nothing to be found. But the result is still the same. This young woman's life is forever changed, and there is no one to make certain she is cared for except *me*."

"And I'm certain," Jack finally spoke up from where he'd been standing a step or two behind Tristan, "that your superiors would be very interested in knowing how much time you've been wasting here trying to find something that simply doesn't exist. And your methods would surely come under scrutiny."

"Who are *you*?" Wixom asked.

"It doesn't matter who I am. All you need to know about me is that I too served faithfully in the colonies, and I also have connections to parliament. I know well enough how to find out who gave you your orders and why. And I will climb the chain of command until I make certain that you cretins are justly punished for the unethical and appalling way you have misrepresented the uniforms you wear."

"You wouldn't!" the lieutenant insisted, and Tristan relished the fear in his eyes that he was trying to hide.

"Oh, I would!" Jack said. "And I will! Leave town by morning and forget that you ever came here, or by noon I will be on my way to London to begin a quest that will end with your courts-martial, and I will make certain that young May is there to testify as to your deplorable means of conspiring to manipulate false information." Jack hesitated for a long moment before he demanded, "What's it going to be?"

"It's your word against mine," Wixom said in a tone that barely concealed his defeat.

"Is it?" Jack countered loudly enough to reverberate through the eerily silent pub as everyone was apparently listening.

None of the officers spoke. They obviously had no defense. Tristan said, "Your accusations of treason have no bearing in this community. The three of you are like snakes trying to incite fear and distrust when there is nothing here to be found. These are good people who are just trying to live their lives in peace, and your presence here will not be tolerated any longer."

"Hear hear," the innkeeper bellowed from where he was leaning against the wall nearby, his arms folded over his broad chest. "I've been wantin' t' kick them out for weeks now. I think I've had about enough o' their pretendin' t' be all high and mighty. They're just rats. And I generally just shoots rats when they show up around here."

Several male voices resounded with words of agreement, and the three officers looked suddenly nervous, realizing they were vastly outnumbered and some form of riot might break out. Wixom stood and brushed his hands over his coat and lifted his chin. "I believe we will gather our things and be on our way. I see no reason to stay here and deal with this kind of ridiculous defiance."

"What an excellent idea," Jack said, and a round of applause rose from the room.

The officers went to their rooms on the upper floor to get their things, and they scurried back down and out the door within minutes, with a few of the town's merchants—all strong and burly fellows—following behind them to make certain they immediately left town. Tristan and Jack were suddenly surrounded by the men of the village, all offering to buy them drinks and congratulating them on *finally doing what needed to be done*. Tristan was amazed to hear how many people had been harassed by the officers and how long it had been going on. Those who were present told stories of those who were not, chronicling the appalling behavior of Lieutenant Wixom and his lapdogs. It seemed to be the universal opinion that no one in the area could have ever committed treason, that smuggling would be impossible to carry out without obvious evidence, and that the entire issue had all been a bunch of nonsense. Relief washed over Tristan as the worry and concern he'd felt ever since he'd discovered evidence of smuggling completely vanished. He felt impressed by how careful the people involved had been at covering their tracks. And since they were all officially done with the smuggling business, the matter was now put to rest.

When Tristan and Jack finally left the pub, it was no longer raining.

"Connections to parliament?" Tristan asked with a chuckle as they mounted their horses.

"So I lied," Jack said. "But I promise to put my dishonest and treasonous ways behind me."

"I'm with you on that," Tristan agreed, and they rode home more slowly, recounting their performance and its positive results.

"Who would have guessed?" Jack said as the house was coming into view. "Back when I was patching you up from that bullet you took, who would have guessed we would both end up traitors?"

"It certainly wasn't part of my plan for the future," Tristan said with a chuckle before he added more seriously, "but now that we're here, I'm actually glad to be where I am; I'm glad to understand the colonists' cause and to know that in some small way I might have helped their efforts. I'm proud to be an Englishman, but I do not agree with the king's methods or motives in this regard, and I'm grateful to have a friend with whom I can speak freely of such things. In my heart I hope the colonists succeed . . . that they can gain their independence."

"I agree," Jack said. "And I believe they will. I just hope that their fight for freedom doesn't go on much longer."

"Amen," Tristan said, and they hurried on when Jack commented on how late it was.

Tristan wondered as he went into the house if Olivia might have been worried about him. He went to her room and knocked very quietly on the door, thinking of the time when she'd been recovering from a bullet wound, and the hours he'd spent at her bedside, praying for all of this to be over. And now it was.

Olivia pulled open the door and immediately wrapped her arms around him, exhaling loudly with relief. "I was afraid you'd been arrested . . . or worse."

"I'm fine," he said. "Everything is fine." He hugged her tightly then took hold of her shoulders. "It's over, Olivia. It's really over."

"How?" she asked, her eyes wide with hope.

"Let's sit down," he said, and they went into her sitting room and closed the doors so as not to be overheard.

Tristan started at the beginning and recounted his earlier conversation with Jack, and his gratitude for Jack's knowledge and perspective that had helped Tristan realize that May's tragic experience was the perfect excuse to put an end to all of this. He told her everything about their encounter with the officers, who had hastily left town, and of the resounding support of every man who had been in the pub, which had seemed a fair representation of the entire community.

Olivia shared his joy and amazement. She wept in his arms as she absorbed the full depth of her relief at having all of this behind them. When she quieted down, Tristan said, "There's something I need to say; something that I didn't fully realize until I was speaking to Jack earlier."

"What is it?" she asked, lifting her head from his shoulder to look at him squarely.

"When I first discovered your involvement in this cause, I told you I didn't agree with it but I would support you in order to help keep you safe."

"And you have!" she insisted.

"I've done my best," he said. "But what you need to know is that . . . I don't entirely disagree with the cause. Looking back, I can now see that I felt conflicted even while I was in the colonies, but perhaps I was afraid to admit it—even to myself. I want you to know that I understand why you did what you did—even if you've still never told me exactly how you became involved in all of this to begin with."

"One day," she said with a smile, "I'll tell you everything. For now, it doesn't matter."

"No, it doesn't matter," he said. "It's behind us. But you need to know that I sincerely hope the colonists succeed. And Jack feels the same way."

"I'm *very* glad to know that," Olivia said. "Even if we must carefully keep our opinions to ourselves and mind our business in order to remain safe, I'm glad to know that our thinking is the same."

"So am I," he said and kissed her. "And now with all of this nonsense out of the way, we can just enjoy the fact that we are getting married soon."

"Indeed we are," she said and kissed him again.

"Speaking of romance," Tristan said, "Jack confessed to me that he's rather taken with Winnie."

"Really?" Olivia said with a conspiratorial smile. "That's very interesting . . . especially since Winnie has admitted to me that she's rather taken with Jack."

Tristan chuckled. "Wouldn't it be marvelous if they decided to marry and stay here forever?"

"That *would* be marvelous," Olivia said and put her head on Tristan's shoulder. "I love you," she added.

"Oh, and I love you!" he said, feeling happier than he'd ever imagined possible.

\* \* \* \* \*

The following day, everything appeared completely normal on the surface, but Olivia was overcome by how much had changed since yesterday, and how differently she felt. When bedtime came, Olivia sat on the edge of her bed, hesitant to get into her nightgown. She felt the need to speak with Walter and wanted to do so privately. She knew from experience that the best time to do that was just before he went to sleep. But she didn't want to alert Tristan to her going to his father's room. They had shared supper with Walter as they usually did, and each time she'd met Tristan's eyes she'd been pleasantly reminded that the danger and worry was finally behind them. It still felt too good to be true, but she felt a peaceful calm in her heart that she'd not felt since the day that Tristan had discovered her illegal doings. When Lawrence had declared that it was time for him to help Walter get ready for bed, Olivia had pleaded exhaustion herself as opposed to spending some time with Tristan as she usually did. He'd kissed her good night and she'd come to her room. But now she needed to get back to Walter's room unnoticed before he fell asleep. She didn't want to wait even another day to tell him what he needed to know.

Olivia left her room and moved carefully through the long halls to Walter's room without the use of a lamp or candle, not wanting to be noticed. She found Lawrence making certain that Walter was comfortable, but he'd not yet given Walter his nighttime medicine. It was far from the first time that Olivia had shown up at this time of day, and Lawrence seemed pleased to see her—as did Walter. Lawrence left so they could talk privately, and Olivia was left in charge of seeing that Walter got his medicine before she would extinguish the lamps in his room so that he could go to sleep.

Walter smiled at Olivia as she sat on the bed beside him and took his hand. "There's something I need to tell you," she said and saw the concern in his expression, but she knew she just had to forge ahead and get it over with.

* * * * *

Tristan went to his father's room for breakfast—as he usually did—and he was met by Lawrence at the door who told him that Walter was feeling tired since he'd had a restless night.

"Is he all right?" Tristan asked.

"Yes, fine," Lawrence said with a smile. "He's just resting. I've already told Olivia and she asked me to tell you that she'll be in the breakfast room."

"Very well," Tristan said. "Tell my father I'll see him later, then."

"I will," Lawrence said and quietly closed the door.

Tristan tried not to feel uneasy over this unusual situation and focused instead on seeing Olivia. It didn't matter that he'd seen her just before she'd gone to bed last night; he always felt better when he was with her. He found her in the breakfast room, along with Winnie and Jack. The three of them had just begun eating, and he quickly kissed Olivia in greeting before he sat down to join them and said, "I don't recall my father ever not being up to seeing me in the mornings. I admit that I feel concerned."

"I checked on him earlier," Jack said. "He's fine. It's possible that he's become so accustomed to the medicine he takes that helps him sleep that it's not working as well as it used to. I'll keep a close eye on him, Tristan; I promise."

"Thank you," Tristan said, feeling better.

The four of them shared a delightful conversation over breakfast, while Tristan enjoyed watching the interaction between Jack and Winnie—now that he knew they were both interested in each other. But more than that he enjoyed the undeniable relief he could see in Olivia's eyes. A burden had been lifted from both their shoulders, and he could feel the lightness in himself as much as he could see it in the woman he loved. Between himself and Olivia, they had each spoken privately to everyone involved to give them the latest update, and now it was officially put to rest. Now all they had to do was take care of his father and anticipate their wedding day.

By lunchtime, Walter was feeling better and they all ate lunch with him in his room as usual. Tristan noted that every day his father was becoming more able to form some simple words—even though it took some effort—and Tristan was becoming more able to understand what he was trying to say. The improved communication between them was one of many reasons Tristan felt cause to hope.

After lunch, they left Walter to take his nap and Olivia insisted they needed to meet with Mrs. Higley—who was expecting them—to go over their wedding plans and make certain that everything was under control.

"As long as I can marry you," he said, "I don't really care about the flavor of the cake."

"Perhaps not," she said, smiling brightly, "but you have to offer your opinions nevertheless."

"Then I concede," he said but stopped her in the hallway to kiss her with as much passion as he dared until they were married. Olivia laughed softly and kissed him again before they moved on to their meeting with Mrs. Higley, which ended up taking most of the afternoon. By the time they were done, they knew Walter would be awake again and probably finished with his afternoon exercises with Jack. They went together to his room to visit until supper and found him looking rather grim.

"Is something wrong?" Tristan asked, taking a quick glance at the other people seated in the room. Winnie and Lawrence also looked rather grim. Jack looked completely ignorant of what the problem might be. At least that meant it wasn't likely a medical concern.

"I need . . . to . . . tell you . . . something," Walter said, his words barely discernible, his focus on Tristan.

"Is this private?" Jack asked, coming to his feet.

"No," Walter said and Jack sat back down. "Want . . . you all . . . here." It was becoming increasingly evident that Walter had come to trust Jack completely through all the time they'd shared and the help Jack had given him. He was not only Tristan's friend; he had become a friend to everyone else in the room as well.

Olivia took a chair, and Tristan sat on the edge of the bed beside his father. "What is it?" Tristan asked and was surprised to have Walter hand him a letter.

Noting Tristan's curiosity, Walter glanced to Lawrence, as if to give him a cue to speak. "He asked me to help him write that this morning," Lawrence said and Tristan now knew that Walter *hadn't* been overly tired this morning. He felt a chill rush over his shoulders as it seemed that there was some kind of conspiracy taking place.

"Read it," Walter said.

Tristan unfolded the three pieces of paper that had been folded together and glanced down to see his name at the beginning of the letter. He was about to ask if his father wanted him to read it silently or aloud when words from the first couple of sentences jumped into his mind like heavy stones being thrown into a still pond. At the quickening of his heart, Tristan reread the words, expecting to realize that he'd mixed up the meaning in his mind. But there it was, written in his father's hand, clear as daylight: *You need to know that all of this is my fault. I am the source of treason in this house.*

"What?" Tristan demanded, looking at his father, his heart pounding so hard he felt sure the others in the room could hear it.

"Read it!" Walter insisted in his strongest possible slurred voice.

Tristan looked back down at the letter and noticed the papers quivering as a result of the sudden trembling of his hands. He reread those first two sentences and felt his entire belief about his father's devotion to king and country come tumbling down around him. He recalled in a flash many pieces of conversations he'd had with his father or had overheard where it had been unmistakably clear that he was against this colonist rebellion. He just couldn't believe this was true. A quick glance at the others in the room showed him that everyone but Jack already knew what was in the letter. Olivia was dabbing at her eyes but looking at the floor.

Knowing the letter was meant to explain, he forced himself to keep reading. He wondered if he should read aloud for Jack's benefit, but he couldn't bring himself to attach his voice to what he was learning. He was astonished to read that his father's dear and trusted friend Mr. Cornaby had come to Walter not long after Tristan's departure with ideas about this colonist revolution that had begun to make Walter see that he didn't necessarily agree with the reasons for this war. In spite of his deep concern for his son, Walter had become involved with a carefully laid out operation to assist the colonists without ever allowing any evidence to be traced back to them. Walter had engaged a few men to help him, men he trusted completely, men who had worked for him for many years. And the smuggling had begun. When Walter's health had suddenly declined, he had reluctantly turned to Olivia to take his place. He trusted her completely, and she had been eager to do anything to help ease his burdens. Her idea to dress as a man had left them both confident that her identity would never be discovered, and Walter had sincerely believed that she would never be in any danger. Lawrence had been aware of Walter's involvement from the beginning, due to the close relationship they'd always shared. And Winnie had been involved for as long as Olivia had been. Mrs. Higley had known from the start, and she had been a great champion of the colonists' cause. And through it all, their greatest concern had always been Tristan's safety; they had all hoped and prayed that he would return home and they would never have to face the guilt of wondering if their commission of treason might have aided a cause that could have taken his life.

Walter concluded the letter with a firm declaration that he had no regrets over his convictions—except for the worry it had brought upon those involved through recent months, and most especially Olivia's suffering from the bullet wound that might have killed her if Tristan hadn't known how to help. Walter had known all along that Olivia had not been ill. The servants who had been aware of the truth had been quietly communicating to him all that had been taking place. Walter hadn't wanted Tristan to be disappointed in him, and he'd feared that it would come between them and damage what little time they might have left together as father and son. But now, after all that had happened, Walter had come to the decision that he couldn't pass from this life with such a secret between them. And he certainly didn't want any secrets between Tristan and Olivia as they began their life together. Walter wrote that he felt like a coward now for not having just told Tristan the truth once he'd learned that Tristan had discovered what was going on. He apologized profusely for any grief he may have caused for Tristan and everyone else involved, and he pleaded for Tristan's forgiveness.

Tristan finished reading the letter and stared at that word *forgiveness* for a full minute or more before he looked up at his father to see his face wet with tears. It was easy for Tristan to say, "Of course I forgive you." Walter's tears increased and his countenance glowed with relief even while his eyes still showed concern and a worried expectation. When Tristan realized he had no idea what to say next, he stood and added, "I . . . need some time . . . to . . . I don't know. I just . . . need some time."

He left the room with the letter in his hand and without looking at anyone. He just needed to be alone to allow all of this to catch up with his limited ability to comprehend something that he'd never imagined possible. He figured that the others could fill Jack in on what the letter contained if they chose to.

Tristan went to the library since it was a room where he knew he could be comfortable, but he also knew that it was the first place anyone would look for him, so he locked the door before he sank onto one of the sofas and hung his head, squeezing his eyes closed while he prayed to be able to understand all of this. He finally found it possible to read the letter again. And again. For an hour, or maybe two, he sorted all of this new information into everything he already knew—and what he'd believed. In the end he was surprised to feel a warm peace settle over him. While he was astonished to realize how dramatically his father's beliefs had changed and how much he'd been involved in the difficulties they'd been facing, the conclusion was that he and his father were of the same mind in regard to this issue. Walter had not wanted any secrets between them, but did he know that Tristan had also dramatically changed his beliefs? That he too was a traitor—not just in his actions as he'd fought to protect Olivia and his household, but also in his mind and in his heart. And he felt a deep gratitude for all that Olivia had done to support her father and try to ease his concerns through all that had been going on. She truly was an amazing woman, and he was glad to know that they could move forward with their lives, completely free of these burdens.

He was just considering what he might say to his father to set his mind at ease when a knock at the door startled him. "It's Jack. May I come in?"

Tristan stood to unlock the door and open it.

"Are you all right?" Jack asked.

"Better than I expected to be," Tristan said. "Did they tell you what—"

"They told me everything," Jack said. "If you ask me, it's all rather remarkable."

"It is, isn't it," Tristan stated, overcome again with that warm peace. "I need to talk to my father before he goes to sleep."

"Yes, I believe you do," Jack said with a smile. "And you missed supper. Olivia told me to tell you she would eat with you after you've spoken to your father." His smile broadened. "Funny how she can predict you so accurately."

"Or remarkable," Tristan said and held out his hand toward Jack, who took it firmly. "Thank you, my friend—for everything."

"I didn't do anything," Jack said. "I'm just . . . here . . . relishing in treason with the rest of you." He chuckled.

"Exactly," Tristan said and chuckled too before he headed up the stairs to tell his father how very proud he was to be the son of such a fine man. They could never publicly declare their beliefs, but as a family they were united in a quiet hope for a better world for those who were fighting for their rightful freedom.

TRISTAN AND OLIVIA WERE MARRIED on a cloudless day with skies of brilliant blue. Olivia found it difficult not to cry when Tristan spoke his vows with such conviction and when he kissed her to seal their marriage. She could see his love for her glowing in his eyes, and the years of believing that Tristan would never be hers vanished completely, leaving nothing behind but a deep gratitude for having been given a second chance.

Walter had a seat in a comfortable chair that had been placed at the front of the guests in attendance. Olivia stole a couple of glances at him during the ceremony and was pleased to see how happy he appeared. Having him here for this monumental occasion in all their lives meant more than she could ever put into words, and she knew that Tristan felt the same.

Tristan's sisters and their families were also present, and even though Tristan wasn't close with them, she knew it meant a great deal to him to have them there. The effort it had taken them to travel from their distant homes expressed their love and support of him as he stepped into a new season of life.

Every member of the household was also present—right down to every maid and houseboy. They all worked hard to keep everything functioning from day to day, and Olivia knew that Tristan was glad to be able to provide a good living for these people. They both agreed that everyone should be a part of this great celebration. May was among them and looking well; she'd made some new friends among the servants, and Mrs. Higley had taken over her care like a mother hen.

There were also guests from the community, people that had known Tristan and his father for many years. It was a fairly large crowd, but the ballroom where they'd had rows of chairs set up was huge, and it looked especially lovely with the flowers and ribbons that had been added as decor to evoke the proper mood for a wedding.

Throughout the celebrations afterward, Olivia's happiness felt too enormous to hold. Tristan kept her at his side while they visited with well-wishers and loved ones. Walter appeared to be enjoying himself thoroughly. Lawrence was remaining near him to be certain he had what he needed, and he was helping Walter communicate with people who were not accustomed to his new way of speaking. But Walter didn't appear to be at all self-conscious. He'd come to accept his malady for what it was and had progressed beyond any embarrassment. Overall he was doing well and had more than once expressed how grateful he was to be alive and to be able to attend his son's wedding.

Olivia couldn't help noticing how Jack and Winnie were hovering close together continually, holding hands and often whispering to each other. Now that everyone knew they were courting, they all felt certain it was only a matter of time before they were married. Olivia was overjoyed with such an outcome; she wanted Winnie to be as happy as she was now, and she knew that Jack was a good man.

When Tristan and Olivia finally found a few minutes to themselves, they fed each other wedding cake and both kept laughing for no apparent reason. Their happiness just couldn't be contained. For only a moment, Olivia considered all they had been through, but she quickly banished any thoughts of Muriel and treason and danger. They had come past all of that, and the future held nothing but the hope of a good life.

\* \* \* \* \*

Walter lived more than a year beyond Tristan and Olivia's marriage, and he frequently declared that it had been one of the best years of his life. Jack took very good care of him and helped keep him healthy as far as it was possible. Tristan's dear friend spent time with Walter every day except for the week he was away on his honeymoon with Winnie. During that time Tristan took over Jack's duties and enjoyed the extra time with his father.

Before Walter finally passed away, he held his grandson in his arms and wept over the miracle. The boy would be named after him, and he was tangible evidence of the love that Tristan and Olivia shared.

Not long after Walter's passing, word came that Dr. Brown had suffered an onset of apoplexy—with very similar results to that which had afflicted Walter. The irony was almost laughable—considering how unkind and dismissive he had been toward Walter—except that they all knew how difficult it could be, and as a household they agreed to pray for this man despite how much they disliked him.

The timing seemed evidence that once again God's hand was in their lives. Now that Jack no longer needed to care for Walter, it was easy for him to officially take on the work of being a much-needed doctor in the community. Word quickly spread that Jack Barburry was available as a physician, and he had no trouble acquiring patients. Jack discussed with Tristan the possibility of moving into town, but Tristan very much wanted Jack to stay and live under the same roof. Considering how much he enjoyed Jack's friendship, he feared he would rarely see him if he lived elsewhere. And neither Jack nor Tristan could fathom separating Olivia and Winnie. Tristan insisted that the house was so huge that it was ridiculous for Jack and Winnie to leave. A room in the manor was designated as a clinic and quickly transformed to suit that purpose. Since the manor was some distance from the village, Jack found a young man in need of employment who agreed to be his messenger. Word quickly spread through the area that if anyone was in need of urgent medical care—any time of the day or night—they could go to this young man's home and he would quickly ride to the manor and fetch the doctor. This system fell swiftly into place and worked well. Jack was delivering babies, stitching wounds, and treating illnesses. And Tristan often accompanied him as an unofficial apprentice. He wasn't certain yet whether he wanted to take his wife and child to London while he went through official medical training, but in the meantime, he knew that he could learn a great deal from Jack, who had already proven to be an excellent teacher. Tristan enjoyed feeling useful in this way, and he easily managed overseeing the estate and also working with Jack in a way that they both enjoyed.

Winnie gave birth to a boy ten months following her marriage to Jack, and everyone in the house was thrilled to have another child under the roof. The prospect of these boys growing up together gave their parents great joy.

Tristan and Jack occasionally reminisced about the way they'd met in the colonies, and the irony of how the friendship they'd gained there had brought them to this place, sharing a home and enriching each other's lives. They were happy. Their wives were happy. And their involvement with treason became more and more a secret they spoke of only occasionally and in whispers. They quietly celebrated when news came that the colonists had won their revolution against the king. Those in Tristan's household who had put themselves in danger to aid the colonists' cause all agreed that they had certainly earned their freedom, and they deserved to enjoy it.

# ABOUT THE AUTHOR

ANITA STANSFIELD HAS MORE THAN fifty published books and is the recipient of many awards, including two Lifetime Achievement Awards. Her books go far beyond being enjoyable, memorable stories. Anita resonates particularly well with a broad range of devoted readers because of her sensitive and insightful examination of contemporary issues that are faced by many of those readers, even when her venue is a historical romance. Readers come away from her compelling stories equipped with new ideas about how to enrich their own lives, regardless of their circumstances.

Anita was born and raised in Provo, Utah. She is the mother of five and has a growing number of grandchildren. She also writes for the general trade market under the name Elizabeth D. Michaels.

For more information and a complete list of her publications, go to anitastansfield.blogspot.com or anitastansfield.com, where you can sign up to receive email updates. You can also follow her on Facebook and Twitter.